D0262064

County Council Library

Chisholm, P.F.

A FAMINE OF HORSES

A FAMINE OF HORSES

P. F. Chisholm

Hodder & Stoughton
LONDON SYDNEY AUCKLAND

First published in 1994 by Hodder and Stoughton, a division of Hodder Headline PLC

10 9 8 7 6 5 4 3 2 1

British Library Cataloguing in Publication Data

Chisholm, P. F.
Famine of Horses
I. Title
823 [F]

ISBN 0-340-60912-5

Typeset by Phoenix Typesetting, Ilkley, West Yorkshire.

Printed and bound in Great Britain by
Mackays of Chatham plc, Chatham, Kent

Hodder and Stoughton Ltd
A Division of Hodder Headline
47 Bedford Square
London WC1B 3DP

Historical Note

Anyone who wants to know the true history of the Anglo-Scottish Borders in the Sixteenth Century should read George MacDonald Fraser's superbly lucid and entertaining account: "The Steel Bonnets" (1971). Those who wish to meet the real Sir Robert Carey can read his Memoirs (edited by F.H. Mares, 1972) and some of his letters in the Calendar of Border Papers.

Sunday, 18th June 1592, noon

Henry Dodd let the water drip off the end of his nose as he stared at a trail in the long sodden grasses. It was simple enough: two horses, both burdened, though from a long slide mark by a little hump he thought the bigger of the two was carrying a pack rather than being ridden by a man who could have avoided it. The prints kept close enough for the one to be leading the other.

He looked up and squinted at the low hills north of the border where the Picts' Wall ran. They melted into the grey sky so it seemed there was no difference between the earth and the cloud and a lesser man might have made comparisons between them and the area of moss and waste between, where the purely theoretical change between England and Scotland took place.

Sergeant Henry Dodd, however, had no time for such fancyings. He was mortally certain that the two men, or possibly one and a packhorse, had been where they had no business to be, and he wanted to know why.

Blinking intently at the traces, he turned his horse and let her find her own path amongst tussocks and rabbit holes, following the trail before it was washed into mud.

Behind him his six patrolmen muttered into their chests and followed in sodden misery. They had been on their way home to Carlisle from a dull inspection of the fords on the River Sark when the Sergeant had seen the trail and taken it into his head to follow it. By the time they got to the guardroom, Lowther's men would have taken the best beer and the least stale loaves and if there was cheese or meat left, it would be a wonder.

Dodd crested a small rise and paused. Ahead of him three crows yarped in alarm and flapped into the sky from a little stand of gorse, to which the trail led directly.

"Sergeant . . ." began Red Sandy Dodd, nervously.

"We're still in England."

"We could send some men out this afternoon . . ."

Dodd twisted in the saddle and looked gravely at his brother, who shrugged, smiled and subsided. The sergeant turned and kicked his reluctant mare down the slope towards the gorse.

The others followed, sighing.

Beside the stand of gorse was a stone marked about by the prints of hooves where horses had stood. From there into the gorse there was a swathe of flattened and rubbed grass, stained here and there by smears of brown almost completely turned back to mud now. None of the horses wanted to approach, they neighed and sidled at the smell. The Sergeant's mare tipped her hip and snorted long and liquidly in warning.

Dodd leaned on his saddle crupper and nodded at the youngest of them.

"Right, Storey, go and fetch it out."

Bessie's Andrew Storey had a pleasant round face with a few carefully nurtured brown whiskers about the upper lip and he looked denser than he was.

"In there, sir?"

You're struggling against fate, said the Sergeant's dour look.

"Ay," he answered.

Dodd turned away to inspect the marks in the ground again. Bessie's Andrew looked at the gorse and knew his horse had more sense than to venture in. He slid down from his saddle, knocking his helmet from its hook as he went and muttered as it landed in a puddle.

"Bessie'll have your guts if yon man's got plague," said Bangtail Graham cheerily. Dodd grunted at him.

Nobody else spoke as Storey squelched through the scrub, following the trail, pushing spines aside with his elbows and sidling through the gaps as best he could. His sword caught on a low branch and another spined branch whipped back as he let go of it and caught him round the back of the head. Still cursing he disappeared from sight.

"There's a body here, Sergeant," he called at last.

"Is there now," said Dodd in tones of sarcastic wonder. "Whose?"

"I'm not sure, sir. The face . . ." There was a pause and a sound of swallowing. "The face is pecked, sir."

"Guess."

"I dunno, sir. From the look of his jack, I'd say it might be a Graham."

There was a general shifting in saddles. Dodd sighed deeply as Bangtail Graham came up beside him looking worried and intent. The other men looked covertly at the two of them from under their lashes.

"Which Graham?"

"Dunno, sir. He was shot in the back."

More silence.

"Fetch him out then, man," said Dodd gently, "it's wet out here."

Sunday, 18th June 1592, noon

Barnabus Cooke had bruises and blisters on his backside and was filled with loathing for his master. The rain fell without cease, as it had since they left Newcastle, the horses were sulky and unwilling, two of the packs had been so ill-stowed by the grooms at their last inn that they forever threatened to break loose. In the meantime the expensive brocade trim on his cloak (that his master had told him not to bring) was ruined, and his velvet doublet would need an hour of brushing if it was not to dry to a lumpish roughness and his ruff was a choking wad of soaked linen that he had not the heart to take off and squeeze dry.

His master came trotting up to ride beside him and smiled. "Only another ten miles, Barnabus, and we'll be in Carlisle."

Ten more miles, *only ten*, thought Barnabus in despair,

what's sir's bum made of then, cured leather? "Yes, Sir Robert," he said. "Any chance of a rest?"

"Not around here, Barnabus," said Sir Robert Carey, looking about as if he was in some dubious alley in London. "Best keep going and rest once we're inside the castle."

Barnabus looked about as well, seeing nothing but disgusting empty green hills, close-packed small farms, coppices of trees, rain, sky, rain. No sign of civilisation except the miserable stone walls the barbarian northerners used in place of proper hedges, and the occasional ominous tower in the distance.

Behind him trailed the four garrison men from Berwick that Sir Robert's brother had sent to meet them at Newcastle, and behind that Barnabus's nephew Simon whose mother had terrorised him into taking her baby to learn him gentle ways. That was while he and Sir Robert had been at Court, serving Her Majesty Queen Elizabeth, eating palace food and standing about in anterooms and galleries while Barnabus raked in fees from the unwary who thought, mistakenly, that the Queen's favourite cousin might be able to put a good word in her ear. That was in the happy profitable time before the letter came for Sir Robert via the Carlisle Warden's messenger riding post. Barnabus had been sent out to buy black velvet and see if Mr Bullard would give Carey a bit more credit and make a new suit in two days flat.

To be fair Sir Robert had offered to get Barnabus a job with his friend the Earl of Cumberland if he didn't want to go into foreign northern parts. He'd even offered to pay some of the back wages he owed, but Barnabus Cooke had been too much of a fool to grab the offer and stay in London where he could understand what men said.

The four Berwick men were muttering incomprehensibly to each other again. One came cantering past Barnabus, spraying him with mud, to talk urgently to Sir Robert.

Barnabus hunched his back and shifted forwards a little to try and take the weight off the worst worn parts of him. Sir Robert was talking quickly with the soldier, his voice suddenly tinged with an ugly northern harshness, so Barnabus could no longer understand him either.

There were men with lances on one of the hills nearby, he could see that now. Sir Robert was staring at them, narrowing his eyes, peering north, then south.

Barnabus began to feel a little sick. Everyone was behaving exactly as if they were in Blackfriars coming out of a primero game and the alley was blocked by armed men.

There were eight lancers, to be precise.

Sir Robert was riding alongside him now.

"Have Simon come up behind me," he said in a low voice. "Where's your gun?"

Barnabus collected his scattered wits. "In the . . . er . . . in the case, sir."

"I told you to have it ready."

"Well, but . . . it's raining, sir"

"Is it loaded?"

Barnabus was offended. "Of course." He saw that Sir Robert already had his own dag out under his cloak, and was winding the lock with a little square key he carried on his belt. Suddenly Sir Robert's insistence on expensive modern wheel-lock guns without powderpans made sense – who could keep a powderpan dry in this weather?

"Sir," ventured Barnabus, beginning to think, "if it's footpads, I've my daggers."

Sir Robert nodded. "Good man," he said. "Go to the rear with Robson. If there are eight on the hill, there's another four behind us, somewhere. If they come up fast, kill them."

"What, all four, sir?"

"As many as you can, Barnabus."

"Right sir."

Sir Robert turned his horse to go to the front, stopped.

"Aim for the faces, they'll be wearing padded jacks."

"Yes sir."

Heart thudding under his wrecked doublet, Barnabus slowed his horse until he was level with Simon, sent the boy up ahead and then nodded to the Berwick man who joined him.

"Spot of bother coming then, eh?" he said brightly, hoping the rain would disguise the fact that he was sweating.

The Berwick man frowned at him, shook his head. "Ah

wouldna like tae ride for Carlisle at this distance."

"No," said Barnabus with feeling, "Nor me."

"It's aye the packs they'll be after."

Barnabus made a face. The three pack ponies were trudging along under a remarkable quantity of clothes and gear, including, Barnabus was sure from the weight, a certain amount of weaponry.

"Why didn't Sir John send more men?"asked Barnabus, "Seeing it's his brother."

There was a cold stare from the Berwick man.

"He didnae have more men to send."

"Well," said Barnabus desperately, "we're still in England, ain't we? They can't be Scots, surely?"

The Berwick man rolled his eyes and did not deign to answer.

They rode along and the men with the lances paced with them. Sir Robert was casting increasingly anxious glances to the rear. At last, one of the broader of the strangers detached from the group and rode down through the scrub to stop beside a flowing pothole. Sir Robert held up his hand to stop his own procession and trotted forwards, smiling blithely. That was a thing the Court taught you, reflected Barnabus, drying his hands on his padded breeches and taking out one of his daggers covertly under his cloak. To paste a smile on your face and keep it there, no matter what.

The two men talked while Barnabus tried to see in two directions at once. Was that a movement behind a rock there, in the rain? The sticky squelching was only the rearmost pony shifting his feet, and that . . . no, it was a rabbit.

Out of the corner of his eye he saw Sir Robert laugh, lean forward and . . . thank God, shake the man's hand. Barnabus let his breath puff out once more, and resheathed his dagger with fingers that were trembling so much it took him three tries.

Sir Robert waved them on towards him, while the broad northerner did the same with his men. Snorting protestingly the pack ponies let themselves be led forward to pick between the pools and ridges, while the strangers came down from their hillock. Four more materialised from the south, but walking not galloping.

"My brother-in-law Lord Scrope," said Sir Robert loudly, "has very kindly sent Mr Thomas Carleton, Captain of Bewcastle, to escort us the last few miles into Carlisle, the country being somewhat unsettled since the death of his father."

The Berwick men grunted and relaxed a little. Barnabus suddenly felt his gut congeal as he puzzled out the implications. Footpads were one thing, highwaymen were another thing, but a country where the Lord Warden of the West March had to send an escort for the area around his own city . . . What in God's name was Carey doing here?

"Welcome to Carlisle," said the Captain of Bewcastle, looking like a beer barrel but sitting his horse as if he were born on it and ignoring the little rivers running down the curves of his helmet. "I see the weather's kept nice for you."

Sunday, 18th June 1592, afternoon

Bangtail Graham had gone into the gorse to help young Storey and after a while and a great deal more profanity, the two of them came struggling out with the dripping corpse between them. It was well stiff, but in a bent position, as if the lad had been frozen while making a bow for the first time in his life. Dodd gestured for them to lay it down on its side, and dismounted to take a closer look.

He'd been shot from behind, that was clear enough. There was a gaping hole in the chest and white ribs visible in the mess of red, mixed with tatters of shirt, doublet and leather jack with the padding quilted in the Graham pattern. The crows had not had time to wreck his face completely: there was no mistaking the long jaw and sallow skin of a Graham. No doubt the eyes would have been grey.

Red Sandy had ridden up behind Dodd to peer at the body.

"Devil take it," he said. "Is that . . .?"

"Ay," said Bangtail, wiping his hands on the seat of his

horse, looking upset and disgusted, "it's Sweetmilk Geordie."

"Oh Christ," said somebody.

"Jock of the Peartree's youngest boy," said Dodd heavily.

Bangtail nodded. "He'll not be happy."

Dodd blinked through the thinning rain at the grubby sky and wondered briefly what particular thing he had done was warranting this, in God's ineffable judgement. Storey was openly worried, while the other men were gathering closer and looking over their shoulders as if they were expecting a feud to explode immediately like a siege bomb. Which it would, of course, but in due time. Dodd coughed and shook his head at Archie Give-it-Them who had his hand on his swordhilt.

"Sim's Will Croser, I want your horse."

Sim's Will was the next youngest to Storey and slid from his mount resignedly, grabbing his steel bonnet from the pommel and putting it on. As if he had shouted an order, the others all put on their own helmets. Dodd thought about it and decided to stay with his squelching cap. Why deliberately look more martial than you were?

Croser was taking his own cloak off, but Storey said, "His cloak's in the gorse still."

Sim's Will crashed into the gorse to fetch it, while Dodd walked all around the corpse and toed him. Dead and gone since yesterday, no doubt of it. The pale leather of the jack was stained black around the small hole in the back where the bullet went in.

Croser had returned and was laying the cloth on the ground. Storey and Bangtail moved the corpse onto it and bundled it up, a makeshift shroud. Bangtail tried to cross Sweetmilk's arms on what was left of his chest. The corpse was not co-operative so he made the Sign of the Cross on his own. Croser covered his horse's eyes and led him forwards, while Story and Bangtail huffed and heaved to get Sweetmilk slung over the animal's back before he knew what was happening. Sweetmilk fitted nicely, which helped. By the time the hobby's small but sharp brain had taken note of the blood and the weight and it had begun to hop and kick, Croser had wrapped his stirrup leathers round Sweetmilk Graham's wrists and ankles and after a couple of protesting whinnies, it quieted and stood looking offended at Croser.

"Lead your horse, Sim's Will," said Dodd. "Archie and Bangtail to the front, Archie goes ahead a way, Bessie's Andrew and myself with you, Red Sandy and Long George at the back. Anyone asks, it was a Bell we found."

They paced on towards the ford of the Esk at Longtown, hoping they would meet no Grahams.

Longtown was quiet and the ford seemed clear of danger, though the water was higher than usual. Archie Give-it-Them splashed across, scrambled up the bank, and cantered on down the path. Dodd waited a minute, then gestured for the rest of them to go on. Then just as they were in the middle of the ford, Archie came galloping back on the opposite bank, with five fingers raised, and then a thumb pointing down, meaning he'd seen ten men ahead, and as Dodd made to draw his sword, five more came out of the bushes on foot. Bugger, thought Dodd.

"I'm the Sergeant of the Carlisle Guard," he shouted. "We're on Warden's business."

Bangtail's horse was already out on the bank, but Sim's Will, Bessie's Andrew and Dodd were still in mid-stream because Sim's Will was having trouble leading his hobby through the high water. Bessie's Andrew stared open-mouthed at the lances surrounding them, stock still. Dodd swung about and brought his crop down on the laden animal's rump. It whinnied, pranced sideways and at last Croser hauled the snorting animal up the other bank. Dodd and Andrew Storey followed.

"Surely they wouldna dare . . ." stuttered Bessie's Andrew.

Well, at least, Dodd thought, feeling his pulse in his temples and wishing he'd put his helmet on while he had the chance, if they were planning to dare, they would have done it while we were still sloshing about in the Esk.

A long-faced, grey-eyed, grey-haired ruffian in a patched and mended jack and a dull blued steel helmet trotted forward, his two younger sons behind him. The third they had across Croser's hobby, of course. Surely nothing he'd done recently deserved this much trouble, Dodd thought protestingly. Just in time he saw that the idiot lad Storey was reaching for his sword, and he spurred his horse up behind and cuffed the boy out of the saddle.

"If you want a fight, you can fight them alone," he said.

Jock of the Peartree smiled. He had four teeth missing and one chipped and a nose that had been broken at least three times. Storey picked himself up out of the mud resentfully.

"Now then, Jock Graham," said Dodd civilly.

"Is that one of mine ye have there, Sergeant Dodd?

Dodd did not look at the corpse. "It's one of the Bells, I think," he said. "We're taking him to Carlisle . . ."

"I'll have him."

Dodd sucked his teeth and thought. He liked silence, and the little jinks of harness and the creaking noise made by men in leather jacks leaning forward with their spears only confirmed the blessedness of it. Behind them the Esk was purling its way to the marshes about Rockcliffe castle and thence to the sea. There were hardly any men in the fields with the wet, most of them at the summerings anyway, a few women peering out of their huts further down the road. Jock folded his arms and narrowed his eyes impatiently. Dodd could see no reason for hurry, the man was dead after all.

"Well Jock," he said at last, "I'd need to ask the Warden's permission . . ."

"Now."

Dodd sighed, his gloomy face lengthening with weariness.

"What makes you so interested in a Bell?"

"I'm nae interested in any dead Bell, nor you neither Sergeant, and ye know it. I think he's a Graham," said Jock. "That's good enough for me. I've five men out . . ."

"On a raid?"

"They were in Carlisle to buy horses."

"Ah," said Dodd agreeably, "I see. Well, Jock, as you know, I'd like to oblige you, but I canna. If you had found him, that would be one thing. But we found him and that makes him Warden business for the moment."

"If ye drop him accidental off the horse, and I come upon him, then I've found him, eh?" suggested Jock.

Dodd looked at his men. "If it was myself and none other, then I'd oblige you, Jock." He glared at Bangtail who seemed dangerously close to opening his mouth. If Jock of the Peartree knew for sure that his favourite son was dead, there was no telling what he might do . . . God help the man that killed Sweetmilk, Dodd thought, for nobody else will dare.

He leaned on the crupper again, calculating ways and means. They were about five miles from Carlisle which was over-far for a race as far as he was concerned, if he could avoid it, and nobody in their right senses wanted to mix it with the Graham surname. Storey might, but then Storey had family reasons.

Jock of the Peartree was speaking. "What use d'ye have for a corpse in Carlisle?" he demanded. "There's a man that'll foul no more bills and it's late to think of stretching a rope wi' him."

"It's the law, Jock," Sergeant Dodd explained, all sweet reason, with a trickle of either rain or sweat itching his back under his shirt. On the other hand they were at least talking, and it was probable even the Grahams might think twice about killing the Sergeant of the Carlisle Guard and his men. Possible at any rate. "The law says there should be an inquest for him and an inquest there will be. If he's yours, ye can have him to bury in two days."

As if that closed the conversation, Dodd clucked at his horse, waved the men on, and rode slowly past the Grahams. Collectively holding their breath and praying that the Grahams were not in a mood for a fight, the patrolmen followed after, with Croser's mare pecking irritably at the leading rein as she bore her cloak-wrapped burden. The prickling down Dodd's spine continued until he heard Jock of the Peartree shout,

"Two days, Henry Dodd, or I'll burn your wife from your land."

Red Sandy winced, but Dodd merely looked back once and then continued. Bangtail Graham, who was Jock's nephew by marriage, had the grace to look embarrassed.

"It's his way of talking, sir . . ."

Dodd's face cracked open a little.

"God help your uncle if he goes up against my wife and

her kin, Bangtail," he said, before slouching deep into the saddle and seeming to fall asleep.

Sunday, 18th June 1592, evening

They reached Carlisle as the rain slackened off a little and the day slumped towards evening. The cobbles were slippery and treacherous and none of the townsfolk were impressed by Dodd or his men, making way with very ill grace.

"What will we do with him?" asked Red Sandy as they passed through the gate by the uneven towers of the Citadel. "We canna take him to Fenwick or any other undertaker, Jock will hear ye lied to him by morning."

Most of the shopkeepers on English street were too busy shutting up their shops to pay much attention to them.

"I never lied to him." said Dodd, "I said I thought it was a Bell. I canna help it if I made a mistake."

Red Sandy grinned and waited.

"We'll take him to the castle and find a storeroom to put him in until the inquest."

Once past the Captain's Tower into Carlisle keep, they found the courtyard and its rabble of huts full of disorderly folk. Lowther was back from an inspection of the Bewcastle waste, and the castle guard was being changed. Carleton and his men were in town as well. Dodd and his men threaded quietly through the confusion to the Queen Mary Tower, where he, Bessie's Andrew and Red Sandy hauled Sweetmilk awkwardly up the stairs and into one of the empty chambers that unexpectedly had tallow dips lit around the walls. They rolled the corpse onto the bed and covered it up with the counterpane.

"He'll ruin the bedcover . . ." muttered Bessie's Andrew, whose mother gave him a hard life.

"Aw shut your worriting, Andrew," said Red Sandy. "Any fool knows a corpse that cold doesna bleed and, besides, that counterpane's older than you are, or it should be, the state it's in."

When they clattered down the stairs and out under the rusted portcullis, they found Bangtail and Long George waiting for them in great excitement.

"Ten new horses in the stables?" Not even Dodd could hide his blazing curiosity which he showed by rubbing his cheek with his knuckles. They hurried to the stables by the New Barracks to look at the beasts.

Four of them were easy enough, being long-coated hobbies with Berwick garrison brands on them; the other six were puzzles, no doubt about it, great tall animals that stood with their heads hanging down in weariness as they munched at their fodder and steam still coming off them, though they had been unsaddled and rubbed down already. One in particular was a large-boned handsome warhorse that looked almost a different kind of animal from the ugly little hobbies he was sharing stables with. Nobody in the entire West March owned a horse like that. Nor did anyone recognise the brands but there were no strange grooms about to question and so they all went back to the barracks in search of vittles.

As expected, Lowther's men had made free with their rations and the ale had succumbed to the usual vinegar fly, so they went back through the Captain's Gate to the outer ward where Bessie Storey had her strictly illegal but long-tolerated alehouse hard by the crosswall.

An hour later, Dodd's belly was gratefully full of Bessie's incomparable stew and ale, and he was already hoarse with argument over the likely stamina of the six new horses and how a cross with one of his hobbies might turn out.

"See, you'd get the southern speed and a bit of extra bone . . ." Red Sandy was explaining when he noticed Dodd had gone silent and was trying to become invisible in the back of the booth. Red Sandy looked at the door and saw a boy in Scrope's livery craning his neck.

"Sergeant Dodd, Sergeant Dodd . . ." called the boy.

"He's here," said Bessie's Andrew, waving, no doubt getting his revenge for the gorse bush.

The boy came barging over through the press, neat work with his elbows.

"Sergeant Dodd," he squeaked, stopped and managed to drop his voice. "The Warden wants you, he wants you in the Keep, sir."

"Now?" asked Dodd, wondering why he had paid good cash to be Sergeant of the Warden's Guard and whether he could find some fool to sell the office to and recover his money.

"He wants you to meet his new Deputy."

"I already know Richard Lowther."

"No sir." The boy's face was alight with pleasure at knowing something Dodd didn't. The conversations round about them suddenly sputtered and died. "It's not him."

"What?" demanded Dodd, who had been straining himself to be pleasant to Lowther in anticipation of his confirmation in the Deputyship.

"I thought he was set to get it," protested Red Sandy, concerned about his own investment, "I thought the old Lord promised him . . .'

The boy shook his head. "It's not him."

"Well who is it then?" demanded Bangtail.

Cunning disfigured the child's face. "I dinna ken," he said.

Dodd picked up his cap which had been steaming next to the fire. "Is it still raining outside?"

"Yes sir, but he wants . . ."

Sighing, Dodd unfolded his lanky body from the booth and began pushing and sidling between the drinkers to get to the door. Argument and betting on the new Deputy's identity exploded behind him with Bangtail's voice full of glee above the rest, "God, Lowther'll be in a bate in the morning. He's already sold his offices."

At the door, digging his cloak out of the steaming heap, Dodd looked narrowly at the boy.

"Are you one of Bangtail's kin?"

"Second cousin, once removed, sir."

"Graham?"

"Yes sir, Young Hutchin Graham."

That was an ill to-name to be saddled with, thought Dodd, he'd be called Young Hutchin when he was seventy and bent like willow.

"Then you'll be Hutchin the Bastard's boy?"

"Yes sir."

"You know who my Lord Scrope's new deputy is, don't you?"

"I might," allowed Young Hutchin carefully.

They stepped away from Bessie's door and dodged to the covered way from the drawbridge to the Captain's Tower. The rain had slackened off to a fine mizzle and the dusk was stretching itself out above the clouds. The boy grinned.

"It's not one of the Warden's relatives."

"Of course it is," said Dodd. "Why else would he make a mortal enemy of Richard Lowther."

Young Hutchin shook his head and looked smug. Dodd sighed and gave him a penny. Perhaps he wouldn't make it to seventy.

"It's one of his wife's kin. He's just ridden up from London and the Queen's Court and the strange horses in the stable are . . ."

"Good Christ!" said Dodd disgustedly, "It's a Carey. It's not Sir John is it? Say to me Scrope hasn't made John Carey Deputy Warden in the West March as well?"

"Oh no, sir, that one's still just Marshal of Berwick Castle. It's his youngest brother Robert."

"Who?"

"Robert Carey. Sir Robert, I heard. Lady Scrope's his nearest sister in age and she thinks the world of him and he's no money and would like to be away from Court, so I heard, so she made my Lord offer him the place . . . They've put him in the Queen Mary Tower for the night, in the main bedchamber."

"Ah."

They were let in through the Captain's Gate at the shout of their usual password, crossed the yard and came to the stair to the door of the Keep where Scrope's apartments were. At the foot Dodd gave Young Hutchin another penny.

"Fetch your cousin Bangtail, my brother Red Sandy and Long George Ridley, oh and Archie Give-it-Them if he's sober and tell them to shift the baggage that's in the Queen Mary

Tower into one of the feed huts for the night. Tell them to do it now, not when they've finished their quarts."

"Ay sir. What is it?"

"A package," said Dodd gravely. "Go on, run."

Dodd waited until the boy had disappeared through the Captain's Gate, reflecting that whoever Hutchin the Bastard's mother had been, she must have been uncommonly fine-looking for her looks and hair to survive two generations of Graham breeding so well. The lad had better never go near the Scottish King's Court with that tow head and blue eyes, not until he'd put on enough bone to defend himself.

He opened the heavy door and went into the big main room. Two of Scrope's attendants were there and a round ugly little man was huddled up on a stool by the fire in the vast fireplace finishing mulled ale from a leather tankard. Next to him was a soft-looking lad, sitting on a pile of rushes, dispiritedly oiling some harness and in the corner, four louts with Berwick stamped on their voices were arguing the toss over whether a shod horse went better than an unshod one in a race. The ferret-faced man on the stool slapped his knees, stood up and said something in what sounded like English, if spoken by a man with a head-cold and the hiccups. Dodd couldn't understand a word seeing it was some kind of southern talk, but the boy did and the two hurried out into the rain, the boy tripping on some of the harness straps.

Dodd passed through with a polite nod to John Ogle, the Warden's steward, and climbed the spiral staircase in the furthest corner.

At Scrope's impatient "Enter" he pushed open the oak door with the mysterious axe-mark in it and went in. The air was full of woollen steam from the heavy cloak hanging by the fire and Scrope's hangings were given a courtly glamour by the fat wax candles all about the room. At least it was warm there.

Scrope, as usual, was sitting hunched like a heron in his carved chair by the desk while Richard Bell the clerk packed up papers behind him. Two other men looked up as he came in. Captain Carleton was standing, and a stranger was sitting at his ease on the cushioned bench.

"Good evening, Sergeant," said Scrope, "any news from the patrol?"

"The Sark fords are high for the time of year and I doubt anyone's been across them this summer, except perhaps the horse smuggler we've heard tell of," said Dodd. "We met Jock of the Peartree with fifteen men by the Esk ford at Longtown."

"What was he doing there?" asked Scrope.

"Looking for lost cows?" suggested Thomas Carleton sarcastically. He had parked his bulky body in front of the fire, blocking most of the heat, and wore a face full of repressed amusement.

"He said he'd five men that had gone to Carlisle to buy horses."

Carleton snorted. "Good luck to them. We've a famine of horses hereabouts."

"I trust you sent him packing," said Lord Scrope. Dodd said nothing. The man sitting on the bench with his mud-caked boots stretched out in front of him and crossed at the ankle smiled slightly. His face was long and beaky with something indefinably familiar about it, he had dark red-brown wavy hair, and very bright blue eyes, and a neatly trimmed little Court beard and moustache.

"Was there anything else, my lord?" asked Dodd patiently.

"No . . . Yes. Sir Robert, may I present to you Henry Dodd, Sergeant of the Guard. Henry, this is my brother-in-law Sir Robert Carey, who will be my Deputy Warden."

Dodd made a stiff-necked bow, Carey came to his feet, returned the courtesy, held out his hand and smiled. There was one who'd be expensive to put in livery, thought Dodd. He was taller by an inch or two than Dodd, who found himself in the unfamiliar position of looking up at someone. He took the proffered hand, which was long, white and nicely manicured, with three rings on it, and shook it.

"Sir Robert," said Dodd non-committally.

"Apologies for hauling you up here on such a foul evening," said Carey affably. "Captain Carleton says he's too busy to take me for a tour of the area tomorrow, and I was hoping you would oblige?"

It was on the tip of Dodd's tongue to say that he had a lot less time than Carleton, and stay out of trouble, but then he reflected. After all, this was the Warden's brother-in-law, a courtier come riding up from London, and not just any courtier but one of Lord Hunsdon's boys. He might even be grateful for a friendly face. Perhaps if he got on well with this Court sprig, who seemingly was the new Deputy Warden, Dodd might snaffle a couple of the offices in the Deputy's gift to sell on. And Lowther was a miserable bastard in any case.

"No trouble, sir."

"Dodd, is it? From Upper Tynedale."

"My grandfather's land, sir. Mine comes to me from my wife, I've a tower and some acres not far from Gilsland."

"Bell or Armstrong land?"

Dodd coughed. "Ay sir," he said stonily. "English Armstrongs. And a few Dodds." He hated nosiness, particularly from courtiers. Though Carey looked little like a courtier in his dark green woollen doublet and paned hose; just the lace on his collar and the jewels gave the game away.

There was a clatter of light boots on the stair and Scrope's lady came through the door in a hurry, her doublet bodice open at the neck and her satin apron awry. Scrope looked up and smiled fondly; she was a pleasing small creature with black ringlets making ciphers on her white skin. At the sight of Carey her face lit up like a beacon.

"Robin!" she shouted and ran into his arms like a girl. Carleton's lip curled at the sight, which had cost Richard Lowther at least fifty pounds and much credit. Carey grinned, kissed her, lifted her up and kissed her again. She giggled and batted him away.

"Was it a hard journey?" she asked. "How is the Queen, did you meet John?"

"Yes, well enough, no." said Carey methodically.

"Philadelphia . . ." began Scrope.

"I may greet my brother, I think," said Lady Scrope haughtily. Carey whispered in her ear and she frowned, then picked up a work bag from near the fire, sat down on her stool and began rapidly stitching at a piece of white linen, her steel needle with its tail of black flashing hypnotically before Dodd's eyes. "And I wanted to speak to him privately as well."

"When we . . ."

"How much did you want?" asked Carey. Lady Scrope tutted at him.

"Not money," she said primly. "I do not always lose at primero, you know."

"Oh no?" said Carey sceptically. "I swear on my honour I have seen you draw to a flush with no points on three separate occasions."

Dodd, who had heard some of the legends about Lady Scrope's gambling, hid a smile.

"My lord has been teaching me better play," said Lady Scrope with dignity, a blatant lie as far as Dodd was concerned, since Lord Scrope was even worse than she was.

Carey raised his eyebrows severely.

"My lord," said Dodd across the argument, "I must have a private word . . ."

"Later, Sergeant, later," said Scrope irritably. "I have some business with Sir Robert, my dear . . ."

Philadelphia made three minute stitches and finished off the end, unfurled a new length from her bobbin, snipped, threaded and began stitching again. A blackworked peapod was taking shape like magic on the linen. "Pray continue," she said. "My business can wait a little."

Dodd decided he had been dismissed and turned to go, wondering what the disturbance downstairs might be. Carleton came with him. They were stopped by Carey's voice.

"Sergeant," he called, "shall I meet you at dawn in the yard tomorrow?"

Dodd thought about it and sighed. "Ay sir."

He reached for the door and nearly had it slammed in his face. There on the threshold stood Sir Richard Lowther, resplendent in tawny velvet and red gown, his greying hair further frosted with rain and murder in his face.

"What is this I hear," he said, dangerously quiet into the instant silence, "about the Deputyship?"

Scrope was on his feet, coming forward.

"Ah, Sir Richard," he said, "may I present to you Sir Robert Carey, my brother-in-law and . . . er . . ."

Dodd had backed into a corner, the better to watch the show. Philadelphia had stopped sewing and was also watching intently, Carleton was leaning against a wall, with a cynical grin on his face. Hands on hips, Lowther advanced towards Carey, who was standing, smiling unconcernedly.

"Sir Richard Lowther," he said with a shallow Court bow. "Pleased to make your acquaintance, sir."

"Well I," snarled Lowther, "am not pleased to make yours, *sir*."

Carey's eyebrows went up again. "I'm sorry to hear that."

Scrope coughed frantically, and wriggled his fingers together like knobbled worms. "I am . . . er . . . appointing Sir Robert as my Deputy," he said. "The post is in my gift."

"A bloody foreigner? A *southerner* to be Deputy Warden."

"I was brought up in Berwick, my father Lord Hunsdon is East March Warden," said Carey mildly.

"Oh Christ!" roared Lowther. "One of *those* Careys. That's all we need. What's the old woman up to then, making the poor bloody Borders a sinecure for all her base-born cousins?"

Carey went white and drew his sword. Its long wickedly pointed blade caught the firelight and slid it up and down distractingly. Carleton blinked and stood upright, glanced at Dodd who was ready to move as well. One of those long modern rapiers, he thought professionally, fine for a duel but unreliable for a fight where men were wearing jacks. Would Lowther draw?

"I don't like the way you talk of my family and I don't like the way you talk of the Queen," said Carey very coldly. "Would you care to discuss the matter outside?"

Lowther looked a little surprised, under his rage. His own hand was on his swordhilt, he had not yet committed himself. In the silence that followed, Dodd reflected that it was always interesting to watch the way a man held a sword, providing he wasn't facing you at the time. Beyond the question of whether he knew how to use it, there was the way he stood, was he tense, had he killed before, how angry was he? Carey looked competent with his rapier and not at all a virgin in the way of bloodshed. Of one thing Dodd was morally certain, who had met both of them: his brother, Sir John, would not have drawn, his father would have drawn and struck.

"Gentlemen, gentlemen," said Scrope, breaking out of his trance and moving between them, "I will not have my men duelling. Sir Richard, if you have a quarrel with the way I appoint my officers, please take it up with Her Majesty. Sir Robert, you will put up your weapon."

Carey hesitated a moment, then sheathed his sword. Lowther growled inarticulately, turned on his heel and stamped out of the room. They could hear his boots on the stairs and his bull-bellow as he passed through to the lower room.

All of them let out a breath, except for Carleton who looked disappointed.

"I should have warned you . . ." began Scrope apologetically, but Carey had sat himself carefully down on the bench again, clasped his hands and was looking at them abstractedly.

"Who controls the dispatches to London?" he asked, seemingly irrelevantly.

"That's Lowther's job," Carleton answered him, "fairly bought and paid for."

Carey looked at Scrope regretfully. "My lord, we have a problem."

"Why?" asked Scrope pettishly, "I made him know who was Warden here."

Lady Scrope was sewing again. "Robin means, my lord," she said tactfully, "that Sir Richard will be writing to my Lord Burghley and we can't stop his letter."

Carey smiled fondly at his sister.

"Why should that matter?" Scrope demanded. "I'm the Warden."

"Fully confirmed, with your warrant?" asked Carey.

"Well . . ."

"Not yet," said Philadelphia, raising her eyebrows exactly

like her brother. "There hasn't been time since the old lord died. It was less than a week ago, remember. He isn't even buried yet, he's still in the chapel, poor old soul."

"No warrant?"

"I'm only Warden during pleasure anyway," said Scrope. "What would Burghley do . . ."

Being a man who often edited what he wanted to say, Dodd recognised the symptoms in someone else.

"Well, my lord," said Carey after a deep breath, "if you remember, it was the Earl of Essex who gave me my knighthood. He and Burghley . . . er . . . hate each other.'

"Oh," said Scrope, beginning to understand, "Court factions."

"Of course, Robin is the Queen's favourite . . ." began Philadelphia.

"Heaven preserve me from that," said Carey feelingly. "No, she likes me, but Essex has the . . . er . . . honour at the moment. Even so, she would prefer me back at Court under her eye. This needs to be handled with care, my lord."

"Surely I can appoint my own deputy," said Scrope.

Carey and his sister exchanged glances. "Of course. One thing I must have settled tonight, my lord," he said, "is the question of men. The garrison men my brother lent me must go back to Berwick tomorrow, he's short-handed enough as it is. I need my own men here, appointed to me, paid by me and loyal to me."

Too late Dodd realised that he should have left with Lowther, no matter how fascinated he was. He tried melting into the tapestry, but Carleton did for him, damn his guts.

"Sergeant Dodd here is the loyalest man I know," boomed Carleton with an evil grin.

"Oh Ah could niver . . ."

"Rubbish, man, no deputy could wish for a better guard than you and your soldiers."

"Excellent idea, Captain," drivelled Scrope. "Yes. Sergeant Dodd, you can transfer to Sir Robert's service until he releases you."

Carey had spotted his reaction too, alas. Dodd coughed and did his best to look honest but thick.

"Ay sir," he said, wondering how he could explain it to Janet that he was now in the service of some damned Court sprig, not even securely appointed Deputy Warden. Ah well, no doubt Carey would be heading south in a month or two, with his tail between his legs.

And then how would Dodd deal with Richard Lowther's wrath? It was too much to cope with on top of Sweetmilk Graham's killing.

"Sir," he said to Carey. "I'd best get back to my men and explain to them."

"Of course, Sergeant," said Carey. "How many of them are there?"

"Six, sir."

"Six. Good." Carey coughed a little. "Well, I'll see you in the morning then, Sergeant. Good night."

Dodd clumped down the stairs, shaking his head and hoping he wouldn't need to do any more thinking that night. Then Lowther stopped him in the lower room, looming by the fire, his broad handsome face like a rock carving on a tomb.

"Well, Sergeant?"

"Ay sir."

"What did they say after I left?"

"Say, sir?"

Lowther's grey eyes narrowed.

"Of what did they speak when I was gone?" The words sprang out half-bitten.

Dodd thought for a while.

"Scrope turned me over to the new . . . to Sir Robert as sergeant of his guard, me and my men together."

Lowther humphed to himself.

"You'll not forget where your true interests lie, Sergeant." he said with heavy meaning.

Christ man, thought Dodd to himself, if you're here demanding blackrent off me, say so out clear, ye've not the talent for subtle hinting.

Aloud he said stolidly, "No sir."

"So what did they say?"

Dodd thought again. "It was some chatter about Court factions and Carey said he wasna the Queen's favourite, the Earl of Essex was, and they'd need to be careful of you."

Lowther humphed again. "Was that all?"

Inspiration struck Dodd. "All I understood, sir, seeing they were talking foreign."

"What, southern English."

"No, I can make that out usually: foreign, French maybe or Latin even. I don't know."

Lowther looked sideways at him under his flourishing grey brows and Dodd stared into space. Lowther snapped his fingers at John Ogle who bristled, but came towards them.

"Find me and the sergeant some beer," he said, stepping over a snoring pile of sleuthdogs and sitting on one of the benches. At his gesture Dodd sat down next to him, itching to get back to the barracks and find out what his men had done with Sweetmilk. He gulped the beer when it came, from Scrope's brewhouse, not the garrison's, and not half bad.

"Scrope's mad," said Lowther dourly. "A bloody courtier, what does he know about the Border?"

He knew enough to identify immediately where most of Dodd's surname lived and that Gilsland was full of Armstrongs, Dodd thought, but said nothing and nodded.

"Still, that might not be so ill a thing . . ." muttered Lowther, thinking aloud. "What do you make of him, Sergeant?"

Dodd forebore to point out that he had exchanged perhaps three sentences with the man, and shrugged.

"He's got very polished manners."

"He might not be here long," said Lowther pointedly. Dodd didn't reply because in his present mood he might have said something he would regret later. And Janet would have his guts if he lost his place before he had his investment back. Which on current showing might be well into the next century, assuming he lived that long.

"Keep an eye on him for me, will you Henry?" Lowther said, the firelight catching his pale prominent eyes and the broken veins on his cheeks and nose. To complete the effect, he made a face which might, if practised, have counted for a smile one day.

"Ay sir," said Dodd woodenly.

"Good lad." Lowther clapped him on the shoulder and headed purposefully across the room to the fire, threading between benches and trestle tables.

Dodd hurried out the door. At the dark foot of the stairs outside, he looked about him impatiently.

"Hey Sergeant," came a voice from the door of the new barracks and Dodd changed direction to find four of his men sheltering there, Red Sandy fiddling with a lantern that had almost no wick left.

"Where have you put it then?" Dodd asked, thinking longingly of his bed.

Archie Give-it-Them coughed and the others looked sheepishly at each other. Dodd sighed again.

"Well?" he said.

"We tried, Sergeant," said Bangtail Graham, "but the new Deputy had a man on the door already and he wouldna let us in, but."

There was a long moment of silence. Dodd thought of the thirty good English pounds he had given for the sergeant's post, which was a loan from Janet's father as an investment, and decided that if he lost his place he would ride to Berwick and take ship for the Low Countries.

"Good night," he said, turned on his heel and walked off to the stables to think.

Sunday, 18th June, night

Carey saw his sister up the stairs to the Warden's bedchamber, and she leant on his arm smiling and chattering so happily that he knew how hard it had been for her. Goodwife Biltock was pulling a warming pan out of the great bed.

"God's sake, this weather, June, who could believe it . . ." she was muttering as she turned and saw him. "Oh now," she flustered, dropping a curtsey, "well, Robin, what a sight . . ."

Carey crossed the floor in three strides and picked her up to give her a smacking kiss on the cheek. She cuffed his ear.

"Put me down, bad child, put me . . ."

Carey put her down and handed her his hankerchief, while Philadelphia smiled and brought her to the stool by the fire until she could collect herself.

"Every time I see you," Goodwife Biltock snuffled, scrubbing at her eyes, "every time, silly old cow . . ."

Carey was pouring her wine from the flagon on the plate chest, since women's tears had always had him come out in a sweat. He brought it to her and squatted down beside her.

"So it's true Scrope offered you the deputyship," she said at last. "I never thought . . ."

". . . I could drag myself away from London?" Carey made a wry face. "Nothing easier when I could feast my eyes on you Goodwife . . ."

"Pfff, get away, Robin, your tongue's been worn too smooth at Court. Well you're a sight for sore eyes and no mistake and I see you can find a clean hankerchief now which is more than I could say for you once. Will you stay do you think?"

Carey coughed. "I don't know, Goodwife, it depends."

"You take care for that Lowther fellow . . ."

"Nurse . . ." warned Philadelphia.

"I speak as I find, I'm sure. Where are you lying, Robin, is it warm and dry?"

"Nowhere better in the castle, it's in the Queen Mary Tower."

"Hah, warm and dry, I doubt. They use the place as a store room . . ."

"Do they?" said Carey, straightfaced.

"Oh they do, flour mostly, and I'll be struck dumb with amazement if the lummocks even thought to air the place, let alone light a fire, I'll go and . . ."

"No need, Nurse," said Carey, "I've a man in there already, and my own body servant will be seeing after making it comfortable, you're not to trouble yourself."

"Well, have you eaten?"

"I had a bit with the men in the . . ."

"Oh in the Lord's name, old bread and last year's cheese, and the beer brewed by idiots, I'll go and fetch something out of my lord's kitchen, you stay there, Robin, and dry your hose . . ."

"Would you have it sent up to my chamber, Nurse. I'll be going to bed soon."

Goodwife Biltock opened her mouth to argue, then smiled. "There'll be enough for your servants too," she said. "Be sure you eat your share, I know you. Good night, Robin." She reached over and ruffled his hair, heaved herself up and bustled out, rump swinging beneath a let out gown of Philadelphia's. She looked very fine in green velvet, though worn and of an old style. But then the Goodwife had always liked to look well, even when she was nursing Carey babies.

"Didn't you tell her?" Carey asked as he took her place on the stool.

"No one was sure you were coming until your messenger arrived this morning while we were all in church. I made Scrope send Carleton out. And I didn't want to disappoint her in case the Queen called you back before you got here."

Philadelphia brought up the other stool and settled down facing him.

"Be very careful of Lowther, Robin, he's the reason . . ."

". . . why I'm here. So I gathered."

"I wish you had fought him, right there and then," whispered Philadelphia, screwing up her fists on her apron and causing it to crumple.

"Philly . . ." Carey saw she meant it and changed what he had to say. "It might have been a little messy. Have you ever seen a real sword fight?"

"No, but I've nursed enough sword cuts. I'd nurse Lowther too, I would, nurse him good and proper."

Carey looked away from her vehemence. "What was it you couldn't tell me in your letter?"

"Only that he has this March closed up tight in his fist. He has most of the lucrative offices and he takes the tenths of recovered cattle, not the Warden."

Carey's lips moved in a soundless whistle.

"What's left? Just the thirds from fines."

"What there are of them, we've had no justice out of Liddesdale for fourteen years. Sir John Carmichael . . ."

"He's still the Scots West March Warden?"

"For the moment, but the rumours are he wants to resign."

"Wise man."

"He's well enough, he's an honest decent gentleman, too good for this country. Did you ever meet him?"

"I think I did. Last time I was at King James's Court he was there, I remember."

"He does his best, but the Maxwells and the Johnstones ignore him and the Armstrongs and Grahams . . ."

"Who will bind the wind?"

"Exactly. Old Lord Scrope held it together because towards the end he simply did what Lowther told him and let the rest go hang and Lowther kept the peace as far as it suited him."

"Not far?"

"Well, it's remarkable how often people who offend him get raided and their houses burned."

"Who by?"

"Grahams or Elliots mostly, but Nixons and Crosers too."

Carey rubbed his bottom lip with his thumb. "This is no restful sinecure I think," he said.

"Did you think it would be?"

Carey laughed. "Christ, no, or I'd never have come."

"Don't swear, Robin, you're getting worse than father."

"He warned me that things were rotten here, but he didn't know the details."

"How would he, staying warm in London with the Queen and messing about with players."

"Why Philly, you sound bitter."

She put her face in her hands.

"John does his best in the East March but . . ."

"He makes an ass of himself from time to time and the Berwick townsmen can't stand him, I know."

"We need father to run a good strong Warden's Raid," said his sister ferociously, "burn all their towers down for them. Then they'd behave."

Carey put his arm round her shoulders and held her tight. "You don't need father, you've got me, Philly my dear," he said. "Don't worry."

"You won't let him make you leave?" She was blinking up at him with a frown.

Carey sucked wind through his teeth. "If the Queen orders me back to Westminster, you know I have to go."

"She won't, will she?"

"Not if we can forestall whatever Lowther writes to Burghley."

"You could send a letter with the Berwick men and have John put it in his usual package to London."

"Yes," said Carey, thoughtfully, "I'll do that." He yawned. "I'll do it in the morning before I go out with Dodd. There'll be no time later, I want to inspect my men before I call a paymuster for them. And I must go to bed, Philly, or I'll fall asleep here and you'll have to turf Nurse out of her trundle bed and put me in it."

Philly grinned at him. "Nonsense, she'd carry you down the stairs on her back and dump you with the other servants in the hall and then she'd give you a thick ear in the morning."

"She would," Carey said as he stood up, and kissed his sister on the forehead. "Thank you for your good word to Scrope."

"You don't mind that I made him send for you?"

"Sweetheart, you did me the best favour a sister could, you got me out of London and saved my life."

"Oh?' said Philly naughtily, "And who was she?"

"None of your business. Good night."

Monday, 19th June, morning

Dawn came to Carlisle with a feeble clearing of the sky and a wind to strip the skin and cause a dilemma over cloaks: wear one, be marginally warmer and risk having it ripped from your back by a gust, or leave it off and freeze. Dodd put on an extra shirt, a padded doublet and his better jack and decided to freeze.

Carey was already in the stableyard when he arrived, between two of the castle's rough-coated hobbies, checking girth straps and saddle leathers and passing a knowledgeable hand down the horses' legs. He had on a clean but worn buff jerkin, his well-cut suit of green wool trimmed with olive velvet and his small ruff was freshly starched. He looked repulsively sprightly.

"Do you never shoe your horses, Sergeant?" he asked as Dodd came into view.

Dodd considered an explanation and decided against it. "No sir." Carey patted a foreleg and lifted the foot to inspect the sturdy, well-grown hoof. He smiled quizzically and Dodd relented a little. "Not hobbies, sir."

"I like a sure-footed horse myself," said Carey agreeably and mounted.

As Carlisle's stolid red walls and rabble of huts dropped behind them Carey seemed for some reason to be quite happy. Dodd failed to see why: the vicious wind was harrying clouds across the blue like a defeated army and the land was soused with the rain of the previous days. This was June, for Heaven's sake, and it felt like February. Dodd began to run through his normal tally of worries: lack of money, the hay harvest likely to fail, lack of money, the barley crop poor, the rye and oats only middling and the wheat gone to the Devil, lack of money, pasturage poor and sour and Mildred, one of Janet's work-horses, mysteriously off her feed, Janet in general, lack of money, the dead Graham . . .

Dodd glanced sideways at the present occupant of the Queen Mary Tower. He was riding loosely along, looking all about him, whistling slightly and half-smiling and when his hobby tried an exaggerated shy at a limp dandelion, he rode the hopping good-humouredly and hardly used the whip. He did not look like a man whose sleep had been upset by a corpse in his bed. Why hadn't he mentioned it? And if his servants had dealt with the body, what in God's name had they done with it?

Privately deciding to send Red Sandy out to Gilsland to warn Janet of a possible raid by Jock of the Peartree if he hadn't found the dead man by the evening, Dodd cleared his throat.

"Different from London I doubt, sir."

Carey was deep in thought. "Hm? London? Yes. Have you ever been there?"

"No sir. I've been to Edinburgh though, carrying messages."

"What did you think of the place?"

Dodd tried to be just. "It had some fair houses. Too many . . ."

"Scots?"

"Er . . . people."

Carey grinned. "You wouldn't believe how many people there are in London. And every man jack of them with some complaint to bring as a petition to Her Majesty."

"You've been at Court, sir?"

"Too much. However, the Queen likes me, so I do the best I can."

Dodd struggled for a moment, then gave in. "What's she like, the Queen?"

Carey raised an eyebrow. "Well," he said consideringly, "a scurvy Scotsman might say she is a wild old bat who knows more of governorship and statecraft than the Privy Councils of both realms put together, but *I* say she is like Aurora in her beauty, her hair puts the sun in splendour to shame, her face holds the heavens within its compass and her glance is like the falling dew."

"You say that do you, sir?"

"Certainly I do, frequently, and she laughs at me, tells me that I am her Robin Redbreast and I'm a naughty boy and too plainspoken for the Court."

"Christ."

"And then I kiss her hand and she bids me rise and tells me that my brother is being tedious again and my father should get up to Berwick and birch him well, and that poor fool of a boy Thomas Scrope apparently wants me for a deputy in the West March, which shows he has at least enough sense to cover his little fingernail, which surprised her, and what would I say to wasting my life on the windswept Borders chasing cattle-thieves."

"What did you say, sir?" Dodd asked, fascinated. Carey's eyes danced.

"I groaned, covered my face, fell to my knees and besought her not to send me so far from her glorious countenance, although if it were not for the sorrow of leaving her august presence, I would rejoice in wind, borders and cattle-thieves, and if she be so hard of heart as to drive me away from the fountain of her delight, then I shall go and serve her with all my heart and soul and try and keep Scrope out of trouble.

Despite himself, Dodd cracked a laugh. "Is that how they speak at the Court?"

"If they want to keep out of the Tower, they do. I'm good at it and she likes my looks, so we get on well enough. And here I am, thank God."

He looked around with the air of a man escaped from jail, before some memory, no doubt of Lowther, clouded him over.

"For the moment anyway. Burghley may convince her she wants me back at Court."

Dodd grunted as they turned from the main trail, heading north, taking a wide sweep around the town, and passing the steady stream of folk going out from the city to work in their farms and market gardens.

They were almost back at the south gate when Carey said, "Longtown would be a little far to go now, no doubt."

Here it comes, thought Dodd, bracing himself. "I could take you with some men."

"I thought things were calmer in summer with the men up at the shielings."

"Well they are, sir, but 'tisn't seemly for the Warden's Deputy to be out with no attendant but the Sergeant of the Guard."

"Much going on near the Sark, at the moment? My lord Scrope said you were there yesterday."

Was the man taunting him? "I came on Jock of the Peartree at the Esk ford . . ."

"I know. Any of them get shot in the back?"

In a way it was better to have it out in the open, at least he would know the worst. As often happened to Dodd his mind came up with three dozen things to say, all of which sounded inside him full of the ring of excuses and blame-passing, and in the end he said nothing save a stolid "No sir".

Carey sighed. "All right, Sergeant," he said, "I give in. Let's call vada and I'll see your prime. Tell me about my would-be bedfellow of last night."

"I only put him there for lack of any other place . . ."

"Is there no undertaker in Carlisle?"

"Three," said Dodd, "but they would know him and . . ."

"Who is he . . . was he?"

Dodd told him. It seemed Carey had heard something of Jock Graham's reputation, for he was thoughtful.

"When's the inquest?"

Dodd sighed at the reminder of things he hadn't done yet. "I'll try and fix it for tomorrow: there's no question of the verdict."

"Any hint of the murderer?"

Dodd shrugged. "Jock of the Peartree could likely tell you more about that. Who knows? Who cares?"

Carey gave him an odd look. "I think murder is still against the law, isn't it?"

"Sweetmilk? He's already had three bills fouled against him in his absence for murder in Scotland and he was just gone eighteen. Only the Jedburgh hangman will be sorry he's dead."

"And Jock of the Peartree, no doubt."

"Oh the Grahams will be riding once they know who did it. We've no need to trouble ourselves about Sweetmilk's killer once the inquest's finished and Jock's got the body."

"Why didn't you give him to Jock when you met yesterday?"

Dodd blinked. "Well sir, I wanted the fee and I didnae want to be facing a grieving Jock and fifteen Grahams with only six of my own behind me."

"Fair enough, Sergeant. I want a look at the place where you found the body – can you show me this afternoon?"

"Ay sir, but . . ."

"Excellent." Carey urged his hobby up the cobbles to the castle gate and Dodd had to raise a canter to catch up with him again.

"Sir . . ."

"Yes, Sergeant. Oh I shall want to inspect the men at two hours before midday."

"Inspect the men?"

"Yes. You and your six patrolmen. And I'd be grateful if you could put your heads together and make a list for me of any defensible men within ten miles of Carlisle who dislike Lowther and might come out to support me in a fight."

"But sir . . ."

"Yes, Sergeant?"

"Sir, where's Sweetmilk's body?"

"You'll find him, Sergeant."

Monday, 19th June, morning

Having been given fair warning by Carey, Dodd mustered the men as soon as he rode into the castle, told them what would happen and further his reaction if they failed to show the Courtier how things were done properly on the border and his men scattered looking deeply worried.

Paperwork for the inquest attended to and his temper a little improved by a morning bite of bread and cheese, Dodd checked his tack, his weapons and his armour, and after a nasty scene with his occasional servant, John Ogle's boy, was in reasonable order by ten o'clock.

Carey inspecting men and weapons was an interesting sight. At least it was quick. He had all six of the men stand in a row facing him in the castle courtyard. Then he walked up and down the line, smiling slightly. He picked out Archie Give-it-Them Musgrave, though how he already knew that Archie was the worst for his tackle among them Dodd had no idea. Archie sweated for a quarter of an hour while Carey painstakingly explained why his caliver would inevitably misfire because the pan was clogged, his lance-point needed new rivets, his sword had no edge and was rusty and his jack was a disgrace. Archie thought he had scored when Carey asked what the brown stain on his jack happened to be.

"Armstrong blood, sir."

"How old?"

Archie's talents were not in his brain. "Sir?'

"How old is the blood?"

Archie mumbled. "I killed him in April."

The snotty git, thought Dodd, to pick on poor Archie. Carey nodded for Archie to go back to his position in the line. He then stood with his left hand on his rapier hilt and his right fist on his hip and looked at them thoughtfully.

"Gentlemen," said Carey at length, "I have served in France with the Huguenots, and under Lord Howard of Effingham against the Spanish Armada. I have served at several sieges, I have fought in a number of battles, though I admit most of them were against foreigners and Frenchmen and suchlike rabble. I have commanded men on divers occasions over the past five years and I swear by Almighty God that I have never seen such a pitiful sight as you." He paused to let the insult sink in.

"I was born in London but bred in Berwick," he continued in tones of reproach. "When I took horse to come north, a southerner friend of mine laughed and said I should find your lances would be rotten, your swords rusted, your guns better used as clubs and your armour filthy. And I told him I would fight him if he insulted Borderers again, that I was as sure of finding right fighting men here as any place in England – no, surer – and I come and what do I find?" He took a deep breath and blew it out again, shook his head, mounted his horse without touching the stirrups and rode over to where Dodd sat slumped in his saddle, wishing he was in the Netherlands.

"Sergeant, sit up," said Carey very quietly. "I find your men are a bloody disgrace which is less their fault than yours. You shall mend it, Sergeant, by this time tomorrow."

He rode away, while Dodd wondered if it was worth thirty pounds to him to put his lance up Carey's arse. He had still not found Graham's body.

Carey came by while they were waiting for the blacksmith to get his fire hot enough for riveting and beckoned Dodd over.

"Who's in charge of the armoury?"

"Sir Richard Lowther . . ."

"Who's the armoury clerk?"

"Jemmy Atkinson."

"Is he here?"

Dodd laughed shortly and Carey looked grim. "As soon as you've finished, I want to roust out the armoury and see what sins we can find there."

Dodd's mouth fell open. Sins? Sodom and Gomorrah came to mind, if he was talking about peculation in the armoury. "We'll not have finished with your orders until this evening, sir," he protested feebly.

"I want to see if your longbows are as mildewed as the rest of your weapons, assuming you have any longbows. The rest can wait."

"But sir . . ."

"Yes, Sergeant."

"It's locked."

"So it is, Sergeant."

The Lord Warden was there when they went to the armoury in a group, a little before dinnertime, walking up and down, winding his hands together and blinking worriedly at the Captain's Gate.

"Do you really think this is necessary . . .?" he began as Carey strode over with a crowbar under his arm, followed by his little London servant who was struggling with an odd-looking wooden frame.

"Yes my lord," said Carey briskly, inserting the crowbar in the lock.

"But Sir Richard . . ."

There was a cracking ugly noise as the lock broke and the door creaked open. Everyone peered inside.

Carey was the first to move. He went straight to the racks of calivers and arquebuses. Those near the door were rusted solid. Those further from the door . . . Dodd winced as Carey pulled one down and threw it out into the bright sunlight.

Bangtail whistled.

"Well, Atkinson's found a good woodcarver, that's sure," he said.

More dummy weapons crashed onto the straw-covered cobbles, until there was a pile of them. They were beautifully made, carefully coloured with salts of iron and galls to look like metal. Occasionally Carey would grunt as he found another real weapon and put it on the rack nearest the door. Then he went to the gunpowder kegs and opened them, filled a pouch from each, and brought out the least filthy arquebus.

"Please note, gentlemen," he said taking a satchel from his perspiring servant, "this is the right way to clean an arquebus so it may be fired."

By the time he had done scraping and brushing and oiling, there was an audience gathered round of most of the men of the garrison. Behind him the Carlisle locksmith was working to replace the lock he had broken.

Carey made neat little piles of gunpowder on the ground and called for slowmatch. The boy he had brought with him came running up with a lighted coil. He blew on it and put it to the first pile, which burned sullenly.

"Sawdust," said Carey.

In silence he went down the row of little mounds with his slowmatch. Lord Scrope had his hand over his mouth and was staring like a man at a nest of vipers in his bed. The last pile of gunpowder sputtered and popped grudgingly.

"Hm. Sloppy," said Carey sarcastically, "they must have missed this barrel."

He loaded the arquebus with a half-charge, tamped down a paper wad and used his own fine-grain powder to put in the pan. He then fastened the arquebus carefully on the frame his servant had brought, aimed at the sky, and stepped back.

"Why . . .?" began Scrope.

"In Berwick my brother had two men with their hands and faces blown to rags after their guns exploded," said Carey. The audience immediately moved out of range.

He leaned over to put the fire to the pan, jumped away. The good powder in the pan fizzed and the arquebus fired after a fashion. It did not exactly explode; only the barrel cracked. There was a sigh from the audience.

"What the devil is the meaning of this?" roared a voice from the rear of the crowd.

Carey folded his arms and waited as Lowther shouldered his way through, red-faced.

"How dare you, sir, how dare you interfere with my . . ."

His voice died away as he saw the pile of dummy weapons and the still feebly smouldering mounds of black powder.

"*Your* armoury?" enquired Carey politely.

Lowther looked from him to the Lord Warden who was glaring back at him.

"There is not one single defensible weapon in the place." said Lord Scrope reproachfully, "Not one.'

"Who gave him authority to . . ."

"I did," said Scrope. "He wanted to check on his men's longbows as part of the preparations for my father's funeral."

"I see no longbows."

"That's because there are none," put in Carey. "There's some rotten firewood at the back, but the rest have been sold, no doubt."

Lowther looked about him. Most of the men in the crowd were grinning; Dodd himself was hard put to it to stay stony-faced and the women at the back were whispering and giggling.

"Where's Mr Atkinson?" he asked at last.

"I've no idea," said Carey, "I was hoping you could enlighten us."

Lowther said nothing and Carey turned away to speak to the locksmith.

"Finished?"

"Ay sir," said the locksmith with pride, "I did it just like yer honour said."

Ceremoniously Carey paid him, shut the door to the armoury and locked it, put the key on his belt and gave the other to Scrope.

"Where's mine?" demanded Lowther.

The Carey eyebrows would have driven Dodd wild if he'd been Lowther, they were so expressive.

"The Deputy Warden keeps the key to the armoury," he said blandly, "along with the Warden. Though it hardly seems necessary to lock the place, seeing as there's nothing left to steal."

Lowther turned on his heel and marched away. Most of the crowd heard the rumbling in their bellies and followed. Bangtail Graham and Red Sandy were talking together and Dodd joined them as Carey came towards him.

"How far is it to where you found the body?" Carey asked.

Dodd thought for a moment. "About six miles to the Esk and then another two, maybe."

"That's Solway field, isn't it, where the battle was?"

"You come on old skulls and helmets now and then," Dodd allowed. "It's aye rough ground."

"We'll go tomorrow then, when we're more respectable, after the inquest."

"Ay sir."

"And now, while we're at the whited sepulchres, shall we have a look at the stables and the barracks?"

God, did the man never stop? Dodd's belly was growling heroically.

"Ay sir," he said sullenly.

Carey smiled. "After dinner."

At least the stables were clean, which was a mercy because Carey poked about in a way that Lowther never had, digging deep into feed bins, lifting hooves for signs of footrot, tutting at the miserable stocks of hay and oats which was all they had left and agreeing that the harness was old but in reasonably good condition.

The barracks Carey pronounced as no worse than many he had seen and better than some. Even so, he had two of Scrope's women servants come in with brooms to sweep the ancient rushes from Dodd's section out into the courtyard so the jacks could be sponged and dried and oiled.

When Dodd asked him why on earth he cared about the huswifery of the barracks he told a long story about the Netherlands, how the Dutch seldom got the plague and that he was convinced it was because they kept foul airs out of their houses by cleaning them. Dodd had never heard such a ridiculous story, since everyone knew that plague was the sword of God's wrath, but he decided he could humour a man who would face down Richard Lowther so entertainingly.

The wind helped them to dry off the cleaned jacks and weaponry, and they worked on through the long evening and by torchlight after sunset, while Carey wandered by occasionally, making helpful suggestions and supplying harness oil. He also went down to Carlisle town and bought six longbows and quivers of arrows with his own money, which he announced he would see tried the next day.

At last, dog-tired, with sore hands, worrying over the Graham corpse which had not yet turned up, and beginning to hate Carey, Dodd went to his bed in the tiny chamber that was one of his perks as Sergeant. He would have to be up out of it again in about five hours, he knew.

When he pulled back the curtain, he stopped. A less dour man would have howled at the waxy face with the star-shaped peck in the right cheek that glared up at him from his pillow, but Dodd had no more indignation left in him. He was simply glad to have found the damned thing, rolled it off onto the floor and was asleep three minutes later. At least the bastard Courtier had wrapped it in its cloak again.

Monday, 19th June, evening

Barnabus Cooke had seen his master in action in a new command before and so knew what to expect. By dint of making up to Goodwife Biltock, the only other southerner in the place, he had found an ancient desk in one of the storerooms, and acquired it. After cleaning and polishing and eviction of mice it went into Carey's second chamber in the Queen Mary Tower, followed by a high stool and a rickety little table. Richard Bell, Scrope's nervous elderly clerk, was astonished when he was asked for paper, pens and ink and had none to spare. In the end they made an expedition to the one stationer in town, where they bought paper and ink and some uncut goose feathers on credit.

By evening the pens had been cured in sandbaths and cut by Bell the way Carey liked them, thc floor of his bedroom had been swept again and was newly strewn with fresh rushes. They had decided to sell the mildewed bedcurtains and stained counterpane. Goodwife Biltock brought wormwood and rue to try and clear the place of fleas, but she said there was nothing really to be done about them, other than burning the place out and putting new woodwork in. She brought a large quilt and some of Scrope's hangings to replace the old curtains and announced that Lady Scrope had begun work on a completely new set for her brother. Next on Barnabus's mental list was a fresh palliasse for him and Simon and an uncracked jordan to go under the bed, but that could wait.

Barnabus had lit the rushlights and the fire and was just unpacking the second chest they had brought when Carey walked in and stopped. His face lit up.

"Barnabus, this is splendid. Thank God I can trust at least one of my men."

Barnabus snorted and elaborately examined a shoulder seam that seemed on the point of parting. Carey got the message.

"How can I thank you?" he asked warily.

"You can pay me my back wages, sir."

"God's blood, Barnabus, you know what . . ."

"I know the third chest is heavy, sir," said Barnabus. "And I know you had an argument with my Lord Hunsdon before you left London."

"Aren't you afraid your savings might be stolen in this nest of thieves?"

"If I had any, I might be, sir. But there's a goldsmith in the town will give me a good rate on it and I know what you plan for tomorrow so if I might make so bold and strike while the iron's hot, as it were, I'd rather have what I'm owed now than wait another year . . ."

Carey winced. "I still owe the tailors . . ."

". . . far more money than you can pay, sir," said Barnabus, putting down the cramoisie doublet and picking up the new black velvet one. "However they're in London and . . ."

". . . and you're here and can make my life miserable."

"Yes sir," said Barnabus blandly. "That's about the size of it."

Carey made a face, took his sword off, leaned it against the wall and went to the third chest. He opened it, scattered shirts and hose until it was empty, and then released the false bottom. Barnabus stared at the money with the blood draining from his face.

"Jesus Christ," he said.

"How much do I owe you?"

"Thirty-eight pounds, ten shillings and fourpence, including the money I lent you last month," Barnabus answered mechanically, still hypnotised by the gold and silver in front of him.

Carey counted the cash out, and handed it over.

"Wh . . . where did you get it all from, sir?"

"I robbed a goldsmith on Cheapside."

Although he was fully capable of it, if necessary, Barnabus didn't find this funny. "Lord Hunsdon . . ."

"My father gave me some but the Queen gave me the rest and if I lose it, she'll put me in the Tower. It's a loan, anyway," said Carey sadly, 'and it took an hour of flattery to stop her charging me interest. So for God's sake, keep your mouth shut, Barnabus. If somebody robs me before I can use it and I go into the Tower, you're going into Little Ease and staying there."

"Never, sir," said Barnabus, recovering a bit now Carey had put the false bottom back in the chest. "I'd be in Scotland, you know that."

Carey said "Ha!", went back to the desk and sat down. "They'd rob you blind and send you back naked, that's what I know. Now then, my lord Scrope will be here in a little while when he's had supper with some of the arrangements for the old Lord's funeral which he wants me to organise. Any chance of a bite . . ."

As luck would have it, Simon came in at that moment with part of a raised pie, mutton collops, good bread from Scrope's kitchen and some cheese Lady Scrope herself had made, according to Goodwife Biltock, and some raspberry fool.

Scrope arrived just as Carey was finishing, which was unfortunate because he polished off the fool that Barnabus had had his eye on, leaving him and Simon with the choice of what was left of the pie and bread or a trip into the Keep's hall for whatever Scrope's servants were eating. Scrope sent Simon out for wine, so Barnabus told him to eat in the hall and himself quietly finished what was left of his master's meal. Then he went into the corner where he kept his own chest, found an old shirt and began tying up each coin separately into a band to put round his waist until he could get to the goldsmith's the next day. Proximity to so much money was making him as nervous as a cat at a witchburning.

The talk of the funeral took twice as long as it needed to because Scrope would not keep to the point. Carey dealt with him patiently, sitting at his desk, writing lists and making notes like a clerk, until the question of horses came up.

"What do you mean, my lord, there are no horses? You mean, no black horses?"

Scrope was up off the chair that Biltock claimed Queen Mary had sat on and was pacing up and down the room, the flapping false sleeves on his gown guttering the rushlights.

"I mean, no horses, black, white or piebald. We've what there are in stables but the garrison will need them to form an honour guard, but apart from the six you brought, the horse merchants say they've never known mounts to be so hard to find and the price in Scotland is astonishing, sixty or seventy shillings for a poor scrawny nag, I heard, and whether it's Bothwell being in Lochmaben at the moment or what, I don't know, but horses there are none . . ."

"How many do we need?"

"Six heavy draught horses at least to pull the hearse and fifty more mounts for the procession and we can't use packponies so . . ."

"Where have they gone?"

"Scotland, I expect. I was hoping for black horses, of course, but any beasts not actually grey or piebald will do well enough, we could dye the coats . . ."

"What' the need for horses in Scotland, at the moment?"

Scrope blinked at him. "I don't know. Probably the Maxwells are planning another strike at the Johnstones or the King is planning a Warden Raid at Jedburgh or Bothwell's planning something . . ."

"Bothwell?"

"He took Lochmaben last week, didn't you know?"

"No."

"Did you ever meet him at King James's Court?"

"I did," said Carey feelingly. "Once. No, twice, the bastard fouled me at a football game in front of the King. What's he up to?"

Again Scrope shrugged. "It's some Court faction matter in Scotland. I'm hoping Sir John Carmichael will let me know when he knows what's going on."

"And the Earl of Bothwell's taken Lochmaben, you say? How the devil did he do that?"

"Dressed as a woman, apparently, got inside the Keep and opened it up when his men arrived. The whole Border was laughing about it and Maxwell's enraged but too afraid of Bothwell to do anything about it. They say he's the King of the Witches, you know."

"Nothing would surprise me about Bothwell. So he's got all the horses in the north."

"Well no, the surnames have their herds of course, but they won't loan them out to us no matter what we offer and . . ."

"The surnames are refusing honest money? How much did you offer?"

"Twenty shillings a horse for the two days."

Carey put his pen down. "Aren't you worried about this, my lord?"

Lord Scrope flapped his bony hands. "Philadelphia keeps telling me to be careful, but what can I do? It's all happening in Scotland and until my father's buried and the Queen sends my warrant, my hands are tied."

"With respect, my lord . . ."

"Anyway, we simply must get this funeral organised, I will not have my father dishonoured with a miserable poor funeral. Lowther says he might be able to get horses."

Barnabus winced, knowing how much his master disliked clumsy manipulation, but Carey only took a deep breath.

"Well," he said, "I'll see what I can do."

"And what about your man Dodd killing that Graham fellow?"

"I beg your pardon, my lord?"

"It's all over the castle."

Barnabus prepared to duck, but Carey spoke quite quietly, counting off on his fingers in an oddly clerkish way.

"Firstly, my man Dodd, as you put it, was not my man when he found the body; secondly, I doubt very much he did the killing since he's not a fool and in any case the body was stone cold when it was found, and thirdly, the inquest is fixed for tomorrow and no doubt the Grahams will be coming to fetch the corpse afterwards. Those of them that aren't outlawed, of course."

"Hm, yes, well. I'm very worried about this quarrel between you and Lowther, Robin. He's a dangerous man to cross."

Carey picked up his goblet off the small table beside him a little too carefully. Barnabus who knew how he loathed being called Robin by anyone except women and relatives, grabbed a cloth. All he did was drink.

"My lord," he said formally, "you have two options. You can confirm Lowther as Deputy and let him take back the ruling of your Wardenry as he did while your father was ill. If that's what you plan, let me know and I'll be on my way back to Newcastle as soon as your father's in his grave." Scrope blinked unhappily and twiddled his thumbs.

"Or," continued Carey in the same dangerously quiet voice, "you can ignore his howling, confirm me as your Deputy and support me if I have to fight him."

"Well, I . . ."

"Tell me now, my lord. If my position is insecure I can do nothing at all to help you."

There, thought Barnabus with satisfaction, if you want your father buried nicely, there you are.

"Do you think you can deal with Lowther?"

"Oh yes, my lord. I can deal with Lowther."

"Right," said Scrope, still twiddling. "yes. Right. I'll confirm you as my Deputy of course and I'll support you . . ."

"To the hilt, my lord. Otherwise, I go back to London."

"Yes, to the hilt, of course, right." As if he had only just noticed the compression of Carey's lips, Scrope began wandering to the door. Carey stopped him.

"My lord."

"Er, yes?"

"I want my warrant before dawn tomorrow."

"Warrant. Dawn. Right. I'll tell Richard Bell to have it ready. Yes. Um . . . good night, Robin."

"Good night, my lord."

Scrope shut the door carefully and went on down the stairs. They heard his voice in the lower room and the creak of the heavy main door. Barnabus got ready.

"JESUS CHRIST GODDAMN IT TO HELL!" roared Carey, causing the shutters to rattle as he surged to his feet and kicked the little table across the room. The goblet hit the opposite wall but luckily was empty. Scrope's half full goblet rolled after it, bleeding wine, and Carey had the stool in his hand when Barnabus shouted, "Sir, sir, we've only found the one stool, sir . . ."

He paused, blinked, put the stool down and slammed his fist on the desk instead.

"*Good God!*" he shouted slightly less loudly. "*That* lily-livered halfwitted pillock is Henry Scrope's son, I can't bloody believe it, JESUS GOD . . ."

Barnabus was mopping busily and examining the goblets, only one of which was dented, fortunately. He could take it to the goldsmith when he went tomorrow. What was left of the table would do for firewood. Simon, he noticed, was cowering in the corner by the bed while Carey paced and roared until he had worked his anger off. Those who doubted the rumours about Carey's grandfather being King Henry VIII on the wrong side of the blanket, and not the man who complaisantly married Mary Boleyn, should see him or his father in a temper, Barnabus thought, that would set them right.

He beckoned Simon over and sent the trembling lad out for some more wine. By the time he came back, Carey was calm again and looking wearily at the pile of papers Scrope had brought.

"God's truth," was all he said, "He's set it for Thursday and it's Monday now. How the devil does he think I can organise anything in two days . . .?"

Tuesday, 20th June, before dawn

Dodd was roused out of sweet dreams concerning Janet two hours before dawn and an hour before he would normally get up. He had pulled his jack on and was feeling for his sword before he woke up properly and heard Red Sandy telling him it wasnae a raid, it was yon scurvy git of a Courtier in the yard wanting to inspect them again.

He stumbled out of the barracks to find the scurvy git standing there, flanked by his two body-servants holding torches, waiting patiently for his men to appear.

At least they were lined up quickly since turning out fully armed in the middle of the night was something they did regularly, even if nothing much generally came of it. Lowther had always liked to make a bit of a show of a hot trod.

Once they were there, Carey nodded.

"Not bad," he allowed, "I know the Earl of Essex's soldiers would still be scratching their backsides and wondering where their boots were. Now then."

There followed a full hour of meticulous individual examination followed by shooting practice with the new longbows at the butts on the town racecourse. At the end of it Carey brought them back to the castle, stood in front of them and said simply,

"I find you satisfactory, gentlemen."

The heavy-eyed men brightened considerably. Carey called out Archie and Long George and went into the now busy Keep with them. They returned a few minutes later with a folding card table and stool, Carey carrying a sheaf of papers and what looked like an account book. When the table was set up, he put them down, and nodded at his servant, Barnabus, who led Archie and Long George self-importantly into the Queen Mary Tower and out again a few minutes later, carrying a small but heavy box.

Bangtail and Sandy were talking to each other, covertly watching Dodd, who had his mouth open as his brain caught up with what he saw.

Carey opened up the account book and squinted at the figures. He blinked, his lips moved as he calculated and his face took on an irritated cynical expression. Just then a short figure erupted from the Keep and ran across the yard, comically dressed in shirt, hose, pattens and a flying taffeta gown. He was already gabbling in a high-pitched squeak that it would be quite impossible for anyone without the right training in accounts and mathematics to understand the very precise and detailed figures it was his job to . . .

Carey shut the book and smiled down at him.

"What did you pay for your paymaster's job, Mr Atkinson?" he asked.

"Sir Richard had fifty pounds from me, sir," said Atkinson, surprised into honesty.

"For the two offices, the Armoury and the Paymaster?"

"N – no, sir. Just the Paymaster clerkship."

"And how long have you held this particular lucrative office?"

"Er . . . only four years and . . ."

"Then you have made back your investment at least tenfold and will suffer no loss if you lose it."

"I . . ."

"You have lost it, Atkinson. Get out."

There was a murmur of interest from the men, craning forward to hear this exchange.

"Silence in the ranks," snapped Carey as he seated himself at the table and re-opened the account books. "Sergeant Dodd, you may call your men to muster for their pay."

Goddamn him, Dodd thought, as the men cheered, and Red Sandy looked with morbid curiosity at him. On muster days it was Red Sandy's job to bring in three of their cousins to take the place of the patrolmen who had died and whose pay Dodd kept.

Blandly Carey began to call through the men's names and pay out as each stepped up in front of him. They didn't get all of their backpay, naturally, but they got six months' worth each which was better than they had ever done under old Scrope. Dodd was called last.

"Your pay, Sergeant," said Carey, handing it over. Dodd took the money in silence and turned to go. "Sergeant."

He turned, waited for the axe to fall.

Carey pointed at the dead men's names. "Faggots, I take it."

Dodd's mind reverberated with excuses, sickness, wounds, dilatoriness. In the end he said, "Yes sir."

"Have you a reason for defrauding the Queen?"

Outrage almost made Dodd splutter. It was traditional for the sergeant to take the pay of men who died, how else could he live?

"Yes sir," he said stonily.

"What's that?"

"Poverty."

Carey smiled. "I'm the youngest of seven sons, and the last time I was out of debt was in '89, the year I walked from London to Berwick in twelve days for a bet of two thousand pounds."

Dodd said nothing. Did the bastard Courtier expect him to be impressed?

"I'm not one to go against tradition, Sergeant. You may keep two faggots at any time and no more. Do you understand?" He crossed out one of the names.

Oh God, Janet would have his guts. "Yes sir." He turned to go, but Carey stopped him.

"Sergeant, do you think you could give me that list of men I can call upon to fight by this evening?"

"Any particular surnames?"

"No, Sergeant, surname doesn't matter to me," said Carey heretically. "Dislike of Lowther and a willingness to fight is all I want."

"Well sir . . ."

"I've asked Richard Bell to be your clerk if you need him."

Dodd was relieved. It wasn't exactly that he couldn't write, it was only that not being a gentleman, paperwork of any description always took him several hours and more sweat than a pitched battle.

Carey grinned, shut the book and stood up.

"We've finished here. Don't drink it all at once, gentlemen, that's all I've got. Company dismissed."

Tuesday, 20th June, morning

The men left the castle in a rabble, jingling their purses and planning extensive wanderings among the town's alehouses that night. Naturally they decided to have a magnificent breakfast at Bessie Storey's and they marched into the common room in a bunch, called for quarts and steak for their meals. Oddly enough she seemed to be expecting them and as soon as the last order was in, Bessie's cousin Nancy Storey barred the door. Bessie herself shuttered the windows and rang her bell.

Janet Dodd, broad and resplendent in her red wool market gown, led the wives of Bangtail, Archie, Red Sandy and Long George into the common room. Grim determination on their faces, they split up and moved in on their husbands. At last Dodd cracked. He laughed and laughed until the tears were dripping in his beer, while Janet marched up to him, sat down beside him and held her hand out. Still snorting feebly, Dodd took five shillings beermoney out of his pay and gave the rest into her hard upturned palm.

"I hear he's a fine man, your new Deputy Warden," she said smugly. All around them arose whining and protests, while Bessie stood by with a broad grin on her face, ready to calm marital discord with a cudgel. Her son Andrew had already given her his pay.

"You've met him?" said Dodd in astonishment.

"No, no, Lady Scrope sent her girl Joan with Young Hutchin yesterday to tell me what was afoot. I told the others."

Privately deciding to tan Young Hutchin's arse for him next time they met, Henry drank his beer without comment.

Janet put hers down with a sigh of satisfaction. "Lord, Bessie knows how to brew, I wish I had her skill. Is he married, the new Deputy?" she asked.

"No."

She elbowed him in the ribs. "Come on, Henry," she said, "what's the difference? By tomorrow you'd be in the same state, only you would have drunk and gambled the money and I would be after you with a broom handle."

"That fine Courtier found out about my faggots."

Janet made a face. "I minded me that was what he was after, I even brought in three of my brothers, only I saw we couldna get them into the castle in time, so I sent them home. The Borders are very tickle at the moment, the Middle March was hit yesterday, but only four horses stolen and they lost a man because they hadna paid the Warden first. Did he leave you any faggots?"

"Two. He said that's all I'm to take the pay off."

"It's not so bad, then. Dinna be so glum."

"Ha. Yon Courtier had us cleaning ourselves like bloody Dutch housewives yesterday, you wouldna ken the barracks now, and even Archie's gun is gleaming bright," Dodd said grudgingly.

Janet seemed to find this funny.

"I heard he took on that Turk Lowther too, and bought you new bows. Ay well, think upon it, Dodd. He has to make his mark which he's now done. He's paid you cash and where he got it, I don't know for I'm certain there's been no Queen's paychest come into the city for the last six months. Would Lowther have paid cash?"

Dodd laughed at the idea and started to unbend a little. "How's the farm?"

"Mildred died."

His good humour promptly dried up again. "What was wrong with her?"

Janet looked worried. "I had the knacker's man take her and he didn't know either. At least Shilling's well enough. What's this I hear about us getting raided?"

"Was that from Young Hutchin?"

"He said I might want to have some of my brothers to stay with me and a couple of men to go out to the summer pastures for a week or so, just in case. There's a lot of broken men about, he said."

Mostly Hutchin's relations, but it was kindly of the boy, Dodd thought, deciding to let him live. Henry found himself close to wishing Lowther had got the deputyship after all. A comfortable if unprofitable life was now all back to front and looked likely to get worse and for lack of rest and unaccustomed labour he was falling asleep where he sat.

"At least we can afford to buy a new horse," Janet said, after counting the money.

"Now there's a novel idea," said Henry Dodd, blinking into his leather beaker. "*Buy* a horse with *money* instead of me having to ride about the countryside at dead of night with your brothers . . .?"

Janet grinned at him. "I'll keep it to meself if you will."

Tuesday, 20th June, morning

The inquest, such as it was, took half an hour. Scrope sat in his capacity as Warden at the courtroom in the town hall; Bangtail came forward, identified himself as Cuthbert Graham, known as Bangtail, identified the corpse as his second cousin by marriage George Graham, known as Sweetmilk, youngest son of John Graham of the Peartree. Dodd explained of his own knowing that the man had been shot in the back by person or persons unknown and Scrope adjourned the case to the next Warden's Day.

A black-haired ill-favoured man at the back of the court came forward to claim the body, and took a long hard stare at Dodd as he passed by. Dodd thought it was Francis Graham of Moat, one of Sweetmilk's cousins, and his nearest available relative that wasn't outlawed and at risk of arrest in England.

By the time the clouds had cleared and the sun shone down for the first time in a week, Carey, Dodd and all six of his men were out on the road to Longtown ford where the Esk began spreading itself like a blowzy wife on the way to Rockcliffe Marsh and the Solway Firth.

At the ford Carey stopped and looked around.

"This is where you met Jock?"

"Ay," said Dodd, not relishing the moment, "they had us neatly."

Carey said nothing but chirruped to his horse, let him find his own way down into the water and splashed across and up the muddy bank. The rest of them followed. Unseasonable rain had washed away most of the traces, but there were still a few old prints in sheltered spots.

When Dodd gestured wordlessly at Sweetmilk's bushes Carey stopped, leaned on his crupper and looked all around him. A gust of wind nearly took his hat off, but he rammed it down again and slid from the saddle.

"Tell me the tale, Sergeant."

Dodd told it and Carey followed his movements exactly, then beckoned for Bessie's Andrew and Bangtail to follow him into the gorse. Bangtail rolled his eyeballs but obeyed: it was remarkable how gold could sweeten a man's disposition. After a struggle with his worst nature, Sergeant Dodd also dismounted and followed them. The springy branch which had caught Bessie's Andrew nearly took his cap off and he swore.

"Wait a minute, Sergeant," said Carey, examining the branch as if it was the first he'd ever seen. "No," he said, disappointed. "Pity."

In the centre was a flattened place and some broken branches.

"Tell me what you saw."

Bessie's Andrew looked bewildered.

"I saw a corpse, sir."

"Yes, but how did you see it? How was it lying?"

The lad swallowed. "The crows had pecked it."

Carey was patient with him. "I know, but which way was it lying? Was it on its back, or . . ."

"On his side."

"Which side?"

"God, I don't know, right side I think."

"Then the right cheek was to the ground."

"Ay."

"Was it stiff?"

"Stiff as a board, sir."

"Well, how did you get it on a horse to bring it back then?"

"Sir?"

"If the body was stiff, how did you put it over a horse? Did you have to break him . . ."

"Och no sir, nothing like that."

"Then how . . ."

"It was bent over already," snapped Dodd. "Like this." He showed the mad Courtier and the mad Courtier grinned like a Bedlamite.

"Would you say he'd been brought here on a horse?"

"Well, of course, he was, sir," said Dodd. "I told ye, I followed the tracks of two nags from the ford . . ."

"But he was dead when he was put on the horse and then brought here; not, for instance, alive when he came and dead when his killer left him?"

What was the man driving at? "Ay sir. I'd say so, the tracks of one of the horses didn't look like a beast was being ridden, more a beast burdened."

"Excellent. So he was killed somewhere else and dumped here, on an old battlefield in the hope that after a few months anyone who came on the bones would think they died fifty years ago."

"I suppose so, sir," said Dodd who couldn't see any point in this expedition at all. "There weren't any traces of blood or suchlike around about here either."

Carey nodded. "What did he have on him?"

Bessie's Andrew blushed. Dodd saw it and hoped Carey wouldn't. Unfortunately he did.

"So what did you take off him, Bessie's Andrew?" Carcy asked ominously.

"Nothing sir, I . . ."

Carey folded his arms and waited. Dodd was glaring at Storey who looked terrified.

"Well, nothing much, sir . . ."

"What did you take off him?" Carey didn't raise his voice.

Bessie's Andrew muttered something.

"Speak up, boy," growled Dodd.

"He . . . er . . . he had a ring."

"*A* ring?" Carey's eyebrows were very sarcastic. Dodd wondered if it was the eyebrows that broke Bessie's Andrew's spirit.

"Well, he had three rings, gold and silver and one with a little ruby in it," stammered the boy in a rush, "and he had a purse with some Scots silver in it, about five shillings worth and he had a dagger with a good hilt . . ."

"By God," said Bangtail admiringly, "that was quick work picking him clean, lad."

Bessie's Andrew stared at the ground miserably. "And that's all, sir."

"*All?*"

Dodd was impressed for the first time. Bessie's Andrew's face twisted. "He had a good jewel on his cap. No more, I swear it."

Carey reached out and patted Storey's shoulder comfortingly. "The Papists say that confession makes a man's soul easier in his body. Don't you feel better?"

"No sir. Me mam'll kill me."

"Why?"

"I only gave her the rings sir, but I took a liking to the jewel and the dagger and the silver . . ."

"Of course you did," said Carey softly. "Now, Storey, look at me. Do I look like a man of my word?"

"Ay sir."

"Then you believe me if I swear on my honour that if you ever rob a corpse while you're in my service, I will personally flog you."

Bessie's Andrew went white. His large Adam's apple bobbed convulsively as he nodded.

"And," Carey continued, "if there's a second offence, I will hang you. For March treason. Do you understand?"

Bessie's Andrew squeaked something.

"What?"

"Y – yes sir."

"Which applies to any man in my service whatsoever," said Carey, glaring at Bangtail and then at Dodd. "You'll see the men know that."

"Yes sir," said Dodd. "When did you want to flog him?"

"It depends if he's told the truth this time and if he hands over what he took."

Bessie's Andrew's face was the colour of mildewed parchment. "But my mother . . ."

"Blame it on me." Carey was inflexible.

"Och God . . ."

"You can bring me what you took after we get back. I might be merciful this time, since you were not, after all, in my service when you stole Sweetmilk's jewels."

Carey seemed to dismiss the wretched Bessie's Andrew from his mind completely. He was pulling at the branches near where the corpse had lain, turning them about. One of the spines stabbed him through the leather of his glove and he cursed.

"What are you looking for, sir?" asked Bangtail. "More gold?"

"That or bits of cloth. Anything that shouldn't be in a gorse bush."

They all looked. It was Bessie's Andrew who found the only thing that Carey found interesting, which was a long shining thread of gold. Carey put it away in his belt pouch and they searched fruitlessly for a little while before struggling back out of the bushes again to find the men also wandering about, checking hopefully for plunder from the old battlefield. There was none of course, the field had been picked clean for fifty years by crows and men. And nobody had bothered to set a watch, which caused Carey to lecture them again.

It was sad to think of all the fighting and the men who had died fifty years before, among them a couple of great-uncles of his, Dodd thought. Some of them were sucked into the mosses round about, quagmires they knew well enough but could not avoid in a pitched battle. That was a bad death – to go looking for a fight and end up with a mouthful of mud and foul water. Those would be angry ghosts. Nothing short of a loaded dag would have persuaded Dodd to venture near the place after dark, and he might have taken his chances with a bullet. He was relieved when Carey gave the signal to mount and they rode away, back to the ford.

Bessie's Andrew was sent ahead to scout and prevent ugly surprises like the last one and the ever-venturesome Bangtail took the chance to ride alongside the Deputy Warden.

"Sir?"

"Yes, Bangtail."

"How did you know so fine that Bessie's Andrew was lying?"

Carey smiled and looked mysterious. "Never lie to a courtier, Bangtail. We're all experts at the game.

Dodd grunted to himself. He thought he knew another reason why Carey had been so sure of Andrew Storey's perfidy. After all, he'd had the chance to take a good look at the corpse, and rings long-worn leave dents on a man's fingers.

At Carlisle, Carey dismissed them and hurried into the Keep calling for Bell. Once they were safely in the barracks, and Bessie's Andrew had taken his jack off and put it on a stand, Dodd turned to him and punched him hard in the gut. Bessie's Andrew sank to the floor mewing and gasping. Dodd kicked him a couple of times for good luck.

"And that's for keeping the gear from *me*," he snarled.

Tuesday, 20th June, afternoon

With Carey gone about some urgent business, Dodd rubbed down his own horse, saw the animals were properly watered, fed and clean, and then wandered, belly rumbling, down towards Bessie's again. Time enough to eat the garrison rations when he had no more money left. He was still in a bad temper and cursing Bessie's Andrew: if the ill-starred wean had behaved properly with his windfall and shared it with his sergeant, Dodd could have given Janet a little ring with a ruby in it which she would have liked. On the other hand, he might then have had to ask for it back . . .

He was sauntering along, thinking about that with his long dour face like the past week's weather, when he saw something that cheered him at once.

There, astride Shilling his old hobby, rode the splendid sight of his wife Janet, market pannier full of salt and string and a sugar loaf poking out the top, her eyes and the dagger at her waist daring any man to try robbing her. Unlike the Graham women, she felt no need of carrying a gun to keep her safe. Dodd liked his woman to look well and Janet was in her red dress with the black trim, a neat little ruff round her neck, and a fine false front to her petticoat made of part of the old Lord Scrope's court cloak, which the young lord had disdained since it was out of fashion, Philadelphia had accepted, her maid taken as a perk and Janet snapped up as a bargain the month before. Her white apron was of linen she had woven herself and was a credit to her. The red kirtle suited her high colour and the snapping pale blue eyes and Armstrong sandy hair. If her teeth were a little crooked and her hips broad enough to be fashionable without need of a bumroll (though she wore one of course) and her boots heavy and hobnailed, what of it? He put his hand to the horse's bridle and Shilling whickered at him and tried to find an apple in the front of his jerkin. Janet smiled at him.

"Now then wife," said Dodd, grinning lecherously at her. "I heard you were out on patrol."

"We were looking at the place where we found a body."

Janet frowned. "Was that the body of Sweetmilk Graham you've not yet told me of?"

"It was."

"Will Jock raid us, do you think?"

"Why should he?" demanded Dodd, "It wasn't me that killed his son."

Janet looked dubious. "What about lying to him at the ford?"

Christ, how did she hear so much? "He'll know it was because I was not inclined to a fight. And where are you off to?"

"To see my lover," said Janet with a naughty look. Dodd growled. She slid from the horse and began leading the animal, holding her skirts high above the mud.

"How's the wheat?" Henry asked, walking beside her and enjoying the view.

Janet began to suck her bottom lip through a gap in her teeth and her brow knitted.

"Sick," she said. "We might get by with the oats and the barley if there's no more rain. I'll leave that field fallow next year."

"But it's infield," protested Dodd.

"Give it time to clean itself. I might run some pigs on it. The beans are doing poorly too."

"What will you do to replace Mildred?"

"I've heard tell there's one for sale."

"Not reived?"

Janet shrugged. "Not branded, any road. That's why I want to buy him."

"Buy," said Dodd and shook his head.

Janet giggled. "Will you want to come with me or would it go against your credit to be seen giving money for a beast?"

Dodd considered. Janet was almost as good a judge of horseflesh as he was himself, and knew most of the horses from round about and wasn't likely to be sold a stolen animal, at least not unknowingly. But she was only a woman. If it had been a cow . . .

"I'll come with you," he said.

They turned down a small wynd leading to one of the many ruined churches of Carlisle: this one had a churchman in it, a book-a-bosom man who spent most of his time travelling about the country catching up with the weddings and christenings.

"Good afternoon, Reverend Turnbull," said Janet politely, "we've come about the horse."

Now Dodd was no different from any other man. He may have had a longer and more ill-tempered face than most, but he could fall in love. He fell in love immediately, with the elegant long-legged creature that was tethered inside the porch of the church. The colour was unusual, a piebald black, the neck high and arched, the legs strong and firm, hooves as healthy as you could wish and best of all, he still had his stones.

Janet's face was bland. "Where was he stolen?"

The Reverend Turnbull looked offended. "Mrs Dodd, I would never try to sell you or the Sergeant a . . . stolen animal. I swear to you on my honour as a man of the cloth, that he was honestly bought. Besides, do you think an animal like that could be reived and the Sergeant not know about it?"

Dodd turned away so the churchman wouldn't see his face which he knew would be full of ardour. With a horse like that he could win the victor's bell at any race he chose to enter, he thought, and the fees he could charge at stud . . .

"Well?" said Janet.

"Eh?" Dodd had his hands on the horse's rump, running them down the beautiful muscles, feeling the tail which needed grooming to rid it of burrs.

"Have you heard of a horse like that being reived recently?"

"Reived . . . no, no, I'd have heard for sure. There now, there, I've no apples, I'm sorry . . ."

"Dodd," growled Janet. Henry paid no attention.

"He's an English beast, surely," he said. "Never Scots, not looking like that, unless he's out of the King's stable."

"Is he?"

"Is he what?"

"Is he out of the King's stable, Reverend?"

The churchman laughed fondly. "No, no, he's an English horse, from Berwick, I know that from the man that sold him to me."

Dodd took the reins and swung himself up onto the horse's back, rode in a tight circle before the church. He had a lovely gait, a mettlesome manner though he might have been short of horsefeed recently, and a mouth as soft as a lady's glove.

"Who was that?" asked Janet.

"Oh, a peddler I know. He told me he came from further south than that, but he bought him in Berwick."

"Why bring him here? Wouldn't he get a better price from the Marshal of Berwick Castle?" Janet demanded suspiciously.

"I think he may have had some notion of crossing the border with him to sell to the Scots, but I convinced him he should not break the law and I bought him to sell on."

Dodd slid from the horse's back again and patted his proud neck.

"Hm," said Janet, took Henry Dodd's arm and moved him out of earshot. "Henry Dodd, wake up. Yon animal must be stolen."

"Not from here," said Dodd, "I'd know."

"From Northumberland then."

Dodd shook his head and smiled. "Get a bill of sale on him and he's ours legally."

"Oh, you . . ."

"Janet, he's beautiful, he'll run like the wind and his foals will be . . ."

"I know you in this state with a horse, you'd blather like

a man possessed and pay three times the right price. If you promise me he isn't stolen from this March, I'll buy him, but you get away from here or the Reverend will see you've lost your heart."

Henry smiled lopsidedly. "I can't promise he's not reived, but I'm sure as I can be."

"We may have trouble keeping hold of him, you know, once the Grahams and the Elliots know we've got him."

Dodd shrugged. "I'm not mad, Janet. I'll have him cover as many mares as I can in the time, then I'll enter him at the next race and sell him after to the Keeper of Hermitage or Lord Maxwell."

Janet laughed. "Against the law."

Dodd had the grace to look embarrassed. "Or the Captain of Bewcastle or the new Deputy or someone strong enough to hold him."

Janet punched him gently in the ribs and kissed his cheek. "He's a light thing to look upon, isn't he."

Dodd forced himself to turn about, bid the churchman a gruff good day and walk away while Janet leapt hard-faced into the bargaining.

Afterwards, she took the horses by back routes to the castle so that fewer unscrupulous eyes would see the beauty, and tethered both in Bessie's yard. When she went in she found Henry, Red Sandy, Long George and Archie Give-it-Them all playing primero with a tall handsome chestnut-haired man she didn't know, who talked and laughed more than anyone she had ever met, and had skyblue eyes to melt your heart.

She sat down, watched the play which was tame, and waited to be noticed.

"Oh Janet," said Dodd happily, drinking from his favourite leather mug. "Sir Robert, this is my wife; wife, this is Sir Robert Carey, the new Deputy Warden."

Janet rose to curtsey to him and instantly took to him when he too rose and made his bow in return, smiling and addressing her courteously as Mrs Dodd rather than Goodwife. That arrogant lump Lowther would have grunted at her and told her to fetch him another quart. Though she would hardly need to be introduced to him.

"Get me another quart, wife," said Dodd, oiled enough to make a point of it. Janet smiled, thinking what babes men were, picked up the jug and went to where Bessie was tapping another barrel, with her bodice sleeves unlaced and laid over a stool, the sleeves of her smock pushed back.

"How are you, goodwife?" Janet asked politely.

Bessie shook her head, her lips pressed tight, from which Janet concluded that her Andrew was in trouble and she didn't want to talk about it.

The primero game was still in progress. Someone had dealt a new hand and Carey glanced at his, and called, "Vada. I've a flush here."

Everyone laid down his cards, but Red Sandy held the highest points and pulled in the pot, grumbling at Carey's sport-stopping flush.

Carey stood. "Good night, gentlemen," he said, "you've cleaned me out."

"You could stay and try and win it back," said Red Sandy unsubtly.

Carey smiled. "Another night, Sandy Dodd, I shall take you on and mend my fortunes, but not tonight. Thank you for your list, Sergeant."

Janet watched him go, wondering how much his extremely well-cut dark cramoisie doublet and hose had cost him in London, and who had starched his ruff so nicely. He surely was a great deal easier on the eye than Lowther or Carleton. Archie had taken the pack and was shuffling the cards methodically, his tongue stuck out and his breath held in his effort not to drop them from his enormous hands.

"I'm for home," she announced, "I'll want to be there before nightfall with things as they are."

Dodd followed her out where they ran smack into Bangtail coming from the midden. He smiled weakly at her and rejoined the game.

"There he is," she said pointing at where the beautiful horse was whickering and pulling at his tethering reins. Dodd went up and patted the silky neck, his face filled with happy dreams of golden bells and showers of silver. "What shall we call him?"

Dodd had unhitched him and was walking him up and down again.

"He walks so nicely," Janet said consideringly, with her head on one side, "like your new Deputy Warden, somehow."

Dodd grinned at the poetic fancy. "There's his name. Courtier. How about it?"

"I like it," said Janet approvingly, "they'll know he's out of the common. Do you want to keep him with you in the castle or shall I take him back to Gilsland?"

Dodd hesitated. "Lowther might spot him and take a fancy to him. Or the new Deputy. Better keep him in our tower. But will you be all right on the road back, it's a long way and I canna come with ye."

"I willna be alone. My cousin Willie's Simon is here today, I heard. I'll offer him a good meal at Gilsland and a bed for the night if he'll bear me company."

Dodd nodded approvingly. It would help if some thought the horse belonged to the Armstrongs rather than him.

Janet kissed him and then took the horses out of the yard. Dodd went back into Bessie's and set about losing the rest of his pay. He didn't succeed, if only because Bangtail had already gone. Archie Give-it-Them said he'd muttered something about an errand for his wife and Dodd was too pleased at the possibility of winning to wonder at it.

Wednesday, 21st June, 2 a.m.

That night Dodd dreamed he was about to be hanged for some crime he could not remember. He could hear the Reverend Turnbull intoning his neck-verse in a huckster's gabble.

"Have mercy upon me, oh God, according to thy loving kindness; according unto the multitude of thy tender mercies blot out my transgressions.

"Wash me thoroughly from my iniquity and cleanse me from my sin . . ."

He was just trying desperately to think of something to say as his last words when the drums leading him to the gigantic scaffold turned out to be a fist hammering on the door of his little chamber.

"Sergeant!" roared Carey's voice, "Up and rouse out your men."

Dodd was already hauling on his hose and shrugging on his doublet. He put on his second-best jack, the one Janet had spent hours reinforcing with bits of secondhand mail where ordinary steel plates would chafe. By the time his eyes were properly open he had laced himself up, buckled on his sword and found his helmet under the bed, and he was following Carey down the dark passage past the tackroom to the barracks door, as the Carlisle bell started ringing.

"Where's the raid?" hc asked.

"A boy came in a quarter of an hour ago and he said the Grahams lifted ten head of cattle and three horses out of Lanercost at midnight."

"How many reivers?"

"Between ten and twenty men, he thought."

"Forty in all then," said Dodd, and Carey nodded. He was already booted and spurred and his own jack seemed well-worn and serviceable. No way of telling the man's courage though when it came to it, Dodd thought, he wished he'd seen Carey in a fight before having to follow him on a hot trod. What was wrong with a cold trod, anyway, they had six days to follow in for it to be legal, and nobody blinked much at a day or two to spare? Which would be worse? A fire-eater or a man who was all bully and brag and no blows? His face settling into its customary sullenness, Dodd decided he was hoping for a coward who would follow the trod well back and discharge his duty without too much sweat. But seeing Carey's grin and the sparkle in his eyes, Dodd began to feel uneasy.

By the time the men had turned out and were in the castle yard, with sleepy hobbies snorting and stamping protestingly and blowing up their barrels to prevent their girths being fastened, another boy had ridden in with news of a herd of horses gone missing from Walter Ridley's fields and a farmhouse broken into on the way. Estimates of the Graham's strength ranged from fifteen to forty men and Dodd nodded.

"Where are the Elliots?" he asked.

Carey turned to the most recent arrival, a lad of about twelve on his father's fastest pony, his face flushed with the ride and the excitement.

"We didna see them," he said.

"The Grahams don't always ride with the Elliots, though Sergeant?" Carey asked, raising his voice to be heard above the clanging of the bell.

"Not always," Dodd allowed, "Usually. It could be Johnstones or even Nixons or Scotch Armstrongs. Tom's Watt Ridley," he called to the other boy, "Did your uncle say aught about the Scots?"

"Only he hadna seen none," said Tom's Watt, helpfully. "It was all Grahams."

Dodd sucked his teeth.

"Are these out of Liddesdale, Tom's Watt?"

"Oh ay."

Red Sandy came bustling up, with his steel bonnet in his hands and a crossbow under his arm, followed by his two sleuthhounds. The two dogs were bouncing around him, panting and leaping up with their paws and making the odd excited strangulated squeaks of dogs that have been taught not to give tongue.

"No sign of Bangtail," he said, "no sign of Richard Lowther either. The Warden says Sir Robert's to lead the whole castle guard."

Carey nodded and looked pleased. If he had any worries about it they didn't show.

"Sergeant, if you were the Graham leader, where would you be taking the animals?" asked Carey.

"Into Liddesdale across the Bewcastle Waste," said Dodd instantly. "There's plenty of nice valleys in the dale with pens for holding booty in, no better hiding hole."

"I take it we don't want to be pursuing them directly into Liddesdale?" said Carey.

Dodd winced while Red Sandy looked appalled.

"No sir."

"Name me a meeting place within two miles of the mouth of Liddesdale."

Dodd named the Longtownmoor meeting stone which was a mile from Netherby, held by an unfortunate Milburn who paid blackrent to everyone.

Carey smiled at Tom's Watt, drew him aside, spoke for a time and gave him a ring from his hand before drawing his gloves on. Dodd mounted up and trotted between his men to see all of them were properly equipped. The few who owned calivers had left them behind because of the rain. Dodd himself took the burning peat turf on the end of his lance that signified a hot trod. The horn he was supposed to blow in warning if they had to cross over into Scotland was at his belt.

"Sergeant, do you know the Bewcastle Waste well?"

Dodd considered. "Ay sir. Well enough." Red Sandy snorted at this modesty.

"Up here by me, then. I know it not at all and am in your hands."

With the Carlisle bell still clanging irregularly into the night behind them, they walked their horses through the town, glared at by cats interrupted in their own reiving. Once through the gates they came to a canter northwards, the darkness about them sparsely sequined with signal beacons.

They picked up a trail of several dozen cattle a little to the south of Lanercost, the hounds lolloping and panting along and giving no tongue as they had been trained. At least Carey seemed in no hurry to close with the Grahams. As soon as he could the Graham leader dodged into the Waste, and as the sky greyed and the rain fell again, Dodd was threading through the bogs and scrub with Carey uncharacteristically quiet beside him. He rode well enough, Dodd allowed grudgingly, perhaps a little too straight in the saddle for endurance, a little too reluctant to let his mount judge her own pace.

Always Carey wanted to be round to the east of them

and the strategy seemed to be working for the Grahams let themselves be herded westwards rather than northwards. Dawn was theoretical rather than real as they wove in and out of ditches and up hills, while the Grahams doubled back and crossed water to try and lose the hounds, all of it cruelly rough country. By the time it was full morning, Carey at last had lost some of his bounce, and began to take on the experienced loosebacked slouch of Dodd and his men.

By the sourness of his expression, Henry Dodd's men could tell he was enjoying himself, countering every Graham turn and ruse, and reading the man's mind ahead of himself, until he lifted his head, turned while Carey urged his hobby through another little stream, and nodded with supreme satisfaction.

"There they are, sir."

Ahead of them they could make out against the grey wet curtains drooling out of the clouds, the lances and lowing of the raiding party.

"Where are we?" Carey asked, a little breathless.

"One mile south of the meeting stone," said Henry and nodded to the right, "Liddesdale's that way sir."

"No sign of Elliots or Armstrongs."

"Doesna mean there are none," said Dodd, hoping his various cousins by marriage might remember who he was if they were there.

"What are they doing now?"

"Rounding up the cattle again, sir, ready to take them into the Debateable Land."

"How long will it take them?"

"Five minutes."

Carey scraped his thumb on his lower lip where his nicely trimmed courtier's goatee was invading upland pastures. Like all of them Carey was caked in mud and the slogging through the Waste seemed to have dulled even his enthusiasm for movement. They had come about in a broad anticlockwise arc.

"What do you think of them, Sergeant?"

Dodd blinked into the rain and considered.

"They're slow, sir." A thought came to him unbidden

but he suppressed it. As Lowther had said to him many times, it wasn't his job to think.

"Could be the cattle."

"No, see, sir, I could have had the cattle into Scotland by now."

Carey raised an aristocratic eyebrow.

"Are they waiting for us?"

"Might be," said Dodd reluctantly, "I don't know. They might be waiting for us."

"So the betting is they've got someone to back them hiding in the valley?"

"Ay sir."

"Where have they set the ambush?"

"I'm not sure, sir," said Dodd cautiously.

Carey smiled. "As an expert, speaking from your past experience."

Dodd sucked his teeth again, thought and pronounced his opinion. By the end of his explanation, Carey had begun to look worried. He peered over his shoulder at the miserable pale sun where it was struggling against the clouds and squinted at the western horizon. For a moment it almost seemed to Dodd that he was listening. Far away came the peewits of green plover disturbed by the reivers. Carey urged his tired horse to a fast canter up a slight knoll, stood in his stirrups, looked all around, and came trotting back cheerfully again.

"Let's have them then," he said.

"Now sir?"

"Yes, Sergeant." He stood in his stirrups again. "Gentlemen," he said at large to the men, "we're taking back the cattle. With God's help, we have friends on the other side of the Grahams who will come and join the fun." He didn't mention the possibility that the Grahams might have friends too.

There was the clatter and creak of harness as men tightened the straps on their helmets, loosened their swords, gripped their lances. None except Carey had firearms but Carey's were a beautiful pair of dags with a Tower gunsmith's mark on them, ready shotted and wound.

"Nineteen of us?" said Dodd.

"Twenty," said Carey quietly, letting his horse back and snort nervously as he took one gun in each hand. Bloody show-off, thought Dodd, I hope the recoil breaks his wrist.

"There's twenty-five of them at least from their trail," Red Sandy said reasonably, "and ten others and the Elliots unaccounted for . . . We could likely come to some arrangement . . ."

Carey's eyes narrowed. "Now we come to it," he said, "do I have grey hair? Is my face red? Do I look like Richard Lowther to you?"

"No sir, but . . ."

"Which is it to be? Do I shout come on, or do I shout go on and shoot the first coward who hesitates?"

Red Sandy flushed. "'Tis only business . . ."

"No, it's theft." Carey's lip curled. "Christ, I knew you were dishonest and I knew you were sloppy. God as my witness, I never thought you were scared . . ."

Red Sandy darkened to ruby. He backed his horse into the group of men, put his lance in rest.

"All right," said Carey, taking a deep breath, "Let's have the bastards." He spurred his horse to the gallop. Dodd thought of Lowther's gratitude and then decided he didn't care and kicked his hobby till it ran and caught up to Carey in a shower of mud. There were horsemen on the Longtownmoor.

"Elliots?" he yelled, pointing at them.

Carey laughed. "Who knows?" he shouted back.

They had been spotted. Carey put a gun under his arm, winded his own horn three times, dropped it and took the gun again. The strange horsemen shimmered and shifted down the slope in the distance. The raiders put a shot in among the cattle to scatter them and bent low over their horses' necks as they rode hard for Liddesdale. They seemed to think the other group were their friends the Elliots. In the last few seconds Dodd saw the Grahams suddenly haul their horses up short. At that moment, Dodd, Carey and the men were amongst them. Carey shot one Graham in the face, misfired with his other dag from the wet. Ducking a lance, he thrust his guns back in the saddle case and drew his sword which was the long slender article that Dodd had seen him draw on Lowther. He wielded it more with his forearm than his shoulder. Unexpectedly, he managed to run at least one man through under the arm with it: the blade flickered in and out again like a needle. Dodd with his broadsword was mournfully and methodically cutting and kicking his way through the press of men, and Archie Give-it-Them successfully ran a Graham through the thigh with his lance, which broke off.

By which time Thomas Carleton and a number of Musgraves and Fenwicks had surrounded the mêlée and when the Elliots came swarming out of the valley a few seconds later, the reivers had all either run or surrendered, except for the three of them that were dead and one badly wounded. Seeing the situation, the Elliots swung round and rode away back into Liddesdale again as fast as they could, with a few Carletons whooping dangerously after them.

Dodd came upon Carey wiping sweat and rain off his face with a hankerchief while he stood by his horse to let it catch its breath. He was glaring disgustedly at his pretty rapier which had broken off on somebody's jack.

"Five prisoners," Dodd reported, "Young Jock Graham, Young Wattie, Sim's Sim, Henharrow Geordie and . . . er . . . Ekie Graham." Pray that Carey didn't know Ekie Graham was Bangtail's half-brother.

"Where are the horses?" demanded Carey.

"Well, they're here, sir . . ."

"Not the ones we rode, Sergeant, the ones they stole. It's all cattle here."

Dodd looked about. "Ahh," he groaned. Carey's lips were pressed tight together as he strode over to where the prisoners were being tied in a line by Long George and Captain Carleton's younger brother.

"You," he snapped to Young Jock, who was the tallest and the spottiest and had the best jack and helmet, "where's your father?"

Young Jock grinned impudently. "Wouldn't you like to know, eh, Courtier?"

Long George slapped him across the face. "Speak civil to the Deputy Warden," he said.

Young Jock spat on the ground. Carey looked at him narrow-eyed for a moment, suddenly not seeming angry any more. He turned to Red Sandy who was bustling up with ropes over his shoulder.

"Take a list of the Fenwicks, Musgraves and Carletons that helped us," said Carey, "see they get their share for backing a hot trod."

Long George was amused. "Och sir, Captain Carleton'll see to that, never fear."

Captain Carleton was overseeing the gathering up of the Graham weapons and horses. His voice boomed over the moor, saying that the wounded man could bide there until his friends came back for him.

"The prisoners, sir? Shall I find some trees?" asked Red Sandy.

"Trees?"

"To hang them on." Dodd gestured with his thumb. "We caught them red-hand on a lawful hot trod, we have the right."

Carey put his hankerchief away while he thought about it. Archie Give-it-Them put a rope round Young Jock's neck and mounted his horse ready to lead them. Young Jock looked surprised and worried for the first time. He seemed to have a boil in his ear which he was trying to scratch with one shoulder.

"Not today, Sergeant," said Carey, clapping a hand on Dodd's shoulder comfortingly, "they'll hang at Carlisle after a fair hearing."

Red Sandy stared at him in shock. "But sir . . ." he began.

"Gentlemen, gentlemen," Carey reproved them, "be practical. I want to find out where the reived horses have gone." He slapped his horse's neck, and mounted the tired beast gently. "They can't tell me anything if they've long necks and black tongues, now can they? Have them run back to Carlisle."

He sent the prisoners off with ten men and with the remaining nine he set about recapturing the cattle. These were long experienced in being raided and had settled down out of their stampede to munch at what fodder they could find.

Dodd and his men urged their weary horses round about the cattle to gather them again, with the dogs darting and nipping among the legs to help them. It took a while, but they had the cattle running in a stream southwards when Dodd cantered up to the Deputy Warden and asked if he wanted them brought through the Waste again.

"No," said Carey, "we'll bring them through Lanercost valley and through the pass, and not too fast or the milch cows will take sick."

Dodd privately objected to being told something he had known before he was eight, but only turned his horse and yipped angrily at an enterprising calf.

At Lanercost Carey took his Warden's one tenth fee in the form of a cow and a soft-eyed heifer after a ferocious argument over which cattle exactly belonged to the Ogle there, seeing he had not yet got round to branding some of them. A similar argument and arrangement followed with Walter Ridley, whose nephew Tom's Watt watched with interest. Driving their fees ahead of them, they caught up to the prisoners, almost into Carlisle. The reivers were gasping and dripping with the brisk run over rough ground forced on them by the grinning Archie Give-it-Them.

"Yah, get on with you, ye're soft as southerners," he was sneering happily at their protests when Carey came trotting alongside.

"Bastard," croaked Young Jock over his sweat-soaked shoulder when he caught sight of Carey. "Fucking bastard Courtier . . ."

Carey raised an eyebrow a fraction, tutted, looked critically at the prisoners and told Archie to take them for a little run round the walls of Carlisle before he put them in the dungeons, since they still seemed so fresh and lippy.

Wednesday, 21st June, 2 a.m.

At the same time as Dodd was hearing his neck-verse in his dream, Janet Dodd was shaken awake by one of her women, a young cousin by the name of Rowan Armstrong.

"Mistress, mistress," she hissed, "Topped Hobbie's ridden in, there's reivers coming."

Janet was instantly awake. She pulled her stays over her head and her petticoat, while Rowan fumbled her kirtle off the chest. "How far?"

"A few miles away. He could hear them but not see them."

"What are they doing out on a night like this? Are the men awake?"

"I told him to fetch up Geordie."

"Good girl." A horn sounded from the barnekin, loud and urgent. Janet disappeared in the midst of her kirtle, reappeared, her fingers flying among the lacings. She went to the narrow window, opened the shutter and leaned out into the muggy darkness – cloud and no moon, a fine soaking rain. "Did Topped Hobbie say who it was coming?"

"He thought it was Grahams, but he doesn't know. He thought he heard Jock of the Peartree's voice, mistress."

Janet pulled her lip through the gap in her teeth. "You go and wake the other maids, get yourself dressed and booted, then go help them bring in the cattle and the sheep nearby."

"What about the horses, mistress?"

"Shilling and Courtier are both in the lower room of the tower already."

The horn stopped blowing, there were torches being lit in the barnekin. She peered out into the blackness as she pulled on her boots. "Geordie," she shrieked.

"Yes, Janet," her brother's voice sounded strained.

"Is the beacon lit?"

"As soon as we can get the kindling to catch, Janet. There are other beacons alight already, the March is up."

"Are the men in harness?"

"They will be. We'll ride out and fight them in . . ."

"You will not. You will bring in every beast we have and bar the gate, then get on the wall with your bows."

"We canna catch them all in the time."

"Bring in what you can."

"But if he fires us . . ."

"Every roof is wet through. Do as I say."

Janet ran down the stairs with her skirts hitched over her belt, out the door of the tower and into the barnekin which was already filling with desperately lowing cows, two half-panicked horses and frightened women trying to control over-excited children. Janet ran out of the gate and climbed on a stone to direct the running traffic of cattle, horses, men, boys, chickens, pigs, children, and, she would have sworn, rats as well. They could hear hooves; she waited as long as she dared, then shook her head.

"Come in, Geordie and Simon and Little Robert, leave the rest!" she yelled. "Come on in."

Her cousin and her brother came galloping out of the mirk on their own horses, and Willie's Simon had an arrow in his arm. Janet waited on them as the hooves and the shouting grew louder, slid through the narrow gate last of all, helped Geordie shut it and bar it and barricade it with settles from the hall, as a couple of arrows thudded into the wood. There was whooping and the flicker of torches on the other side.

"Go to the kitchen," she told Willie's Simon who was white-faced and gripping the place where the arrow had pinned the muscle of his upper arm to his jack. "Kat Pringle will see to it. Give your crossbow to the best shot among the men. Where's Little Robert?"

"I thought he was already in," said Geordie as he took the crossbow and began winding it up. Willie's Simon slid awkwardly from his horse and walked away.

"He's not in the tower," Janet said, frowning. "He must be outside still, God help him, I hope he has the sense to lay low."

There was loud shouting outside and the noise of a scuffle. Janet looked about for a ladder to the fighting platform, and then motioned Geordie to go up it first.

"Janet . . ." he began to protest.

"Shut up." He obeyed, climbed the ladder and stayed crouched like the other men on the platform, while she climbed up behind and squatted beside him. She peered cautiously over the pointed wooden stakes.

On the hill something was burning: no doubt it was Clem Pringle's farm, since it was traditional to set light to it. The stones that made the walls were set hard as rock together from repeated firings.

There were some men riding about, some torches set in the earth to give them light, two torches in two roofs, trying stubbornly to spread through the sodden turves. A little further off she could hear protesting lowing and whistles.

"Jock!" she shouted, "Jock of the Peartree!"

An arrow on fire sped over the wall, nearly setting her hair ablaze and she squatted lower, crawled further along.

"I want to talk to you, Jock." Before the next arrow could come, she moved again. Somebody put the other one out.

"Where's my horse?" came a shout from the other side.

"If you can see him, shoot him," Janet whispered to Geordie.

"Steady Janet, do we want a feud with the Grahams?"

"You fool, we're already at feud with them."

"Oh Christ."

"Don't blaspheme in my house."

"But you . . ."

"Shut up. *Jock!*" she roared.

"Janet Dodd, I have Little Robert here and I want my horse back. In fact, I want all your horses."

"What?" She peeped over the palisade and there he was in the torchlight, the young fool, fifteen years old and no sense, kneeling in the mud with four Graham lances at his throat and back, and blood purling down his face from a slice on the head.

"I bought him fair and square," she shouted. "If I'd known he was yours I wouldna touch him on the end of a lance. But I bought and paid for him."

"What did you pay?"

"Five English pounds."

"I dinna believe you, Janet, no one would sell my Caspar for so little, he's the cream of Scotland. Your man Sergeant Dodd took him off my son when he shot him dead from behind."

"He'd nothing to do with it, you know that."

"I don't, Janet. Sweetmilk's dead, your man had the body and lied to me about it. Who else would kill Sweetmilk, he was the gentlest wean I ever had."

God give me strength and patience, Janet thought, remembering Sweetmilk in a brawl at the last Warden's Day. "Jock, would you keep hold of a horse from a man you'd murdered like that?"

There was silence on the other side.

After a while Janet stood up. "Give me Little Robert back, Jock."

Jock's voice was mocking. "I'll let you buy him off me with all the mounts you have in there and for a sign what a patient man I am, I'll not even take the kine."

Janet closed her eyes so as not to see Little Robert trying not to wriggle when the lancepoints poked him as their wielders' horses moved.

"I canna give you Shilling," she said. "He's sick with what killed Mildred."

"Fair enough. Ye've five mounts to give me then: my Caspar, and the nags your two brothers were riding and the two from the Pringles. Do it now or I'll use this one for pricking practice."

Down in the barnekin Willie's Simon was staring up at her, his arm bandaged and in a sling. She nodded at him. Anger in every inch of his back, he went to the tiny postern door in the base of the tower and led out their beautiful Courtier, which Jock called Caspar. The other horses were still out in the courtyard.

Janet beckoned Simon up onto the fighting platform and waited until all the crossbows were wound up. Rowan had one as well: she was a good shot and Janet told her to pick out Jock and keep her bow aimed at him.

"Send Little Robert forward," she shouted, "and you all fall back ten paces."

Down on the ground, everyone was watching as she peeked through a shot-hole while the horses stamped and snorted and pulled at their halters.

At a prodding from Jock's lance, Little Robert got unsteadily to his feet and staggered forwards. Janet had Clemmie Pringle, Kat's vast husband and Wide Mary on either side of the gate, ready to shut it if there should be treachery. She opened it, then smacked each horse hard on the rump and shrieked. The horses broke forwards through the gate, snorting and panicking.

"Run, Little Robert!" she yelled.

He ran, dodging to and fro and between Caspar and Sim's Redmane, a lance stuck in the mud behind him, he tripled his speed and fell into Janet's arms as the gate shut behind him. There was nothing wrong with him bar his headwound, a little rough handling and stark fear, so she passed him to Clemmie Pringle to take to Kat, and climbed the ladder again.

There was confusion as the Grahams caught their booty and then the sound of hooves riding off. "Stay where you are," she snarled, when Geordie began to unwind his crossbow. "How do we know this isn't some trick?"

"Why would they trick us, Janet?" Geordie asked reasonably, "They've got what they came for."

"Henry'll be fit to be tied," said a voice in the background.

Janet pretended she hadn't heard. "We'll wait until morning and then we'll out that little fire and see the damage and I'll take Shilling to Carlisle.

"The March is up," said Geordie, "Lowther's on the trod already if they didna pay him for this. Why go to . . ."

"Did ye not hear what I told you? There's a new Deputy there and I've business with one of Dodd's men."

"God help him," muttered one of the other men.

Wednesday, 21st June, 9 a.m.

Lady Philadelphia Scrope was glaring worriedly at her embroidery hoop as she sat on a padded stool in the Queen Mary Tower and finished a rampant blackwork bee. She heard her brother's boots coming heavily up the stairs, tripping once. There was a pause at the door before he opened it and came in.

Almost laughing with relief at the sight of him, she put down her work and ran to hug him. He was rank with sweat, horse and human, and the oddly bitter scents of sodden leather and iron, he was spattered from head to foot with mud and blood, but none of it fresh enough to be his, thank God. The only thing not some shade of brown on him, other than the grubby rag of his collar, was his face which was white with weariness.

"You caught them," she said joyfully, "You caught the reivers."

Robin's swordbelt clattered onto a chest and the pieces of rapier fell out.

"Bloody thing broke," grunted her brother, stripping off his gloves and fighting the laces of his helmet which had shrunk in the rain so that the knots became inextricable. He started to swear but Philadelphia delved in her workbag, brought out her little broidery shears and snipped the laces, so he could take it off and shake out his hair. She helped him with the ones on his jack which had also shrunk, took it off his shoulders for him, acting the squire as she had on occasion for her husband, and set it on its stand. As always it surprised her with its weight: you expected a steel helmet to be heavy, but you couldn't see the metal plates in a jack under the padded leather. She set to work on his doublet points.

He swatted at her feebly.

"For God's sake, Philly, I can do it myself. And where's Barnabus?"

"He had to go a message." The room was beginning to steam up.

"Christ, who sent my own bloody servant off . . ."

"And anyway, he told me himself he's not much of a hand with armour and suchlike, you never took him to the Netherlands with you remember. I'm much better at it than he is."

"I can't afford to lend you any more . . ."

Resisting the impulse to punch him, Philadelphia sat him on the stool, which made him wince satisfactorily, and hauled off his left boot.

"Be quiet," she said. "Behind the screen is my lord's own hip bath with hot water in it. The cold is in the ewer next to it, don't knock it over. There's a towel and a fresh shirt airing on a hook by the chest, and your other suit, the good cramoisie, and your other boots and – come on, Robert, *pull* will you? – a fresh pair of hose. Don't worry about the leaves in the water, they're lovage, they'll soothe your saddle burns . . ." She put the boots down near the door.

"How do you know I've got saddle burns?"

"And on the table by the bath is a posset . . ."

"I hate possets."

"Which you will drink and a mess of eggs on sippets of toast with herbs in, which I made myself . . ."

"Which I must eat?"

"Which you will eat or I'll wave your shirt out the window like the mother on a wedding morning. My lord wants to hear the whole tale when you've finished. Leave your soiled linen on the floor as you usually do and I'll send Barnabus as soon as he's back."

"Why the cramoisie suit?"

She hid a pert little grin. "For a good and sufficient reason which I will tell you as soon as you've finished with the Warden. Don't forget to comb your hair."

She dodged his attempt to stop her and cross-examine her about whatever female plot she was working, humphed at him like a mother of five and then her skirts swished through the door and she was gone.

Wondering what she meant about his shirt, he pulled the clammy thing off and found its lower half spotted with fresh blood in a dozen places. Shuddering he hobbled to the screen, holding up his hose with one hand and feeling the damage tenderly with the other.

Wednesday, 21st June, 10 a.m.

It was unjust, thought Dodd, after Carey had supervised the penning of their fees in the little fold within the Carlisle castle walls, the feeding, watering and rubbing down of their tired hobbies, and the feeding, watering and congratulating of the men and gone wearily to the Queen Mary Tower. What was unjust was that he had servants to help him clean up after fighting, whereas John Ogle's boy who was supposed to look after Dodd's needs had disappeared to Carlisle town. Dodd was reduced to a quick scour under the barracks pump which got the worst off; he left his jack to Bessie's Andrew and received with sour silence Bangtail's explanations of the whorehouse he'd been in when the summons came to go out on the hot trod.

He thought he'd done well for himself until he saw the blasted Courtier, hair combed, sweet-smelling as a maid on her wedding morning, and spruce in a fresh ruff and a fine London suit the colour of a summer pudding, with one of Scrope's spare swords on his belt. It was enough to make a man puke.

Captains Carleton and Dick Musgrave, and the bad penny Sir Richard Lowther, were all present at the meeting in the Warden's council chamber. Carey told the tale of the raid and the capture of five Grahams red-handed with a fine blend of modesty and fact-improving. It was not a long tale; shorter by far than the reports Lowther generally gave, in which he explained why the trods he led always, for some excellent reason, just missed catching the reivers.

"What will you do with your fees?" asked Lowther.

"We might kill the older cow to salt down, but the other two we'll sell to buy powder and guns," said Carey.

"And the Grahams?" asked Scrope.

"We can keep them until the next Day of Truce," said Carey. "Then I can swear of my own knowing that they were raiders and hang them where their deaths will do most good."

Scrope nodded at the sense of this. "That's why you didn't hang them on the spot."

"Yes, my lord," said Carey. "I also wanted to talk to them."

"Oh?" asked Lowther, "Why?"

"Horses," answered Carey. "I'm concerned about horses. Not just the ones we lack for your father's funeral, my lord, but the fact that we seem to have a general famine of horses."

"I heard there was a horse plague in Scotland," said Lowther.

"Did you?" said Carey, "I've not heard of it. Where is it worst?"

Lowther shrugged. "I don't know. It would account for the lack of horses . . ."

"It would," said Carey slowly, 'but what concerns me is that the Grahams might be reiving horses for a different reason."

"Why?" Scrope's fingers were at their anxious self-knitting again.

"For a large-scale long-range raid at the next opportunity," said Carey. "If they want to ride deep into England, they'll need remounts, especially for the return when they'll be driving spoil and at risk of meeting us."

Lowther's eyes had gone so small they almost disappeared under his grey eyebrows.

"What happened this raid . . ." Carey shook his head. "They used the cattle as bait, knowing we'd follow, with Elliots to spring the trap just outside Liddesdale. Luckily Captain Carleton was there . . ."

"No luck about it," growled Carleton, deep in his chest, "I got your message.' Lowther glared at him.

". . . so we caught them. But meanwhile the main band of Grahams were winnowing the border of horses and taking them off north to Liddesdale. From the preliminary complaints, I'd say they had enough for a journey of a hundred miles or more and back again, depending on how many reivers there are."

"When would this happen?" asked Scrope.

"Well, they won't want the horses for long because feeding that many animals could beggar them for their winter horsefeed. And further, the perfect date would be one when all the gentlemen of the March will be otherwise engaged." He said the last couple of words with a great deal of emphasis and looked at Scrope.

"Oh Lord," said the Warden with deep dismay. "You mean on the day of my father's funeral?"

"Yes, my lord. I would also point out that the preparations are not ready, even if we had the horses for the bier."

"I thought you were supposed to be arranging it," sneered Lowther. Carey did not rise to this.

"I have been a little busy, Sir Richard."

"Yes, yes, quite," said Scrope. "Are you saying that you want me to postpone the funeral?"

"Yes, my lord. For a few days only. Hold it on Sunday rather than tomorrow. If you made a proclamation at the Market Cross this noon and sent fast messengers to the gentlemen expected for the service warning them to be ready for a long-range raid . . ."

"On the evidence of the theft of a few nags?" protested Lowther. "It's hardly conclusive that they'd be trying any such thing. And this is the wrong time of year."

"It looks bad to me," grunted Carleton.

"What about the body?" continued Lowther, "Won't it start to stink?"

Scrope was offended. "My revered father's corpse has been embalmed of course, a few days should do no harm."

"And I'd rather postpone the funeral unnecessarily than have to explain to the Queen why we allowed the broken men of the Debateable Land to foray deep into England," said Carey sincerely.

Lowther, who had never met her, rolled his eyes but Scrope, who had, was nodding anxiously.

"I think you're right, Sir Robert, we'll postpone the funeral until Sunday. I'll see to the proclamations and messages. Will you make any other arrangements necessary, and deal with the complaints from this raid."

"Yes, my lord."

The meeting broke up and Carleton caught up with Carey as he hurried to the door.

"Here's your ring back, Sir Robert. Now, I'm sending a message to my cousin that keeps a stud in Northumberland – he has some draft horses with good dark coats he'd be willing to lend us for a fee. They'll be here by Saturday."

"Thank you, Captain. That solves the foremost of my worries . . ."

"Oh ay? What about this long-range raid?"

Carey shrugged. "There's little I can do about that save be ready for them if they come. Though I'd give a lot to know where they're gathering."

"If it's Bothwell planning it, they'll be riding from Lochmaben."

Carey shook his head. "I doubt it's the Earl. He's in such bad odour with the Scottish king since that mad attack on Holyrood Palace last year, he'll want to keep the Queen of England as sweet as he can. No, I think it's Jock of the Peartree planning this and Sweetmilk was concerned in it somehow when he was killed."

Carleton nodded. "I heard that the Grahams were blaming Dodd for the murder, poor man."

"You don't think he did it either?"

"God, no," Carleton laughed. "Any man of any sense that had a Graham corpse on his hands like that would take him down to the Rockcliffe marshes and throw him in the deepest bog he could find, not take him up to the old battlefield and try and hide him in a gorse bush." Carleton shook his head, his broad face full of mirth. "Me, I'd leave him on Elliot or Armstrong land and let them take the heat. Dodd's no jewel, but he's not mad."

As they went down the stair, Carey put his hand to his head as he remembered something.

"By the way, Captain, you've a right to a part of our fee for helping the trod, haven't you?"

Carleton clapped a massive paw on Carey's shoulder.

"Lad," he said, "watching you and Dodd and the garrison mixing it with those Grahams was almost worth the fee to me.

Pay me a quarter of whatever you make on the heifer and the younger cow. I haven't enjoyed myself so much for months, and you won me a pound off my brother."

"Oh?" smiled Carey, "what did you bet on?"

"Whether you'd dare attack, what else?"

Carey laughed. "At least it wasn't on whether I'd fall off my horse."

Carleton's face was full of pleasure. "Nay, Sir Robert, I won that bet the day before yesterday."

Wednesday, 21st June, 10 a.m.

Philadelphia Scrope was waiting impatiently for the men to stop blathering and come out of the council room at the back of the keep. She stopped Robert, who was looking very fine, if a bit baggy under the eyes, and took him mysteriously by the arm.

"All right, Philly," said her brother resignedly, "what's the surprise."

"Come with me."

"Philly, I've about a hundred things to do and at least fifty letters to write and Richard Bell promised me he could only be my clerk this morning, so . . ."

"It'll take no more than ten minutes."

Carey sighed and suffered himself to be led. They went out through the Captain's gate and down the covered way a little to Bessie's handsome inn and through the arch to the courtyard.

Behind them three of Dodd's men came tumbling out of the inn's common room, teasing a fourth for missing out on his share of the trod fee. The men headed for the drawbridge gate shouting crude jokes about the origins of Bangtail's nickname and how they would improve it, looking very pleased with themselves. Carey watched them go approvingly and when Philly pulled impatiently on his arm, he turned the way she was pointing him.

A tall woman in a fine woollen riding habit of dark moss

green and a lace edged ruff was standing with her back to him, talking to a sandy-haired young man with broad shoulders and a terrible collection of spots, pockmarks and freckles. Carey stopped dead when he saw them.

"Philadelphia . . ." he growled.

She grinned naughtily at him and went over to the woman. "Lady Widdrington," she said, "how splendid to see you."

They embraced, and Lady Elizabeth Widdrington saw Carey over Philly's shoulder. Philly could feel the indrawn breath and had a good view of the blush creeping up from under Lady Widdrington's ruff to colour her rather long face to a surprising semblance of beauty.

Lady Elizabeth curtseyed to Robert, who automatically swept her an elegant court bow. He paused, took breath to speak, then paused again. Philadelphia decided to take a hand.

"There, Robin," she said blandly, "you can go back to your dull old papers now."

Lady Widdrington was the first to recover her senses.

"Sir Robert," she said formally, "I believe I should congratulate you on your Deputyship. I hope you don't miss London and the Court."

He made a little bow and laughed with delight.

"Only you," he said, instincts reasserting themselves, "could have brought me here so quickly to the land of cattle-thieves. I'd hoped I could find an excuse to chase a few raiders into Northumberland and catch them dramatically on your doorstep . . ."

"And if necessary you would have paid them to go that way," said Lady Widdrington drily. Carey laughed again.

"Absolutely."

"Of course, I'm only here for my Lord Scrope's funeral. Your sister invited me."

Philly managed to look both smug and shocked. "It was Sir Henry I invited."

"In the certainty that his gout would prevent him coming," said Robert. "Honestly, Philadelphia, your plots are transparent."

"Who cares so long as they work," said Philly. "Will you come to dinner, Lady Widdrington. I'm hoping my brother remembered to bring some new madrigal sheets with him, and if he didn't I'll make him listen to one of our border minstrels instead."

"No, please, save me," said Robert. "I brought the madrigals and they're well beyond my voice so good luck to you."

"You're invited too, Robin," said Philly inflexibly. "We need a tenor. Now . . ."

What she was about to suggest next nobody ever found out. There was a sudden shouting and commotion further down the street, near the drawbridge gate.

A woman had come riding in at a gallop, sandy red hair flying. She hauled her horse back on his haunches when she saw Dodd's men staring at her from the gate. Then she leaped from the saddle and caught one of them by the front of his jack. She let fly with a punch and booted him in the groin for good measure. The man tried to defend himself, hurt his hand on her stays, got another boot in his kneecap, and rolled away. He ran limping up the street with the woman in full pursuit, her homespun skirts kilted up in her belt, and Carey saw it was Bangtail Graham and that his enemy was Janet Dodd.

Automatically he stepped out of the courtyard into the street.

"What the . . .?"

Bangtail ran behind Carey and dodged another punch.

"It wasna me, it wasna me . . ." he was shouting, "I only told my brother . . ."

Janet Dodd sneered at him as she circled round. "Get out from behind that man, Bangtail, you bastard, you lily-livered git, you've lost me five horses, a house and half a field of grain trampled . . ."

"Mrs Dodd, Mrs Dodd . . ." Carey tried to remonstrate.

"I've no quarrel with you Deputy but if ye protect yon treacherous blabbermouthed . . ."

"What's he done?"

Behind Janet, Carey could see Sergeant Dodd sprinting down from the Castle yard.

Bangtail unwisely made a break for it from behind Carey's broad back, and Janet was on him. Philly, Lady Widdrington and Young Henry Widdrington watched with open-mouthed curiosity. Bangtail tried his best, even marked Janet's cheek, but he was born down and kicked again before Dodd came up behind his wife and grabbed her round the middle, swung her about like a dancer in the volta, dodged a fist, and roared in her ear, "Goddam it wife, what's wrong?"

"He sold us to Jock of the Peartree," she shouted. "That filthy bastard Graham told Jock . . ."

"I never . . ." protested Bangtail.

"What? What happened?" Dodd was shaking his wife's shoulders. "Are you saying Jock raided us last night?"

"Five horses," shrieked Janet, "five horses, Clem Pringle's house burned again, half the barley trampled into the mud, poor Margaret miscarrying her bairn with the fright, Willie's Simon with an arrow in his arm because yon strilpit nyaff couldna keep his mouth shut . . ."

"Jock of the Peartree did this?"

Carey watched with interest. Dodd perpetually looked as if he had lost a shilling and found a penny, but he was beginning to suspect that that often denoted good humour. Now the long jaw and surly face were darkening and the thin mouth whitening with rage.

"I talked to him from the wall," Janet said catching her breath. "Courtier's his horse, he called him Caspar. You said you'd know if he was reived from this country, you said you'd know . . . Stay there, Bangtail, or I'll gut you . . ."

"You never gave him Courtier," shouted Dodd.

"I had nae choice, he caught Little Robert and ransomed him for all the horses except poor Shilling," Janet wailed. "He said Courtier was his and he said he was proof you'd killed Sweetmilk . . ."

"Jock of the Peartree has *Courtier* . . .?"

"Oh Christ," muttered Carey under his breath, having listened to Dodd boast about the beautiful stallion most of the way back to Carlisle that morning.

"Wake up, Dodd, wake up. It's not just the horse, it's the

Grahams thinking you were the one who murdered Sweetmilk. Ye think it's bad now? What will ye do when they come and burn the tower and us all in our beds . . .?"

Looking at his Sergeant, Carey could already hear the hooves thundering and the lances clattering. Dodd's face was now completely white.

"Mrs Dodd, Sergeant," Carey appealed, stepping between them with his hands out and his most courtly appeasing smile on his face. He managed to have got between both Dodds and Bangtail who was nursing a bleeding nose and his groin and looking terrified. "Please. If you've been raided . . ."

"What business is it of yours?" demanded Dodd, "I'll have my own justice. Janet did you send to your father?"

"I did and I also . . ."

By this time a small audience had formed, including Elizabeth, Philly and Henry Widdrington, plus Scrope himself, glimpsed like a nervous crane fly beyond thc crowd.

"If you will come into the castle," hissed Carey, "we'll see what we can . . ."

"Keep yer long neb out of my affairs, Courtier," snarled Dodd.

Carey was tired: in particular he was very weary of Dodd's sullenness. Without any of the usual warning signs his patience suddenly snapped. He drew his borrowed sword, stepped up close to Dodd and put the point against the man's belly.

There was a moment of shocked silence. Scrope winced and began backing away. Out of the corner of his eye, Carey saw Janet's hand go to the hilt of her knife.

"Now," he said very softly. "Firstly, Sergeant, you will address me as sir if you wish to speak to me. Secondly, this ugly street brawl will stop. Thirdly, you will come into my office now, with me, where we will consider what is to be done. And fourthly, Dodd, if you tell me this is not my affair once more, I'll run you through. Mrs Dodd unless you want to be a widow, you'll put up your weapon."

For a moment the whole thing held in the balance, and then Janet said, "What *is* your interest, Sir Robert?"

"If the Sergeant of the Warden's Guard is raided by any

man, Scots, English or Debateable, that makes it my affair. I will not have it."

"You'll lead the trod?"

"I will."

Janet smiled, which was in some ways more frightening than her rage.

"*If* there's a trod," added Carey.

"What does the Warden say?"

Scrope was trying to become invisible at the entrance to a wynd. Carey glared at him.

"Oh I agree," said Scrope, rearranging his gown. "Absolutely. Can't have the Sergeant raided. It's an insult to the Wardenry."

Thank you Thomas, thought Carey, watching Dodd intently. Dodd was still tense, but seemed to be thinking. He nodded. Carey put his sword away and the audience began to wander off on important appointments, since the thrilling prospect of a fight between the Warden's Deputy, the Sergeant and his wife seemed to have faded. Philly was speaking in a low tactful voice to the Widdringtons and leading them into Bessie's. God damn the luck, that Elizabeth should have had to see such a brawl.

"Now please, come up to my chamber," he said to the Dodds. "No need to broadcast to Jock what trouble he's in." Not very subtle flattery, but it worked well enough.

Both Dodds nodded at that and they all walked docilely towards the castle. Missing someone important, Carey fell back a little and spotted Bangtail limping down an alley. He darted after the man, grabbed his collar and twisted his arm up his back, propelled him along in front. Bangtail gibbered excuses.

"Silence," hissed Carey, "or I'll break your arm."

"But I never . . ."

"I'll give you to Janet Dodd."

"Yes sir."

Scrope disappeared, muttering about arrangements for the funeral. Carey barged Bangtail up the stairs of the Queen Mary Tower, followed by the Dodds. Once into his second chamber, he ordered Richard Bell the clerk out, pulled up a stool for Janet to sit on, kicked the door to the stairs shut, dropped Bangtail in a heap on the floor and then sat at his desk. The others stood looking at each other.

"Barnabus!" Carey roared.

The servant's ferret-like face poked nervously round the door.

"Fetch wine and four goblets. Send Young Hutchin to bring in Mrs Dodd's horse and have him rubbed down and settled with some fodder in the stables."

It was interesting to watch how they waited. Janet ignored the proffered seat and stood with her arms folded and her hip cocked and her long wiry ginger hair adrift from its pins down her back with a colour on her cheeks that the Court ladies spent hours in front of their mirrors to achieve. Dodd simply stood in a lanky slouch, his fingers tapping occasionally on his belt buckle. Bangtail had the sense to stay where he'd been dropped, pinching his nose to stop the blood.

Barnabus came in with the wine and four silver goblets from Carey's own silver chest. He had a napkin over his arm and at Carey's imperceptible nod he poured, bowed and removed himself.

Carey rose, passed around the goblets as if he were hosting a dinner party in London. Bangtail took his with considerable surprise and some gratitude.

"Sergeant Dodd, Mrs Dodd, Mr Graham," said Carey formally. Bangtail blinked, seemed to get the message and scrambled to his feet. He quailed at Janet's glare but remained standing. "I give you the return of the Sergeant's horses and confusion to Jock of the Peartree."

"Ay," muttered Dodd. Bangtail coughed, Janet said nothing. They all drank.

Carey seated himself once more, cleared some bills of complaint away and looked up again.

"We will never again have a scene like that in public." Janet took breath to speak but Carey simply carried on. "I don't care if King James is hammering over the border with the entire Scots lordship at his back and Bangtail is to blame, it will not happen again. Is that understood?"

Dodd nodded, Janet simply pursed her lips.

"Please, Mrs Dodd, be seated." She sat. "Now give me the story."

He heard the tale in silence, turned to Bangtail.

"Mr Graham. You were not with us on the hot trod as your duty was, where were you?"

"I was sick," Bangtail said full of aggrievement, "I was sick in my bed with an ague . . ."

"That's not the tale you told me," snorted Dodd, "An hour ago you said you were at the bawdy house asleep and never heard the bell."

Bangtail reddened and looked at the floor.

"Somebody told the Graham family who had this horse Sweetmilk rode," said Carey reasonably. "Who else knew you had the animal, Sergeant?"

Dodd counted off on his fingers. "Me, my wife, the lousy git that sold him to her – Reverend Turnbull – anyone who was in Bessie's courtyard last night."

"You saw Courtier," said Janet accusingly to Bangtail, "You came in from the midden while I was talking to Dodd."

"Ay," growled Dodd, "and then you were off somewhere in an almighty hurry. Ye left the game."

"But I didna, I swear it on my oath . . ." Janet looked as if she was about to interrupt. Carey glared at her and she contained herself. Bangtail was waving his arms and clearly winding himself up for a magnificent weaving together of diverse falsehoods.

"Bangtail Cuthbert Graham," said Carey very quietly, "I take very seriously any man who forswears himself to me. I don't care who else you lie to, but not to me. Do you understand?"

"Ay sir," mumbled Bangtail.

"Now, I ask you again and for the last time. Did you tell anyone of the Sergeant's new horse?"

Bangtail's boot toe scraped in the rushes and kicked a flowerhead into the fireplace.

"I might . . . I might have mentioned it by accident to Ekie last night – that's my half-brother – I think I was talking of

. . . of well, fine horseflesh and where you could get it and I might have said the Sergeant's wife had a stallion that was as fine as the King of Scotland's own. And that's all."

Dodd remained ominously silent, while Janet simply snorted. Carey let the silence run for a bit. Bangtail flushed, looked at the floor, squashed a stray rush with his other boot toe, coughed and added, "I might have said I thought it was Jock's new stallion, Caspar, but I asked him not to tell."

Janet let out a single derisory "Ha!" and subsided again.

"How many men would we need to take your horses back from Jock of the Peartree?" Carey asked Dodd. The Sergeant considered for a minute, his considerable military sense at last beginning to work.

"It's well too late to stop him reaching Liddesdale, especially with only horses to drive," he said mournfully. "And to pry him out of Liddesdale with the notice he's had – I wouldna like to try it with less than a thousand men, sir."

Privately Carey thought that was optimistic. "Bangtail, how many men can your uncle have in the saddle by this afternoon?"

Bangtail looked shifty. "I don't know . . ."

"I think you do know, Bangtail," Carey said with quiet venom, "and I'm waiting to hear it from you if you want to keep your neck the length it is now."

"What would you hang me for, sir?" demanded Bangtail. "I never did . . ."

"March treason, what else?" said Carey, smiling unpleasantly. "For bringing in raiders."

"Oh." Bangtail thought for a little longer. "By this afternoon he'd have 800 men or so, plus however many Elliots felt like turning out, and another 300 in the morning, if he calls in the Debateable Land broken men or the Johnstones. If Old Wat Scott of Harden comes in for him, well, it's another 500 at least and . . ."

"Going into Liddesdale on a foray with Jock warned and his kinship behind him . . ." Carey shook his head.

"I can bring in a hundred Dodds myself," said Henry, "and Janet's brothers and father can call on another two hundred, all English Armstrongs. And Kinmont Willie would listen to her, he's an uncle and he likes her and he can have a thousand men in the saddle by morning if he wants . . ."

Carey shut his eyes momentarily at the thought of the West March descending into bloody chaos three days after he arrived.

"Are ye saying it's too hard to go and fetch Courtier back from Jock of the Peartree?" asked Janet. Carey felt his temper rise again, she was near as dammit giving him the lie. He took a breath and held it, let it out again.

"No, Mrs Dodd. I am saying that to go into Liddesdale bald-headed and crying for vengeance is simply stupid, since Jock will have laid an ambush and called out every man he could last night in the hope that you and the Sergeant would do precisely what you wanted to do. He'll cut all your kin to pieces, take prisoners for ransom and go off laughing to run Dodd's horse at the next race he can."

They exchanged glances and looked at the floor.

"So there's nothing ye can do," said Janet.

"On the contrary, since your husband is my man, there is a great deal I can and will do. In fact, I give you my word on it. You'll have your horses back."

Sergeant Dodd nodded grudgingly. Janet still looked dubious but hadn't the courage to call him a liar. That was good enough for Carey, he didn't expect to be believed without having to prove himself.

"Meantime, I want you both to make me out a bill of complaint for the Day of Truce."

Janet nodded. "You'll see it's called then, will you, sir?"

"Naturally. Richard Bell can help you if you need . . ."

"I know how to make a bill of complaint, sir," said Dodd huffily.

"I'm sorry, Sergeant, of course you do," said Carey at his most charming. "If you see to it now, I can promise you the bill will be called at the next Day of Truce."

They took the hint. "Thank you, sir," said Janet. Dodd grunted assent, and Carey ushered them to the door. "Send someone to Janet's father and your brothers, Sergeant, we don't want them wasting their time."

"Ay sir."

Both Dodds clattered in silence down the stairs. Bangtail began sliding out the door to follow them, but Carey blocked his passage.

"But I thought . . ."

"Bangtail," said Carey, full of regret, "If you were capable of thought, you wouldn't *be* here. What possessed you? Never mind. You stay here under lock and key until we get the Sergeant's horses back."

"In jail, sir?" Bangtail protested.

"In jail."

"I'll give ye my parole."

Carey shook his head. "I'd like to take it, but I daren't."

"Och sir, don't put me in the jail, its . . ."

"If I have any more bloody rubbish from you, Bangtail, I'll chain you as well. Now come on. And cheer up, I expect it'll only be for a couple of days."

Wednesday, 21st June, 11 a.m.

The castle dungeon was extremely damp after all the rain and stank as badly as most jails. Carey shoved Bangtail into the last empty cell, slammed the door and peered through the Judas hole. Bangtail was sitting on the bare bench, chewing nervously on one of his nails.

One of Lowther's men, whom Carey vaguely remembered was a Fenwick, came in carrying a bag full of loaves of bread and a small cheese. Behind him Young Hutchin was staggering under a firkin of ale. Both of them looked surprised to see him there, so he leaned against a wall and watched as they cut up the cheese and threw the food into each cell.

"Hey," shouted Young Jock Graham, "where's the butter, man? Lowther promised . . ."

"Shut up," growled Fenwick, "the Deputy's here."

"Well, I want to talk to him."

"It isna . . ."

"I want to talk to Young Jock too," said Carey agreeably. "Let me in."

Fenwick did so, and Carey went in and stood at a safe distance. Jock of the Peartree's third eldest living son was a lanky long-faced man with greasy black hair, about twenty-three and just past the uneasy borderline between youth and maturity. No doubt he already had a collection of foul bills and complaints against him as long as his arm. Young Jock did not seem pleased to see the Deputy.

"Who're ye?" he demanded. "Where's Lowther?"

"I'm the new Deputy Warden," said Carey, "I'm also the man that captured you and didn't hang you on the spot. You should thank me."

Young Jock grunted ungratefully and sank his teeth into the cheese. Three weevils popped their heads out and wriggled and he spat them into the straw and stamped on them, then swallowed the rest.

"What d'ye want?"

"I want," said Carey thoughtfully, "a full account of where your father has taken the horses he reived last night and also what he's planning to do with them."

Young Jock stared at him as if he was mad. At that moment, Young Hutchin knocked and came through the door with a leather mug full of ale, which Young Jock took and gulped down.

"Now then, Young Hutchin," Jock was picking absent-mindedly at his ear.

"I'm sorry to see you here, Jock," said the boy. "Can I get you anything else?"

"Ay, you can find me the keys and a nice sharp dagger." Young Jock examined his fingernail for trophies.

Hutchin smiled and left while Carey hummed a little tune.

"What are ye waiting for, Courtier." Jock was delving at his ear again.

"I'm waiting for you to tell me what I asked."

Young Jock spat messily near Carey's boots.

"You can wait there until you die, ye bastard, I'm telling you nothing."

"It could save your neck."

"Go to the devil, Courtier, my neck's safe enough."

Young Jock set himself to eating and Carey nodded, banged on the door to be let out and watched carefully while Fenwick locked it after him.

On his way out, he paused to shout through the Judas hole at Bangtail.

"I want to know what's going on, Bangtail, and you'll tell me."

"I willna," said Bangtail feebly.

"You surely will," said Carey ominously. "One way or another, with the use of your legs or without them."

Wednesday, 21st June, 11 a.m.

When she came down the steps of the Queen Mary Tower, Janet was met by Lady Scrope and a gentlewoman she didn't know. She was intending to see after poor old Shilling who had run like a hero all the way to Carlisle and might need comforting, but when she curtseyed to the ladies, she found her hand taken and the Warden's wife was speaking to her gently.

"Mrs Dodd," said Philadelphia, "I'm sorry to hear of the raid, is there anything I can do to help?"

Janet flushed a little. "Well," she said, "the new Deputy has promised he'll get my horses back but whether he will or not . . ."

Lady Scrope grimaced a little. "Knowing my brother, he'll half kill himself to do it if he promised to. Who was it sold you the beast that belonged to Sweetmilk?"

"Reverend Turnbull, may God rot his bowels."

"That's the book-a-bosom man isn't it?"

Janet nodded. Lady Scrope exchanged glances with the other woman. A certain amount of mischief appeared on Lady Scrope's pointed little face.

"Shall we go and speak to him, then?"

Janet found herself borne along by the ladies; Lady Widdrington was asking practical questions about the girl

Margaret's miscarriage and the state of their barley crop which distracted Janet's confused mind until she came to the wynd that led down to the church.

"It's very kind of you to take so much trouble, Lady Scrope," she began, "but I think I can . . ."

"Hush, Mrs Dodd," said Lady Scrope, "We only want to give Sir Robert what help we can to get back your horses."

"And this needs doing quickly because when Reverend Turnbull hears what happened, he'll be out of Carlisle as fast as his legs will run," added Lady Widdrington. "Ah, look," she said kindly, "he's heard already, I think. Is that him, Mrs Dodd?"

The Reverend Turnbull was at that moment shutting the door to the little priest's house next to the church, wearing a pack on his back and carrying a stout walking stick. Janet nodded.

The Reverend Thomas Turnbull had had very little to do with real ladies in a not always reverend past, but he knew them when he saw them. With the Warden's wife on one side, and a tall long-nosed lady on the other, he found himself accompanied into his church and sat down on one of the porch benches. It wasn't that he didn't think of running nor that he couldn't perhaps have outrun them – ladies seldom or never ran, so far as he knew, and their petticoats would have tripped them up – it was that he didn't somehow feel he could do it with the Warden's wife holding his arm confidingly under hers and the tall one glinting down at him with a pair of piercing and intelligent grey eyes.

When he sat down the third woman, whom he recognised with a sinking feeling as Janet Dodd, helpfully took his walking stick and laid it on the ground near her foot. Lady Scrope sat down next to him, still trapping his arm, while the tall one continued to pin his soul to the back of his head with her eyes. Janet Dodd crossed her arms and tipped her hip threateningly.

"I'm s–sorry, Mrs Dodd," he stammered at once, deciding immediate surrender would save time, "I had no idea the horse would cause you such trouble. I'd have cut my throat before I sold it to you if I'd known, truly I would . . ."

"Well, tell us who you bought the horse from and we'll forgive you," said Lady Scrope gently.

"And tell the truth," added the tall woman.

Reverend Turnbull bridled a little as he sat. "Madam," he said with as much dignity as he could muster, "I am a man of the cloth and . . ."

"As capable of lying as any other man," snorted the tall woman.

"Now Lady Widdrington," said Philadelphia Scrope reprovingly, "I'm sure the Reverend will tell us the truth. You will, won't you?" she said winningly to him. "I'll get into trouble with my brother if I give him the wrong information."

"And so will you," added Lady Widdrington ominously to the Reverend.

Turnbull shook his head. "I bought the beast from a cadger named Swanders and I'd no reason to think him reived at all. He said he was from Fairburn's stud in Northumberland and had been sold because of an unchancy temper and . . ."

"Why didn't they geld him then?" enquired Lady Widdrington.

Turnbull coughed. "I didna think to ask, your ladyship, I admit it, I was a trusting fool but the Good Book teaches us that it's better to trust than to be ower suspicious."

"Does it?" said Lady Widdrington with interest. "Where does it say that?"

Turnbull's mind was blank. He could barely make out the words of the marriage service and much of the Bible was a wasteland to him.

Lady Scrope got him off the spot.

"Do you know where this man Swanders may be?"

Without question he was halfway back to Berwick by this time, no doubt laughing at Turnbull as he went.

"I dinna ken, your ladyship, I wish I did and that's the truth."

"Oh ay," muttered Janet.

"What did you pay for the horse?"

"Er . . . four pounds English," lied Turnbull. "See, I didna expect to make much profit and it was all to go to the repair of the church roof, which lets in the weather something terrible."

"Oh be quiet," growled Janet Dodd. "You know you paid two pounds for the creature and so do we."

How did they know, wondered Turnbull, when God had made them poor foolish women? How dare they show such disrespect to a man of the cloth.

"Well, it doesn't matter now," said Lady Scrope soothingly. "You can give what's left of your three pounds profit back to Janet Dodd and then claim the money off Swanders the next time you see him."

Turnbull's mouth fell open with dismay.

"B–but it's all spent," he protested.

"Is it now?" said Lady Widdrington. "And what exactly did you spend it on?"

A happy night at Madam Hetherington's bawdy house, among other things, but Turnbull couldn't bring himself to say so. He muttered the first thing that came into his mind.

"Charity?" said Lady Widdrington. "Well, that's very Godly of you. Mrs Dodd, when do you think your husband and some of his patrol would be ready to come and talk to Reverend Turnbull?"

"Oh, I can run and fetch him now," said Mrs Dodd, turning to go, "I'm sure if the lads pick him up and shake him something will fall out."

"Och Chri . . . well, I might have some of it about me."

The ladies turned their backs obligingly as Turnbull unstrapped the pouch from his thigh and the bright silver rolled out in the crusting mud. Lady Widdrington scooped up most of it and gave the money to Janet Dodd.

"You can owe the rest, Mr Turnbull," she said, "I wouldn't want you to be travelling the Border completely empty-handed."

"No. I thank you," said Turnbull feebly.

"Good day, then. I expect you'll want to be out of Carlisle before Sergeant Dodd tracks you down," said Lady Widdrington and added formally, "God go with you."

"Ay, well, good day, ladies."

Turnbull trudged up the wynd feeling as if he had already walked ten miles and wondering how one started proceedings against witches. He thought he heard the sound of laughter behind him but decided he must have been mistaken.

"You know what I find so odd?" said Lady Scrope after a while. They were gathered in a private room of the Bear and Ragged Staff, near the drawbridge gate of the castle. The windows of their private room overlooked the moat so they could watch the pleasant sight of the fish who were a thrifty source of food to anyone that could catch them and were therefore as cunning as foxes.

"What?" asked Lady Widdrington as she cautiously drank the beverage sold to her as wine.

"Why didn't this man Swanders go to Thomas the Merchant Hetherington? Or if he did, why didn't Thomas the Merchant buy such a beautiful piece of horseflesh as this Courtier was supposed to be?"

"Ay," said Janet slowly, "now that is odd."

"He'll have known we'd have paid good money for the animal." Lady Scrope went on, "Seven or eight pounds, likely enough, if he was good; God knows we've been searching out decent horses ever since the old Lord got sick."

Lady Widdrington put down her goblet. "Shall we ask him?"

Wednesday, 21st June, 12 noon

Thomas the Merchant Hetherington happened to be completing his accounts for some important clients when his servant came in to announce that the Ladies Scrope and Widdrington would like to see him. He was honoured and a little puzzled. He was a man who could see a way to make money at anything: the kind of man who bought up and forestalled barley when there was going to be a bad harvest, who paid cash down in advance for the entire shearing of the West March sheep and then joyfully twisted the cods of the Lancashire woolbuyers who came to do business with him and him alone because there was nobody else. However, stay laces and pots of red lead for improving ladies' appearances he left strictly to the common cadgers and peddlers, since they were small, retail items and invariably low profit. He dabbled in horses but only because he loved them.

The ladies came in and he bowed low.

"How may I serve you, your ladyships?" he said in a voice as unctuous as he could make it.

"We are here on the same errand," said Lady Scrope, "in search of good horses."

You and me both, thought Thomas the Merchant.

"We heard that Mrs Dodd had bought a beautiful animal from the Reverend Turnbull and we were wondering if you knew where it came from?" said Lady Scrope blithely. Lady Widdrington frowned at her across the room.

"Surely," said Thomas the Merchant with a warm smile, "this is really a matter I should discuss with your husband, my lady Scrope, since . . ."

"Of course," said Lady Scrope, nodding vigorously, "I would never dream of buying a horse without his advice and permission." Lady Widdrington made what sounded like a repressed snort.

"But I do so want to help him find the right horses for his father's funeral and he's so busy with other matters, I thought I could save him a little time."

"But it's just been postponed to Sunday."

"We'll still need horses."

Suddenly Thomas the Merchant was alert. He was as sensitive and shy of trouble as a fallow deer and could sense it on the wind in much the same way. He looked from Lady Scrope to Lady Widdrington and back again. Damn me, if Janet Dodd isn't outside, waiting on them, he thought suddenly.

Thomas the Merchant normally backed his hunches, to great effect, but that was only because he meticulously checked on them first. He turned from the high desk he used standing up, as if he were a mere clerk which was what he had been twenty years before.

"It's a little close in here, mesdames," he said, to cover the move. As he opened the little diamond paned window, he looked down in the street, and there, of course, was Sergeant Dodd's wild-looking Armstrong wife.

"Alas," he said smoothly, "I canna help ye ladies. I know nothing of Turnbull's horse save that he bought him, perhaps unwisely, from Swanders the Peddler."

"Do you know where Swanders got it."

"Presumably," said Thomas the Merchant, steepling his fingers and smiling kindly at their womanly obtuseness, 'presumably he stole it from the Grahams, or so it seems."

"He might have another source of horses."

"He might," allowed Thomas the Merchant, "but I doubt it."

"Why?" asked Lady Widdrington suddenly.

"Er . . ."

"Why do you doubt it, you seem very sure."

Thomas the Merchant was nettled. "Because, madam, I ken verra well where every single nag in this March was born, raised, and who it was sold to and stolen from, I make it my business to know."

"Do you?" said Lady Widdrington kindly. "Then you knew when Swanders showed you the animal in question that he belonged to Sweetmilk Graham. Why didn't you buy him to give back to the Grahams – surely they'd like that?"

Thomas the Merchant moved with dignity to the door and opened it.

"I verra much regret that some ill-affected fellow has been telling you ladies the old scandal about the Grahams and myself, but that was tried and I was cleared of the charge at the last but one Warden's Day."

"Oh," said Lady Widdrington, not moving, "and what scandal was that? I live in Northumberland and I'm not familiar with the gossip in this town."

Give ye two days and ye'll know the lot, madam, Thomas the Merchant thought to himself, but didn't say.

"He was accused of collecting blackmail money for the Grahams," explained Lady Scrope.

Thomas the Merchant found himself being examined at leisure by Lady Widdrington's steely grey eyes. He examined her in return. Her face was too long and her chin too pronounced for beauty but she was a striking-looking woman, with soft pale brown hair showing under her white cap and feathered hat. He disliked tall women, being a little on the short side himself.

"I fear I canna give you ladies the information you're seeking," he said humbly, "as I have not the faintest idea what you're talking about. If ye will excuse me now, I have a great deal to do."

Lady Scrope moved to the door, but Lady Widdrington stayed still for a moment. Then she smiled suddenly, not a particularly sweet smile.

"What an opportunity you've missed to be sure, Mr Hetherington," she said and he bowed to her. Both ladies gave him the barest token of a curtsey and sailed out, the hems of their gowns whispering on his expensive rush-matting. When they had gone he sat down and stared into space for a while, thinking of the price of gunpowder and where firearms could be had. At last he made a decision and began writing a letter to a cousin of his in York.

Wednesday, 21st June, afternoon

Barnabus brought his master bread and cheese to eat immediately after he came out of the castle jail. Carey, to his surprise, gave him the afternoon off. While Carey and Richard Bell disappeared into the Queen Mary Tower to attack the tottering pile of papers and the arrangements for the postponed funeral, Barnabus hung around the castle twiddling his thumbs. He found a young lad with shining fair hair sitting in the stables, polishing some horse tack and borrowed him from the stablemaster to act as his guide. Then Young Hutchin and he wandered down to the market place.

At noon the town crier made the announcement at the Market Cross that his lordship, Henry Lord Scrope, quondam Warden of this March, would be buried on Sunday and not the next day which caused Young Hutchin to blink and raise his eyebrows.

"He's lying in state at the cathedral," explained Young Hutchin slowly and carefully so Barnabus could understand him, "so anybody that wants can be sure the old bugger's dead as a doorpost and not as sweet."

"Not much liked hereabouts, eh?" asked Barnabus, munching on a flat pennyloaf (referred to by Hutchin as a stottiecake) with salt herring in it, since it was a fishday. Young Hutchin grinned and shook his head, but didn't add any information.

"Well," Barnabus patted his belly as he finished, "Now what shall we do?"

"I could show you round about the town, Mr Cooke," said Young Hutchin, "so ye can find your way."

"Lead on."

No one who knew his way around London town could be in the least confused by Carlisle which was barely a village by comparison. They wandered down Castle Street and looked at the cathedral, which was in a little better condition than St Paul's and examined what was left of the abbey. English Street was where the best shops were and Barnabus had been there before to buy paper and ink for his master with Richard Bell and also to visit the goldsmith's. Young Hutchin's eyes shone as he peered through the thick bars of the goldsmith's grill and counted the rather poor silver plate and gold jewellery displayed there. Barnabus wondered if the goldsmith also dealt in receiving stolen goods, as some of his London colleagues did, but Young Hutchin when asked, explained virtuously that he knew nothing of such sinfulness.

They examined the glowering two towers of the citadel, with their cannon, defending the road called Botchergate which led to Newcastle and ultimately to London. Then they retraced their steps and bore right up Scotch Street which was a poorer place altogether, though well-supplied with ale houses, horse dealers and smiths.

All about them flowed the townsfolk, greatly thinned in their numbers by the men who had gone out to work the fields round about. The women kept many of the shops, particularly the fish and butcher's shops, and some of the fish they were selling actually looked and smelled quite fresh.

Barnabus remembered they were only a few miles from Solway and no doubt there were fishermen who went out to harvest the Irish sea. Perhaps Wednesdays and Fridays would not be such a trial here as they were in London, where the trotting trains from Tilbury and East Anglia could not bring in the fish any quicker than two days old.

They were passing by a wynd with the strong smell of herring saltworks coming from it when Barnabus said to Young Hutchin, "Where would I go to . . . er . . . find a woman?"

Young Hutchin grinned cynically. "Depends on the woman, master," he said. "What kind of woman was ye thinking of?"

Barnabus coughed. Well, Devil take it, he'd just been paid and what else was there to spend his money on? There was no bear or bull-baiting in this backwater and there certainly wasn't a theatre. "I was thinking of a . . . helpful sort of woman," he said. "The kind that might take pity on a poor southerner far from home."

Young Hutchin nodded in perfect comprehension. "Ay, well there's two bawdy houses, ye ken, but neither of them have lassies that are much in the way of beauty if ye're used to London ways . . ."

"Are they poxed?" asked Barnabus.

Young Hutchin raised his eyebrows and for a second he looked astonishingly like Carey, who could be no relation.

"Now, master, how would I know such a thing, being only a poor lad meself."

"You might have heard where the nearest of them is, so I can go and inspect them myself," said Barnabus, gravely.

"Nay, master, I'm too innocent for . . ."

Barnabus sighed and produced a groat. "I could likely find the place myself," he said, "or ask someone else?"

Young Hutchin took the groat smoothly and led the way down the nearest wynd.

Barnabus liked the boy's technique. For instance, he was perfectly well aware that he was being led on a deliberately twisting and complex route so he would have difficulty finding the place again and that Young Hutchin had tipped the wink to one of the lads sitting in the street minding his family's pigs that he was bringing in custom. He didn't mind in the least, it made him feel nicely at home, though every time he looked up he saw a nasty unsmoky sky and almost every wynd off Scotch Street eventually ended in red brick wall.

Down one of the culs-de-sac they came on a brightly painted house with red lattices, a painted wooden sign of a rainbow and a girl sitting on the step. She stood up and smiled at him, leaned over so her large breasts could press enticingly over the top of her stays, and in a reek of cheap perfume, said, "Can I help you, sir?"

His breath coming short, on account of being away from the stews of Southwark for so long, Barnabus nodded. To Young Hutchin he said, "You stay here, my son, we wouldn't want your innocence being corrupted, would we?"

"What, wait here in the street?" asked Young Hutchin with dismay.

"Tch. You're far too young to go into a place like that," said Barnabus gravely, perfectly well aware that Young Hutchin might even lodge there when he wasn't in the castle, being the age he was, even if he might not be able to do much about it yet. On the other hand, Barnabus as a sturdy lad of thirteen had many fond memories of the Falcon in Southwark and in particular of a girl called Mary. Perhaps he sold his . . . No, he didn't look the type and in any case Barnabus doubted that the more sophisticated London perversions had got this far north. Anyway, it was the principle of the thing.

"I'd never shirk my responsibilities to you, my son," he added preachily, "and you're not getting corrupted on my money today. Besides, if you stay outside and give me a list of everyone who comes in and goes out while I'm there, you could earn yourself enough for two women in the one bed."

That caused Young Hutchin to brighten considerably and he settled down on the step as Barnabus went in. He was met by a grey-haired woman of formidable expression, dressed in a tawny velvet kirtle with a damask forepart and embroidery on her stomacher, her hair covered by a cap and a long-crowned hat in the Scottish fashion, with a pheasant's feather. Her ruff was edged with lace and starched with yellow starch and altogether she was as magnificent a woman as complete flouting of the sumptuary laws could make her. London work, as well, Barnabus estimated, his eyes narrowing, it seemed Hutchin had brought him to the most expensive place in town. No matter. Barnabus regarded money invested on good whores as money well-spent. No doubt the Scots went to the other bawdy house, wherever that was, since he could hear none of their accents which he was just beginning to be able to tell from an English Borders accent.

"Welcome to this house," said the woman in a clear southern voice, somewhere in London, Barnabus judged in surprise. "How may I serve you, sir?"

The common room where the whores paraded was nicely floored with fresh rushes and had a fireplace, though no fire since the weather had turned warm and muggy. There was a man there, no doubt acting as security against anyone who tried to leave without paying, a young, clever-faced man, with a weather-beaten face, black ringlets and long fingers. There was something familiar about him but Barnabus couldn't place the resemblance. He was throwing dice idly and Barnabus watched how he scooped up the ivories and tossed them and hid a smile to himself. It seemed coney-catchers were another universal thing. It was enough to bring tears to his eyes.

"Shall we have a game, sir?" asked the man in friendly fashion, "To pass the time until the whores are ready?"

Barnabus swallowed a laugh. "Well," he said, "I've only a little bit more than the price of a woman here, but I'll keep you company."

He sat down, took the wine he was brought and sipped it cautiously, and waited for the other man to make the first throw.

"I'm Barnabus Cooke," he explained, "servant to Sir Robert Carey, the new Deputy." Since they almost certainly knew that already, he didn't see any reason not to confirm it.

"I'm Daniel Swanders," said the man, "peddler by trade, but I'm waiting about here for a while until whatever's happening in Scotland has finished happening."

Barnabus nodded pleasantly, betraying no interest at all. He calculated they'd give him about twenty minutes to win some money before the whores arrived and then after he'd finished with a woman, Daniel Swanders would have a friend arrive, and he'd be brought into some plot to cheat the friend at dice since he was such a good player. Barnabus felt a warm pleasant feeling lift his heart nearly as much as the prospect of seeing to some womanflesh; it was almost like being back in London again.

Two hours later, comfortable and easy in his skin with only a tiny niggling doubt chewing in the hole at the back of his mind where he'd locked up his consciencc, Barnabus Cooke walked out of the Carlisle bawdy house, known as the Rainbow, about two pounds richer than when he came in. Daniel Swanders was still inside, examining his four identical dice with great puzzlement, since they seemed to have betrayed him for the first timc in his life, and his friend was trying to be jovial with Barnabus and offering to see him home. Barnabus, who had last fallen for that game when he was twelve years old, loosened his knife and explained to the importunate friend that he already had a guide to see him back to the castle and his master was expecting him to wait at dinner.

As they walked back up the wynd, past the courtyards redolent with herring and mackerel drying on the racks, Barnabus said quietly to Young Hutchin, "Can you use a knife?"

Young Hutchin looked insulted. "Ay, master, of course I can."

"Good," said Barnabus. "Now, we're being followed by a large co from near the bawdy house, ain't we?"

Hutchin stopped to kick a stone, dribbled it round a post in the street and back again. Good, Barnabus thought, liking the boy's style.

"You know 'im, don't you," said Barnabus, as usual losing his careful Court voice in the excitement.

"I might. I dinna ken his name, but," said Hutchin.

My eye, thought Barnabus, it's probably your own brother.

"Now then," said Barnabus as he stopped to examine a cooking pot hanging on an awning for sale, "I don't want to 'urt 'im, I just want to 'ave a little talk wiv 'im, see?" Young Hutchin looked bewildered and Barnabus got a grip on his tongue and repeated himself more clearly. Young Hutchin nodded nervously. "This is what's going to 'appen. I'm going down that alley there to take a piss, and you carry on and give 'im whatever signal you've arranged between yourselves." Young Hutchin's mouth opened to protest his utter innocence but he wasn't able to stop his fair skin colouring up. Barnabus had often given thanks that he wasn't liable to blushing with his sallow complexion. The pockmarks helped as well.

"Don't worry," he reassured the boy, "I was doing your job down in London before you was born. Now, as soon as you see him go in after me, you follow and put your knife against his back first opportunity you get."

"I canna . . ." began Young Hutchin indignantly. The large man was standing by another shop, staring elaborately at the sky. Barnabus hid a grin.

"I'm not asking you to knife the bugger; did I say that? No, so don't jump to conclusions, I want you to prick him enough to let him know you're there and tell him to stop what he's doing."

"But . . ."

"Listen, son. If you don't want to do it, just say so now and you can hop along up the castle and we'll say no more about it. But if you want to learn something from a real craftsman, you do as I say and I'll pay you for it too out of my dice winnings."

Hutchin's mouth dropped open. "You *won* the dice game?" he gasped.

"'Course I did, I told you, I'm a craftsman. Well, what do you say?"

"I'll help ye," said Young Hutchin.

"Just one thing to bear in mind, my son. I don't want to kill this man, but I will if I have to, and the thing that'll make me have to kill him is you buggering me about, you got that? And if you do that, son, I'll find you and I'll teach you better manners, you got that?"

"Yes, master," said Young Hutchin in a subdued tone.

"Never mind," said Barnabus kindly, "you're doing your

best, don't worry, it gets easier as you know more."

Arthur Musgrave saw his quarry disappearing down a wynd that was almost blocked out by the heavy buildings straining towards each other overhead. He'd had the all clear from Young Hutchin. He hurried after the plump ferret-faced southerner, taking out his cudgel as he went, hoping this would square it with Madam Hetherington who was enraged at him and Danny losing the bawdy house stake. He paused to take his bearings, wondered where the bastard Londoner had got to and felt a heavy weight thump down on his shoulders from above. The lights went out.

Fighting his way clear of the cloak, he got his head free only to find somebody's knee crunching into his nose. He lost his temper and managed to grab the Londoner by the doublet front and bash him against the wattle and daub wall of one of the houses, making a man-shaped dent in the plaster. Suddenly he felt the cold prickle of a knife at his back and stopped still.

Somebody's fist smashed into his gut three or four times and he toppled onto his face, mewing and fighting to breathe. The cloak went over his head again, his belt was undone with unbelievable speed and then wrapped around his body and arms at the bend of the elbow and buckled tight, all before he'd even managed to breathe once. So he lay there, choked with muddy cloak, waiting for the worst and found himself being lifted upright.

It was the bastard bloody southerner again, with that mangling of consonants and dropping of aitches which made him impossible to understand.

"Speak slower, man," he shouted, wincing at the pain in his belly and tasting blood from his battered nose, "I canna understand ye."

"I don't want your purse because I know there's nothing in it and I don't want your life yet," repeated Barnabus patiently, "I want to know who's the King of Carlisle."

"What?"

The would-be footpad tangled up in Barnabus' cloak couldn't show the bewilderment he felt, but Young Hutchin's face said it all.

"Bloody hell," said Barnabus, "are you telling me there isn't one? Isn't there anybody collecting rent off the thieves here to keep them safe from the law?"

Young Hutchin snorted with laughter. "No, master, generally it's the thieves that collect the rent from the lawful folk."

"If ye mean surnames, mine's Musgrave, and my father's cousin to Captain Musgrave, so if ye . . ."

"Shut up," said Barnabus, kicking him. "Young Hutchin, are you saying that none of the thieves and beggars in Carlisle are properly organised?"

Young Hutchin nodded. "There's never been enough of them in the city," he explained. "Outside, well, I suppose every man takes a hand in a bit of cattle-lifting and horse-thieving now and again, even the Warden or the Captain of Bewcastle."

"Especially the Captain of Bewcastle," muttered Arthur Musgrave, who hated all Carletons.

"Who do you work for then?" demanded Barnabus of Arthur, "Your father?"

Arthur Musgrave's father was humiliated by Arthur's inability to get on with horses and had kicked him out of the house five years before. "No," said Arthur, "it's Madam Hetherington's stake you've got there."

"*The* madam?"

"Ay."

Barnabus nodded. It stood to reason, of course, seeing she was a southerner. Well, that changed his plans a bit.

"All right, on yer feet," he said, giving Arthur Musgrave a heft and leading back into Scotch Street. A few people glanced at them but didn't feel inclined to interfere. It gave Barnabus great satisfaction to navigate his way back to the Rainbow without Hutchin's help, and yell for Madam Hetherington.

A moment later she appeared on the top step with a primed caliver and lit slowmatch in her hand. Barnabus grinned at her and toed Arthur forwards until he landed on the bottom step, and lay there, feebly struggling.

"I've got no argument with you, Madam," he said cheerily. "And just to show what a generous sort of man I am, here's half of your stake back." He took out the twenty shillings he'd earned and tossed the half-full leather purse onto the step at her feet.

Madam Hetherington's eyes narrowed and the gun did not move. "Why?" she demanded.

"Well, I've charged you the money for the useful lesson in diceplay I gave your lads . . ."

"No, why did you come back?"

Barnabus's smile went from ear to ear of his narrow face. "I want to be a friend, not a coney," he said, "I know you won't try this on me again, but I'd like to be welcome here to join the girls if I want."

Madam Hetherington finally smiled. "I welcome anyone with the money to pay me."

"Seriously," said Barnabus.

"And I would be willing to pay for more lessons in diceplay."

Barnabus twinkled his fingers together. "Delighted to oblige, I'm sure, mistress."

Wednesday, 21st June, late afternoon

The muggy clouds chose to part as Philadelphia Scrope's guests moved from the eight covers of meat and fish she had provided to the marmalades of quince and wet comfits. They admired her marzipan subtlety of a peel tower, complete with armed men, as an amusing variation on the usual themes. Sportingly they agreed not to eat it since it would keep to be used again on the Sunday as part of the old lord's funeral banquet. As the yellow sunlight found the little narrow windows and drove probing fingers into the council chamber cum dining room, it lighted on her brother's chestnut curls and laughing face. He put up a hand in protest and squinted at Elizabeth Widdrington who was frowning with mock severity.

"I refuse to believe that streams can chase you round the countryside," she said.

"On my honour they did," said Robin, picking up a date stuffed with marzipan and nibbling it, "and what's more the hills followed us too, so the ones we struggled up on the way north turned themselves round and we had to struggle up them again on the way back south." He winced slightly, put the date down and ate a piece of cheese instead.

"Did you find you were being adopted by a herd of brambles and gorse bushes as well?" asked young Henry Widdrington. "When I go out on a hot trod, I'd swear they follow me as lovingly as if I was their mother. Then when I fall off my horse one of them rushes forward bravely to break my fall."

Listening to the laughter, Philadelphia felt a little wistful. She loved giving dinner parties and the pity of it was, there were so few people she could invite in Carlisle; most of them were dull merchants or tedious coarse creatures like Thomas Carleton who would keep beginning tales of conquests at Madam Hetherington's and then remember where he was and fall silent at the best bit. It was a pity she had no pretty well-bred girl she could bring in to make up the numbers for Henry Widdrington, but she was used to there being an oversupply of men. After all, very few ladies would want to live in the West March and those that were bred to it were poor dinner party material. London was so much more fun. Somehow her husband's 3,700 pounds per annum from his estates wasn't the compensation her father had told her it would be.

"And all this on account of one horse stolen from the Grahams?" asked Elizabeth Widdrington.

"I don't think so," said Robin, "I think it was a long-planned raid for remounts and where they're planning to go with them, I wish I knew."

They were also eating up the food she had made ready for the funeral feast which couldn't keep until the Sunday – it was typical of men when they high handedly postponed funerals that it never occurred to them to think of things like perishable fish – and it would serve her brother right if he got indigestion. Though as usual, he was too busy talking and being charming to eat very much.

They had sat down at 2.30, fashionably late, and when Lord Scrope had said grace, her guests had flatteringly spent most of the first twenty minutes eating and occasionally asking each other to pass the salt. She was particularly fond of the salt cellar, being newly inherited from the old lord, a massive silver bowl with ancient figures in armour on it and some elaborate crosses, but she would have to check on the kitchen supplies of salt to see what had happened there.

Elizabeth Widdrington caught her eye questioningly and she nodded with a smile that she should broach their expedition of the morning.

"Did you know that Janet Dodd bought the horse from that little priest, Reverend Turnbull?" asked Elizabeth casually.

"Damn," said Carey. "I'm sorry, Philly," he added at his sister's automatic frown, "I meant to go and question the man about where he got the nag but it clean slipped my mind and I expect he's halfway to Berwick by now . . ."

"We went and asked him a few questions," offered Elizabeth. "And yes, he was on his way, but he very kindly stayed for us and told us what we wanted to know."

Robert's face lit up. "*You* talked to him?"

"Wasn't that a little dangerous?" asked Henry Widdrington with a frown.

"Oh never fear, Henry, I went with Lady Scrope and Mrs Dodd," Elizabeth said, hiding a smile at her stepson's concern. "He was very helpful."

"I'm sure he was," murmured Robert, "poor man. I would have been."

"He told us he'd bought the horse from a peddler called Swanders and . . ."

"Good God!" said Robert. "Sorry Philly, are you saying that Daniel Swanders is in Carlisle now?"

"I don't know." Elizabeth took a French biscuit and broke it in half. "Do you know him?"

"Yes, yes I do. He's a Berwick man though, deals in anything small and portable or that has four legs and can walk. My brother almost hanged him once for bringing in of Scots raiders only he got enough respectable men to swear for him and got away with it."

"How did he do that?" asked Henry naïvely.

"He bribed them, Henry," said his stepmother. "Most of them do that can."

"The thing was, Janet was surprised that he didn't go straight to Thomas the Merchant to sell such a good animal since Thomas has been our agent to find decent horseflesh and would know we'd want him," added Philadelphia.

"Good point," said Carey, "and why didn't he?"

"We went to speak to Thomas the Merchant as well," said Elizabeth, biting elegantly into her half biscuit, "and I'm certain he lied in his teeth to us."

"Did he now?" said Robert with an answering smile. "That was bad of him."

"I do object to it," Elizabeth agreed.

God help Thomas the Merchant for offending Elizabeth Widdrington, Philadelphia thought at the look in Carey's eyes.

"What he *said* was that he didn't know what we were talking about and he'd been cleared of the accusation that he collects blackrent for the Grahams," added Elizabeth, finishing the biscuit and brushing her fingers. "He gave me the impression that he was a mite too big for his boots as well."

"Hm."

Thomas Lord Scrope had been listening to this. "I don't know why this horse is so important to the Grahams or you. It's just a horse, isn't it? Dammit, don't horses go missing every day of the week?"

"It's only important because the Grahams think important," said Philly, resisting the impulse to shake her obtuse husband, "and because it was apparently the horse that Sweetmilk was riding when he was murdered."

"Which makes me even more interested to know why Swanders happened to have it," said Carey.

"Yes," said Scrope, standing up and wandering restlessly to the virginals kept under cover in the corner of the room, "but why does anyone care that Sweetmilk was murdered? Apart from the hangman, that is?"

"Well, my lord," said Carey with a patience Philly hadn't seen in him before, "firstly the Grahams seem to believe that it was Sergeant Dodd did the killing because he had the horse, or his wife did. Secondly because of the way the killing was done."

"Shot wasn't he?"

"Yes. But from behind."

"Best way to do it, I've always thought, especially dealing with a Graham."

Carey coughed. "Well, my lord, I'd agree, except that I had a chance to look at the body and the back was black with powder burns and further, the body wasn't robbed."

Scrope began to press the keys gently, listening for sour notes. He found one and began hunting for the tuning key.

"Is that important?"

"It means he was shot from very close behind him, which argues that he knew his murderer and didn't mind him being there. And then whoever did it wasn't interested in theft, which cuts out practically anyone on the borders."

"That or he was afraid the jewels would be recognised," added Elizabeth Widdrington.

"And then," continued Carey, as he dug in a canvas bag for the latest madrigal sheets he had carried with him faithfully from London, "there's where he put the body. After all, Solway field's a very odd place. The marshes or the sea would give him a better chance of the body never being found. It's almost as if he couldn't think of anywhere else. And how did Swanders come by the horse?"

"Killed Sweetmilk?" asked Henry Widdrington, picking up one of the sheets and squinting at it.

"Not Swanders. He doesn't own a dag. A knife in the ribs would be more his mark. Can you take the bass part?"

Henry Widdrington whistled at the music. "I can try."

Elizabeth had already taken the alto sheet. At least Robert had had the sense not to buy the four-way sheets which had the different parts printed as if on a four sided box, thought Philly – they were almost impossible to make out.

Robert carried the complete song to Scrope who was still fiddling with the fah string and humming to himself.

"Ah, mm, yes. Yes I see, dear me, they get more intricate

every year, look at this bit . . . Philly, you mustn't let your throat tighten on the higher notes, you know, or it will come out like cats."

Robert laughed. "It usually comes out like cats anyway," he said, "but it's all the rage at Court at the moment, God help . . . I'm sorry, Philly."

Robert had a good tenor voice which went well with Philadelphia's high true but weak soprano. Elizabeth Widdrington had a powerful alto, but was out of practice at sight-reading and Henry Widdrington, with his still unformed bass, had a tendency to lose his place and blush furiously under his spots. Scrope who had an extraordinary reach on any keyboard and could sight read anything first time, though his voice was appalling, took each of them through twice separately, rapping with his toe to give the time. At last they all took deep breaths, waited on Lord Scrope's signal and launched into "When Philomela Lost Her Love". After three collapses and Philadelphia's helpless attack of giggles when she got lost amongst the fa-la-las they managed to work through to the end and stood looking at each other with satisfaction. Then they sang it again with gusto and the beautiful intertwining medley of voices briefly turned the grim old Carlisle keep into an antechamber of Westminster.

Philly saw the happy dreamy smile on her husband's face as the music fitted itself together into the filmy light-hearted bubble of a song that it was, and it touched her heart. She decided she would nag Scrope into travelling to London for the Christmas season if she possibly could and if not then, for the Hilary term. If necessary she would fabricate a lawsuit. It was such a pity he was born the eldest son of Henry Lord Scrope: his life would have been easier and happier if he could have been of the class of folk that supplied Royal musicians rather than soldiers and lawmen for the Crown. Still, God had made him what he was and no doubt He knew what He was about.

They tried three more of the madrigals, and then a fiendishly difficult one in Latin by the Queen's Chapelmaster, William Byrd, until the sun had set and Carey could no longer hide his frequent yawns.

"I'm sorry, Robin," said Philly, conscience-stricken, "you've been up since two this morning, I know. We can sing again tomorrow or play a little primero."

Robert laughed and insisted he wasn't tired, so Elizabeth Widdrington did the tactful thing and announced that she had been up since at least two hours before dawn herself and if Sir Robert was able to go with only four hours sleep a night like the Queen, she certainly couldn't.

They left, making their bows and complimenting Philadelphia until she was alone in spirit, even if not in body. Thomas was adrift on seas of music, his spidery restless fingers become wizardly and loving as they coaxed long rambling digressions and ruminations ad libitum from the virginals. Philly kissed the top of his head and bade him good night and knew perfectly well as she went to her chamber and woke Alyson her tiring woman to unlace her stays, that he had forgotten altogether anything except the music. She slept with the waves of it carrying her into dreams as if she were a boat.

Thursday, 22nd June, before dawn

Coming as he did from the only respectable branch of Grahams, Bangtail had not been in jail before, not even as a pledge for somebody else's good behaviour. The noise of singing from upstairs came down to him somehow fiendishly magnified by a quirk of the stone, the bench was hard as a rock because it was rock and the thin straw palliasse he had been given because he was one of the Guard also contained some voracious lice and fleas. Scratching, deafened and uncomfortable, he felt the blackness of the cell as a demon on his chest and woke half a dozen times out of a dream of being pressed to death for not pleading at his trial. It was no comfort to him that if Carey did press charges of March treason against him – and if he was found guilty, which might be a foregone conclusion with this new Deputy – he would hang for it. In which case he would struggle for breath on the end of a rope rather than feel his ribs and pelvis crushed under the weight of twenty flagstones . . .

Sitting on the bench, rubbing his sandy eyes, and trying to convince himself that the walls were not really coming towards him, Bangtail ventured to call out to his half-brother Ekie, in whom the Graham blood had run true and who was certain sure to hang, if only for the various bills against him that had been fouled in his absence.

"Ekie?" he asked, "Ekie, are ye there?"

"God Almighty," growled Ekie, "the bastard Courtier's shut his goddamned screeching at last and now you wake me up. What is it, Bangtail?"

"What should I say, Ekie?"

"Eh?"

"Shut up," yelled somebody else, "some of us want to sleep."

"I mean when the Deputy comes to question me, should I tell him about Netherby and the Earl?"

"Jesus Christ, I don't care. Tell the git what you want, it willna make no odds."

"I think he thinks the horses are for a foray into England."

There was a moment's silence and then somebody snorted with laughter, Young Jock's voice by the depth of it.

"Does he now? Well, let the man think what he likes."

The others laughed.

"He'll want to know," persisted Bangtail.

Ekie sighed. "Bangtail," he said, "a' your brains are in yer balls. D'ye think *we* know where the Earl of Bothwell's planning to raid? D'ye think he'd tell us when he knows fine half of the men he's got would sell him out sooner than fart? All anybody kens is it's a long way to ride and there's fighting and treasure at the end."

"Oh," said Bangtail sadly.

"Tell him ye don't know where we're going and leave it at that and let him plump up the watches and guard all the fords and passes and tire himself out while we do the Earl of Bothwell's business, whatever it is."

Young Jock Graham didn't know Carey very well, of that Bangtail was sure, but he didn't dare ask any more and lay down on the pallet again. After a lot of scratching he slept.

He woke blearily when the door clattered and crashed open

and Carey came in, followed by Dodd with a lantern. Jesus, wasn't sunrise early enough for them, it was still black as pitch outside. Bangtail was too tired and miserable to protest when Dodd picked him up by the scruff of his jerkin's neck and propelled him through the door so hard he banged his head painfully on the opposite door. He kept his feet and heard the protests from the other prisoners.

"Go back to sleep," said Carey, "I only want to talk to my friend Bangtail here."

There was a great deal of unsympathetic laughter.

"Tell him nothing, Bangtail," said Ekie.

"You got your pinniwinks on you, Courtier, you'll need them for Bangtail," said Young Jock.

"Ay," said Ekie, "but I know where I'd put them, I'd crack his nuts for him, that's what I'd do . . ."

"Shut up," yelled Bangtail, beginning to shake as Dodd clapped his wrists in manacles and Carey motioned him out the thrice barred door behind the Sergeant.

They wound up in Carey's own office chamber where his servant, looking as heavy-eyed as Bangtail felt, was just on his way to fetch some morning bread and ale from the buttery. Carey sat at his desk and looked sadly at Bangtail.

"What the devil are pinniwinks?" he asked.

Bangtail's mouth was too dry to answer so Dodd said grimly, "Thumbscrews."

It was impossible to say what Carey thought of thumbscrews by looking at his face. Bangtail supposed it was too much to hope that the Courtier was one of those eccentric folk who disapproved of torture.

"Are there any in the castle?" asked Carey casually.

Dodd sucked his teeth. "I dinna ken," he said, "there might be. There's the Boot somewhere in the armoury."

Please God, thought Bangtail incoherently, don't let them give me the Boot, oh please God . . .

"Good," said Carey. "In fact I think I tripped on the frame when I was in there, though the wedges and the mallet were missing."

"We can have the carpenter find ye some," said Dodd

helpfully. "Do ye want me to go and ask him, sir?"

Oh God, oh God, oh God, thought Bangtail, wondering if they could see his legs shaking.

"No," said Carey slowly, "no need to waken the man just yet. There's plenty of time, after all."

"Ay sir."

"And it's possible we may not need them?" At last he looked at Bangtail, his eyebrows making a question.

"N–no sir," Bangtail managed to say.

"What can you tell me, Bangtail."

I'm a Graham, he thought desperately, we're tough and stubborn folk . . . Oh God, oh God, oh God . . .

"Wh–what do ye want to know, sir?"

"Tell me what you did after you saw the horse Janet Dodd bought."

"W–well, sir, I knew it was Caspar right away, though somebody had put a few extra white patches on him so he looked piebald, but ye could niver mistake the face of the animal, it were so noble and his legs and his . . . Anyway, I was in a state, so I did the first thing I thought of which was to ride to Netherby tower to tell . . . er . . . to tell Ekie."

"Why not go directly to Jock?"

"I wasn't sure I should do it, sir, I knew what might happen, I wanted to talk to Ekie first, but Ekie said I should tell him since Sweetmilk was riding Caspar when he disappeared. He was allus the favourite, you know, sir, best dressed, best mounted."

"Was Young Jock or any of the others jealous of him?"

"Well they might have been, sir, but Sweetmilk is . . . was so sweet-natured, ye couldna help liking him even if he did talk too much. So I talked to Jock of the Peartree and he thanked me and said he'd remember me if we ever met in a fight and I went back to Carlisle but the gate was shut. I was sleeping outside in a bush, but then the bell rang and ye all went riding out on the hot trod so I slipped in behind ye and went to Madam Hetherington's."

Bangtail tried to spread his hands to show he'd finished but the manacles stopped him.

Carey had steepled his long white fingers and rested his chin gently on them. There was silence for a while, during which Barnabus Cooke came yawning back with a platter of bread and ale. Bangtail looked at it longingly, not having eaten since the previous morning, but Carey sank his teeth into a hunk of fresh white bread, spread with butter and a sliced sausage, and it didn't seem to occur to him to offer any to Bangtail. Dodd drank some of the mild ale and ate a sausage on its own, rather ostentatiously, Bangtail thought, who was drooling at the smell of fresh-baked bread.

"Well?" said Carey, swallowing, drinking and dabbing his moustache and beard with a napkin like the pansified southerner he was.

"Well, sir?"

"Shall I fetch the Boot?" asked Dodd.

Carey sighed. "I hate to cripple a strong well-made pair of legs like his, but . . ."

"Wh–what clsc do you want, sir, plcasc, I . . ."

"What's going on at Netherby?"

"S–sir?"

"Who's there, why do they want horses?"

Bangtail gulped and tried to think. Carey watched him patiently, his usually humorous face unreadable.

Dodd growled. "You're with us, or agin us, Bangtail."

What would Ekie do to him? Was it even a secret who was at Netherby? Anyway, what could the bastard Courtier do about it?

"Th–the Earl of Bothwell.'

There was a flicker of something on Carey's face. Dodd made an mmphmm noise in his throat.

"Who else?" demanded Carey.

"Och, his own followers of course, like Jock Hepburn and Geordie Irwin of Bonshaw, and there's Johnstone and Old Wat of Harden and a fair few broken men from Liddesdale and the Debateable Land like Skinabake Armstrong and his lot."

"And what does he want all these men and horses for?" enquired Carey softly from behind his fingers.

Bangtail's face twisted in despair, "I dinna ken, Deputy, I wish to God I did and that's the truth, but nobody knows except the Earl himself and his man Hepburn and Old Wat, and not me that's certain and I'd tell ye if I knew it, I swear to God I would, but I dinna and if ye put me in the Boot I'll know no more . . . Oh God."

He put his face in his hands and tried not to cry. "Ekie said none of them know, but he could be lying . . ."

"If *you're* lying to me, Bangtail . . ." said Carey menacingly.

"Och no, sir, I'm not lying, I got no reason to, I'm not in the rode, see ye, and it's no gain to me whatever they do, though I heard tell that Captain Musgrave's helping out with a few remounts for Young Jock and Long Nebbed Robert, on a share, ye know, but that's all I know and I tellt ye the truth, as God's my judge . . ."

"All right," said Carey, "no need to take the Lord's name in vain any more."

"It's not in vain, sir," said Bangtail, shocked, "I dinna swear sir, not falsely, my word's as good as any other man's in the March."

"I thought there was a complete dispensation for that on swearing to the Warden or his men."

Bangtail blinked. "Eh?"

"He means," translated Dodd, "that he knows fine ye'll swear your oath till you're blue in the face to the Warden but it doesna count in men's minds if ye go and break it the next day. Not the way it would if ye swore to Jock of the Peartree or some other man that was your equal."

"Well, it's not false, I swear by God and the Holy Bible, I told you all I know and that's that," said Bangtail sullenly. "If ye dinna believe me, then ye can fetch in the Boot and go to hell."

Surprisingly Carey smiled. "Well said, Bangtail." He nodded to Dodd, who grabbed Bangtail's arm and led him to the door.

"Will ye let me go?" he asked hopefully.

"Not yet, Bangtail," said Carey, the bastard Courtier, while his bastard servant finished what was left of his bread and sausage and the ale, God damn him. "When I've checked your story. Not that I don't believe you, but you could be mistaken, and you don't know the most important thing. Perhaps you could find out for me?"

"In jail?"

"Where else? I can hardly lodge Young Jock and Ekie in the town, they'd be out of the place in an hour."

"I doubt they know, sir," said Bangtail, "And they willna tell me if they see me come back . . . er . . ."

"Untouched, as it were," said Carey. "We can arrange that."

"Well no, sir, I didna mean . . ."

"No hard feelings, Bangtail," said Sergeant Dodd as he pushed Bangtail down the stairs and punched him on the face, "I wouldna want you under suspicion from Ekie."

Thursday, 22nd June, 10 a.m.

Thomas the Merchant had been seriously considering a quiet trip to his newly bought manor in Cumberland, but he knew a man in a hurry when he saw one and so he let the finely ruffed green-suited gentleman and his servant come sweeping into his study and called his own servant to fetch wine.

"How may I serve you, sir?" he asked.

The gentleman smiled. "Do you know me, Mr Hetherington?"

"I have not had the pleasure . . ."

"I am the new Deputy Warden."

"Ah," said Thomas the Merchant, smiling in perfect understanding, "I see."

"I am in search of some help."

"Of course," murmured Thomas the Merchant, pulling his ledger from the shelf, the one that gave details of his interests in the Carlisle garrisons. "I am delighted to see you, sir. Who was it recommended you to see me? Captain Carleton or Sir Richard?"

Carey opened his mouth to answer and then shut it again, wondering if Thomas the Merchant was carrying on the same conversation he was. Barnabus solicitously pulled up a gracefully carved chair that was standing by the wall and he sat down in it.

The two of them looked at each other for a moment. "Well," said Thomas the Merchant, dusting his fingers, "As you know, I have always been very generous when it comes to the gentlemen who protect us from the Scots."

Carey's eyebrows went up but he said nothing, which made Thomas the Merchant a little uneasy. Thomas's servant entered with the wine, served it out and made his bows. Carey drank cautiously, then drank again looking pleased and surprised.

Let's get on with it, thought Thomas, surprised that the conversation was taking so long. "Have you a sum in mind, sir?"

"For what?" asked the Courtier. Behind him his servant was looking nervous.

"For your . . . er . . . pension, of course," said Thomas, astonished at such obtuseness, "I must warn you that business has been very bad this year and I cannot afford to pay you as much as I paid Lowther while the old lord was sick. Shall we say three pounds a week, English?"

"For me?" asked Carey slowly.

Thomas sighed. "And of course, for your servant, I can offer one pound a week – really sir, I can afford no more." Thomas was hoping wildly that Lowther hadn't told him the truth about what he was really getting from Thomas the Merchant.

He noticed that Carey's fingers had gone bone white on the metal of the goblet. Well, happiness took people differently, perhaps Thomas had made the mistake of offering too much. Alas, too late now. Carey's servant had backed into a corner next to the door and was looking terrified. Good, thought Thomas, that's the way to deal with serving men, keep them in fear of you and then they have no time to be plotting rebellion or . . .

"Have I understood you correctly, Mr Hetherington?" asked Carey in a soft, almost breathless voice. "Are you offering me a free gift of 156 pounds per annum?"

Thomas the Merchant beamed. This one would last about three minutes; what possessed the Queen to send someone so naïve into the cockpit of her kingdom?

"Well, nothing in this life is free, sir, except the Grace of

God," he said. "I naturally hope to gain your . . . er . . . goodwill, perhaps even your friendship."

"And on the right occasions a little blindness, perhaps even the occasional tip-off."

Did he have to spell it out so baldly? "Yes," said Thomas, embarrassed at such crassness, "of course."

Carey put the goblet down on the little chest nearby so carefully you would think it made of Venetian glass, "And you have the same arrangement with Lowther, Carleton? Any others in the castle?"

"Naturally, although of course the matter is in confidence."

Carey longed to bring his fist down on Thomas's desk hard enough to make the windows rattle and the ledger hop in the air like a scared goat. He didn't do it, though he knew Barnabus was tensed ready for him to roar. The insult of it! How dare the man? How dare he even *think* of buying the Queen's cousin for less than ten pounds a week? And how dare he do it with such arrogant presumption, as if he were discussing no more than a business partnership.

Carey held onto his wrath because he had learned to his cost how it put men against him. In any case people had offered to buy his services often enough before, after being filtered expensively by Barnabus: at Court his friendship with the Queen, although it lacked the intensity of men like the Earl of Essex or even Sir Walter Raleigh, was still a valuable commodity. The Queen herself, when he was tactfully putting in a good word for some striving office seeker, would caustically ask him how much his words were priced at now and to be sure to make a profit. It never made any real difference so far as he could see, the Queen listened gravely to his request and would then decide for herself. Still people were occasionally willing to pay for the influence they sought so desperately. . . . And yet in over ten years of attendance at Court, he had never been approached so crassly or arrogantly by anyone.

"Mr Hetherington," he began, and then changed his mind. He was up off his chair and had crossed the room to Thomas the Merchant's desk and swept the ledger out from under his long thin nose before the Merchant could do no more than take in a gasp of surprise. Carey flipped quickly through the pages, squinting at the crabbed Secretary hand, lighted on a few names and laughed. "I'd be in noble company, I see. I wonder, does her Majesty know you have the Wardens of the West and Middle Marches in your pay?"

"Er . . .?" began Thomas the Merchant.

It was tempting to throw the ledger in the greasy skinny man's face and march out, but Carey saw a better way of continuing to call his own tune. He shut the ledger and tapped it.

"I want information, Mr Hetherington, much more than I want money. And it's not my way to enter into this kind of . . . business arrangement." His servant made a desperate little whimper. "And so, I'll thank you to tell me all you know about the horse that Janet Dodd bought, the one that came from Jock of the Peartree's stable. To begin with."

"Er . . ." Thomas the Merchant was staring wildly at Carey as if at a chimaera, which indeed Robert Carey was, thought Barnabus bitterly, being the only man ever at Court capable of turning down a bribe.

Carey leaned over him threateningly. Thomas the Merchant made a feeble swipe for his ledger, but Carey skimmed it across the room to Barnabus who scrambled and caught it.

"Now then," said Carey with his hand suggestively on the hilt of his sword, "let's hear the tale."

Thomas the Merchant sat down on his high stool again and blinked at the fine set of plate he displayed every day on the chest in his room.

"A cadger brought the horse to me," he admitted at last, "and I refused him because I had . . . er . . . seen him before, ridden by Sweetmilk. I wanted no trouble with the Grahams . . ."

"I thought they were clients of yours."

"Sir!" protested Thomas. "The accusation was found clean six months ago and . . ."

"Never mind. When did you see the horse being ridden by Sweetmilk?"

"Oh. Er . . . on Saturday."

"Where?"

"Where what? Oh, ay sir, he was riding out the gate on the nag."

"Who with?"

Thomas the Merchant was sweating, gazing sincerely into Carey's eyes. "Alone."

"And when was the horse offered to you?"

"On Sunday. Naturally I refused to do business on the Sabbath."

"Naturally," agreed Carey drily. "But you were suspicious?"

Thomas the Merchant smiled. "A little," he admitted. "It was a coincidence. I wanted nothing to do with any criminal proceedings."

"Of course."

Carey moved to the door, motioned his servant to give him the precious ledger and walked out of the door – simply took it in his hand and walked out of the door. Thomas the Merchant was appalled at such high-handedness.

"Sir, sir," he protested, rushing after him, "my ledger, I must have it . . ."

"No, no, Mr Hetherington," said Carey, with a smile and a familiar patting of the calfskin binding, "I'm taking your ledger as a pledge for your good behaviour, as my hostage, Mr Hetherington."

"But . . ."

The rat-faced servant barred his passage.

"I wouldn't if I was you, sir," said Barnabus, sympathetically, "I know, he's a little high-handed at times. It comes of being so closely related to Her Majesty, you know. His father is her half-brother, or so they say."

Thomas wasn't interested in Carey's ancestry.

"My ledger . . . What shall I do . . ."

"Amazing how memory can serve you, sir, if you let it. I'd bet good money that if you sat down and rewrote it, you'd end up with exactly the same ledger."

"But . . ."

"Also, I might as well warn you, Sir Robert is wary of taking regular money, but he might be persuaded to accept a gift." The servant grinned widely, showing a very black set of teeth. "I can usually convince him if I set my mind to it."

This Thomas understood. He nodded sadly. "But my ledger . . ."

"Well, you've lost it for the moment, sir, you might as well . . ."

Carey poked his head back round the door.

"I forgot to ask. What was the name of the peddler you didn't buy the horse from?"

"Daniel Swanders."

Carey's face lit up.

"Splendid. At least that's the truth," he said. "Do you know where he is?"

"No sir."

"Let me know if you find out. Goodbye to you."

The servant was looking transfixed. Without another word, he hurried after his master and when Thomas the Merchant looked down into the street, he saw the two men conferring together, before Carey laughed and set off purposefully towards Scotch Street.

Thursday, 22nd June 11 a.m.

Barnabus had run back to the castle, stored the ledger in Carey's lock-up chest, and run back again to find Carey drinking ale at a small boozing ken on the corner of Scotch Street.

"You know the establishment, do you?" said Carey, nodding at Barnabus to sit down and refresh himself.

"Of course, sir."

Carey smiled. "Tell me about it."

"There's a backdoor leading into a courtyard and then into another alley and it's backed onto the castle wall. Madam Hetherington . . ."

"Good God, another one?"

"Yes sir, I believe she's a distant cousin."

"Go on."

"Madam Hetherington is from London and it's a very well-ordered house: she has six girls, one Irish, two Scots, one French and two English. . ."

"Pox?"

"Not as far as I could see," Carey grunted and drank. "It's expensive, a shilling a room, not including food or drink or clean sheets. . ."

Carey was surprised. "She provides clean sheets, does she?"

"Only if you pay for it," said Barnabus, who hadn't bothered. "There's a man called Arthur Musgrave acts as her henchman and this man Daniel Swanders . . ."

"Late of Berwick town . . ."

". . .was playing dice there when I went yesterday."

"Any good?"

"He had a couple of bales of crooked dice, a highman and a lowman and one with a bristle on the pip, but he hasn't the way of using them properly yet. I was going to give him lessons."

Carey laughed. "I'm sure you'll make a fine teacher."

"Well, it offends me, sir. I like to see a craft practised well and he was trying but it was no good. Madam Hetherington says she'll pay me for the teaching, if you take my meaning, sir."

"I have no intention of offending Madam Hetherington," said Carey. "She might well object to me arresting someone in her house. On the other hand, I want a quiet chat with Swanders."

By the light in his eyes and the impatient tapping of his fingers on his swordhilt, Barnabus was beginning to suspect that his master was cooking up some dangerous scheme. He had looked very much the same when he was planning to escape from the Queen's suffocating care of him with the Earl of Cumberland and go and serve against the Armada. That adventure had very nearly been the death of him, though not, oddly enough, from Spanish steel nor even English provisions, but rather a jail fever picked up on board ship. He had collapsed at Tilbury after leaving the fleet when the Armada was safely fleeing northwards, and had had to be brought back to Westminster in a litter.

Suddenly he leaned forward.
"This is what we'll do."

Thursday, 22nd June, noon

Daniel Swanders had only just crawled blearily out of a tangle of blankets next to the fire in the kitchen of Madam Hetherington's. The girls were all at their meal at the big table, laughing and chatting and making occasional snide comments to each other. The curling tongs were heating up on the hearth and a couple of pints of ointment, guaranteed to help a man's prowess, were being strained into little pots by Madam Hetherington's cook. The smell was awful: rendered lard and lavender, rosemary and pepper.

Daniel Swanders liked where he was: he was a strongly made young man with long hair to hide one ragged ear. Women usually took to his laughing face, and he was a peddler by choice and nature. He was never so happy as when he was persuading maidens to part with more than they planned for more ribbons, laces and beads than they needed, and if possible, with rather more than money later. His idea of heaven had been taking refuge in a bawdy house, rather than doing the obvious thing and running away. The only trouble was that none of the girls saw fit to give away what they normally sold and he knew Madam Hetherington would geld him personally if he tried to force one of them.

"Good morning, ladies," he yawned as he pulled on his jerkin and shambled to the table. "Any room for a little one."

Madam Hetherington was sitting in splendour in a carved chair with arms at the head of the table, almost as if she was the paterfamilias of the household. Which she was, really, thought Daniel, touching his forehead to her in respect. As usual the meal was Scots porridge with salt and very mild beer. Daniel Swanders wished he could get tobacco in Carlisle, but the nearest place for that was Edinburgh where he was not welcome at the moment. Or rather he would be a bit too welcome, but he hated the whole idea of his ear being nailed to the pillory and having to pull free because it had hurt so much the last time.

The girls shoved up for him, packing their petticoat-covered bumrolls together and making an enchanting sight with their hair pinned roughly and their breasts pushed up by their corsets. Two of them were magnificent that way and with typical female perversity, Madam Hetherington insisted that they wore high-necked smocks, the better to entice the customer into wanting to undress them.

By the time Daniel had finished his porridge and beer, Arthur Musgrave had gone into the courtyard to chop firewood and the girls were fluttering about in a complication of underwear, hairbrushes, make-up and pins, making ready for the day's trade. Daniel sat back on the bench and watched them with admiration: perhaps if he did well with the ugly Londoner and learnt better dice play, Madam Hetherington would let him take Grainne or possibly Maria to bed, or perhaps, if he was very successful, both of them. Lost in happy dreams, he only noticed the Londoner had turned up when Madam Hetherington spoke to him sharply.

"This is Barnabus Cooke, Daniel," she said, "Are you listening?"

"Yes mistress," said Daniel humbly, "I'm sorry, I was only admiring Maria."

"Maria, cover yourself, you're not working now. I want you to pay attention to what Barnabus teaches you, since he's a master craftsman at this game."

"Yes mistress."

Barnabus Cooke gave him a considering look and then said, "Madam Hetherington, I'm happy to teach Swanders some of my secrets but they're worthless if everyone knows them, so . . ."

"Of course," agreed Madam Hetherington, "you may use the private banqueting room at the back, no one is using it."

Arthur Musgrave came struggling in with his arms full of firewood and glowered at Barnabus who smiled back and raised his hat.

"I was going to suggest the courtyard, but the private room is even better," he said. "Come on, Daniel."

The smell of roast beef and wine always clung to the walls of the private room which occasionally saw some very strange behaviour. Barnabus carefully cleared the rushes away from the floor at one end of the big table and then went to the glass-paned window and opened it.

"Well, here we are," he said loudly, breathing deeply. "Let's begin with the basics of palming dice. After all, it's no good using highmen if you can't swap them for lowmen when your opponent is playing, is it?"

Daniel nodded and sat down next to Barnabus on the bench. Barnabus brought out half a dozen dice from his own purse and separated them into their various families, asking Daniel to identify them. He then began a game with three pewter beakers taken from the sideboard, and one of the dice where he switched them round and magically moved the die from one to the other.

"This is called Find the Lady," said Barnabus wisely, "and it's not much good for catching coneys in London now, since even the coneys have heard of it, but you might find it worthwhile here or in Scotland. The idea is they bet on where the Lady – the die – is going to end up. See it's all done with the fingers, like that. All right? Now you try."

Daniel tried and found it much harder than he had thought at first and very different from the way he usually palmed dice. For ten minutes he moved the beakers and tried to shift the dice without being spotted by Barnabus's beady eye, and although Barnabus said he was improving, he felt a little the way he had when his father had first begun teaching him the ways of persuading people to buy. There was so much to learn, so little time, and so many men who were better at it than him, he became quite depressed. Though that could have been the effect of living with so many beautiful girls and no money to pay them.

He was trying again to move a die from his sleeve to the table and back again without being spotted, when he heard the sound of someone at the window. He turned to look and saw to his horror that Robert Carey was sitting on the sill with one knee drawn up, ready to jump down.

Barnabus had drawn a knife, but Daniel was in too much of a panic to be afraid of it. He simply fell backwards off the bench, scattering dice in all directions, rolled, headed for the door. By some miracle, he got through it first, slammed it, tried to lock it, dropped the key in his haste and ran up the stairs to the bedrooms, with Carey hot on his heels.

It was Maria's room they barged into, and she already had her first client of the day. Daniel dodged, tried to hide behind the bed, but Carey skidded to a halt and stared.

"What the Devil . . ." wailed the man on the bed, whose shirt had tangled round his armpits as Maria worked on him. He sat up, throwing Maria aside and tried desperately to pull down his shirt.

Carey had turned his back.

"I'm very sorry, my lord," he said in a strangled voice, "I was chasing a horse-thief . . . I had no idea."

Barnabus, who had seen Burghley's hunchbacked son Robert Cecil in circumstances too wonderful to tell and was not at all concerned, went behind the bed like a ferret and hauled out Daniel, with a knife at his neck.

"You've caused a lot of trouble, you," he hissed into Daniel's ear as he twisted Daniel's arm behind him very painfully. "That's the Lord Warden of the West March you've offended. What did you think you was doing, running like that, we only wanted a little chat. Guilty conscience, that's what it is. Come on."

"For God's sake," said Thomas Lord Scrope, realising he looked worse standing up than he did in bed, sat down again and pulled the covers up to hide his embarrassment, "Robin. You won't tell Philly, please. I know she's your sister, but . . ."

Carey still had his back turned, but his fists were clenched. At last he turned with a perfectly calm expression on his face.

"Don't worry, my lord," he said, "I would never do anything to hurt her."

Scrope winced and looked at the floor. "She's a good woman," he said lamely, "she'd never . . . well, you know. I'm only flesh and blood . . ."

Carey had got a proper grip on himself. "I think we should both forget that this happened, my lord," he said.

Scrope's face was full of relief. "Er . . . yes, forget it, absolutely right, of course."

Barnabus was at the door with Daniel, not being too careful with his knife point either. Daniel squawked and struggled as he nearly lost his earlobe but the pain from his arm stopped him. Carey took a step closer to the bed.

"One thing, though, my lord," he said very quietly.

"Er, yes, Robin," said Scrope vaguely. He was being distracted by Maria's busy fingers under the covers, Daniel saw jealously.

"If you pox my sister, I will personally see to it that you never have the opportunity again. Do you understand me?"

"Well . . . er . . ."

"I'll make a woman of you, my lord, is that clear?"

Thomas Lord Scrope quivered and shrank back under the bedclothes.

Carey didn't wait to see his reaction, but waved Barnabus on and walked out of the room, shutting it very carefully behind him.

They processed down the passage, where they met Madam Hetherington, with her dag.

"What do you think you're doing?" she demanded. "And who are you?"

"I am the Deputy Warden of the West March and I am arresting your man Daniel Swanders, for horse theft and murder."

"He's not my man, he's only staying here," said Madam Hetherington quickly.

"So we are absolutely clear, madam, I have . . . ahem . . . checked the matter with the Lord Warden, who is in agreement. I apologise for the disruption to your establishment, but I had hoped to take him quietly out of the courtyard, without bothering you at all. Circumstances . . ."

Madam Hetherington's eyes narrowed. "Are you taking him to the castle, sir?"

"Not yet. I would like to use your private room, if that's possible."

Madam Hetherington nodded curtly, led the way down the passage and handed him the key to the room.

"Please make sure he only bleeds into the rushes," she said curtly, opened the door for them courteously, and left them. Barnabus kicked Daniel into the room, Carey shut the door and locked it. Barnabus shut the window and stood with his arms folded.

Carey was staring into space, his face working oddly. Barnabus wondered if there was going to be an explosion, and there was. It was Carey roaring with laughter.

"Oh Barnabus, did you see his face . . . Jesus, I nearly died."

"I think so did he, sir," said Barnabus primly. "Very unhealthy for any man, that sort of shock." Carey creased up again.

"Oh . . . oh . . . God, I must stop this, it's a very serious matter . . . with his shirt up and his prick all covered with lard . . ." Carey bent over and howled.

Daniel had picked himself up off the floor, felt his ear where blood was oozing and rubbed his arm and shoulder. He smiled at them uncertainly, took two of the dice from the floor near his feet and tossed them from hand to hand.

Carey was recovering himself, wiping his eyes with his hankerchief, blowing his nose and coughing. "Oh Lord, oh Lord, I wish I could tell Philly. No, Barnabus, I know I can't, but . . . All right. Enough. To business."

Carey hitched the padding of his trunkhose onto the table and stared down its length at him. Daniel sat on the bench and continued to juggle, staring back guilelessly.

The silence suddenly became very thick, a little decorated round the edges by sounds of chatter from the kitchen and the creaking of beds upstairs.

"Get on, Robin," Daniel said at last, "ye know me. I take it, you're saying was it me killed Sweetmilk Graham and stole his horse? You know I'd never be mad enough to do such a thing."

Carey sighed. Barnabus had at first stared at his impudence in using Carey's nickname, then narrowed his eyes suspiciously.

"Danny," said Carey, "I don't know you. I knew you five years ago, but how do I know what you might have done since then? I've fought in three separate wars since then, and what I couldn't have done in 1587, I might well be capable of now given reason enough. So tell me what happened. And please, Daniel, tell me the truth."

Daniel Swanders had been travelling on foot across the little nook of a border that lay north and west of the Solway firth, around the site of the Battle of Solway Moss. It was the Saturday, and he was on his way back to Carlisle from some successful business conducted with both the Maxwells and the Johnstones, involving horses, which it was forbidden to export to Scotland, and whisky which was heavily taxed. Thomas the Merchant trusted no one with the whisky which would follow later as part of a pack train, so Daniel was travelling light.

He thought he was very lucky at about sunset, when he saw two horses in the distance, lightly tethered to the root of a gorse bush and no one guarding them.

He came up on them cautiously, using the cover, watching to see if a guard should appear. Both of them looked tired, as if they had been ridden hard for a while. One was an ordinary hobby, a sturdy short beast with shaggy coat, no different from any of the others that rode the borders, but the other horse was another matter altogether. He was a beautiful tall animal, with a graceful neck and a noble head, a black coat with a white blaze on his forehead and two white socks and every line of him proclaimed speed, endurance and even intelligence. He was a horse any lord would covet. He was also a stallion, which meant he must have a sweet nature and that meant that his worth at stud was enough to give a man heart failure.

Daniel wrestled with his conscience for at least four seconds, before conscience won out over caution. It would have been a crime to leave the animal behind him and not even try to steal him.

There was still no sign of any owner or rider, so Daniel simply walked up to the beautiful creature, untied him, offered him an apple from his pack, let himself be smelled and inspected, and then jumped on his back. The stallion hopped a little, then snorted and turned his head eagerly north, so Daniel let him have his head, went to a trot.

A yell from behind made him turn in the saddle. A tall man was struggling out of the gorse bush: he was in his doublet, and he had his fighting jack in one hand and a cloth in the other which he was waving.

Daniel didn't wait to see any more, put his heels to the horse's flank and galloped away.

"He's a beauty, he's the Lord God's own delight to ride, you know, Robin, so fast and so smooth," said Daniel, waving his arms in horse-shaped gestures at Carey and Barnabus. "I had him hammering over rough country and I could have been in my bed at home, oh he'll bear away a few bells in his time, that horse, mark my words."

Daniel brought the horse round in a wide circle, coming only a few miles short of Netherby tower at one point, before he got on the southern road to Carlisle. All the time he was nervous, in case the horse's rightful owner came after him on the hobby, but he needn't have worried. Nobody chased him and he rode happily to Carlisle. He got there too late to get in before the gate was shut, so he stayed the night in one of the little inns that made up part of the overspill at the southern gate, beside the River Calder, and then first thing on the Sunday morning he went proudly to Thomas the Merchant to sell him the horse.

"I couldna hope to keep him," Daniel said sadly, "not having a tower of my own nor a surname to back me, but oh it broke my heart . . ."

Much to Daniel's surprise, Thomas the Merchant went white when he saw the animal and refused point blank to have anything to do with him. This Daniel had not expected, but when he asked if the horse belonged to some important man on the border, Thomas the Merchant simply shook his head and bade him be gone.

"So then I thought I'd see the Reverend Turnbull who's a

book-a-bosom man that sometimes travels with me, and ask his advice, him being educated and all. And I thought it might be best to be rid of the horse, in case it belonged to old Wat of Harden or Cessford or some unchancy bastard like that."

"Jock of the Peartree," said Carey.

"Ay, I know it now," agreed Daniel ruefully, "and Turnbull said he couldna offer what the beast was worth, but he could offer me two pounds English because it was all he had, and then he'd sell it on for me and split the profit. So I agreed and then because I was nearly sure the horse was owned by some headman of a riding surname, I decided it might be healthier to wait a while in Carlisle, here, until the fuss was over with."

Carey looked at him gravely for a long time, so long that Daniel became nervous.

"Well, what more do you want?" he demanded. "That's what happened, it's God's truth, that's all. And I've admitted to horse-stealing, what more do you want?"

"I'm not quite certain what the legal position is when you steal a horse from the thief that stole it," said Carey, "but you haven't told me the most important thing."

"What's that?" Daniel was wary.

"Who you saw in the gorse bush?"

Daniel threw up his hands, palms upwards. "If I'd known him, I'd tell you, of course I would, especially when the bastard must have done a murder for the beast. But I didnae know him, I'd never seen him before. And he didna look like a Borderer, forbye."

"Why not?"

Daniel shrugged. "Too glossy, too elegant, with his pretty doublet with the gold thread in it, looking like some sodomite of a courtier, is what he looked like, saving your presence, sir." He grinned disrespectfully at Carey, who looked stern.

"Could you recognise him again?"

"Oh ay," said Daniel, "I could, if you think I make a good witness."

"Experienced, anyway," muttered Carey, tapping his forefinger on his front teeth and staring out the window with an abstracted expression on his face. "Tell me, how well known are you in these parts, how long have you been here?"

Daniel winced a little. "Well, I only left Berwick a couple of weeks ago."

"And why did you leave?"

"Er . . . well . . . your brother's very hot against horse-smuggling at the moment and he's never liked me. I'd had a couple of nasty frights so I thought I'd go where it was a mite calmer."

"And you came *here*, to the *West March*."

Daniel coughed. "You know what I mean."

"How did you know Thomas the Merchant?"

"I didn't. I had a letter of introduction from Mr Fairburn in Northumberland, and this was the first job I did for him."

"Do you know anything of Netherby castle and what they're doing there?"

Daniel shook his head. "No, I've never been there."

"Have you ever met Jock of the Peartree, Old Wat of Harden or the Earl of Bothwell?"

"No, never, thank God, and I hope I never do."

Carey was stroking his neat court beard thoughtfully. "Do you know anything of the reason why the Earl of Bothwell might want a couple of hundred horses at the moment?"

Daniel shook his head.

Carey beckoned Barnabus over into a corner with him, while Daniel continued to play with Barnabus's dice. He'd pocketed a couple of them, Barnabus noticed.

"I'm very worried," Carey said, "I want to know three things: what the Earl of Bothwell is up to . . ."

"I thought the Earl wanted to keep the Queen sweet at the moment, sir."

"Barnabus, the man's mad. He'd probably think he could charm her round."

"And could he, sir?"

"Who knows? If I understood that well how Her Majesty's mind works, I'd be rich. He's got good legs, he might. He surely thinks so, anyway."

Barnabus nodded. "And the other things, sir?"

"The other problem is Dodd's horses. I gave my word on

it that he'd get them back, and I'll lay all Westminster to a Scotsman's purse the nags are eating their heads off at Netherby right now. And I don't like the sound of Jock of the Peartree believing Dodd was the man that killed Sweetmilk, so I want to find out who really did it."

"What are you planning, sir?" asked Barnabus warily, knowing the symptoms of old.

Carey grinned at him, confirming all his fears. "It seems the answers to all of my riddles lie at Netherby and so . . ."

"Oh no sir, we're not going to Netherby tower?"

"You're not, I am."

"Sir . . ."

"Shh. Listen. I'll borrow Daniel's clothes and his pack and you can shave off my beard and brown my face and hands and then . . ."

"Sir, sir, 'ow do you know you can trust 'im, 'e's a thief and he's a northerner and . . ."

"He's a relative of mine. Also, we'll have his clothes and we'll give him to Madam Hetherington to keep safe for us."

"What do you mean, sir, relative? What sort?"

"Ask my father."

"Oho, it's like that is it?"

"It's like that, and if you gossip about it, I'll skin you."

Thinking about a certain young woman at Court who would no doubt be married very shortly, Barnabus muttered that it was a wise Carey that knew all his children. Carey pretended he hadn't heard.

"But look sir," he said conscientiously trying again, "why couldn't you send Swanders in there instead of you, if you need a spy so bad, I mean, if they topple to you, you're done for, ain't you? Daniel . . ."

"It'd be worse for him. They'd likely hang him if they thought he was a spy, but they might not kill me. Anyway, I want to know who killed Sweetmilk Graham so I can bring him to justice and get Jock of the Peartree off Dodd's back. There's the makings of a very nasty feud there, when they've finished with their raid."

"What about the Earl of Bothwell, you said yourself 'e's

mad and I've heard tell 'e's a witch besides, won't 'e know who you are?"

Carey shook his head. "I doubt it. It's four years since I was at King James's Court and he met me with a number of other gentlemen. There was the football match, but I don't see why he'd remember that either. I've got unfinished business with him anyway."

"What sort of unfinished business?"

"He practically broke my shin bone taking the ball off me."

"Sir, you can't . . ."

"Oh shut up, Barnabus, I know you mean well, but my mind's made up."

"Well can I come with you . . ."

"Absolutely not. What would Daniel Swanders the peddler be doing with a servant from London – you'd stick out like a sore thumb."

"So would you, sir, you don't sound like . . ."

"Ah was brought up in Berwick, Barnabus, " said Carey switching to a nearly incomprehensible Northumberland accent, "An' I rode a couple of raids meself when I were a lad."

"Oh bloody hell, sir."

"Don't swear," said Carey primly, "Lady Scrope doesn't like it. Now you run out and find an apothecary; buy some walnut juice and borrow shaving tackle from Madam Hetherington on your way back. I'll talk to Daniel."

Barnabus left the bawdy house at a dead run and sprinted through an alleyway into English Street, heading for the castle. Once there he quartered the place looking for Lady Widdrington and found her at last in the kitchen supervising the making of sweetmeats for the funeral feast. He panted out his tale to her, she took it all in and frowned.

"He's mad," she said.

"Yes ma'am," said Barnabus disloyally. "Ma'am, will you come and talk him out of it . . ."

"I can't go to Madam Hetherington's, Barnabus, I'd cause no end of talk. Do you know the Golden Bell inn, just outside the gate? Make sure he stops off there and I'll do my best."

Barnabus sprinted back down Castle Street and English Street, bought the walnut juice at one of the apothecaries, made a quick detour to an armourers in Scotch Street and came panting and blowing into Madam Hetherington's an hour after he left.

When he'd recovered a little, he found Carey and Daniel Swanders drinking and eating an excellent dinner of baked chicken and a bag pudding, reminiscing in harsh Northumbrian voices about some escapade they had both been involved in as boys.

"What kept you, Barnabus?" asked Carey, switching back to his normal way of speaking, "I was starting to get worried."

It was so odd to hear him: one minute he was a northerner to the life and the next minute he was as understandable as any of the Queen's courtiers. Barnabus sat down to what was left of the meal and got his composure back.

"I couldn't tell you weren't a Northumbrian myself, sir," he said, "but what about a native, couldn't he tell?"

Daniel shook his head. "No, it's wonderful how he can do it, I wouldna ken if I didna ken, you follow."

Carey looked complacent.

"I was telling Daniel earlier, there's a little man in my father's company of players, what's his name, can never remember what it is, said I could have been a player if I'd been born in a lower station of life. He had me read to him endlessly in my Northumbrian voice, so he could get the sound of it for some play he was working on, which I told him was too conscientious for the London mob, best get some pretty boys in petticoats and a good thundering battle for the end and he'd do well enough. My father thinks the world of him, God knows why, dullest man I ever met."

"Can you do any accent, sir?" Barnabus asked, fascinated.

Carey swallowed what he was eating and smiled. "If I've heard it for a few days, yes. It's a gift like singing, makes it easier to learn French or Italian too. It's all in the rhythm. My father's little player prosed to me for an hour about it, and I'd have kicked him out, only father had told me to be polite to him. He was odd that way: he used to track down foreigners, Welshmen, Cornishmen, Yorkshiremen and pay them by the hour to read to him and talk to him, just so he could catch the rhythm of their voices. Wasted effort, I called it, but he seemed to think it was important."

"What are you going to do, sir?"

"Today? I'll change clothes with Daniel here, you shave my beard and brown my face a bit . . ."

"I bought some hair dye too, sir," said Barnabus. While sprinting around Carlisle he had realised that the harder he argued against one of his master's schemes, the more determined Carey became. He had decided to leave any dissuading to Lady Widdrington. "After all, they might have heard that Swanders is a black-haired man."

"True enough, well done. We'll do all that and when it's dry and I look the part, we'll leave Carlisle and go north. Daniel stays here with Madam Hetherington and I've promised to pay her enough so she'll let him have one of her girls for the night, the sinful git." Daniel smiled slyly. "You wait for me outside Carlisle in one of the inns and when I come back tomorrow morning, we'll decide what to do."

It broke Barnabus's heart to shave Carey's lovely trim little beard and then brown his skin with the walnut juice. Dying Carey's hair took longer than they expected, what with having to ask Madam Hetherington for a basin and two ewers and waiting for the water to be heated. To his horror, Barnabus found some nits and would have had at them with a fine-toothed comb, but Carey told him to leave them since no one would believe a cadger that hadn't a few headlice.

"You'll look a sight for the old lord's funeral."

"Oh, the brown comes off your skin with lemon juice," said Carey, "and I can hide my hair under my hat. Nobody will notice, they'll all be too busy worrying what they look like themselves."

While Carey waited bare-chested for his hair and skin to dry, Daniel explained his price system and he memorised the commonest items, laughing heartily when Daniel explained what some of them had really cost him, in case he needed to bargain down.

Barnabus had drawn the curtains while Carey and Daniel Swanders stripped off and swapped clothes. Daniel and he were almost exactly of a size, with Daniel perhaps an inch or two shorter. Swanders tried on Carey's doublet and posed in front of the mirror they'd had brought in while Carey laughed at him and told him the Queen would love him until she found out he couldn't dance, sang like a crow and had stolen all her jewels.

By this time Carey was scratching a little in Daniel's coarse hemp shirt, and putting on his worn homespun woollen hose and greasy leather jerkin. He pulled Daniel's blue statute cap down over his ears, looked at himself in the mirror and laughed again.

"I got you these sir," said Barnabus diffidently, taking out the knives he had bought. "See here, this one goes behind your neck, this one's on your belt and this one's in your sleeve. The two hidden ones are for throwing . . ."

"I'm not the dead shot you are, Barnabus . . ."

"It don't matter, sir, aim for the body and if they stick in anywhere they'll distract 'im long enough for you to make a run for it. Which you will do, won't you, sir, if they rumble you."

"Not if I can help it, since they'll have horses and I won't."

"Aren't you even going to ride?"

"Well Daniel hasn't any horses, and I can't ride one of my own, it would be spotted as coming from the south and somebody would ask questions. I can't ride anything from the Castle stables because of the brands. And I don't want to buy another horse, even if there were any to be had, which there aren't."

Barnabus sighed unhappily. "Can I wait for you a mile or two outside, then sir, with a horse in case you need to . . ."

"Barnabus, Barnabus, I appreciate your concern, I really do, but you'd get caught. Bothwell will have riders all around the place watching in case anybody tries to steal all his stolen horses back from him and you'd be caught and then they'd beat you up and I'd have to tell them the story to stop them and it would all be very embarrassing. You stay in Carlisle until I get back, do you understand?"

"Yes sir," said Barnabus mutinously, thinking bleakly of having to face Carey's father with an explanation of how his youngest son happened to wind up kicking in the wind by his neck from Netherby's gatehouse.

"Right," said Carey, "here's my purse with my rings in it, you arrange things with Madam Hetherington and pay her whatever she asks for looking after Daniel, and then you go back to the castle and tell everybody I'm sick in bed . . ."

"Can't I even come a little way with you?"

"Oh all right, if you must, you can meet me in the alley-way."

Carey took Daniel's pack, winced a little at its weight, then opened the window and climbed out into the little courtyard.

Barnabus went unhappily to negotiate with Madam Hetherington.

Thursday 22nd June, late afternoon

Even Barnabus had to admit, walking through Carlisle, that Carey made an uncommonly convincing peddler. He even flirted with one of the girls selling meat pies and had her shrieking at an incomprehensible Northumbrian joke.

It took some argument to get Carey, afire with impatience to put his head in the noose, to pause for a beer at the Golden Bell. As soon as they entered the common room, a tall figure in fine grey wool, piped with murrey, snapped her fingers at Barnabus and beckoned them over.

"What the . . ." hissed Carey. "God's blood, you told her, you sneaking little bastard, I'll tan your backside for you . . ."

"Well, Danny," said Barnabus, deliberately insolent, "I don't know what good getting in a fight with me would do you, but if that's what you want, I'm game."

Carey growled at him. Lady Widdrington had lifted her head haughtily and was beckoning again.

"I think there's business to be done with the lady, mate,"

said Barnabus, "Ain't you going to find out what it is?"

In fact, Barnabus nearly gave himself a rupture trying not to laugh as he watched his elegant master slouch over to Lady Widdrington, haul off his statute cap and make an ugly-looking bow. In a minute he had his pack off his back and had opened the top and was delving in the depths. She apparently wanted a thimble, and when he pulled out five in a little packet, she examined them carefully and asked if he was mad.

Barnabus loafed over with the beer, so as not to miss the fun.

His face hidden by digging in the pack, Carey was muttering his reasons for sneaking into Netherby to Lady Widdrington who listened with regal calmness.

"I see why you want to do it," she said, to Barnabus's shocked disappointment, "but have you thought it through?"

"I think so, ma'am," said Carey, producing a card wound with stay laces.

"Do you? Well, I don't. What's your excuse for going to Netherby? Why are you there at all? To sell Bothwell broidery silks and some pretty ribbons for his hair?"

This nonplussed Carey who had been so charmed at the idea of getting into Netherby, he had not in fact thought it through. Lady Widdrington examined the laces and talked rapidly out of the side of her mouth.

"In the stables are three northern horses, with Fairburn brands on them, and also the Widdrington mark which might not be known here. They are my horses which I am lending to you as cover. You take them into Netherby and offer them to Bothwell and if he's as anxious for remounts as you say he is, then he'll be delighted. We'll work out a way of getting them back later."

Carey opened his mouth to argue, stopped, thought, then nodded intently.

"Now you'll have trouble getting out in the morning, because if the raid is due in the next couple of days, I expect Bothwell will simply close up the castle and let no one out for any reason. He may be mad but he isn't stupid. So if you find it hard to get out, put all of this powder . . ." She put down a twist of paper next to some lace bobbins, ". . . into your wine or beer and it'll give you all the symptoms of a man with the first stages of the plague – fever, headache, sneezing, and if you complain of pains in your neck, groin and armpits that should frighten the life out of them."

"It isn't . . . er . . . plague . . .?"

"No, Robin, it's poison, a very mild one and you'll feel very ill too, but that will help convince them. They'll kick you out of Netherby themselves and then you'll have to do the best you can. If I haven't heard from you by late afternoon tomorrow, I'll tell Scrope and we'll come and get you out."

"Elizabeth, my dear . . ."

"One of the hardest things to disguise in a voice is endearment," interrupted Elizabeth Widdrington frostily. "This is a lunatic scheme, but if your heart is set on it, well . . . And I most certainly will not pay five pence for stay laces Daniel Swanders may have paid a penny for at the most, what can he be thinking of? I'll take this thimble though."

She picked up a small ivory thimble and paid for it, and then watched impassively as Carey thanked her with extravagant obsequity and started shoving his things back in the pack.

"Go carefully with those silk stockings, they fray and they're your stock in trade, remember. I'll leave, and Barnabus will go for the horses, while you stay here. Barnabus will walk them up to the gate with me and then he'll go on round the walls and wait for you at Eden bridge. You follow when you've drunk your beer."

Carey was smiling fondly at her. Many men might have resented her high-handedness, but he was used to managing women. He thought she never looked handsomer than when she was taking charge of something.

"Is there anything else I can do to help?" she asked.

"I wish I could kiss you," said Carey. That put colour in the lady's cheeks. It was a good thing the light was so bad, no doubt to assist the diceplayers in the corner. Barnabus would have been over there to investigate if Lady Widdrington hadn't included him in her plan.

"It would be unseemly," said Lady Widdrington sternly. "If any cadger . . . I'd have my steward throw him out."

"No steward here, my lady," said Carey with a wicked grin, caught her hand and bent over it with a kiss. "Now you'd better slap me."

She was a quick-thinking woman, thought Barnabus approvingly, because she didn't slap him, she boxed his ears as she would any servant who behaved like that. One of the innkeeper's large sons came looming over with a cudgel in his hand.

"Is he bothering ye, ma'am?" he asked.

"Yes, he is," said Lady Widdrington coldly, wiping her hand with her napkin, "but I think he's drunk. You'd better throw him out."

"Tut, and it's only the afternoon too," said the innkeeper's son primly.

It did Barnabus's heart good to see his master frogmarched to the door and kicked into the mud outside, where he landed on his face. For good measure, Barnabus picked up the pack, stuffed the rest of the gear inside along with the twist of paper, and slung it after him.

"And stay out," he ordered sternly. "That'll learn you better manners wiv her ladyship."

Knowing Carey, he turned away quickly, but he wasn't quick enough to avoid the clot of mud that hit his back. Not such a bad shot as all that, he thought, though of course knives were a different matter.

He went back to Lady Widdrington, who was drinking a tot of whisky on the house, to settle her nerves after her nasty experience, with the landlord making excuses and promising that the drunken sot would never be allowed to darken his respectable door again. Lady Widdrington nodded and generously said that she couldn't possibly hold it against him since the man had no doubt been drinking all day somewhere else and had been the best her servant could find.

Once the landlord had subsided and gone back to his

less prestigious but more valuable customers, Barnabus attended on her assiduously, and murmured the story of Carey's visit to Thomas the Merchant.

"I think he was in too much of a hurry, ma'am," he said. "I think Thomas hadn't told us the half of what he knew, but once he heard the name Swanders confirmed, of course sir had to be off."

"He is like that," agreed Lady Widdrington, "Straight into the thick of it at top speed. Well, he's done it before and never a scratch on him, so God must be watching over him."

"Ma'am," said Barnabus slowly, "I don't want to pry, but . . . er . . . why didn't you stop him?"

"Stop Robin Carey when he's got the bit between his teeth?" she smiled at him. "Could you?"

"Well no, ma'am, though I tried. But I thought . . ."

"I wouldn't back the Queen herself against him, once he's in that state. In fact she couldn't stop him running off to fight the Armada though she threatened him with the Tower. So if I can't prevent him, I can help him to do whatever mad scheme he's hatched more efficiently." She let out a little sigh and clasped her hands together. They were not very ladylike hands, being large, square and strong, though they were as white and neat as lemon juice and buffing could make them.

"I see, ma'am," said Barnabus sympathetically, who did indeed see. "Do you think he'll manage it?"

She folded her lips consideringly as he refilled her larger goblet with wine, mopped a tiny spill with a cloth. Eventually, Barnabus thought, her long nose and determined chin would begin to curl towards each other as she got old and her teeth fell out.

"I don't know, Barnabus," she said at last, her voice firm and quiet. "At worst they might shoot him or hang him, or even torture him if they take it into their heads he might tell them something they want to know. At best they might ransom him, if he can overcome his pride long enough to tell them who he is. I'm sure Scrope will buy him free if he has to."

Barnabus who remembered the scene at the bawdy house

wasn't so sure, but didn't feel inclined to say so. He bowed to her and she smiled radiantly at him.

"And of course, he might even succeed. After all, he has unexpectedness on his side. I think he will if God watches over him as He always has so far."

That was good enough for Barnabus and he smiled back.

"Come along," said Lady Widdrington. "You'd best get those horses for me. They're in the end stable, if Young Hutchin got it right, the bay, the dapple mare and the chestnut."

She walked to the door with her back straight as an arquebusier's ramrod.

Thursday 22nd June, late afternoon

Young Hutchin had had a very trying day. Somehow he had lost track of the new Deputy in the morning, which had annoyed Richard Lowther very much indeed. In the afternoon, he hung around the stables on the grounds that if Carey was planning to go anywhere, he'd need a mount, and as his own horses were all there, he hadn't gone yet. Even though the stable master set him to the eternal chore of harness cleaning, it had been well worth it. Elizabeth Widdrington had come sweeping in and ordered him to put halters on two of her own animals and the oldest saddle and bridle in the place on the third.

He followed her obediently out of the castle, wondering what on earth was going on, while she went to the Golden Bell in the little squabble of huts outside the Carlisle citadel gate. When she dismissed him, he followed his instinct and skulked around near the inn doorway, to be rewarded by the sight of Barnabus Cooke and another much taller man going in. Peering through one of the windows, he saw them all talking to each other and then, when the stranger kissed the lady's hand, he recognised the way of moving rather than the face and realised with shock that he was looking at the Deputy Warden in disguise. Moments later he had to dodge back behind the stable yard gateway, as Carey made his undignified exit.

Filled with relief and the glorious certainty that Lowther would reward him well, he hung about the stable block until Barnabus Cooke came for the horses and then followed him cautiously well back, dodging into doorways and booths every few moments. He had a healthy respect for Barnabus.

However, Barnabus was preoccupied and didn't seem to notice him. He went round outside the walls with the horses, past the racecourse and up to the Eden bridge, where he tethered them to a stone and sat down to wait.

Young Hutchin hid behind a dry stone wall and waited. In a few minutes a cadger with the long bouncy stride of the Deputy Warden came walking past him, still wiping mud off his face and jerkin. As Carey came close to Barnabus, Young Hutchin trailed him behind the wall, hardly daring to breathe.

"One peep out of you, Barnabus, and you're a dead man." warned Carey as he swung his pack from his back and began strapping it onto one of the horses. In tactful silence Barnabus helped him, but at last, as Carey swung up into the saddle he held a stirrup and asked, "Sir, what'll you do if they torture you?"

Carey looked down at him with his eyebrows up. His face looked very odd without its goatee beard. At least he didn't have a receding chin like Lord Scrope.

"I see no earthly reason why they should, Barnabus," he said, "but if they do I expect I'll tell them who I am and they'll have a good laugh at my expense."

"Will Scrope ransom you?"

Carey laughed. "Eventually. Or I'll escape."

"Be careful, sir. Do you think you'll get there in time?"

"Oh Lord, Barnabus, it's only ten miles. Even you could ride ten miles before sunset if you didn't fall off too often."

"Well sir, if you ride like that, with your hand on your hip so prettily and your back so straight, they'll know you're fake before you're close enough for them to see the walnut juice."

Carey had the grace to look embarrassed, put his hand down and slouched a bit.

"Better?" he asked.

"I suppose. Sir."

"Well, then, off you go Barnabus, and tell them all I'm sick or something."

"What should I say to Sergeant Dodd?"

Carey thought for a moment. "I don't think he's in it with them, whatever it is, but you could wait until after sunset. Use your judgement, Barnabus."

"All right, sir."

"See you tomorrow, God willing."

"Amen," said Barnabus fervently as Carey chirruped to the horses he was leading and clopped his way over the flimsy bridge northwards.

Young Hutchin waited for a long while after Barnabus had set off back to Carlisle. He was in a quandary. Should he run across country to Netherby and warn his Uncle Jock what was going on, or should he go back into the castle and tell Richard Lowther as he'd been paid to. In the end he decided to go to Lowther, because if Carey happened to catch him on the way, then nobody would know what the Deputy Warden was up to until it was too late. Also it wasn't nearly so far to run.

It took him an hour to find out where Richard Lowther had gone and to track him down to the cousin's house where he was having dinner. He was then sent to the kitchen to wait while another boy was ordered to tell Lowther of the message and in all, the sun had set and the Carlisle gate was shut by the time he made his bow to Lowther and gabbled out the news to him.

Lowther's bushy eyebrows almost met over his nose.

"He's going to Netherby dressed as a peddler? Good God, why?"

Young Hutchin shrugged. "He's mad, but he could . . ."

"I know what he could do, lad, none better. Ay. You did right coming to me."

"What are you going to do, sir?"

"None of your business, Young Hutchin. Here's some drink money for you, and a job well done. Off you go, don't spend it all at once and if I catch you in the bawdy house again I'll leather you and send you back to your father."

Heart glowing at the bright silver in his hand, Young Hutchin ran off, leaving Richard Lowther very thoughtful as he sat down at his cousin's table again.

Thursday, 22nd June, evening

As Carey rode out of the Cleughfoot Wood and into sight of Netherby tower, with the pretty little stonebuilt farmhouse nearby, he knew perfectly well he was being paced by two men who had spotted him not far from Longtown. As he slowed his horse to an ambling walk, they came in close behind him but didn't stop him.

In the horse paddock outside Netherby tower was a most remarkable press of horses, with Grahams and Johnstones bringing in bales of hay for their fodder, and feeding them oats and horse nuts besides, which must have cost a fortune at that time of year.

Outside the paddock was a kicking yelling scrum of men, in their shirts and hose. Carey paused to watch. There was some nasty work going on in centre of that mêlée. Suddenly, from the middle of them a wild figure burst, dribbling the ball in front of him. As the scrum broke apart leaving a couple of fist fights, he wove between two large Grahams bearing down on him, dodged back and faked neatly as a Johnstone poked a foot in front of him. For a moment it seemed he would be caught, but he elbowed the fourth defender out of his way as he pounded on alone to the open goal made by two piles of doublets at the far end of the field.

The man in goal looked horrified, dodged back and forth, fell for a lovely feint and dived in the wrong direction as the Earl of Bothwell kicked the ball straight into goal.

Some of the players cheered; the others looked sulky. Carey dismounted and led his horses forward to the edge of the field and watched as an argument developed over whether it was a fair goal or not.

"Who's winning?" he asked the massive black-bearded ruffian who was watching with his arms folded and a deep frown on his face.

"The Earl's men," said the man.

"Do ye not think it would be better if ye had to have a defender or two between you and the goal when you played the ball."

"What for?"

"It might make it more interesting, and ye'd have less motive for fouls."

"More motive for fights after, though," commented the broad man after some thought, "as if it were nae bad enough now."

The Earl was shouting at the leader of the opposing team.

"And who're ye?" demanded the black-bearded man, swinging round to look at him.

"Daniel Swanders, at your service," said Carey, taking off his cap.

"What're ye doing here?"

"I heard ye were after horses. Are you the laird?"

"Nay, lad, that's Wattie Graham there, with the red face shouting at the Earl. I'm Walter Scott of Harden. Ye're not from this country."

"No, master, I'm from Berwick."

"Ay, thought so. The horses yourn?"

"Ay master."

"Mphm."

The football match seemed to be breaking up, as the Earl's side had seemingly won by five goals to none. The losers were sullen and some of them were nursing bruised shins and the man who'd taken the full force of the Earl's elbow in his stomach was still coughing.

Francis Stuart, Earl of Bothwell was a large handsome man with brown hair and a long face never at rest, its features oddly blurred by the continual succession of emotions crossing it, like weather. He was in a good mood from winning the football match and after slapping Wattie Graham on the back and promising him a rematch, he spotted Carey and came striding over to inspect him. Carey tensed a little: it wasn't very likely the Earl would recognise him, he thought, having met the man only once, officially, and the Earl being the kind who is usually so wrapped up in his own importance that anyone not immediately useful to him is nothing more than a fleshly ghost. But still, Bothwell was the only one there who knew Carey at all.

Carey doffed his cap and made a clumsy bow and repeated his story about the horses. He found himself being looked up and down in silence for a moment.

"What's the price on them?" asked Bothwell, his guttural Scottish bringing back memories of King James's Court that Carey would have preferred to forget. At least he could understand it, once his ear was in, and it made it easier for him to slip into the Berwick manner of speaking that southerners thought of as Scottish in their ignorance.

"Well, sir, I thought . . ."

Bothwell laughed. "Makes no matter what ye think, man, I havnae got it. So now."

That was no surprise. Carey smiled ingratiatingly. "Sir, I thought I could lend them to ye, for the raid, and then get them back with a little extra for the trouble after. As an investment, see."

Bothwell's eyes narrowed suspiciously. "What do ye know of the raid?"

"Nothing, your honour, nothing. Only I canna see why ye would be collecting horses for fun."

Bothwell barked with laughter. "And the pack?"

Carey coughed. "Well, I'm a peddler by trade, sir, I thought ye might let me open it and offer what I have to your ladies."

"And yourself?"

"Myself, sir?"

"You look a sturdy man, yourself, can you back a horse, hold a lance?"

Carey hesitated. What would Daniel say? He decided on cunning. "I can ride as well as any man, but it's no' my trade, see."

"There's more than cows where I'm riding, ye could come well out of it."

"Well sir . . ."

"Tell me later," said the Earl generously and clapped Carey's shoulder. "Put your horses in the paddock with the others. If ye ride with us, ye've got your own remounts and I'll see ye have a jack and a lance. If ye dinna, ye must bide here till we come back, if ye follow me?"

"Ay sir."

There was a clanging of a bell from the castle and Carey trotted his horses over to the paddock, then joined the general rush of football players and watchers and horse tenders into the barnekin and so up the rickety wooden steps to the main room of the keep.

Crammed up tight on a bench at a greasy trestle table between a man with only one ear and another Scott, who was one of Old Wat's younger sons, Carey knew perfectly well that no one trusted him. With the number of outlaws around, it was a wonder anyone could trust enough to put their heads down to eat. Broad wooden platters lined the tables filled with porridge garnished with bacon and peas. Carey reached behind him for his pack and pulled out Daniel's wooden bowl and spoon, drew his knife and wiped it on his hose, which only made it greasier.

The braying of a trumpet behind him almost made him jump out of his skin. He craned his head round to see the dinner procession of servants in their blue caps, bearing steaming dishes: he caught the smell of cock-a-leekie and a roasted kid and even some bread. Odd to see all that food go by and know none of it was for him. It was a hard job for the servants to pass between the packed benches and up to the high table where the Earl sat, with his cronies on one side of him and Wattie Graham of Netherby on his right, then Old Walter Scott of Harden, each of them flanked by his eldest sons and the young laird of Johnstone. There didn't seem to be a woman in the place, though Carey couldn't blame their menfolk if they wanted them out of sight.

As the procession reached the high table and the chief men were served, the Earl stood up and threw half a breadroll at a nervous-looking priest in the corner.

"Say a grace for us, Reverend," he shouted.

The Reverend stood up and gabbled some Latin, which was in fact a part of the old wedding service, if Carey's feeble classical knowledge served him right. Everyone shouted Amen, bent their heads and began shovelling food into their guts as if they were half starved.

There was indeed a shortage of food: Carey was slow to help himself and wound up with watery porridge, a few bits of leek and kale and a minute piece of bacon that had hidden under a lump of oatmeal. He gulped the skimpy portion down, and hoped it wouldn't give him the bellyache.

At the high table the Earl of Bothwell was laughing at some joke told by the man beside him; a man, Carey saw with narrowed eyes, who wore a gold threaded brocade doublet and a snowy white falling band in the French style. Unfortunately, about five of the men around Bothwell, including Wattie Graham, had some gold thread in their doublets, being well-able to afford finery on their ill-gotten gains.

"Where are ye from?" demanded the earless man beside him. Carey trotted out his story again and the man nodded.

"One-Lug Johnstone," he explained with his mouth full. "And that's Old Wat's Clemmie Scott."

The man on the other side who had been digging his elbows into Carey's ribs as he struggled with a tough piece of bacon, nodded politely.

"Ye've come up from Carlisle," continued One-Lug, waving for an ale pot and being ignored by the group at the end of the table who had managed to lay hold of it. "What's the news there?"

"Old Scrope's dead," began Carey.

"Ay, so I heard, Devil keep him. His son's the Warden now, I heard tell. How's Lowther?"

"The Warden's got a new Deputy," said Carey.

"Not Lowther?" One-Lug found that very funny and beckoned over two friends of his who'd been playing football. "Listen to this, Jemmie, the man's saying Lowther's not Deputy Warden."

"Who is it then?" demanded Jemmie.

Carey coughed. "Some courtier the Queen's sent up from London," he said modestly, "they say he willna last the year out."

"Nor the month." All three of them were hysterical with laughter at the idea. "Och save me," said One-Lug, in what he thought was a London accent, "Please don't stick that lance in me, Mr Graham, it hurts."

"A cow?" added Jemmie. "Why, what on earth's a cow?"

"Och, my lord Warden, the rude men have stolen my horses . . ."

Carey laughed with them until Old Wat's Clemmie finished chewing on his lump of bacon, swallowed what he could, spat out what he couldn't onto the floor and grunted, "He faced down Sergeant Dodd at the castle yesterday, I saw him."

Ice trickling down his spine, Carey looked as interested as he could.

"What with, a cannon?" asked One-Lug.

"A sword. Mind you, it was to stop Dodd going out after his horses, when Jock of the Peartree was all set to catch him at the Strength of Liddesdale, lying out in the cold wood all night for nothing, thanks to the damned Courtier. They say he's a sodomite . . ."

"Ye canna be a courtier without ye sell your bum," agreed Jemmie wisely. "He must have annoyed the old Queen something powerful."

"If ye ask me," said Old Wat's Clemmie, "he was short of money to pay his tailor's bills, if ye looked at him with his great fat hose and his little doublet, ye never saw such a pretty suit."

"Ye canna pay a London tailor with a cow."

"What do ye know about it, the Edinburgh tailors take horses."

While the argument raged across him, Carey scraped the last of the porridge off his bowl with his finger and put it away in his pack. He looked around the room idly and froze still.

Bothwell was talking to one of the lesser Grahams who had acted as servants to bring in the meal, gesturing in Carey's direction. The boy came struggling down to Carey just as he was helping to clear the trestle tables. The middle of the floor was being swept clean of rushes and sprinkled with sand.

Bothwell had moved: he had the laird's own carved armchair, was drinking wine from a goblet and beside him sat a sinewy grey-bearded man with a broken nose. The Graham boy who had come for Carey, threaded past the men who were now rearranging the benches ready for the evening's entertainment, which was a cockfight. Carey saw the combatants being brought in, still in their cages, crowing defiance and fluttering aggressively and concluded that at least one of them had been got at.

Remembering Bothwell's vanity, when he came up onto the dais, he bobbed his knee to the Earl and stood holding his cap and successfully looking scared.

"There's the man, Jock," said Bothwell, "he must have left Carlisle but a few hours gone."

Jock of the Peartree spent a good minute examining Carey, who smiled ingratiatingly and hoped the walnut juice wouldn't dissolve in his sweat. The keep was infernally hot with all the bodies packed into it.

"I heard," said Jock of the Peartree in a very level voice, "That you was the man sold Sergeant Dodd's wife Sweetmilk's horse."

With a swooping in his gut, Carey remembered that she had in fact bought it from the Reverend Turnbull and that some sort of Reverend had said grace. He wanted to turn and look for him but didn't. In any case, he didn't know what Turnbull looked like.

"No, master," he said, bringing his voice down from a squeak, "I didnae."

"That's the word," said Jock. "You say you know nothing about it?"

"Nowt, sir."

Jock watched him at his leisure for a while. Carey thought frantically. Surely to God, if Turnbull was here, he wouldn't have admitted to his part in the trafficking in that thrice damned nag. Had he? Had he bought his own safety by selling them an intruder? Turnbull was the book-a-bosom priest

Daniel sometimes travelled with, he must have known Carey wasn't Daniel Swanders . . . Why should he? Carey had given the name only to Wat of Harden . . . Don't speculate, ask.

"Sir, who was it said it was me had the animal?"

Jock and the Earl exchanged glances. "That was the word in Carlisle, last we heard," said the Earl. "Do ye tell me on your honour that you never had the horse?"

"Never clapped eyes on him, on my honour, my lord," said Carey, only slightly mendaciously.

Jock snorted slightly. "Do ye know aught ye could tell us about Sweetmilk's killing?" he asked.

"No sir," said Carey, "but it wasnae Sergeant Dodd."

"How do ye know that?"

"If what I've heard is right, sir, he wouldna make such a bodge of it."

The Earl laughed. "Any other news out of Carlisle?"

"Er . . . they postponed the funeral of the old lord."

"I know that. They think we're riding into England," said Bothwell.

"Are ye not?" asked Carey guilelessly, heart hammering again.

Bothwell smiled, a little coldly. "That's for me to know and you to learn in due course, Daniel."

"Yes sir."

"Are you riding with us, Daniel?"

No help for it. "Yes sir, though I'm not a right fighting man if I'm honest with ye."

Bothwell clapped him on the shoulder again and grinned: he had remarkably good, even teeth and it gave his smile an odd glaring quality. Carey smiled back.

"If ye want custom, wait about a bit and Wattie Graham will take you to see the women, they're all agog for whatever's in your pack."

Wattie Graham was as good as his word: as the betting round the makeshift cockpit reached manic proportions, Carey followed the laird up the winding stair to the next floor, where his womenfolk were hiding from the untrustworthy men down below.

There was a crowd of them, perhaps ten or eleven, and a bewildering number of Jeans and Marys with an occasional Maud and one Susan, sitting on little stools at a trestle table eating their own meal which looked even worse than the one still rattling about Carey's stomach. There was no sign of even a speck of bacon in it.

Wattie's wife, Alison Graham, came to meet them at the door. Her broad, lined face lit up at sight of him and she took his hand in her own small rough one and led him into the feminine billow of skirts and aprons.

Surrounded by them, Carey opened the pack, laid out what it contained in the way Daniel had shown him and gave tongue like a London stallman.

"Ribbons, silks, beads and bracelets, laces, creams, garters and needles, what d'ye lack ladies, come buy."

They giggled and elbowed each other. Mrs Graham fingered the ribbons and another girl picked up a packet of hairpins.

"How much for these?" she asked, and Carey told her.

It was bedlam for a while after that, as Carey told prices, held bargaining sessions over quantities of needles and some perfumed soap direct from Castile, as he insisted, although he knew perfectly well it was boiled up in York, and so did they.

At the end of the hour he had made Daniel a profit of about five shillings, and despite a throbbing head and a dry throat, he was feeling well-pleased with himself.

Mrs Graham brought him a goblet of sour wine well-watered, which he drank gratefully and then told him to sit down and he'd shortly get better fare than he would downstairs.

"Unless you want to go and watch the cockfighting?" said another girl, Jeanie Scott, extremely pregnant and glowing with it.

Carey grinned and decided to risk it. "Nay, mistress," he said, "I laid my bets before I came up."

"Don't you want to see which wins?"

"I know which cock'll win," said Carey, "it's the one that wasna given beer beforehand to slow him down."

They all laughed knowingly at that. "What's the news from Carlisle?" asked Alison Graham.

"I wasna there but ten days," said Carey, "I don't know the doings yet."

"Is it right Jock of the Peartree raided the Dodds?" asked Jeanie Scott.

"Och, you know he did," said another woman impatiently, "He was a' full of it when he came back."

"I heard Janet Dodd say her Cousin Willie's Simon had an arrow in his arm during the raid," ventured Carey. "And a woman called Margaret lost her bairn with the excitement."

Jeanie Scott tutted sadly. "That would be Margaret Pringle, Clem Pringle's sister, poor lass. I hope she's not poorly with it. D'ye know how she fares, cadger?"

Carey shook his head.

"How's Young Jock?" asked another girl, a thin, small pale creature, with a startling head of burnished gold hair. One of her wrists was tightly bandaged.

"He's in the jail at Carlisle," said Carey cautiously.

"They havena chained him?"

"Not that I know."

"Now Mary," said Alison gently, "dinna disturb yourself so much."

Mary seemed on the brink of tears, which surprised Carey. "I couldna bear it to lose another brother . . . Will the Warden hang Young Jock, d'ye think."

Carey shrugged. "He was caught with the red hand, Mistress, the Deputy could have hanged him on the spot."

"Ay, you listen to him," said Alison stoutly, "and dinna concern yourself; Lowther'll see him well enough, mark my words, it's only a matter of waiting."

"But after Sweetmilk . . ." began Mary, and the tears started trickling down her face. From the red rims round her eyes it looked something she did often.

Alison rolled her eyes. "Now Mary, Sweetmilk's dead and gone and that's the end of it. He's with God now and your dad'll get his revenge once he finds the man that did the killing."

Mary only cried harder and put her head on Susan's shoulder.

"Is she Sweetmilk's betrothed?" asked Carey privately of Jeanie Scott, fetching out a hanky from his pack that was edged with lace and handing it to Mary. Service at Court had made it almost a reflex with him, when he saw a woman crying, although naturally what he really wanted to do was to cut and run.

Jeanie didn't look sympathetic. "No, she's Sweetmilk's sister and what she's in such a taking about, I'm sure I dinna ken."

It was Mary who had bought a packet of extra-long staylaces as Carey was sure Mrs Graham had noticed. She was mopping her eyes again: Carey saw her fingernails were bitten down to the quick.

"It's a sad thing to lose a brother," added Jeanie briskly, "but God knows, it's worse to lose a wean, and she's a fancy man here too, if I'm any judge."

"Is she not married yet?" added Carey in surprise.

"Nay, she's only sixteen, she's but a flighty maid with her head full of stories. Jock has her betrothed to an Elliot but she doesna want him. She'll change her tune in time."

"Better to marry than burn, the preachers say," said Carey meaningfully.

Jeanie Scott eyed him. "Ay," she said at last, "that's the way of it."

"Do you know who killed Sweetmilk?"

Jeanie shrugged and patted her stomach. "Save for the way it was done, it could have been a Storey or a Bell or a Maxwell or anyone that found him with cows that didna belong to him."

"Hey, peddler," sang out another Mary, "how much for the whalebone?"

There was a little more selling and then the girl called Susan came in with a large wobbling junket, sweetened with rosewater and honey. They served it to him, laughing at his expression and told him a fine figure of a man like himself needed better feeding than what they were getting downstairs and it would settle his stomach nicely. Three of them had messages for friends in Carlisle, Jeanie Scott wanted him to tell the midwife Mrs Croser that the babe was head down at last, and a fifth wanted to know what a roll of green velvet would cost and if he could get it for her from Edinburgh next time he went. Carey promised he would find out from Thomas the Merchant which seemed to please them.

At last with his pack a good bit lighter than before and his purse considerably heavier, Carey went to the door. Mrs Graham followed him with a roll of cloth.

"Here," she said, "ye dinna want to jingle among that lot downstairs, roll your money in this."

He did as she suggested and behind the door, he slipped it down inside his shirt and tied it round his waist. At the bottom of the stairs he found Wattie Graham, frowning.

"Ye took your time."

Carey shrugged. "I canna rush the ladies when they canna make up their minds," he said reasonably. "Who won the cockfight?"

"The Duke of Guise, Old Wat of Harden's best cock," said Wattie Graham dourly, "and if ye ask me, it was fixed."

Carey went over to One-Lug and Jemmie to collect his winnings, and then agreed to join a game of primero with them. As soon as he took the cards in his hands, he knew they had been marked with pin pricks on the back and had to hide a smile. With a quick shuffle, he had the system worked out, and it was one that the London card-sharps had abandoned five years before.

It was quite pleasant to let himself slip into a card-playing frame of mind, finding a clearer colder self as he watched the cards and the play and calculated the odds according to the Italian book he had read ten years before and which had saved his life. At Court it could sometimes be far more dangerous to win than to lose: he won steadily but had never taken more than he lost off the Earl of Leicester, nor from his successor at Court, the Earl of Essex. Sir Walter Raleigh was a different matter: he had spotted Carey's careful odds playing at once and had insisted on learning it from him.

Carey ended the evening by paying back to Old Wat's

Clemmie and One-Lug and Jemmie exactly what he had won off them at the cockfight, which made them feel they were somehow one up on him. There was music as well: a scrawny old man with a plaited beard took up a little harp like the ones they had in Ireland and strummed and sang a whining ugly song about a fight of some sort. There followed a scurrilous and probably truthful ballad about Scrope and his personal habits and a wistful lament for Sweetmilk Graham that had Jock of the Peartree dabbing his eyes and nodding and sighing.

It hardly seemed possible for the number of men they had fed there to be able to sleep, even after some of them had been set to watch the horses and guard the Longtown ford. And to Carey's frustration, there was still no word on where the raid was headed. But there was no help for it, and so with his pack pillowing his head and a thread from it wound round his thumb, his dagger in his hand and Daniel's thin greasy cloak wrapped round him, he lay down to sleep, with One-Lug's boots by his head and Jemmie's backside wedging him into the wall. Which hardly seemed a coincidence, though if they were watching him they were doing it in their sleep. For a long time he was too tight-strung to shut his eyes as he lay in the smoky darkness listening to an orchestra of snores and grunts and farting. In the end, even he slept.

Friday 23rd June, before dawn

All her life Elizabeth Widdrington had risen well before dawn to dress herself and pray in the quiet pale time before the world sprang to life. It calmed her and gave her space to breathe before she must plunge into managing her husband's house and lands and nursing her husband himself. It was a precious thing to be able to speak to God without interruption by maid-servants wanting to know if the linen should be washed despite the rain and menservants needing the tools out of the lockup.

Of course, sometimes she was hard put to it to keep her mind on her prayers: Philadelphia's brother would keep marching into her thoughts. It had been a long time since her lawfully arranged husband Sir Henry had been well enough for the marriage bed and sometimes she despaired of ever having children. At twenty-eight she was getting on for childbearing . . . And there was the memory of Robert Carey again, courteously determined, blue eyes smoky and intent, whispering his desire to her in the little garden at the palace, while the rain of that stormy summer fell and the whole land held its breath and waited for the Armada. And afterwards . . . No, she wouldn't think of it.

She rose and started to dress. On this particular morning she was in one of the little apartments in the Carlisle Keep, since Lady Scrope refused to hear of her lodging in the town. As always she padded silently about in her shift, not needing a tiring woman since her stays laced unfashionably at the front, and once she was into her grey-woollen gown and her ruff tied at her neck, she crept out through Philadelphia and Thomas Scrope's chamber with her boots in her hand. The two of them were invisible behind the curtains of their bed and the maidservant snoring at a high pitch by the wall. None of them woke as she opened the heavy door and went down the stair.

It was a little more difficult to pick her way amongst the servants asleep in the rushes in the main room, but she managed it with no more than a few grunts and a feeble grope after her by one of the men. She was on the point of opening the heavy main door, when she heard stealthy footsteps and whispered conversation, and the rattle of keys.

She froze, then as she heard them open the iron door to the jail and go in directly beneath her, she pulled on her boots, opened the door a little, to peer out.

Sir Richard Lowther was emerging from under the wooden steps that led to the door she was hiding behind. At his back were five tousled bearded men – no, six. The last she knew was Bangtail Graham and the others must be the raiders Sir Robert Carey had captured the day before yesterday.

Lowther beckoned them to stand around him.

"He's gone to Netherby," he explained, "dressed as a

peddler, by name Daniel Swanders. Now you'd know him again, wouldn't you Young Jock."

"Oh ay," said Young Jock, "I'd know him."

"I can't spare you more than one horse, so Young Jock will have to ride and the rest will have to follow, but . . ."

Elizabeth Widdrington opened the door, walked out onto the steps and stopped, looking down at them.

Richard Lowther looked up at her, not at all worried.

"Good morning, Sir Richard," she said.

"Good morning, Lady Widdrington," he said.

"What are you doing?"

It was hard for him to refuse to answer a direct question, though it was obvious enough he thought it none of her business.

"These men have got bail, Lady Widdrington," he said, "I'm letting them go home to their families."

"Bail?" she asked archly.

"My lord Scrope agreed it last night."

Damn the man for his vagueness. Even when he was sick, Scrope's father would have wanted to know the reason for Lowther's interest.

"They've given their words of honour they'll come when their bills are called at the next Day of Truce, and they cost the castle six pence a day each to guard and feed."

"Is the gate open yet?"

"Not yet. Soon enough."

No she was not going to let him give one of their precious horses to Jock of the Peartree's sons. Let the raiders walk to Netherby on their own two feet that God gave them.

She came down the steps as the whole group of them went to stand by the gate and wait for it to open. At least Lowther hadn't the authority to open it before time. As they passed her she stopped Bangtail.

"Where's the Sergeant?" she demanded.

"He has a little chamber by the barracks door," said Bangtail, "Why did ye want him, missus? Can I help."

"I doubt it, but you could wait and see if I have a message for you if you want to earn yourself a little drinkmoney."

"Ay missus."

Elizabeth hurried across the yard to the bright new barracks building and opened up the door to find Janet Dodd standing in the passage in her kirtle with her stays half laced, head down as she brushed her red hair.

"Janet, where's your husband?"

"In there," said Janet, surprised at seeing a gentlewoman up so early. "Why, what's the matter, my lady?"

"Would you go in and see if he's decent. I must speak to both of you at once."

"Yes ma'am."

Janet peeked round the door, turned to Elizabeth.

"He's dressed and drinking his beer, and if I were you, I'd wait until he comes out, he's ay like a bear in the morning."

"I'm sorry, this is very urgent."

From behind the door that led to the main part of the barracks came the hawking and moaning of the garrison waking up. Brooking no argument, Elizabeth gestured Janet ahead of her into the tiny chamber and followed herself.

Dodd was sitting on the little sagging bed with his chin on his hand, drinking miserably.

"Goddamn it, woman, can ye never find better than sour . . . Oh, sorry, ma'am." To be fair to him, Dodd pulled at the open front of his doublet and made to stand up, but Elizabeth shook her head, shut the door firmly behind her.

"Lowther's freeing the men you and Sir Robert caught the day before yesterday. They'll be out at the gate as soon as it opens."

Dodd looked cynical. "That's no surprise, he's well in with the Grahams and wants to stay that way. Why? What do you care?"

Elizabeth charitably ignored his insolence. "I care because Robert Carey went to Netherby last night in disguise as a peddler."

That woke him up. He sat bolt upright. "Good Chri . . . why?"

"Didn't Barnabus tell you last night? To see about getting your horses back and finding the man that really did kill

Sweetmilk. And also to know where Bothwell is planning to raid."

"The man's mad," said Dodd definitely.

"I never thought he'd do that when he gave his word," said Janet, clearly appalled. "They'll half-kill him if they find out."

"Which they will do as soon as Young Jock and his men get to Netherby."

"Stark staring lunatic," continued Dodd. "That Earl of Bothwell could hang him as soon as look at him, I've known him do it for less."

"Who else knows of this?" asked Janet.

"Myself and Robert's servant Barnabus Cooke, who's still abed as far as I know. And Lowther, somehow."

"Cooke's a Londoner," said Dodd, "Canna ride better than a hog in breeches. What's to be done?"

"Stop Lowther."

Dodd sucked his teeth. "I dinna see why he should pay me any mind, but I'll try for ye, my lady. Good God almighty . . . Sorry ma'am. Disguised as a peddler, would ye credit it?"

Elizabeth left them there with Janet doing up Dodd's laces and finding his cap, while she hurried back to the keep, threaded through the wakening servants and ran up the stairs to the Scropes' chamber.

It took her five minutes to shake the maidservant awake and the maid took another five to waken Philadelphia who climbed tottering out of the high bed and blinked at Elizabeth.

"Wh – what's wrong?" she asked. "Is it a raid?"

"No, it's your brother."

"What's he done?"

Elizabeth told her, including what Lowther was up to. Philly's eyes widened, her hand went to her mouth.

"But the Earl will hang him."

"Robin didn't think so."

"He doesn't know the Earl of Bothwell, he's a wicked Godless man and cruel with it. Thomas, Thomas, wake up."

"I'm awake," came Scrope's tetchy voice from behind the curtains. "What's that mad brother of yours done?"

Elizabeth fidgeted about the room while Philadelphia explained. The two voices rose and fell, one irritable, one pleading. At last Scrope poked his head out of the curtains, causing his nightcap to fall off.

"I said they could have bail and I'm not going back on it," he snarled. "Lowther can let them out but they're not to have horses."

"But Robin . . ." wailed Philly.

"Your precious Robin can look after himself. He should have thought of it before. Man's mad, going into Netherby dressed as a servant . . ."

"A peddler . . ."

"I don't care if he went dressed as the bloody Queen of France, I'm not getting him out of some schoolboy scrape."

There was a thump as Scrope flounced back onto the pillows.

"Anyway," came the reedy voice, "I'm unwell. I think I have an ague."

Philadelphia scrambled out of bed again, leaving the curtains drawn, and fluttered about the chamber, trying to get dressed while she crumpled up her little face and bewailed her husband. Elizabeth waited for a moment, then decided there was no help to be got there, made an impatient "Tchah!" noise, and went down the stairs again.

Out in the courtyard she found Dodd having a shouting match with Lowther by the gate, watched by a group of highly amused Grahams.

"Ye canna let them out and have him taken, he's the Deputy Warden," he was shouting.

"I can and I will," growled Lowther, "And what's more, *I'm* rightfully the Deputy Warden, not that upstart Londoner, or I will be by the end of today, I think."

"That's telling him," laughed Young Jock, "Do ye want the man roasted a bit for impudence before we hang him."

"No," said Lowther, "hang him up first, then roast him, don't take any chances with the young pup."

"Jesus Christ, at least ransom him, we need to know where the raid's going . . ."

"Shut your mouth, Sergeant Dodd," said Lowther, "I know where the raid's headed and so does Captain Musgrave."

"Bothwell could be lying to ye . . ."

Lowther smiled slowly. "He's not lying, not with what it is he's hoping to steal."

"And what's that?" put in Elizabeth. "If you really do know, which I doubt."

Lowther laughed at her rudely. "I'm not telling ye, all women are blabbermouths and ladies nae different. If ye were my wife I'd tan your hide for asking what's men's business and none of yours."

Lady Widdrington paled and her lips tightened. She looked as if she was swallowing a great many large words with great effort.

Young Jock, Ekie and all the Grahams were helpless with laughter. Dodd stepped towards them with his fist raised, but Lowther got in his way, still grinning.

"These are out on bail now, Sergeant," he said, "and as Deputy Warden I forbid you to leave the castle today. Do you understand me?"

"What?" Dodd's eyes were fairly bugging with rage. "Are you making me a prisoner in my own keep . . .?"

"It's not your keep, it's mine, and I'm the authority here. In fact . . ." Lowther's pale eyes narrowed. "I don't trust you not to do something foolish, Sergeant Dodd. Here, Ekie, Young Jock – fetch the Sergeant into the jail for me, will ye?"

"By God, Lowther, I'll have your guts . . ." roared Dodd as the Grahams grabbed him by the arms and manhandled him through the door to the ground floor of the keep. At least Bangtail had the grace to hang back, biting his fist, but he made no move to help his Sergeant. There was a series of thumps and muffled yells. Janet lunged forward, but Elizabeth caught her.

"Up," she said, "into the keep."

"But they're beating him . . ."

"He'll survive," said Elizabeth callously. "They're only taking a little revenge for what he did to them. Do you want to wind up in there too? You will if you make Lowther think of it. Come with me."

By main force she had Janet up the steps and through the door before Lowther came out again, rattling his keys suggestively and looking pleased with himself. He paused when Lord Scrope leaned out of a high window in the keep and yelled that he was not to take a single nag from the stables, but then shrugged. They watched him through a shot hole in the wall as he swaggered over to the barracks, no doubt in search of his breakfast, followed by the mob of Grahams.

"What can we do?"

Elizabeth was still watching. The Grahams were moving in a body to the gate: as it opened, they were out into Carlisle town and from there, once the town gates opened, on the road to Netherby.

Friday, 23rd June, before dawn

Carey awoke out of too little sleep, knowing someone was stealing his pillow. He knew before he was properly awake that he couldn't allow that: gripped it tighter, rolled and pushed himself onto his feet with his back to the wall and his dagger ready.

"Ah well," said Jemmie's voice, "it was worth a try. Don't stick me, peddler, I was only wondering."

Carey showed his teeth and waited until Jemmie had backed off. One-Lug lifted himself up on an elbow and cursed both of them, then lay down and went back to sleep. Old Wat's Clemmie hadn't even stirred.

With the inside of his mouth as full of muck as a badly run stables and his head pounding, Carey thought of trying for another hour's sleep, but decided against it. Instead he picked his way across the crammed bodies, scratching his face where the newly shaved beard was coming back and his body where the fleas had savaged him. Once outside there was blessed fresh clean air, only a little tainted with the staggering quantities of manure produced by the men and horses packed into Netherby, and the stars rioting across the sky, with just a little paleness at the eastern edge.

Carey wished he could wash his face, but couldn't find water, so wandered towards the cow byres set against the barnekin wall where there were lights and movement.

Sleepy women were trudging about there with pails and stools. Alison Graham was standing by the big milk churns and she nodded curtly at him as he slouched towards her.

"Ye're up early," she said to him. "Any of the other men up and doing, eh cadger?"

"One of them tried to steal my pack, but no," said Carey ruefully. "Any water about fit to drink."

She gestured at some buckets standing by for the cows and he went and dunked his head, drank enough to clear out his mouth.

"Is Mary with you?" he asked, "Mary Graham?"

"In with Bluebell at the moment, why?"

"I wanted to ask her about Sweetmilk."

"Why?"

"In case I heard anything, in my travels. I do, you know,"

Alison Graham looked him up and down suspiciously. "If ye're trying . . ."

"God curse me if I lie, missus, I only want to talk to her."

After a moment she nodded. As she took the buckets from the girl bringing them over on a yoke, lifted and poured them without visible effort, she said, "She only has to squeal and the crows'll be feeding on you by midday."

Carey nodded, did his best to look harmless and went into the byre where Bluebell and two other cows were ready to be milked. Following the sound of retching, he came on Mary in the corner, being helplessly sick on an empty stomach. She had her fist clenched on a lace she wore about her neck. Carey watched silently for a moment, knowing perfectly well what was wrong since he had seen the malady before. At last Mary stopped, spat, and sat down on her stool, with her head rested against the cow's flank. As if nothing had happened she started milking away with her sleeves rolled up and the muscles in her white arms catching light off the lantern on the hook above as she worked, though she favoured her bandaged wrist.

She jumped when he coughed.

"Can I sit and talk with ye, missus," he asked gently.

She shrugged and carried on. Carey squatted down with his back to the wall. They watched the milk spurt in white streams, the round sweet smell of it mixing with the smell of hay from the cow's breath.

"When's the babe due?" asked Carey after a while, deciding to bet his shirt on a guess.

Mary Graham gave a little sigh and closed her eyes.

"What babe?" she asked. Squersh, squersh, went the milk and the cow chewed contentedly on her fodder.

Carey said nothing for a while. "I wish ye could help me, for then I might help you," he said at last. "It's a Christmas baby, is it no'?"

She shrugged, turned her face away from him. Her head was bare like most of the maids in the north, and the straight red-gold hair knotted up tightly with wisps falling into her face as she worked.

"What did Sweetmilk say?"

That opened the dyke. Her fingers paused in their rhythm, her shoulders went up then down, and he saw water that was not sweat dripping off her chin.

"He said . . ." she whispered, "he said he'd kill the father."

"Did he know who the father was?"

No answer.

"Can ye tell me?"

"Why should I, if I didna tell my brother and my own father doesnae ken yet."

"Was it one of Bothwell's men?"

There was a telltale little gasp. "How did ye know?"

"If it was one of the men from about here, ye could marry him and if he was married already he could take the bairn for you."

"I may lose it yet."

Carey said nothing. Privately he believed that only women who longed for babes ever lost them: the more embarrassing a child was likely to be, the more certain its survival. Unless the mother went to a witch, but he thought this girl not ruthless enough for that. And not brave enough.

"They say pennyroyal mint will shift it. Do you have any about you, cadger?"

"No," said Carey, coldly. Mary Graham sneered at him and went on with the other two teats. The cow shifted experimentally and tipped her hoof. Mary banged unmercifully on the leg and the cow lowed in protest.

"Would you marry the father if he asked?" pressed Carey, hoping she wouldn't slap him.

She didn't quite: she scowled at him and turned her shoulder to him.

"Not if he was the Earl himself," she whispered fiercely.

Carey nodded. That at least removed the prime suspect, but it confirmed that she must know who killed Sweetmilk. Not that she was likely to tell, even if her father beat her which he no doubt would. Poor lass.

He let her finish milking the cow and when she rose from her stool and rubbed her back, he too rose to go.

"Make yourself useful, peddler," she said to him, "take this over to Mistress Graham for me."

Embarrassed into women's work, Carey took the buckets and carried them out of the byre. Without a yoke to take the surprising weight and steady them he slopped some of the milk and Alison Graham sniffed at him, lifted each one and poured it out and sent him back to swill the buckets with water and take them in to Mary again. He knew perfectly well she'd tell him nothing more and he wasn't her servant, so when he had done as he was bid, he walked out into the dawn again and yawned and stretched.

"What will you do about Mary's bairn?" he asked Mrs Graham when she snorted at him like an irritable horse.

"Why? Are you offering for her hand?" demanded the mistress. "She'll take it if ye do."

"Er . . . no . . ."

"Then leave her alone. She's enough to contend with."

"Yes missus," said Carey meekly.

Friday, 23rd June, dawn

Dodd was sitting glumly in the cell recently vacated by Bangtail, looking at the neat pile of turds in the corner. He had worn out his fury kicking the stout door and now his toes were sore as well as his stomach and his face and he hadn't had breakfast.

The rattle of keys did not make him look up, since he expected it was Lowther come to gloat.

"Wake up, Dodd," snapped his wife's voice, "unless ye want to bide there until your hanging."

Looking up produced the extraordinary sight of three very angry women. If Dodd had been classically trained, he would have thought of the three Fates or possibly the Furies. His wife was holding a small loaf and a leather bottle, and the other two, Lady Scrope and Lady Widdrington, were neat, pale and grim-faced.

"Lowther's put one of his men at the gate," said Lady Widdrington, "but Lady Scrope tells me there's another way out of the castle, some secret passage to the Tile Tower."

This was the first Dodd had heard of it, but he supposed it wasn't the kind of thing generally bandied around. Lady Widdrington put a purse into his hand, and when he got into the passage, he found his wife had piled his jack and sword and helmet into a corner. He drank the ale from the bottle she handed him and gave her a kiss.

"We haven't much time," said Lady Scrope. "My husband says he's got an ague and won't do anything, and Lowther's got the whole castle locked up tight."

"It's too late to stop the Grahams getting to Netherby even on foot," said Dodd gloomily.

Janet was helping him into his jack, Lady Widdrington handed him his helmet and sword, even Lady Scrope was helping with the lacings. It was an extraordinary situation to be in.

"I know that," said Lady Widdrington impatiently. "All we can do now is stop Bothwell from hanging him when he finds out."

"How can we do that?" asked Dodd. "He's an unchancy bastard to meddle with, that Earl and I dinna . . ."

"Dodd, be quiet and listen," snapped his wife, which annoyed him since she was supposed to listen to him. But he couldn't quite bring himself to tell her off since she was breaking him out of jail.

They seemingly had a plan. Surrounding him with their skirts and selves, and with one of Lady Scrope's velvet cloaks over his head, they simply walked him quickly round to the empty inside of the keep, through the servants' quarters and to the place in the wall where the well was enclosed, supplying independent water to all the keep. Janet unbolted and pulled down the shutter.

"Through there," said Lady Scrope.

"What?" asked Dodd, appalled.

"If you climb through the gap," said Lady Scrope brightly, "and feel about with your feet, you'll find the rungs of a ladder set into the wall. Climb down until you find another hole in the wall on the opposite side. That's the entrance to the tunnel that goes to the Tile Tower."

Dodd peered through the hole, which was black and smelled very wet and mouldy.

"Christ Jesus," he said. To his surprise, no one told him not to swear. He would have thought there would be a chorus.

"When you get to the Tile Tower," continued Elizabeth Widdrington coldly, "it's up to you how you get out of the city, but I doubt Lowther knows of this since it's knowledge passed from Warden to Warden. So he'll expect you to try for the gate. I'll have Bangtail try and make the attempt, and no doubt he'll wind up in here which will serve him right."

"What for?"

"For existing," said Janet.

Dodd wasn't sure if it had been Bangtail who punched him in the kidneys when he was arguing with the Grahams about being locked up in his own jail, but wasn't inclined to give anybody the benefit of the doubt.

"What then?" he asked. "If it's too late to warn Carey to be out of Netherby and Scrope willna move, what can I do?"

They told him. He hated the sound of it, but he had to agree there didn't seem anything else to be done. Lady Widdrington gave him one of Carey's rings in case he needed to produce proof. Janet produced a rope which she passed around his middle and then kissed his face.

"God keep you, husband," she said.

"Bloody hell," said Dodd, blinking at the hole he was supposed to climb through. Would his shoulders go, or would he be left stuck and kicking? He poked his head through, eased his shoulders, and found that with some wriggling, they fitted. Some bits of stone slipped and fell: there was an awfully long wait, it seemed, before the splash. The place was pitch black. He spread his arms wide, feeling about, and sure enough there were rungs in the wall a little to the side.

Pulling back with long streaks of mould on his back and chest, he found a lantern being lit by Elizabeth Widdrington. As he was about to snarl he couldn't be expected to do anything without light, he was nonplussed by this. They really expected him to do it.

Oh God, what would they do if he refused? He looked at their soft white faces, set like saints' faces in an unreformed church, and decided he didn't want to find out. And besides, he wouldn't put it past Janet to go herself, she was in such a rage and what she would say to him afterwards, he hated to think. A short life and a miserable one, whatever I do, thought Henry Dodd glumly.

He brought up a stool, climbed on it, poked his shoulders through again and felt for the rungs of the ladder. The first one he found and tested for its strength, promptly came out of the wall at one side.

"The mortar's rotten," he said, thinking maybe he could survive Janet's fury.

"Get on with it," hissed Lady Widdrington, "someone's coming."

It was all very well for her, she wasn't risking her neck in some horrible deep well . . . The second rung seemed firm enough to take his weight. He swallowed hard, got a grip on it with both hands and heaved himself through the little hole, the sword on his belt catching and scraping.

Almost at once, Lady Widdrington put the lantern on the ledge and fitted the shutter back in the hole. He heard the bolts going home as he hung by his hands from the top rung. That was when he thought of taking off his jack, sword and helmet and lowering them down on the rope, but it was too late to do it. Scrabbling desperately with his toes for one below him, he thought that all except the top rungs had fallen out, but at last he found a foothold and could distribute his weight.

He passed the end of the rope round the top rung and felt down gingerly for the next rung. That one held, he went down a little further, gasping a bit with fear. The rung after that was rotten but the three below it were firm enough.

It might have taken him two minutes or half an hour to climb down to the little ledge he could dimly see in the light of the lantern above. He couldn't bring it with him, he didn't have the hands. Once on the ledge he got his breath back and looked about. There were some rotten wooden boards propped up against the wall, and then he saw the opening of the tunnel on the other side, just as Lady Widdrington had said.

It wasn't badly planned, he thought to distract himself as he inched round the ledge towards it. Any besiegers who found the passage would have to reverse what he was doing to get in and it would be a simple matter for the defenders to drop things down on them from above and knock them off. And the ledge was deliberately made too narrow to stand and use a bow. God, it was narrow, and the well was still too deep to see the water. And then, if the garrison wanted to use the passage to make a foray, or get food, they would have control of the well shaft and they could put down planks across the yawning hold so it wasn't so dangerous.

Dodd crouched down by the opening, put his head into it and banged his nose on something metal. Cursing and feeling with his hand, he discovered an iron grill, firmly set in the rock.

"Oh Christ, it's been blocked up . . ."

Sense told him otherwise. If the passage was to be blocked up, they would have done it properly with bricks and mortar, this was a defence. Which meant it could be lifted, perhaps like a portcullis. The light from the lantern high above him was guttering, but he couldn't bring himself to climb and fetch it and trim the wick. Somewhere by the opening there had to be a . . . His hand fell onto a lever, and he pulled it down. It was stuck.

"Come on," he muttered, wrenching at it. At last it creaked and groaned and the iron grill lifted a little. Just like a portcullis. Sweating freely and feeling sick from the smell of mould, Dodd pulled at the lever again, heard a crunching of gears as the ratchet within the mechanism caught its teeth, and the iron grill lifted up a little higher, and then suddenly something worked and it pulled right out of the way. There were long sharp spikes along the bottom.

Terrified of being spitted like an animal in a trap, Dodd looked around for something to wedge it with, pulled one of the rotten planks towards him and jammed it in the groove.

The passage was tiny and slimy and horrible. He didn't want to go in. On the other hand, he couldn't climb back up either.

"Carey, you bastard," he moaned, pushed his sword in its scabbard in front, put his head in and scraped his shoulders through. There was an ominous creak and whine from the iron gate. Dodd whimpered and crawled forwards on his elbows as fast as he could, heard the rattle and cracking as the rusty chain broke and the wood splintered, and brought his feet up under him just in time, scraping a long hole in his hose and grazing his knees. The iron grill slammed into the holes behind him, and he wanted to be sick.

He didn't, it was too unpleasant a thought, having to crawl through it. The passage was bad enough as it was, slimy and stinking of rats and excrement, with little spines of limestone sticking up and hurting his hands and spines of limestone hanging down to bang his head. Why the hell was he doing this for Carey, he didn't even like the man, what the devil did he care . . .

The passage opened out a bit after a few yards of eeling along on his belly, so he could crawl on hands and knees, feeling ahead of himself with his sword, in terror that the roof might have fallen in. There was one place where some stones had fallen down, but he managed to slither through there as well, to find a puddle on the other side.

He splashed through that, crawled for another age, cursing Carey, Lowther and both Scropes comprehensively, and then the point of his sword rammed into solid stone blocking the way. Not knowing whether his eyes were open or shut, except by the way his sweat was stinging them, he felt the stones. Masonry, tightly packed. He must be at the Tile Tower by now, surely. And surely to God, there was a way out. He felt around, found a small slimy drain that was producing a stink to fell an ox. He thought he must suffocate from it and his head was starting to spin.

The wall in front of him stayed obstinately immovable. Dodd pushed and heaved with his neck muscles cramping and his knees giving him hell, almost weeping with frustration. He finally lay down flat to rest, and happened to look upwards.

Either something was wrong with his eyes or there was a tiny squeeze of daylight up there. Above him was no tunnel roof, only a shaft and beside him, now he had calmed down, he could feel some more metal rungs. He sniffed. He thought at last that he knew where he was: this was the garderobe shaft for the Tile Tower, which was one of the lookout towers on the north wall of Carlisle. It was still in use, clearly, by sentries. God, no wonder the tunnel stank and what exactly was it he'd crawled through . . .

"Bastard, bastard, bastard," he muttered in a litany of ill-usage, as he strapped his sword on again and set himself to climb. The rungs were slippery but they seemed firmer than the ones in the well. At last he found the light coming from a little window above a small stone platform. At that point, he could get his bearings. He was in the outer wall where it was at its thickest, seven or eight yards thick, he thought and couldn't remember. There must be a way to the outside, or why bother with a passage?

There was. Part of the wall swivelled and he passed through it. The passage was as narrow as the one from the well, but this one was at least dry. At the end it dipped down where it joined a gutter and when Dodd lowered himself experimentally, he found himself sitting on a ledge about ten feet off the ground to the north of Carlisle, looking out on the Sauceries and the racetrack and the Eden bridge.

Now afraid of twisting his ankle when he had ten miles to run, Dodd lowered himself down on his arms and fingers, dropped into the soft earth and brambles of the ditch and then sat there for five minutes, gasping and shuddering and swearing all sorts of desperate reformations if God would never make him do that again. At last, with his knees killing him and his legs still rubbery, he scrambled up the other side of the ditch and walked across the rough grass to the river.

Once he got to the Eden he mopped off some of the green streaks and filth that covered him from head to foot. There were a few curious stares from some of the women washing linen at the rapids, but none of them saw fit to comment. Then he set off along the old Roman road at a fast jog trot, past the banks and ditch of the old Pict's Wall, heading for Brampton nine miles away where Janet's father lived with his kin, the first of the men on Carey's list of those who disliked Lowther. Nobody enjoyed paying blackrent for protection against raiders Lowther brought in himself, but some resented it more than others. Will the Tod Armstrong, Janet's father, had bent his ear often enough on the subject, God knew.

The day was hot for the first time in weeks, and Dodd thought seriously about hiding his jack in a bush and coming back for it later. In the end he simply couldn't bring himself to do it and risk losing an old friend.

As he loped along, he kept watching for horses though he knew there was less than no hope of finding a loose horse to steal this close to the marauders denned up at Netherby. Most of the men were at the shielings anyway, so not even cows were visible, and the womenfolk hard at work in the fields and gardens near their houses. Some of them unbent their backs to look at him, a couple recognised him, but as they could hear no tolling of the Carlisle bell, they were puzzled to know what to do and simply stood watching. He ignored the ones who called out.

Perhaps his father-in-law would take pity on him and lend him a horse to carry him the further seven miles to Gilsland where he could rouse out his own surname.

God help Carey if he's had the bad taste to get himself hanged before I can bring help to Netherby, was all Dodd could think, as he pounded along the rutted gravel of the Roman road. I'll hunt him down and beat his brains out in Hell itself.

Friday, 23rd June, morning

Elizabeth Widdrington roused her stepson Henry from his lodgings at Bessie's and told him the tale as he ate his bread and cheese. He laughed aloud at the thought of Dodd being banged up in his own jail, until he saw his young stepmother tapping her foot and swallowed his amusement. She's a handsome woman, he thought, a little shocked at himself. What shreds of filial piety Henry had ever felt had been long destroyed by his father's ill-temper and complex doings with the Fenwicks, the Kerrs and every gang of ruffians that chose to terrorise the East March when Sir John Carey's back was turned. As a boy of ten Henry had been prudishly shocked when his father chose to marry again, and found himself a young Cornish girl through the good offices of Lord Hunsdon. But Elizabeth Trevannion had won him over in the end by treating him as a brother, rather than a son.

She was talking again.

"What do you want me to do?" he asked, not sure he had heard it right.

"You and I are going to Thomas the Merchant and we're going to get the full story he's hiding about what he knows of Sweetmilk. And then, depending on what we find, you might go straight to Netherby to tell Jock of the Peartree of it."

Henry choked on a lump of cheese. "But I haven't got a pass to go into Scotland."

"You will by the time you need one, Philadelphia Scrope is seeing to it. Now come along."

Thomas the Merchant had a very fine wooden town house on English Street, solidly built of Irish timber and the walls coloured faint pink with a bull's blood wash. Elizabeth Widdrington swept in, with the top of her high-crowned hat brushing the door lintel and servants scattering behind her like chaff. Henry knew his job for this kind of thing, at least, having collected rents with his stepmother in the past. When an ugly man his own height dared to bar their path, he drew his sword, put it on the man's chest and walked straight on so he had the choice of giving way or being spitted. The man gave way.

At the end of the hallway stood a middle-aged slightly built merchant in rich black brocade, trimmed with citron velvet and green braid, clasping his hands nervously.

"Lady Widdrington, Lady Widdrington, what is the meaning of this . . ."

Henry set his face in an ugly scowl and advanced on the man with his sword. Occasionally he was grateful for the spots and pockmarks that ruined his face for the girls, because they made him look so much more unsavoury than he knew he really was.

"Thomas Hetherington," said Elizabeth in tones that would have skewered a wild boar, "you will tell me what you know about the killing of Sweetmilk Graham and what happened to his horse and you will do it *this instant*! Sit down."

"How dare you come breaking into my house and threatening my servants, I have never been so slighted . . ."

"Then it's about time you were," said Elizabeth. "By God, I have had enough of your patronage and your shilly-shallying and this time you shall tell me what I ask and you shall tell the truth or I will destroy you and everything you own."

Thomas the Merchant's face went putty-coloured. "This is unseemly," he said, and Henry had to give him credit for courage. "Madam, I must ask you to leave or I shall call . . ."

"Oh?" asked Elizabeth, "and whom, pray, shall you call? The Warden? He's in bed. The Grahams? They're busy. However, I am here and I will have no arguments, do you understand?"

"I'll sue, I'll . . ."

Elizabeth smiled very unpleasantly. "Nothing would please me more than to meet you in Westminster Hall. In the meantime, tell me what I ask, God damn you, or I'LL LOSE MY TEMPER."

Henry thought it was wonderful how his God-fearing stepmother could swear when she was angry, but he kept his face straight and his sword ready. She had another advantage, in that she was tall and when she shouted her voice deepened, rather than becoming shrill. Personally, he would have told her everything he knew, down to the place he'd buried his gold, if he was Thomas.

Thomas the Merchant had the sense to sit down. Elizabeth pulled up a heavy chair and sat down opposite him.

"I may have the body of a weak and feeble woman," she said, quoting the Queen whom she greatly admired, "but I have the heart and stomach of a lord, by God, and I'll have your heart and stomach out in the light of day if I must, Thomas the Merchant, and swear you tried to rape me. So. Tell me about Sweetmilk."

Friday, 23rd June, morning

With a couple of hundred stolen horse gathered at Netherby alone – never mind the others being kept further up Liddesdale – there was a stunning amount of work to do. Carey was at the bottom of the heap as far as importance and the backing of a surname was concerned, and so inevitably he found himself lumbered with most of it. He trotted about the churned up paddock, carrying buckets of water and bales of hay while his stomach groaned and rumbled. It was empty because his conversation with Mary Graham had meant he was late for breakfast and all that was left of the porridge was the grey scrapings at the bottom of the pot.

The man in charge of caring for the horses was called Jock Hepburn, a by-blow cousin of Bothwell's, who claimed to have Mary Queen of Scot's second husband the fourth Earl of Bothwell for his father. He explained this to Carey and the sixteen other men who had been set to do the work, told them to call him 'sir' or 'your honour' since he was noble and they weren't, and then sat on the paddock fence, played with the rings on his long noble fingers and shouted orders all morning.

Some surname men were in the paddock too, seeing after favourite animals, but since most of the horses were stolen, the work fell to Carey and his fellows. At least it gave him the chance to mark out Dodd's horses, which he did by the brands. They were standing together, heads down, as horses often did when they were miserable.

Once the feed and water had been brought in, Hepburn took it into his head that the horses needed grooming, since most of them still had mud caked in their coats from when they were reived. In fact, Carey thought, as he worked away with a straw wisp and a brush at the warm rough coat in front of him, Hepburn was perfectly right, but he could have called in some of the idlers playing football in the next field to help: at this rate they'd be at it all day. He was getting a headache and his arms were tiring from unaccustomed work. If Dodd could see me now, he'd surely die laughing, thought Carey grimly as he scrubbed at the hobby's legs, and there's still been no word from Bothwell where we're supposed to be going.

The next horse he went to seemed very skittish, prancing with his front hooves, away from Carey. Carey chucked and gentled the animal, saw a tremor when he put his hoof to the ground. After much backing and shying, he'd calmed the horse enough so he could lift up his leg. What he saw there was thoroughly nasty: white growths and an inflamed reddened frog, and the other forehoof was quite as bad.

Without even thinking, Carey led the horse gently to the side of the paddock, took a halter off the fence and slipped it over the twitching nervous head.

"There now, there now." he murmured, "We'll have it sorted, there now, poor fellow . . ."

Somebody thumped him between the shoulder blades, hard

enough to knock him down. Carey rolled over in the mud, came to his feet with his hand clutching the void at his left hip where his sword should have been.

Jock Hepburn was standing there, flushed and angry.

"Where do ye think ye're going with that horse?"

"He's got footrot and he needs to see a farrier," said Carey, in no mood for an argument.

Jock Hepburn stepped up close and slapped him back-handed. "Sir," he said. "Ye call me sir, ye insolent bastard."

Carey hadn't taken a blow like that since he was a boy. He started forwards with his fists bunched, saw Hepburn back up hurriedly and reach for his sword. He stopped. Rage was making a roaring in his ears and his breath come short, he was about to call the man out there and then, when he caught sight of the Earl of Bothwell hurrying over from his football game and remembered where he was and what he was supposed to be doing.

"What's going on?" demanded the Earl.

"This man was trying to steal a horse."

Bothwell's eyes narrowed. "I said I'd hang anyone that tried to reive one of our horses and I meant it." He paused impressively. "What d'ye have to say for yourself?"

Carey took a deep breath and relaxed his fists. His face was stinging, one of Hepburn's rings had cut his cheek, and his headache was settling in properly.

"Only I'd steal a horse that could run if I was going to," he said, his throat so tight with the effort not to shout he could barely whisper. Bothwell's eyes narrowed at his tone. "My lord," he managed to say, adding, "This one couldna go two miles, his footrot's that bad."

The Earl lifted one of the horse's feet, prodded the sore frog hard enough to make the beast dance and snort.

"Ay," he said at last, "it's true enough. Take the nag up to the tower and ask Jock of the Peartree if he'll take a look. With a good scouring he might be well enough for a pack tomorrow night."

"Ay sir." said Carey, taking hold of the bridle. The Earl stopped him with a heavy hand on his shoulder.

"Ye've too high a stomach on ye for a peddler, Daniel," said Bothwell shrewdly. "What was ye before, at Berwick?"

For a moment Carey couldn't think what to say.

"I've no objection to outlaws, ye know," said Bothwell, and smiled, "I am one myself, after all."

Carey's mind was working furiously. He managed a sheepish grin. "Ah, it wasnae the fighting, sir," he said, "it was the women."

Bothwell laughed explosively. "There y'are, Jock," he said to Hepburn who was looking offended, "dinnae be sa hard on the man, ye've a few fathers after ye and all."

"Husbands, sir," said Carey, "it was husbands." That tickled Bothwell greatly.

He clucked at the horse and led him on to the paddock gate.

"Hey, Daniel," called Bothwell, "stay away from Alison Graham or Wattie'll be after ye with the gelding shears." Carey smiled wanly and lifted his hand to his forehead, leaving the Earl still howling at his own wit.

Carey's back prickled with Hepburn's eyes glaring at him. He tried to slouch a bit more while he went over soft ground to save the horse's feet.

Once at the tower, he tethered the horse at the wall and asked for Jock of the Peartree of one of the boys running past playing wolf-and-sheep.

Jock was inside the main downstairs room with Wattie Graham his brother and Old Wat of Harden who was spread into three men's space on the bench. They were squinting at a sketch map drawn in charcoal. Carey tried to get a look at it, but didn't dare come close enough.

"Master Jock," he said to all of them with his cap in his hand, "The Earl said, would ye look at this horse outside, he's got the footrot."

Jock, very fine in a red velvet doublet, stood up and stretched.

"Ay," he said, "where's the nag?"

Wattie Graham was rolling up the map and Harden stood, scraped back the bench. "It a' makes my head swim," he complained, "I dinna like going so far out of mine own country."

The two of them went ahead through the door, ambling on towards the gate. Carey went ahead of Jock to lead him to the horse, when he saw a commotion outside by the football field. There was a little group of men gesticulating, the Earl at the centre, some of them pointing towards the tower. Screwing up his eyes, Carey saw a lanky frame topped with black hair, and a hand going up characteristically to twiddle in his ear.

Realisation dawned. It was Young Jock, Ekie – all the reivers he had taken red-handed two days before. They were shouting, waving their arms. His own name floated over to him, poking familiarly out of the shouting. Wattie Graham and Wat of Harden were looking at the fuss, turning to look back at him as the shouting reached their ears.

All the world turned cold and clear for Carey. The thought of the horse still tethered to a ring in the wall flickered through his mind, to be dismissed at once. As he had said himself, there was no point stealing a horse that couldn't run.

"Laddie, ye're in my . . ." Jock began behind him.

Carey half turned, drove his elbow into Jock's stomach. Jock, who had eaten a much better breakfast than Carey, went "oof" and sat down. Carey backed into the tower, slammed the door, bolted and barred it, then kicked Jock of the Peartree over again as he struggled wheezing to his feet.

Carey had his dagger in his hand, but decided against using it and put it back. Instead he kicked Jock deliberately in the groin and when he hunched over with his eyes bugging, Carey turned him on his stomach, put a knee in his back, undid Jock's own belt and strapped his arms together behind him before Jock's eyes had uncrossed.

Grabbing a bottle of ale off a table as he went, Carey propelled Jock in front of him by the neck of his jerkin. Behind him there was a thundering on the door.

"Carey!" roared Bothwell's voice, "Carey, God damn you, open up!"

Carey dropped Jock on the floor and put a bench on top of him, then shoved one of the tables up against the door.

Somebody let off a gun outside, and splinters flew from a shot hole, followed by shrieking.

"Halfwits," muttered Carey, looking about for weapons. There were no firearms but there was a longbow with a couple of quivers of arrows hanging on the wall by the door, so he grabbed them gratefully, picked up the struggling Jock and clamped his arm round the man's neck.

Bothwell was shouting orders, Scott of Harden was shouting orders, Wattie Graham was shouting at them not to burn his bloody tower. There was a double thud of shoulders against the iron bound door which had been designed to withstand battering rams.

Jock was going blue, so Carey let him breathe for a moment.

"Now Jock," he said, "I'm sorry to do this to you, but you're my hostage."

Jock struggled feebly at the indignity, so Carey cut off his air again and half-dragged him up the spiral stair to the next floor. An iron barred gate was pegged open there, so Carey unpegged it one handed and it clanged shut, having been recently oiled. He didn't have the key to the lock but he managed to jam it with a chest standing in the corner.

Jock was thrashing about under his arm again, so Carey squeezed until the man's eyes crossed. He could hear a lot more shouting outside. It seemed Wattie Graham was still objecting to his door being bashed in.

"I don't want to kill you," he said reasonably, panting a little as he hauled Jock up the next flight of stairs and past the next iron gate.

Something moved in the corner of his eye: he ducked his head and held his hostage up as a shield and the swinging bolt of wood landed on Jock's skull not Carey's. Carey dropped him and the longbow, dived sideways, glimpsed Alison Graham in a whirl of skirts with a club in one hand and a dagger in the other, her eyes wild.

He charged into her with his shoulder, knocked her against the wall so the breath came out of her, still got a glancing blow about the head with the club and pricked in his arm by the dagger, tried a knee in her groin to no effect and then punched her stomach and bruised his knuckles on her whalebone stays. Christ, where weren't women naturally armoured? No help for it. He punched her on the mouth, and she finally went down, bleeding badly. Please God, he hadn't killed her. No, she was breathing. One of her teeth looked crooked, which was fine since he'd taken the skin off his knuckles on them. He found the bunch of keys on her belt, ripped them off, picked her up under the armpits – Jesus, the weight of her – and hauled her into the linen room where she had been at some wifely pursuit. He locked the door on her, turned back to Jock and found him still googly-eyed from Mrs Graham's blow.

Gasping for breath he shut the gate, tried six of the massive bunch of keys and at last found the one that locked it. He turned and looked for the final flight of stairs up to the roof. There was no staircase, spiral or otherwise, just a ladder at the end of a passage. He could think of only one possible way he could get Jock and himself up there. He choked Jock off again to make sure, trapped his head with a bench from one of the rooms, climbed the ladder and heaved the trapdoor up. Blinking at the sunlight on the roof, he put down the longbow which was miraculously unbroken, the bottle and the two quivers, only half of whose arrows had fallen out. Then he went down the ladder again, heard a deep ominous boom from all the way downstairs. Clearly Bothwell had prevailed on Wattie Graham to let his tower be broken into. Carey picked up Jock by the front of his red velvet doublet. At least he was still stunned.

A treacherous voice inside said perhaps he didn't need Jock of the Peartree on top of his other troubles, and another voice said it was too late now and he might as well be hanged for a sheep.

"Right," he said more to himself for encouragement, than to Jock who couldn't hear yet, "you're coming with me."

He slid Jock up to a sitting position, got hold of his shoulders and hefted Jock onto his back with his legs hanging down in front. There was about thirteen stone of solid muscle and bone to the man and it took two heaves for Carey to stagger to his feet. The ladder looked as if it stretched halfway to the moon.

He climbed one tread at a time, gasping through his teeth, with the sweat making a marsh of his shirt. Halfway up, Jock came to and started to struggle and swear: they swayed dangerously and the ladder creaked.

"STAY STILL!" roared Carey. "Or I'll dump you on your head."

Jock threshed once more, then saw how far they were from the floor and stayed still. Carey went the rest of the way up the ladder, heaved Jock onto the roof.

He kicked Jock in the stomach again to slow him down, turned, pulled up the ladder with his abused arm muscles shrieking at him, heaved the trapdoor into its hole and bolted it, then sat with his back against the parapet and waited until he had stopped crowing for breath and the spots had gone from his vision.

Jock glared at him, sprawled like a trussed chicken on the roof flags, bleeding from his nose and a nasty lump on his head.

"That's better," said Carey and coughed. He didn't think he'd ruptured anything, which was a miracle. His heartbeat seemed to be slowing at last. "Now we can talk, Jock"

Friday, 23rd June, late morning

It so happened that Will the Tod Armstrong was out in the horse paddock of his tower with a young horse that he was breaking on the lungeing rein. His youngest grandson was watching admiringly from the gate. Dodd came at a fast jogtrot to the fence, ducked under it and walked up close to his father-in-law, who took one look at his battered sweaty face and became serious.

"Is Janet all right?" he asked at once. "Where's the raid?"

Never mind Janet, Dodd thought, what about me, I'm half dead of thirst.

"She's fine . . ." he said in between deep breaths, "she's in Carlisle. It's not a raid, exactly, it's the new Deputy Warden and Richard Lowther."

"Sit down, rest yourself. What happened to your horse? Did ye come on foot from Carlisle, ay well, ye're young. Little Will, run down to the house and bring back some beer for your uncle. No, you may not ride the horse, use your legs."

Both Dodd's calves chose that moment to start cramping. He swore and tried rubbing them.

"Walk about a bit," advised Will the Tod, "I mind I ran twenty miles to fetch Kinmont's father once when I was a lad, and if ye stop too suddenly, ye cramp."

Twenty miles, was it? thought Dodd bitterly, ay it would be. Nine and a half miles over rough country and mostly uphill in much less than two hours, and Will the Tod will have done twice that in half the time in his youth.

"Well, what's the news?"

Dodd told him. Will the Tod found the whole thing hilariously funny. His broad red face under its grey-streaked bush of red hair shone with the joke, he slapped his knee, he slapped Dodd's back, he slapped the fence.

"Ye ran from Carlisle to save the *Deputy Warden*?" hooted Will the Tod. "Jesus save me. Why didn't ye run to fetch *his* dad? There's a man that has a quick way with a tower."

"He never burnt yours," Dodd pointed out. There were still bitter memories on the border of Lord Hunsdon's reprisals after the Rising of the Northern Earls.

"Only because I paid him."

"He could have taken the money and still burnt you out."

"Ay well, that's true. So his boy's in trouble, eh?"

Dodd explained, as patiently as he could, that he was.

"What do ye expect me to do about it?"

Dodd suggested, still patiently, that if he could really put sixty men in the saddle at an hour's notice as he'd boasted the last time they met, then he might give the Deputy Warden cause to be grateful to him. Not to mention pleasing his daughter Janet, who was in such a taking about the blasted man, it might have worried a husband less trusting than himself.

"Oh ay, call out my men for the Deputy Warden." Will the Tod found that funny too. Dodd, who had blisters on both his feet and his shoulders, not to mention the damage he'd taken struggling through the secret passage, failed to see the joke. He waited for the bellowing stupid laugh to stop and the said, "Well, sir, if ye've come over to loving Richard Lowther in your old age, I'll be on my way to the Dodds at Gilsland."

Will the Tod's laugh stopped in mid-chuckle. He glowered at his son-in-law.

"Lowther's the man the old lord Warden would have made Deputy Warden. Carey's the young Lord Scrope's friend," explained Dodd through his teeth. "Carey may be a fool of a courtier who's too big for his boots, but he's not Lowther. According to Janet he snuck into Netherby to try and steal back our reived horses because he knew a proper hot trod would be cut to pieces. Now Lowther's let out some raiders Carey took that can identify him to Bothwell, who'll likely string him up."

At least Will the Tod was listening. He nodded and Dodd continued.

"Lowther doesna want to lose his hold over the West March and Carey's bent on taking the power from him. If he can get Carey killed it'll clear the way for him and we'll have him back in the saddle, taking blackrent off us, favouring his kin and bringing in the Grahams and the Johnstones and the Elliots every time any one of us dares to make a squeak about it. There'll be nae chance of justice in this March with Carey gone, believe me. But as it seems ye've made your peace with the Lowthers . . ."

Will the Tod's face darkened. "Make peace with the Lowthers? Never!" he growled. "You're saying, if I bring out my men and save Carey's skin as you ask, we'll stop Richard Lowther from becoming Deputy Warden under the new lord?"

"Ay sir," said Dodd, "that's what I've been saying. For the moment, anyway, seeing how well Lowther's dug in."

Will the Tod clapped Dodd on his back. "I like you, Henry," he said expansively, "ye think well."

"It's your daughter's plan," Dodd muttered.

"Of course it is, but you've the sense to see the sense in it."

And I did all the bloody running and crawling through shit pipes, Dodd thought, but didn't say. Will the Tod stared into space for a moment, and then rubbed his hands together.

"Off ye go, Dodd," he said, "up to the tower and ring the bell. I'll have a horse saddled up for you when ye come back."

Run up there, thought Dodd, despairingly.

"Get on, lad, we havnae got all day. Ye dinna want to get to Netherby and find your man swinging in the breeze."

It was hard going up to the tower now he'd lost the rhythm, but he wasn't going to give Will the Tod any opportunity to tell him more tales of notable runs by Will the Tod in his youth. It half killed him but he gasped his way up the bank, almost fell through the door, found the rope to the bell and started ringing it.

Perhaps he rang it for longer than he need have done, but when he came back down the hill to the house where Will the Tod normally lived, he saw the sight that still lifted his heart no matter how often it happened: the men were coming in at the run from the fields, the women were rushing from their work to the horse paddock to round up the horses – thank God Will the Tod had not been raided by the Grahams, even if he wasn't respectable enough to lend horses to Scrope – and some of the boys were already coming out of the stables with the saddles and bridles, the jacks and helmets.

Will the Tod was standing on a high mounting stone, his thumbs in his broad belt, yelling orders as his family ran purposefully past him in all directions. His second wife, the pretty, nervous little creature whose name Dodd could never remember, came running up with a large ugly gelding snorting behind her and then Will the Tod was in the saddle, closely followed by his five sons, two of his sons-in-law, four nearly grown grandsons, and fifteen assorted cousins already riding in with their families from their own farms nearby.

Henry was brought a large Roman-nosed mare he remembered as having an evil temper at odds with her name which was Rosy, and he mounted up with relief. If God had meant men to run around the countryside he wouldn't have provided them with horses.

"Off you go then, Henry," shouted Will the Tod, waving his lance. "Rouse out the Dodds."

Dodd brought Rosy up alongside Will the Tod, who was letting his mount sidestep and paw the air and roaring with laughter at his surname crowding up around him, all asking where was the raid and whose cows were gone, and how big was it, to be out in daylight? Rosy tried to nip Will the Tod's leg.

"Wait," Dodd said, hauling on the reins, "we've got Netherby to crack. Where will we meet?"

"Longtownmoor meeting stone," said Will the Tod, "where we always meet when we're hitting Liddesdale, ye know that Henry. Shall I send to Kinmont?"

"Send to anybody ye can think of that would like to see Lowther's nose rubbed in the shite."

"Och God, there'd be no room for them all. I'll just send to the ones that werena burnt out of house and home by your young Deputy's father in '69, eh?"

Dodd nodded impatiently, set his heels to the horse's flank, and headed on up the road for Gilsland after a sharp tussle with Rosy's contrariness, which he won. Behind him Will the Tod stood up in his stirrups and addressed his immediate surname in a bellow. Dodd knew when he explained the Deputy Warden's problem because the laughter rolled after him over the hill like the breaker of a sea.

It occurred to him that perhaps Carey would have preferred to hang rather than be rescued from Bothwell's clutches in quite this way.

Friday, 23rd June, noon

Netherby tower was roofed with stone against fire and had a narrow fighting parapet running round it behind the battlements. In the south-east corner was the beacon, a large blackened metal basket raised up on a ten foot pole with a pile of firewood faggots under tarpaulin at the base.

Carey cleared the wood away and tied Jock of the Peartree to the pole in a sitting position, using the rope binding the faggots. The firewood he piled as makeshift barricades across the parapet by the trapdoor.

Every so often he would poke his head over the wall and shoot an arrow at the men with the battering ram, so they'd run for cover. Way down below him, he could see Bothwell, his brocade doublet shining in the sun, foreshortened like a chessman, waving his arms and shouting more orders. He popped his head over and dropped one of the stones kept ready for sieges, close enough to the earl to make him dive for cover.

Arrows came sailing over and clattered harmlessly onto the roof. That roof could have done with some attention, Carey thought, much of the mortar around the stones was cracked and rotten. On a sudden inspiration, he heaved up a couple of the loosest stones and dragged them over to the trapdoor, piled them on top.

"Who the hell are ye?" demanded Jock.

Carey told him.

Jock mulled it over for a bit, then growled: "Ye'll never get out of this."

"I don't know. I've got you as a hostage. You're an important man," said Carey, sitting down again and taking a sip of beer from the leather bottle. He wasn't too worried about thirst since there was a full rainwater butt at the north-western corner, set there to put out besieger's fires. On the other hand, his belly was cramping him.

Jock spat. "D'ye think the Earl willna shoot to save my skin?"

"No," said Carey agreeably, "I think with the mood he's in, he'd perfectly happily shoot through you to get me, but Wattie's your brother . . ."

"They must be aye sentimental in the south," sniffed Jock, "Wattie'd shoot as well."

"Well, I suppose, so would John," admitted Carey, thinking of his pompous whingeing elder brother in a similar situation. "Still, he might hesitate. His aim might be off. He might even talk to me, negotiate some arrangement."

"Are ye hoping for ransom?" demanded Jock of the Peartree.

"No. I hadn't thought about it."

Jock laughed shortly.

"There's no other way ye'll get off this tower still breathing, lad, so ye'd best think about it now and right hard."

It was in fact perfectly true that Carey had no idea how he was going to get off the top of Netherby tower in one piece. When he came to Netherby he had had a vague plan that involved stealing the Dodd and Widdrington horses quietly early in the morning as soon as he knew where Bothwell was planning to raid and making off back to Carlisle as fast as one of them could carry him. Once that was no longer possible, thanks to Lowther's machinations, he had simply reacted according to instinct.

"What do you think I'm worth on the hoof?" Carey asked after a pause.

"Everyone knows Scrope's a rich man. A thousand pounds, perhaps," said Jock consideringly. Carey whistled.

"He might not pay that much."

Jock clearly regarded this as a feeble attempt at bargaining.

"Well, if ye're Lord Hunsdon's son, he'll stump up for you. Of course, first ye've got to get yon Earl to talk civilly to ye, and that might take a while."

"He is very upset. What are my chances?"

"It's always possible," Jock allowed, "a one-legged donkey with spavins could win the Carlisle horserace, but I wouldnae put my shirt on it."

"I think you're a bit of an optimist, Jock," said Carey drily.

Jock laughed again, then winced. "Ye could loosen my arms a bit," he suggested, "I canna feel my hands."

Carey leaned over cautiously and felt one of the hands. It was a little swollen, but not too bad.

"No," he said, "I've got too much respect for you, Jock. I don't want to waste all the care I had of you if you take it in your head to jump off the top of the tower."

"I think it's you'll be making the jump from a high place in the end."

"No," said Carey, leaning his head back and feeling very tired, "he won't hang me." Jock looked dubious. "That'd be too quick for Bothwell."

Jock grunted. "I never said he'd hang you first. That'd be after he'd skelped and roasted you. And I'll be first in with the whip, believe me."

Carey had his eyes half-shut. "Oh, I believe you, Jock. And yet, you know, one reason I came here was so I could find out who killed Sweetmilk."

Jock's face changed. The long craggy canyons in it deepened, the mouth lengthened, and his chin fell on his chest.

"Poor Sweetmilk," he said, "he was such a bonny wee bairn, running after me and laughing." Jock's chin quivered, then hardened again. "Anyway, what do ye care, Deputy, he's one less Graham you've got to chase over the Bewcastle waste."

Carey thought of trying to explain the idea of an impartial law enforcement officer, as interested in the wanton killing of Grahams as in cattle raids and suchlike, but decided it would take too long.

"I don't want you blaming Dodd," he said at last, "and I'm puzzled about it."

"What's to puzzle about, the lad was shot in the back."

Carey shook his head. "You wouldn't be interested, it was only a theory of mine."

Friday, 23rd June, early afternoon

Jock was watching the bottle as Carey drank from it, too stiff-necked to admit he needed a drink. Carey found one of the rags for lighting the beacon, went to the rainbutt to wet it and came back to Jock. He held the bottle for Jock to drink, then mopped the dried blood off Jock's face with the rag. Jock tolerated this in grim silence. On a thought Carey went back to the rainbutt, found two buckets there, filled both of them and brought them to where he was sitting with Jock.

"Does Netherby have any long ladders about?" he asked.

"I hope so."

Carey peered over the parapet again, saw somebody with an arquebus taking aim and ducked down just in time. The crack sounded in the distance, but the bullet didn't even splinter the wall. He picked up one of the buckets and poured it over the side, producing a yell of anger from below, then went and refilled it.

The next time the men with the battering ram from the log pile backed up, Carey shot at them with one of their own arrows. Three more came sailing over the wall, before Bothwell yelled for them to stop.

"Why did you do this?" asked Jock.

"A number of reasons," Carey said. "Firstly, I wanted to know what Bothwell needed all the horses in the West March for."

"Och, that's easy. I'll tell you, since you're going nae further with it. We're running a big raid deep into Scotland, to Falkland Palace, to lift the King and hold him to ransom for a big pot of gold. It's about two hundred miles, so we've all needed remounts."

Carey breathed cautiously. "Right," he said, "you're kidnapping King James."

"Ay," said Jock. "Bothwell says he's worth the Kingdom if we can get him."

"Right," said Carey again. "Of course, Bothwell tried before at Holyrood and he didn't manage it. That's why he's an outlaw."

"He didna have us with him."

"No. Don't you think somebody might notice, a big pack of Border raiders riding into Scotland like that? Don't you think they might take it into their heads to warn the King?"

"Not if we ride fast enough and keep to the waste ground."

"And there are the horses, of course."

"Eh? Oh ay, we've got enough horses now. We'll be off tomorrow."

"Is that so?" Carey's voice was carefully casual. "No, I didn't mean the little nags you've been reiving. I meant the King's horses. But I suppose you're not interested in them."

"No," said Jock, "we're not. It's the King we're reiving."

"Right."

"What theory?" demanded Jock.

"Eh?"

"What theory were ye talking about before? Your theory concerning Sweetmilk."

"You wouldn't be interested."

"How the Devil do you know that if ye won't tell me what it is?"

Carey peeked over again, saw Bothwell, shot at him, missed and ducked down again as two more arquebuses cracked down below.

"I suppose the nearest cannon are in Carlisle?"

"Of course they are," said Jock, "unless your friend Lowther's bringing one up here."

"No, he wouldn't have any powder for it."

"Is that a fact?"

"You know it as well as I do. In fact, I'll bet the powder they're shooting at us with is Carlisle's finest."

Jock grunted. "It's no' very good quality," he complained, "and he charges something shocking for it. What theory?"

Carey sat down facing Jock, with his knees drawn up, examined the skinned knuckles on his right hand and flexed them. He hated punching people in the face, it always hurt your hand so much.

"Did you ever hear of a man called Sir Francis Walsingham, Jock?"

Jock nodded. "Ay, the Queen's Secretary. Sir John Forster in the Middle March did him a good turn, oh, ten, twelve years ago."

"I know. He's dead now, but I was on an embassy with him to Scotland in the summer of '83, it was the first time I went to King James's Court."

"What did you think of it?"

"It was well enough so long as I kept my arse to the wall and a table between me and the King."

Jock laughed. "Took a fancy to ye, did he?"

Carey coughed and looked down. "You could say that."

"Jesus, man, what are ye doing here? Your fortune's made."

Carey shook his head. "I couldn't do it. In fact I damn near puked in his lap when I finally worked out what it was he wanted."

Jock found that very funny. "What did Sir Francis think of it?"

"He was a strange man, you know, Jock. I've met my fair share of puritans, and most of them are hypocrites, but he was not. He was an utterly upright man. He worked night and day to keep the Queen safe, though he hated the thought of obeying a woman . . ."

"Small blame to him," said Jock, "it's unnatural."

Carey thought of the iron grip most border women seemed to have on their menfolk, but didn't say anything. He peered over the parapet and saw Bothwell and Wattie and the other men gathered together talking, while Old Wat of Harden walked up and down. To keep them on their toes he shot a couple of arrows at them. They scattered and dived for cover satisfactorily.

"When I told him what the King wanted from me, he saw to it that I was never alone with him again without it seeming he was doing it, if you follow. And I never knew him to take a bribe."

"What never?"

"Never. When he died his estate was gone and he was deep in debt."

"Why was he at Court then, if he didna take bribes?"

Carey shrugged. "To serve the Queen, he said, because she was the best hope for the True Religion against Papistry. To his mind it was immoral to take money for giving her advice he knew was bad, and immoral to take money for giving advice he would give anyway."

"What's your point?"

"He always told me that truth belonged to God, it was sacred. Every lie, every injustice was an offence to God because it was an offence against truth. The stock of truth in this life is limited like gold, and every time you can dig out a little more of it from the mud and the clay of lies, you bring a little more of God's Grace into the world."

"It's a fine poetical sentiment," said Jock consideringly, "but aye impractical."

"He believed also, that like gold, truth was incorruptible and would always leave traces. And if you were prepared to dig and scrape a bit, you could find out the truth of anything."

"What's this got to do with Sweetmilk?"

"Somebody murdered him and got away with it. To me, that's an offence against justice."

"Justice, truth. What are we doing up here, lad, we should be in church."

Carey ignored him. "It happened I got a good look at his body and I went to see the place where Dodd found it. It was all very odd."

"Why?"

"The shooting for a start. There were powder burns all over the back of his jack, no sign of a struggle. That gives you a bit of truth right there."

Jock swallowed and blinked at the sky. "Why?" he rasped. "It was a quick death, so?"

Carey shook his head. "It was more than that. The dag that killed him must have been right up behind him, close, perhaps less than a foot away. Would you let your enemy get so close to you with a loaded dag?"

Jock thought about it. "I wouldnae," he said finally, "if he's that close, you've a chance of knocking it away or hitting him before the gun can fire, and if he's waving a dag at ye, it's worth a try because he's going to kill ye anyway."

"Precisely," said Carey pedantically, "no gun ever fires instantly: if it's got a powder pan, the flash has to go down into the gun, if it's got a lock, the mechanism has to unwind to make the sparks. Sweetmilk knew that as well as anybody."

Jock nodded slowly. "Ye're saying, he let whoever killed him come up close because he wasnae an enemy, he was a friend."

"Exactly. Or at least someone he knew and had no reason to fear right then."

Jock nodded again. "Go on, Courtier."

Carey peered over the parapet again and saw men hurrying about with lighted torches and faggots of wood. He shot at them, and got one through the leg. He stayed there with his bow, wishing he was a better shot, peering over the parapet and trying to think himself into Bothwell's mind.

"The next point is that he wasn't robbed by whoever killed him."

"He'd been robbed by the time we got the body."

"Yes, that was one of Dodd's men. I have the jewels and rings in Carlisle and I'll send them back to you when I can." He coughed. "If I can."

"Wasna robbed, eh? He was wearing some good stuff."

"I know. So why was he killed? It wasn't a fight, it wasn't to steal his jewels, or even his horse."

"Ah, the horse. I should have known the beauty would be trouble."

"There's a reason why I don't think he was killed for the horse, but I'll come to it. The next point is where the killer left the body. Solway Moss, in a gorse bush."

"Maybe that's where he was killed?"

Carey shook his head. "No, he was killed somewhere else and brought there slung over a horse's back, probably on your Caspar. He stiffened while he was bent over the horse, and there wasn't any blood spattered near where he was found. And why Solway Moss? There are marshes, there's the sea, any number of good places to put a corpse where it'll never be found to cause you trouble. Why there?"

Whatever else he was, Jock was not stupid. "The man didna know of a better place or couldna reach it in the time," he said. "He's a stranger to this country."

"And Daniel Swanders saw someone when he stole Caspar," said Carey. "He saw a man in a rich doublet, cleaning a jack, and what's more, the man didn't chase after him either so Caspar wasn't the reason for the . . ."

"A rich doublet," repeated Jock.

"So," said Carey, counting off on his fingers in a way he had picked up wholesale from Walsingham, "we have signs and portents of the murderer. He was well-known to Sweetmilk so he could get up close behind him with a loaded dag, he was rich, he was a stranger to these parts . . ."

"Good God Almighty," said Jock, putting his head back against the wooden post, "I've been sitting down to eat with my son's killer for this past week."

"It has to be, doesn't it?" said Carey. "It has to be the Earl or one of his men."

"But why . . .?"

"I don't know," said Carey, but he couldn't hide the expression on his face well enough for Jock.

"Ye do know."

"I don't."

"Ay, ye do," said Jock, "and ye'll tell it me, if you've gone this far." He laughed mirthlessly. "Who knows, it could even get you out of this alive."

"Don't lie to me, Jock."

"Well, it could get you a quicker death, any road. Come on."

"Whoever killed Sweetmilk is the father of your daughter Mary's bairn."

"Her *what* " Jock's eyes were glaring with fury and he struggled against the ropes holding him. "WHAT did you say?"

"Your daughter Mary is expecting a babe around Christmas time. Bothwell, or one of his men, is the father." Jock's face was swollen, he seemed to be choking. Carey, who knew perfectly well he was talking for his life, but was a natural gambler, carried on remorselessly. "My thinking is that Sweetmilk found out what had happened to his sister, and challenged the man to a duel. They went off away from Carlisle to fight it out, so Mary wouldn't be shamed by it, and while they were on their way, the man came up behind Sweetmilk when he wasn't expecting it, and shot him. Then he abandoned him at the only place he could think of and came back."

There were tears flowing down Jock's crusty face. "God damn him, God damn him to hell, poor Sweetmilk, I'll skelp the little bitch, I'll . . ."

"You'll marry her off quickly is what you'll do. I think she might have been forced."

"What do you know about it?"

"I've talked to her and I don't think she was willing," Carey, knowing what he did of the Queen's maids of honour, thought she'd probably been perfectly willing at the time, but felt sorry for her. "At best, he persuaded her against her better judgement. At worst he raped her."

"God, so that's what's been ailing her. Why didn't she tell me when Sweetmilk was killed?"

"Afraid of you. Afraid of the man, perhaps he threatened her. Perhaps she still had a liking for him. Who knows?"

Jock shook his head, snortled violently against his running nose. "How can I find the man?"

"Well, I've done a lot of the work," said Carey reasonably, "I've narrowed it down from most of the population of the March to Bothwell or one of his men. And I hate to admit it, but I don't think it was Bothwell either."

"Why not?"

"Mary said she wouldn't marry the father *if* he was the Earl himself, so I think he wasn't. It's not that Bothwell wouldn't do it, but I don't think he did on this occasion. So you've got three or four possible murderers to choose from."

"I suppose it would be wasteful to shoot all of them and be done with it," said Jock thoughtfully. "And it might be a little tickle to do at that. So, how do I find out which one to kill?"

"Who was at Netherby on the Saturday? Who did Sweetmilk ride out with? Who came back?"

"Ah," said Jock, wriggling his shoulders against the wood. "Let me think." If his arms were cramping him, he didn't say anything about it, and Carey wouldn't have risked untying him anyway. He was a grizzled old bastard and tough as doornails, he could suffer.

Carey's belly started rumbling again. It was dinner time and nothing to eat but raw pigeon squabs from the little dovecote on the south western corner. Well, he wasn't that hungry yet. Or perhaps he could light a little fire with the materials for the beacon and roast them.

There was a stealthy clatter on the other side of the roof. Jock didn't seem to have heard, but Carey knew if he'd been a horse, his ears would have swivelled.

He picked up one of the long hardwood poles used for poking the beacon and crept round to the opposite parapet. When he peered over, he saw that the ladder they were trying to use was too short, but that the man climbing it had a caliver under his arm, with the slowmatch lit.

"Halfwits," said Carey again, under his breath, "haven't any of you heard of Pythagoras?"

Very carefully, while the man was still halfway up, he reached with his pole over the wall, hooked it into the top rung of the ladder and pushed. There was a scream, a bang from the caliver, a loud crash and clatter. Carey went back to where Jock was and offered him some water, which Jock drank. Neither of them commented on the ladder.

"Ye canna win," said Jock, "ye canna hold out indefinitely. Sooner or later ye must sleep."

"Oh, it'll be quicker than that," said Carey, "sooner or later they'll work out how to do it."

"And how's that?" demanded Jock.

Carey shook his head. "Besieging's a science, and I'm not going to give you lessons."

"You mean they'll burn ye out."

"Us. They'll burn us out. It's probably only Wattie's objections that's stopping them now."

Jock turned his face away. "What's making ye so cheerful? It's only a matter of time before you die."

Carey couldn't really explain it. He knew perfectly well he'd got himself into a ridiculous situation; that his scheme for finding out what was going on in Netherby had perhaps not been one of his best, and that while Elizabeth might be wondering where he'd got to, there was very little she could do for him. Somehow, with the sun shining down on him and the sight he had of Liddesdale valley glowering to the north, sitting talking to a trussed-up Jock of the Peartree was almost pleasant.

"Well," he said after he'd wandered round the parapet looking for activity down below and seeing nothing, which would have worried him if he'd been a worrying man, "maybe we can narrow it down even more. Tell me what happened here on Saturday."

"Now then. A couple of the women went down to Carlisle to buy oatmeal, but they were back by noon. That was when Mary fell and hurt her hand. And I'd sent Sweetmilk, and Bothwell sent two of his men, Jock Hepburn and Geordie Irwin of Bonshaw, to Carlisle to see if they could scout out who had horses and where they were, and buy a few if they saw some cheap. Sweetmilk was in a taking with something that morning, but he wouldna tell me what it was, so I thought it was some girl or other – it usually is, was," Jock swallowed. "I said he should take Caspar, which the Earl of Bothwell had brought to me as a fee, in case Scrope was interested in buying him and also to . . . er . . . so people could admire him, ye know. So they'd send me their mares."

Carey nodded, twanging his thumb gently on the bowstring. Something was niggling his mind, but he couldn't think what it was.

Jock wriggled again. "That's the last time I saw him alive."

"So it's Geordie Irwin of Bonshaw, or Jock Hepburn. Or the Earl."

"Unless he met somebody at Carlisle, of course. I mind that the Affleck boy, not Robert, he's dead, but his younger brother, Ian, he didn't come here until early Sunday."

"Well it couldn't be him, could it, if I'm right about Mary."

"Oh ay. So it's Geordie Irwin or Jock Hepburn."

"Well?"

"Well what?"

"Which do you think it is?"

"Och, lad, it could be any of them, they're a' bastards. And I'm not convinced it wasna the Earl; he's allus had an eye for women that one, and Mary's a bonny little girl. He wasnae in Netherby on the Saturday either, and I dinna ken where he was."

"What's he got against King James?" asked Carey after a moment.

"The Earl?" Jock laughed shortly. "I think he had a similar problem wi' the King to yours. Only he took it harder."

"And what are his plans if he captures the King?"

"Och, I think it's the Earl of Bothwell for Lord Chancellor and Chamberlain, and Chancellor Robert Melville and his brother for the block. After that . . ." Jock shrugged as far as he could. "I dinna think he knows himself."

"Do you think he will – capture the King, I mean?"

Jock looked at him thoughtfully. "Why? What do ye care?"

"Curious. Come on now, I can hardly warn his perverted Majesty from here, can I?"

"I think he's got a verra good chance of it, with us and with . . ." Jock shook his head, ". . . with his other advantages."

An inside job, thought Carey instantly, there are men at the Scottish Court who will help the Earl. Lord above, what am I supposed to do about this? What can I do?

"And of course there are the horses," said Carey, pursuing a line he had started earlier.

"Ay, ye mentioned them. What horses?"

"Falkland Palace is a hunting lodge. I've been there, the stables are enormous."

"Oh ay?" Jock was pretending indifference, but Carey knew how passionate the Borderers were for horseflesh.

"The King keeps most of his horses there so they're ready for him to ride when he takes a fancy to go hunting."

"What are they like then?"

"Well," said Carey consideringly, "Caspar wouldn't stand out among them."

"No?" Jock didn't believe him.

Carey shook his head. "King James is very particular about his mounts and he has them brought in from France by sea. They're the best horses in Scotland, and perhaps even England too."

"Oh?" Jock was struggling with himself internally. Pride lost and curiosity won out. "How many are there?"

"About six hundred."

"What?"

"It could be more."

"What's the King want with 600 horses?"

"Not all of them are his, a lot belong to the people at Court. But that's the nearest number, I'd say."

"Jesus," said Jock, and Carey could almost see the thoughts whirling past each other in his brain. Clearly Bothwell had neglected to mention the living treasure trove at Falkland: far more valuable than gold to Borderers, because horses could run. Jock coughed and shifted his legs a little. "Would ye happen to know if they're heavily guarded?"

"Not very heavily."

Jock was suspicious again. "Why not? Are they hobbled?"

"No, they're not hobbled. In fact, during the summer most of them are out in the horse paddocks round about the Palace."

"Not inside a barnekin?"

"There'd be no room for a herd that size."

"Why aren't they guarded?"

"Jock," said Carey sadly, "you wouldn't understand if I tried to explain to you what a law-abiding country is like, so I won't try. They're not guarded because no one thereabouts is likely to steal them."

Jock snorted disbelievingly.

"Does Bothwell know about these horses?"

"Of course he does, he's been at Court, same as I have. I expect he didn't want you distracted from King James."

"No," said Jock, a little uncertainly, "he's nothing to worry about anyway. We're going to reive the King out from under the noses of his bad counsellors."

"Of course," said Carey, "and I know you don't care about a charge of High Treason . . ."

Jock's eyes narrowed.

"Well, that's what it is, isn't it?" said Carey, "You live on the Scottish side of the line. If you go out in arms against the King, it's High Treason."

"We're rescuing him from bad counsellors," insisted Jock.

"He's agreed to be rescued, has he? Rescued by Bothwell, I mean, whom he hates because he thinks the Earl's King of the Scottish Witches. He knows all about this scheme, does he?"

"Are ye trying to turn me against the raid?"

Carey leaned forward. "Listen Jock," he said, making sure he stayed out of head-butting distance, "I don't give a turd what you do. If you want to make an enemy of the King – who has a very long memory, by the way, and has been kidnapped before – that's entirely your affair. If the raid goes wrong somehow, and the King comes out to Jedburgh with blood in his eye and an army behind him to hunt down the Grahams and wipe them off the face of the earth, that's nothing but good news to me, alive or dead. If you want to pass up the chance of reiving 600 of the best horses in Scotland in favour of Bothwell's lunatic scheme, I'm not the one to stop you. I just hate to see a man put his head in a noose without knowing the full story."

Jock grunted. There was silence from him, so Carey made another circuit of the parapet. Below he could see smoke and flames licking from near the door. He took the bow from his shoulder, nocked an arrow and waited. Sure enough, six men holding bucklers over their heads appeared from one of the sheds nearby with a battering ram between them, and charged at the door. He shot off four arrows, but they bounced off the shields and after two attempts there was a splintering crash and a chorus of cheers as the door finally gave way.

He went back to Jock, who was staring into space, looking very thoughtful.

"They're into the tower," said Carey. Jock said nothing. Thuds and bangs and a screech of metal below, feet pounding up the stairs, another outburst of clanging and crashing.

In his mind's eye Carey could see the scene one floor below. They'd have released Alison Graham and yes, there was wailing and Wattie yelling threats up through the trapdoor.

He'd been calm before, talking to Jock to keep his mind off what was happening. Now his mouth was dry again and his stomach clenched into a knot. He was no longer hungry.

"Carey," said Jock.

"Hm?" His eye had caught movement over on the hills to the east, a glitter of spears, movement of men. Had the Grahams brought in more of their men to help retake Netherby?

"Do ye think the Earl knew what happened with Sweetmilk?"

Carey shrugged. "I've no idea. He might, he might not. Whichever it is, he won't have told you, you know that."

Jock nodded.

"Would ye agree to be ransomed?"

"I thought you said there'd be no chance . . ."

"I'll pledge for ye. Well?"

Carey laughed, a little desperately. "I've never been ransomed before, but yes."

"He'll likely chain ye up in the dungeon until your family's paid up. It's no' a very nice place."

Carey licked his lips. The whole thing was a disaster. Then he shrugged. "Better than hanging though."

"Untie me then," said Jock. Carey hesitated. "Come on, man, ye havena got all day."

Men with bucklers over their head were trotting in and out of the tower carrying turves and faggots of wood.

Carey undid the ropes holding Jock to the beacon post, but left his hands strapped behind him. He drew his dagger and put it to Jock's neck, then let Jock go over to the trapdoor.

"Bothwell," yelled Jock. There was a pause in the activity below.

"Ye're still alive," said the Earl's voice.

"Ay, of course I'm still alive, if I was dead, I wouldna be speaking to ye, now would I?" snarled Jock.

"What a diplomat," muttered Carey.

"Shut up, ye. *Bothwell.*"

"What do you want, Jock?"

"The Deputy Warden will surrender himself to me if ye'll ransom him after the raid and he'll not talk about it after." Jock glowered at Carey, daring him to disagree. Carey felt his shoulders sag, but nodded.

"How much?"

"A thousand pounds, English."

"No."

"And why the hell not?"

"I'll have him in half an hour anyway, why should I negotiate? You're getting soft, Jock."

Jock made a face, shrugged his shoulders. Carey hadn't really expected Bothwell to say yes, but his stomach squeezed itself up tighter under his breastbone. He tried to avoid wondering what Bothwell would do to him before he was hanged. Maybe not. Maybe the Earl would ransom him anyway.

"He's worth more alive than dead, Bothwell," said Jock.

"I'll be rich enough after the raid," said Bothwell, "and so will ye, if ye can live through the next hour."

There were a couple of echoing cracks from below as Bothwell tried to shoot the trapdoor away.

"It's nae good," shouted Jock, "he's put stones over the hole. Have ye got gunpowder?"

"Jock!" said Carey protestingly.

"My arms are killing me, Carey, let's get this bloody farce over with."

"I'm in no hurry."

There was a sound of crackling and tendrils of smoke started coming up through the cracks around the trapdoor and the holes in the roof. There were more of them than he'd thought, Carey noted, and the smoke was thick and black. Bothwell was using damp turves on top of the dry wood.

"Eh, Wattie must be in a rare mood," said Jock, "and Alison. She'd never let him burn us out if ye hadnae hit her."

"I know," said Carey.

Friday, 23rd June, afternoon

Dodd had split his force into three to come at Netherby from the south west, the south east and the east. Will the Tod took the road north from Longtown that passed beside the river Esk, his son Geordie came in from Dodd's tower at Gilsland with the Dodds but joined up with his own surname and went through Slackbraes wood and Cleughfoot wood. The Dodds went over Slealandsburn and Oakshaw Hill and also passed through the eastern part of the Cleughfoot Wood that cupped itself around Netherby. They rode well-spread out and caught four of the men that Bothwell had stationed to watch.

At Longtownmoor stone, Geordie, Will the Tod and Henry Dodd had agreed that as they didn't know exactly how many men Bothwell had or where they were, their best plan was to hit hard and fast, drive off his horses, capture Bothwell himself if they could and if they couldn't, to trap him in Netherby tower with as few of his men as possible and then negotiate.

The daylight made things difficult for them, experienced night raiders though they all were, since they would be visible further off and they had no torches to signal the onset with. After some argument, they agreed on horncalls when they were ready, which would warn Bothwell, but might confuse him as well, or so they hoped. It might make him think the Carlisle garrison had come out to rescue the Deputy Warden.

And so, being the last to get into position because of having to go over the hill, Dodd put his horn to his lips as soon as he sighted the tower through the trees, and then all three of the groups of men broke from the woods and galloped over fields and barley crops straight up to Netherby tower.

It seemed that Bothwell was distracted, though unfortunately most of his men were already in the barnekin. Geordie and his men got into the horsepaddocks where the vast numbers of horses were – Jesus, there must have been a couple of hundred at least – broke down the fences and drove the horses off into the wood, leaving two men dead behind them.

Will the Tod and Henry rode hard for the barnekin, aiming for the gate. Complete confusion broke out round the tower. Some of the Grahams turned away from what they were doing and shot at them with arquebuses, a couple of the women managed to free the gates. Six men ran outside to help shut the big main gate: there was a sharp fight with ten more who came out with lances to hold them off and then the gate was shut and barred and most of the Grahams outside either surrendered or legged it northwards for Liddesdale and the Debateable Land.

Dodd let them go, he was looking all about him. "Can ye see the Deputy?" he yelled, "Check the trees, where is he? Where's Bothwell?"

"DODD!" came a happy roar that was unmistakably Carey's voice – at least he could still shout. Where the devil was it coming from?

"DODD, I'M UP HERE ON THE ROOF."

By God, so he was. Dodd squinted, shaded his eyes from the sun and saw a smutty wild figure waving his arms from the top of Netherby tower where the smoke was billowing in great black clouds. Some Graham down in the barnekin shot at him with a caliver at a hopeless range and he ducked down. In a moment he was up again.

"DODD, I'VE GOT JOCK OF THE PEARTREE AS MY HOSTAGE. TRY AND . . ." Somebody else tried with an arquebus, and the stone splintered two feet from Carey's hand. ". . . Ah, go to hell you idiots, you'll never hit me at that range . . . TRY AND NEGOTIATE, DODD, BOTHWELL'S INSIDE THE TOWER . . ."

Dodd sat back in the saddle and grinned.

"Och," he said to Will the Tod who was beside him, "they've got him treed."

"That him?" asked Will the Tod curiously. "Are ye sure?"

"Ay," said Dodd, "he doesnae normally look like that, he's generally a very smart man, almost a dandy. But ay, that's him, and he's given 'em a run for their money, if I'm any judge."

"Wattie Graham must be ay annoyed at having to burn his own tower."

"And he's got Jock of the Peartree."

Will the Tod's face was split in the broadest of grins. "Ay, it's a grand thought, Jock made a hostage by the Deputy Warden of Carlisle. That's worth the bother by itself. He's his father's son, true enough."

"I thought ye didn't take to Lord Hunsdon."

"Oh, I wouldna say that, he never burned me and he did burn a few of my enemies when I pointed them out to him. I've got nothing against the Careys, me."

"Good," said Dodd, "but now we have to get the Deputy down from the tower."

"It's a tickle situation, Henry. What's your plan?"

"Talk to Bothwell."

"And if Bothwell willna talk?"

Dodd shrugged. "Avenge Carey and give him a decent burial."

"It'd be a pity."

"Ay."

"So now. I'm the English Armstrong headman, Henry, so I think it's fitting if I do the talking."

Dodd opened his mouth to argue and then thought better of it. He nodded. Will the Tod looked pleased with himself.

"Hey, BOTHWELL!" he roared. "Show your face, I want to talk to ye."

Friday, 23rd June, afternoon

More quickly than seemed possible the smoke had got thicker and thicker until the top of the tower was crowned with a black hood of smoke, a little flurried by the breeze. The day was too still to blow it away, the first truly summer weather for weeks, Carey thought bitterly, when what he needed was a good solid downpour.

Jock coughed hackingly. "When will ye surrender?" he asked. Carey had hustled him back to the beacon post and tied him to it again. Hammering came from below – they must have brought in lances or long poles. Carey backed away from the trapdoor, behind the angle of the roof and his barricade of firewood. He counted out his arrows – he had five left – and laid them in a row in front of him, set his bow before him and waited. Counting the knives still in their scabbards on his wrist and at the back of his neck, he had seven shots at whoever poked his head through the trapdoor, before it was hand to hand.

"Why should I surrender if Bothwell won't ransom me?"

"Och, I'll protect ye, lad. Ye've talked me round wi' that smooth courtier's tongue of yours, I'll not let Bothwell harm ye, nor Wattie. Ye've my word on it."

"Well," said Carey, tempted against his will. A drift of smoke caught him and he coughed.

"Ye'll get us both killed. Ah can save ye, if ye let me lift up the trapdoor and talk to Bothwell. Ye can keep an arrow pointed at my back if ye like. There's no need to die."

That was when Carey and Jock both heard the sound of horns, of hoofbeats, shouting, fighting, the creak and double thud of the barnekin gate. Carey ran to the eastern parapet, peered over, batting furiously at the smoke, and there was Sergeant Dodd, filthy, armed and triumphant, with something like eighty men about him. Carey shouted, waved his arms, shouted again. He'd never have thought he could be so delighted to see that miserable sullen bastard of a Sergeant.

Jock of the Peartree brought him back to reality.

"So the garrison's out," he said dourly. "It makes nae odds to ye, ye bloody fool. Bothwell's still going to have ye either by breaking in the trapdoor or he'll wait until the smoke kills ye. Me, I'd wait."

Carey was coughing again: the smoke reeked and was making his eyes stream. He fanned the air uselessly.

"Us, Jock, you too. Still," he said between hacks, "we can negotiate a bit better because if he kills me, he'll have to fight Dodd and I don't think he wants to with his big raid due tomorrow. So why don't you try talking to him again, Jock?"

"Nay, I tried my best, it's a waste of breath now. Let Dodd and that fat Armstrong father-in-law of his do all the hard work."

The smoke was gouting out of the holes in the roof now, and from round the trapdoor as the fire got a good grip down below on whatever filth they'd put into it. For all the shouting outside, Bothwell seemingly would not be drawn from what he was at.

Jock was choking hard now, wheezing and gasping for breath. Carey watched him, beset with indecision, knowing perfectly well that Jock would rather choke to death than beg to be let up again.

"Oh the hell with it," he said, "Jock, will you swear not to play me false if I let you free?"

"Ay," wheezed Jock, "I swear."

Carey hesitated a moment longer, then went to him, cut the ropes that bound him and undid the belt still holding Jock's arms behind him. Jock whined a little with the pain of returning circulation, brought his arms round very slowly and flexed them. He turned to Carey.

"That was kindly of ye, Courtier," said Jock grudgingly. "Ah wouldnae have done that for ye in this situation."

"No," coughed Carey, "I'm too soft, that's my problem. Get on the other side of the roof until it's over."

"Ay," Jock muttered, moving away, "y'are soft an' all."

There was a heavy thump on the trapdoor. Carey watched through tears and coughing. They must have lit a fire right under it, they weren't about to waste gunpowder when fire would work as well even if it was slower. Once the wood was burned through, the weight of the flagstones would . . .

Something hit him like a mallet in the stomach. It was a block of stone off the roof, shrewdly thrown by Jock, and it took every wisp of air out of him. He tottered, tried to keep his feet, tried to draw his dagger, but Jock moved in, caught him briskly, steadied him, and kneed him hard in the balls.

He landed bruisingly on the hot parapet, agony flaring white in his eyes and no breath even to mew with pain; he tried but failed to puke. Locked in a private battle with what felt like a black spear in his groin, lancing up to his chest, he dimly heard Jock pushing his feeble barricade of firewood aside. There was a scraping sound as Jock pulled the flagstones off the trapdoor, and cursing because the metal and wood were hot, shot the bolts.

Carey was beginning to be able to uncurl when Jock kicked him in the head, grabbed the back of his doublet and some hair and dragged him over the stones, behind the angle of the roof.

"Bothwell," shouted Jock, busily tying Carey's wrists behind him with the ropes that had just been cut off his own arms,

"I've got him. D'ye hear me? The trapdoor's open, ye can come up."

"It could be a trick," came Bothwell's voice, "Carey, what are you up to?"

"He's surrendering unconditionally," said Jock. "In fact, I dinna think he can talk at the moment, he seems verra preoccupied."

"What happened?"

"Och, he's a courtier, wi' notions of honour and such, he only went and untied me arms."

There was a lot of unkind laughter down below. Carey would have felt betrayed, but as Jock was giving him a scientific kicking while he spoke, he found he couldn't think of anything except how to roll up tighter. There were sounds of hissing as water was poured over the fire, cautious scraping sounds of a ladder being brought.

Jock took a fistful of Carey's hair and hauled his head back. "This is for the good of your soul, Courtier. Ah'm teaching ye not to beat up your elders . . ."

Carey blinked away the water springing out of his eyes and, out of pure stupid temper, spat in Jock's face.

"Och, Courtier, Courtier . . ." said Jock regretfully, "ye're a hard man to teach." He banged Carey's face a couple of times on the stone and the ugly world and Jock's ugly face went black.

Carey came to, still cross-eyed and dizzy, and tried to puke again. Jock had sauntered over to the parapet. He was peering out at the barnekin and horse paddock between fading drifts of smoke, still coughing. Carey must have made some sort of moaning noise, because Jock turned to him.

"Och, ye canna complain, ye've had nae worse than ye did to me."

Privately Carey thought he'd had a great deal worse than Jock, but he couldn't see any point in arguing and it was too much effort anyway.

"Thought so," said Jock with satisfaction still gazing outwards at something he could see over the parapet, "Thank God Sergeant Dodd knows what he's at."

One of Carey's eyes was swelling shut and he could do no more than dully wonder through his multifarious pains why Jock had picked up the bow and the remaining arrows and had nocked one on the string. He was still where Jock had hauled him, out of sight of the trapdoor, uncomfortably half-curled, half-sprawled on the roofstones, his head jammed against the parapet wall and his knees pulled up. His hands had already gone numb. A tentative movement of his shoulders to try and free his head got him kicked again, so he stayed where he was. Then the trapdoor moved, shifted, was hefted out of the way.

The head and shoulders that appeared through the hole were Bothwell's, and he was holding a dag with the match ready lit. He and Jock looked at each other for a moment.

"Now," said Jock, "ye're going to talk to Sergeant Dodd, my lord Earl, and in exchange for the men he caught and all our horses which he's rounded up and has started on their way back south and for him agreeing to take himself and his men off again, we'll give him his precious Deputy Warden. Onless ye want to give up on yer raid altogether, because if ye dinna agree then I'm out of it and so are all my kin."

"Why Jock? What do you care about one of Hunsdon's boys? Has he got a knife at your back?"

Jock laughed. "Ye know me better than that, Bothwell. Nay, he's down here on the floor by my feet, feeling right sorry for himself." Carey had tried to wriggle out of range while Jock was busy, so Jock gave him another kick in the back, but the arrow pointed at Bothwell's heart remained rock-steady. Bothwell blinked through the final wisps of smoke, finally spotted Carey, who had decided to play dead for the moment despite the heat of the stones, and laughed heartily.

"Untie him and let me shoot his right hand off, so he never troubles us again."

Jock hesitated. "I'd let ye, my lord," he said, "but he didna kill me when he had the chance and I said I wouldna let you harm him."

"Ye've harmed him yerself, it looks like."

"That's different."

"He wanted to use you as a hostage."

"Nay, I'm no' a good hostage and he knows it. He is, though," grinned Jock. "Are ye fixed on fighting Sergeant Dodd and his men, Bothwell, or would ye rather save the powder for our raid?"

"What did you tell him about it?"

"Jesus, my lord, what do ye take me for, I told him nothing of it," said Jock sincerely. "We've been talking of family matters. It's been verra interesting, eh Courtier?" Jock kicked Carey in the ribs again and smiled blithely at Bothwell.

Friday, 23rd June, afternoon

At last Bothwell climbed up to the fighting platform behind the sharpened logs of the Netherby barnekin and shouted for Sergeant Dodd. Dodd had glimpsed activity at the top of the tower and was wondering irritably if Carey had managed to get himself killed at the last minute.

"I'm the headman . . ." began Will the Tod.

"Shh," said Dodd, "he thinks I've brought the Carlisle garrison too."

"But ye havna. Lowther . . ."

"Let him think it. Ay my lord," yelled Dodd, "what d'ye want?"

"We've got your Deputy Warden prisoner, Sergeant," said Bothwell.

"Is he still alive?"

Bothwell grinned. "Ay. He's not very happy, but he's still alive. Tell me why I shouldnae cut his throat and be done with it."

"Prove he's alive first," said Dodd, his voice hard with suspicion, "I've nae interest in his corpse."

Bothwell nodded, leaned down and gave some orders. Two men appeared behind the pointed logs: Dodd recognised a battered Jock of the Peartree with his knife at the neck of an even more battered Robert Carey.

Dodd relaxed a little. Why on earth hadn't they killed him when they caught him? Ah well, who could fathom the way the mad Earl's mind worked.

"What will ye give me for him?" shouted Bothwell.

"He's only the one man," yelled Will the Tod in return, "and he's no' very valuable."

"Shut up," hissed Dodd, "he's the Deputy Warden and . . ."

"Och, Henry," said Will the Tod, not at all offended, "Janet's right, ye know nothing of bargaining." He raised his voice again. "If ye give him to us, we might consider going away and leaving ye in peace."

Dodd couldn't quite make out expressions at that distance, but he rather thought that one of Carey's eyebrows had gone travelling upwards again.

"What about my horses?" demanded Bothwell.

"What horses?" asked Will the Tod sweetly.

"Don't try my patience, Armstrong, ye ken very well which horses."

"D'ye mean the few nags that belong to ye, or d'ye mean all the peacable innocent men's horses ye've reived in the past week."

"I mean all the horses in the God damned paddock," shouted Bothwell, "or I'll send him out to you in pieces."

"Och, my lord," said Will the Tod, enjoying himself hugely, "we're only discussing it, there's nae need to be offensive."

Dodd rolled his eyes.

Jock of the Peartree leaned over the barnekin wall.

"We'll let ye keep the Dodd horses I took and that's all."

Will the Tod turned to Dodd. "Do ye like the terms, Henry?"

"Get on with it."

"Ts. Young men have nae patience. Your Courtier's got Jock on his side, he'll do well enough."

"He's what?"

"Ay," shouted Will the Tod, "that's good enough for us. We'll gi' ye back all the horses bar the ones that belong to Sergeant Dodd here and we'll go home when we've got our man and we'll no' fight ye unless ye come after us."

Geordie brought back the huge herd of horses from the eaves of Cleughfoot wood, separated out those with Dodd brands, and put the rest back in the paddock. The captured Grahams they left tied to the paddock fence.

They waited. At last the gate opened and Carey was shoved through on foot, limping, weaponless, black with smoke, the left side of his face swollen up, his back straight and his expression unreadable.

Understanding perfectly from the way he walked that somebody – Jock, no doubt – must have been using the Deputy's privates for football practice, Dodd led up a nice quiet soft-paced mare, and held her while Carey set himself, fastened his teeth on his lip, and mounted up very very carefully.

"Can ye ride, sir?" Dodd asked solicitously.

Carey lowered himself down in the saddle like a maiden sitting for the first time on her wedding morning, took a deep breath, held it and nodded. Dodd was sorry to see that the bounce seemed to have quite gone out of him.

He was still every inch the Courtier: once the group of them were out of sight of Netherby, it was very touching the way he took the trouble to thank all of Dodd's surname and Janet's relatives too, Armstrongs though they were. Dodd stayed at his back, feeling a bit as he did when one of his younger brothers had got himself a belting when they were lads: privately, he thought it was funny, but he saw no reason why anybody should add to the man's discomfort by smirking or commenting. So he glowered over Carey's torn and battered shoulder, and not one of his kin disgraced him by cracking a smile.

To keep Carey's mind off things as they rode back to Carlisle, Dodd told him the epic tale of his own arrest, escape from jail and journey through the secret passage, followed by his run to Brampton, very generously only slightly editing the ladies' part in the story. At least Carey was impressed.

"You did it in a jack and helmet, too?" he said, his voice still hoarse with the smoke. "I doubt there's a man in the south that could do the like."

Dodd's long face continued to look as mournful as a hound with the bellyache, but inwardly he was reluctantly flattered. He said, on a friendly impulse, "I'm sorry your plan went awry, Cour . . . sir. It might have worked wi'out Lowther to spike yer guns for ye."

"Oh but, Sergeant," said Carey, wincing and closing his eyes as the horse he was riding pecked at a pothole, "it did work, it worked beautifully. It only went wrong at the very last minute. You watch, you'll see how it all worked out."

He's still mad, thought Dodd dourly, no longer sorry for him.

Friday, 23rd June, evening

Barnabus Cooke was waiting in the Carlisle courtyard when Dodd brought Carey home. Clearly, Lowther had heard what had happened and seemed to think it a good idea to be present, which Barnabus thought was probably a serious mistake. The Lord Warden himself seemed embarrassed at his inaction and he was wandering about in the courtyard too. With the women also there, it was a regular little welcoming party and Barnabus rather thought Carey would have preferred not to see any of them.

However he smiled wanly as he came in, dismounted slowly and carefully, and then held onto the saddle to steady himself.

"Are you wounded anywhere, sir?" Barnabus asked, clicking his fingers imperiously at Hutchin Graham to lead the horses away. Carey shook his head. Dodd came up behind Carey looking as miserable as if he had not just rescued his Deputy Warden. Then Carey spotted Lowther, standing by the barracks door with his arms folded and a look of deep satisfaction all over his face at Carey's condition. The Deputy Warden was in a lamentable state: Daniel Swanders' jerkin and shirt were in tatters and blackened with soot, and Carey couldn't even see out of his left eye which was on the side of his face that was puffed out like a cushion.

The other eye narrowed and its eyebrow went up. This will be interesting, thought Barnabus, and settled back a little to watch the fireworks.

"How are you, Robin?" asked Scrope, breaking the tension between them. "What happened, why did you do it? It was very . . ."

Carey took a deep breath and put his fingers up to rub between his eyebrows. "Thank you, my lord, I'm a lot better than I expect you think I deserve to be."

Scrope coloured. He couldn't seem to look at Carey straight.

"Well, it might have worked . . ." began Scrope generously.

"Ha!" said Lowther.

Carey ignored him elaborately. "Of course it might if you didn't have a traitor claiming to be your Deputy," he said smoothly. "Very unfortunate that he chose to let out the Grahams who could identify me just when I happened to be at Netherby. But I expect he thought he was doing the best he could for his employer."

Scrope looked puzzled and Carey didn't bother to enlighten him. He turned to go to his chambers in the Queen Mary Tower and found his path blocked by Lowther.

"Are ye calling me a traitor?"

Carey blinked at him and smiled his most superior and supercilious smile. It wasn't quite as effective as usual in driving men wild, because only half his face was working properly, but the veins on Lowther's nose throbbed all the same.

"Yes, I am, Lowther," he said, "March traitor, in that you bring in raiders, and traitor to your Queen in that you failed to inform her of important information in your possession. Why, surely you don't mind, do you?"

"We'll see what Burghley has to say about this escapade," huffed Lowther, still not ready to call Carey out to his face.

Carey smiled even more, which must have hurt. "That's right," he said softly, "you dig your own grave and lie in it, Sir Richard. Didn't you know that Burghley and his son support King James's succession to the throne after her Majesty dies? I'm sure my lord Burghley will be fascinated to hear how you tried to stop me discovering Bothwell's plans to raid Falkland

Palace and capture the King of Scotland. So will King James. Please save me the trouble and do it yourself."

Lowther's mouth was open. Carey very gently put out a finger and pushed past him. "Now, I've had a long hard day and I'm tired. If you'll excuse me, I'm going to bed. Good night ladies, good night my lord."

Lovely, Barnabus thought trotting after his master, that'll puzzle him, and you kept your temper as well, you're learning fast, ain't you?

Upstairs in Carey's bedchamber, Barnabus helped him strip off all Swanders' filthy lousy rags and drop them in the corner. Knowing better than to say anything at all, he silently handed Carey cloths and a basin of hot water so he could clean off the soot and tend to the bruises and grazes he could reach. Barnabus dealt with the rest. Somebody knocked on the door just as he finished.

"Oh bloody hell," said Carey, pulling on his night shirt and dressing gown, and sitting down on the side of the bed.

It was Dodd, poking his head round the door. "Sorry to disturb ye sir, but I've spoken to Lady Widdrington and she wants to see you tomorrow and she also says her stepson Henry's waiting at Bessie's to take a message to Chancellor Melville and he has a passport from Scrope so he can go at once."

Carey blinked as he caught up with all this. "Excellent," he croaked at last. "Wait a minute." He hobbled over to his desk in the next room, wrote a few lines, signed it, and folded and sealed it.

"Tell Henry to take the long way round and on no account go anywhere near Liddesdale. The verbal message is that Bothwell's got at least 200 men with remounts, mostly Grahams, and I think there's someone working for Bothwell amongst the courtiers inside the palace."

When Dodd had gone, Barnabus said tactfully, "Shouldn't you warn him about King James's . . . er . . . habits, sir?"

Carey laughed, stopped with a wince and sat down on the bed again. "Not Henry: he's far too spotty for his Majesty's tastes. And Melville's known him since he was a boy, he'll look after him."

"Seems like you've saved the King's life, if he gets through."

"Hmf. Knowing the King he won't pay a blind bit of attention. But I've drawn the raid's sting anyway and he'll never understand how."

"Why's that, sir?" asked Barnabus, wondering if he should call in a surgeon to strap Carey's ribs which were black and blue and looked very much as if they might be cracked.

Carey smiled. "I told Jock of the Peartree about the horses in Falkland Palace. By now he's told all his brothers and nephews and cousins and they'll have lost interest entirely in King James."

He lifted his feet onto the bed, dropped the cloth on the floor. "And I've almost solved the problem of Sweetmilk's murderer and I've made friends with Jock of the Peartree, if you can call it that, and I've . . ."

He snored richly. Barnabus tucked him up and drew the bed curtains. He'd send for the surgeon tomorrow, when Carey would be in a terrible mood, and he'd get Lady Scrope to bring him and Lady Widdrington could continue to organise the funeral which she was doing with her usual briskness.

Simon had made friends with some of the other lads in the castle and reported that Young Hutchin seemed remarkably rich in silver at the moment, which information Barnabus would decide whether to pass onto Carey in the morning.

Saturday, 24th June, morning

Carey woke up late at seven o'clock with a ravenous hunger and ribs that twinged monstrously every time he moved or breathed. Someone had pulled his bedcurtains to let the sun in and left a tray laden with fried collops of ham, grilled eggs, bread, and a flagon of mild beer, which made his mouth water so much he almost drooled as he pulled it towards him.

Ten minutes later it was all gone, despite the way his jaw hurt when he chewed. But his belly was packed tight and his sore face and body receded slightly in significance. Then somebody knocked on the door.

"Enter," said Carey, thinking it was Barnabus. The door opened, and Philadelphia came flying in, her clothes in their usual tumble no matter what the attentions of her tiring woman, and threw herself into his arms, never mind that he was still in his nightshirt and dressing gown.

"I thought they'd hang you, oh Robin, Robin, I was so afraid they'd hang you . . ."

"So was I," said Carey gruffly, "but they didn't, so why weep about it?"

"They hurt you . . ." She was touching his face and he reared back.

"That was Jock of the Peartree," said Carey, "and he's just as sore this morning as I am. Well almost." He handed her his hankerchief from under the pillow and Philly blew her nose, composed herself and flipped bewilderingly into scolding him.

"I hope you're thoroughly embarrassed, Dodd having to come to the rescue like that? Did you hear how he got out of Carlisle through the secret passage nobody knows about except the warden?"

"Yes. Twice."

She wasn't going to leave him in peace, blast her. Carey grabbed his clothes off the chest where they were laid out, shut the bedcurtains and started dressing. Philadelphia continued.

"Well please don't do it again. It was awful waiting here with Lowther keeping the gate with his men and threatening Red Sandy with flogging there and then if he tried anything. You won't do it again, will you, Robin?"

Carey was coughing again. He cursed. There was still smoke in his lungs and it nearly killed him every time he did that. "I don't think anyone in these parts will trust strange peddlers any more. I've probably ruined their trade. Is Red Sandy all right?"

"Scrope made Lowther leave your men alone if they promised to stay in the castle."

"Good, I'm glad they tried."

"How could you do something so dangerous? Scrope said you were mad and he wouldn't get you out of a schoolboy prank."

'I'll bet," muttered Carey to himself.

"What?"

"I said, did he?"

"Yes, he did. I'm still not speaking to him. Stupid man, pretending he had an ague, I hate him. And I hate you too, for worrying us like that."

Carey drew back the curtains again and climbed out of bed to pull on his boots, saying, "You're allowed to hate your brother but you're not supposed to hate your husband, Philly."

"Well, don't give me some romantic nonsense about learning to love him, either. In any case, that's not what I married him for."

"Of course not," said Carey, "you're not a peasant. But you are supposed to respect and obey him, Philly."

"Pah!" She tossed her head and her curly black hair partially escaped from its white cap and fell down her neck. "I've brought some people to see you and first you're going to have a surgeon."

"Oh no, Philly, I don't need a surgeon . . ."

She ignored him and led the man in, a stocky, thickset thug called Mr Little, with hair growing luxuriantly out of his nostrils and up his arms, who prodded and grunted, strapped Carey's ribs, declared that neither his skull nor his nose were cracked, but his cheekbone probably was, which Carey knew already, and let him eight ounces of blood from his left arm to balance up his humours. He offered to put in a clyster to guard against infection and was offended when Carey told him curtly to go and ask Barnabus for his fee.

"Bloody surgeons," he muttered, as he carefully pulled on his shirt and doublet again. He took a quick look down his hose at the damage there, winced at the sight and wondered if he'd ever be the man he was. God knew, the ride back to Carlisle had been Hell, Purgatory and the Spanish Inquisition rolled into one, and every step he took was a punishment. He simply hadn't had the courage to let the surgeon examine his balls.

Somebody else knocked on the door. Damn it, the place was like the Queen's antechamber in Westminster, with all the bloody traffic in it.

"What the hell do you want?" he roared, then coughed when his ribs caught him.

Lady Widdrington marched in, trailing an unwilling but resplendently dressed Thomas the Merchant Hetherington. Behind her, obviously primed, Barnabus shut the door and no doubt stationed himself outside to repel interruptions and, naturally, cram his ear against the panelling.

When she first married her elderly crook of a husband, Elizabeth Widdrington had not known the meaning of the word "tact". He had taught it to her, with the aid of his belt, on several occasions. When her rage had subsided she had decided to learn subtlety and dissimulation, no matter how hard it came to her, since it seemed that was what God wanted.

Clearly God had been training her. When she had seen Robert Carey the night before in the courtyard, her first, chokingly powerful impulse, had been to run to him and hold him and kiss him. She had managed to stay where she was and let him deal on his own with Lowther, whom she wanted to run through with a lance. She still had the marks of her fingernails on her palms to prove her self-control. Now she looked at him and recognised the symptoms of a man whose pride was as badly bruised as his body and who was clinging to his temper by the fingers of one hand.

She still wanted to fold him into her arms and kiss his poor face, but she knew how that would drive him away. So she put one hand out to touch his arm and said, "Thank God you're alive, Sir Robert."

He looked at the floor. She had, after all, tried to dissuade him. No doubt he was waiting for her to tell him she'd told him so.

"Thank you," he managed to say.

"Are you still interested in Sweetmilk?"

Carey looked up. "I beg your pardon?"

"Do you still want to know who killed him? If you've found

out already, I won't waste any more of your time. But if you haven't, Thomas the Merchant has a tale he'd like to tell you."

Good, that distracted him, he'd always liked puzzles and challenges. There went that silly eyebrow of his, ridiculous the effect it had on her.

Carey led the way through to the room he used as an office and sat down behind his desk.

"Well?" he said to Thomas the Merchant, pointedly not offering a seat.

Thomas the Merchant harrumphed, clasped his hands under his belly.

"Early on the Saturday," he began, harrumphed again.

"Yes."

"Jock Hepburn and Mary Graham came to me wanting rings. They were handfasting one another in secret." Thomas look distasteful at this evidence of sin, seemed to consider commenting on it, but changed his mind at Carey's expression. He went on quickly in his resentful drone. "While they were here, Sweetmilk came in, wanting horses and caught them. He was verra put out. He called Jock Hepburn a bastard that had dishonoured his sister, and Hepburn struck him on his face, so he threw down his glove. Hepburn picked it up, but Mary Graham was clinging to Sweetmilk and begging him not to kill her man. He only threw her down and walked out with Hepburn."

Carey's good eye was narrowed with interest. "How were they armed?"

"They werena clad for business. Sweetmilk had his best jack and nae lance and Hepburn was very fine in a French brocade, three pounds the ell, I'd say, and a jack as well, but foreign make. Nice rings too."

"I know," said Carey. "Their arms?"

Thomas the Merchant pulled the corners of his mouth down in thought. "Swords, daggers, the usual."

"Who had a gun?"

"Neither of them."

"Did you look out into the street?"

"I did. Hepburn and Sweetmilk were riding down tae the gate together, with Mary chasing after them on her pony still crying to Sweetmilk not to do it."

"She didn't think Hepburn would win?"

Thomas smiled broadly. "Och, no, he's a bonny man, but Sweetmilk had the experience. I was betting on him meself."

"Think hard, Mr Hetherington. Did any man there have a firearm?"

"Nay, neither of them had more than swords."

"Thank you, Mr Hetherington. I want you to make a proper statement for Richard Bell to take down and I'll be calling you as a witness against Hepburn at the next Warden's Day."

"Sir . . ."

"Quiet. Off you go."

Thomas the Merchant went, but Elizabeth Widdrington stayed for a moment.

"Will you try and arrest Jock Hepburn?"

"Yes," said Carey. "It might have to wait until after Bothwell's raid and we can lift him quietly without too much trouble, but yes."

"Why? He only killed a Graham, an outlaw."

"Sweetmilk wasn't an outlaw, yet. He wasn't killed in a fair fight, he was murdered so Jock Hepburn could avoid a fight."

"Why . . ." Elizabeth paused, "Why did you take so much trouble over it?"

Carey looked down at his hands. "Do you know what justice is?" he asked at last, in an oddly remote voice. "Justice is an accident, really. It's law that's important. Do you know what the rule of law is?"

"I think so. When people obey the laws so there's peace . . ."

Carey was shaking his head. "No. It's the transfer of the duty of revenge to the Queen. It's the officers of the Crown avenging a man's murder, not the man's father or the family. Without law what you have is feud, tangling between themselves, and murder repaying murder down the generations. As we have here. But if the Queen's Officers can be relied on to take revenge for a killing, then the feuding must stop because if you feud against the Queen, it's high treason. That's all. That's all that happens in a law-abiding country: the dead man's family know that the Crown will carry their feud for them. Without it you have bloody chaos."

It was strange to hear anyone talk so intensely of such a dusty subject as law; and yet there was a fire and passion in Carey's words as if the rule of law was infinitely precious to him.

"All we can do to stop the borderers killing each other is give them the promise of justice – which is the accidental result when the Crown hangs the man who did the killing," he said, watching his linked fingers. They were still empty of rings and look oddly bare. "You see, if it was only a bloodfeud, anyone of the right surname would do. But with the law, it should be the man that did the killing, and that's justice. Not just to take vengeance but to take vengeance on the right man."

"So you'll make out a bill for Sweetmilk Graham and go through all the trouble of trying Hepburn and producing witnesses and finding him guilty . . ."

"And then hanging him, when a word to Jock of the Peartree would produce the same result a lot more easily. But that wouldn't be justice, you see, that would only be more feuding, more private revenge which has nothing to do with justice or law or anything else. Justice requires that the man have a trial and face his accusers."

"But you think Jock Hepburn did it."

"Who else was there?" said Carey. Elizabeth opened her mouth to speak, took a breath, and then paused. "But at least at a trial he could argue against my suspicions."

"It's a complicated thing, this law." Elizabeth said, trying to speak lightly. "Do you think you'll be able to explain it to Jock of the Peartree?"

Carey smiled lopsidedly. "No, never in a thousand years."

It was so hard to sit there and not move nearer, not hold her hands out to him. Why was it so hard, even after all this time? After all they had first met in '87 when he was on that difficult and dangerous embassy to King James, and again in the

Armada year when she had been at Court with Philadelphia. They had played at all the light, silly, sweet confections of loverlike convention, half joking, half deadly serious.

He looked awful, but despite the brown walnut stain and clownish bruising, there was something in his blue eyes and the way he smiled that had the power to hypnotise her, make her forget all her faith in God and hard-held virtue, everything. When she had read sceptically the verses about the romantic disease of love poured out by the sonneteers, she had never believed it was such a dangerous uncomfortable beast. But she had been wrong. She looked at the floor so as not to be caught, flushed and struggled. No, she thought harshly, I'm a married woman and unfaithfulness is breaking a vow I made in God's presence. That's all. And now I have to go, so I can think straight.

She stood up. Carey stood as well, moved towards her.

"Thank you," he said gently, "I know what you did for me."

No, she couldn't stand it, in another moment she would burst into tears and tell him how she had paced the castle through the day in terror of his death and let him kiss her and then it would be too late to stop. He wanted to kiss her, any fool could see he needed less than half an excuse to reach out and catch her to him . . . her face as flushed as a girl's, she hung her head, muttered something half-gracious, and fled through the door.

Behind her Carey stared after her, reddening with frustration. Then he yelled, "GOD DAMN IT!" and threw his stool at the wall.

Saturday, 24th June, late afternoon

Lemons, Barnabus thought, lemons, the walnut juice stain comes off with lemons, no problem there, Barnabus, all you need to do is find some lemons. It appeared however, that there were none in Carlisle. The few lemons that had made the long journey from Spain and the south of France, to wind up in the market as slightly wizened specimens, had been snapped up by Lady Scrope the previous week to make syllabubs. Food prices had gone sky high all over Carlisle, what with the unreliable harvest weather, and the arrival of dozens of gentlemen and attendants from all over the March. Thomas the Merchant had bought up most of the spices in Carlisle the night Henry Lord Scrope died and had made a very hard bargain with Lady Scrope.

He'd tried Thomas the Merchant himself, to find Thomas regretful but completely unable to supply him. Nowhere else in Carlisle had any, nor even lemon juice. Mrs Croser, the apothecary and midwife, had told him she was still waiting for new supplies herself.

The gentlemen of the March had finished their final meeting before the funeral procession. They had done eating and drinking and boasting about twelve pointed harts they had brought down in Redesdale and departed, not too unsteadily, to their lodgings. Barnabus lined up the boys who had been serving. After searching them carefully and retrieving four spoons and two wine strainers, he paid them and dismissed them, telling them that any lad that brought him a lemon before evening would be paid sixpence for it.

The boys scattered, talking intently. Barnabus went to Carey's chamber where he finished polishing Carey's best boots and checked the starching and sewing of the new ruff his master was to wear at the funeral. The new black velvet suit was hanging up ready for wear and very fine Carey would look in it too, even if he wasn't ever likely to pay for it. It was quite plain with only a little black braid over the seams and the panes of the hose decorated with brocade. Barnabus would have liked there to be a bit of slashing and a lining of tawny taffeta, but Carey had forbidden it and insisted on cramoisie red silk lining as being more suitable. Eight months in Paris as a youth of nineteen had given Carey very decided ideas about clothes, which ten years of service at Court had confirmed.

Barnabus was just about to make sure that his own best suit of fine dark blue wool was in a reasonable state, when there was a hammering on the door. He opened it to find Goodwife Biltock, bright red with heat and rage standing there, holding Young Hutchin Graham by his right arm twisted up behind his back and his left ear.

"What is the meaning of this, Mr Cooke?" she demanded, sweeping into the room past him.

"Er . . ."

"Why would this young scoundrel want to steal lemons from the kitchen, eh?"

Barnabus knew his mouth was opening and shutting. Goodwife Biltock shoved Young Hutchin into the corner, where he sat rubbing his ear and looking embarrassed. The Goodwife squared up to Barnabus, her broad face on a level with his chest and shook her finger under his nose.

"Sixpence a lemon," she snapped, "I'll sixpence a lemon you, you thieving clapperdudgeon . . ."

Barnabus backed away. "Goodwife, Goodwife . . ."

"Send boys out to steal from the kitchens would you . . ."

"Goodwife, I only said if they could find lemons, I would pay sixpence for them. It's to take the walnut stain off Sir Robert's face and hands, that's all."

As he'd hoped it would, that slowed her down.

"Ah," she said. "Well, fair enough. I can't spare you any lemons, but I can give you verjuice which has the same quality of sourness." She turned to Hutchin Graham. "You, boy!" she barked, "I've got an errand for you, come with me."

As she herded Hutchin out of the door ahead of her she glowered at Barnabus.

"Mind your manners, Mr Cooke," she said, "I know you and where you're from." Barnabus could think of nothing to do except bow. If anything her frown became fiercer. "I'll send this thief back to you with the verjuice. My advice is to beat him well."

"Thank you Goodwife Biltock," said Barnabus faintly.

When Hutchin got back with the little flask of verjuice, Carey had returned from inspecting his men along with Captain Carleton. Barnabus was serving them with what remained of the good wine they had brought north with them: Carleton had parked his bulk on Carey's chair next to the fireplace and Carey was sitting on the bed telling the full tale of his adventures at Netherby. Carleton held his sides and bellowed with laughter when he heard how Carey had been foolish enough to free Jock of the Peartree on his word not to attack and Carey looked wry.

"Well," he said, "I'll know better next time, but it might have saved my life at that. Now then Young Hutchin, what have you got there?"

"Verjuice, sir. From Goodwife Biltock."

"That was kind of her with all she has to do. Give her my thanks and best regards."

Hutchin looked hesitant.

"I'm supposed to give him a beating, sir," said Barnabus helpfully.

"Good lord, why? What's he done?"

"Tried to steal some of the Goodwifc's lemons."

There were volumes of the comprehension in Carey's battered face, but all he said was, "Well, that was very devoted of you, Hutchin, but much more dangerous than simply lifting a few head of cattle. We'll remit the beating for now because I want you to take part in the funeral procession tomorrow."

Young Hutchin who had been looking sullen, stood up straighter.

"We need a groom to ride the lead horse pulling the funeral bier. You'll have a mourning livery and it'll be your job to be sure the horses are calm and go the right way. Can you do it?"

Hutchin was looking for the catch. "Is that all, sir?"

Carey nodded. "Your fee will be the livery: it's a suit of fine black wool which I think will fit you well, and a new linen shirt. We can't arrange for new boots but your own don't look too bad if you give them a polish, and you'll have a black velvet bonnet with a feather."

Hutchin thought carefully."

"Ay sir, I'll do it."

"Excellent. Be here two hours before dawn and Barnabus will see you properly kitted out."

Astonishingly, Hutchin smiled, took off his cap and made quite a presentable bow. He turned to go.

"Oh, and Hutchin."

"Ay Sir?"

"Your Uncle Richard Graham of Brackenhill is coming, so he'll be behind you in the procession."

Hutchin smiled even wider before clattering off down the stairs. Carleton looked quizzically at Carey.

"That young devil is chief of the boys in Carlisle," said Carey in answer to his unspoken question. "If they're planning some bright trick for the funeral, he'll either be in the thick of it or know who is and now he'll see to it that they don't do it."

Carleton nodded. "Ay, there's sense in that."

"Which is also why I got Scrope to invite the Armstrong and Graham headmen."

Carleton smiled. "Well, it's worth a try, any road."

Dodd arrived looking harassed, and Barnabus served him with the last of their wine. He sniffed suspiciously at it, then drank.

There was further tying up of endless loose ends to be done: petty details that somehow always slipped your notice until the last minute. It had invariably been like that when Carey was taking part in an Accession Day Tilt: you thought you'd got everything sorted out and then a hundred things suddenly rose up the night before and sneered at you.

It was getting on towards sunset and Barnabus could see that Carey was tired. However, it seemed he had one further important piece of business to transact.

"Couriers?" asked Dodd.

"The regular service to London from Carlisle. The weak link is the man who rides from Carlisle to Newcastle, before he hands it on to my brother's courier to take the rest of the way."

"Why do you want him stopped?" demanded Carleton suspiciously.

"I want to know what Lowther's saying about me, since he apparently controls the March's correspondence."

"Oh ay," agreed Carleton, "I see."

"And I don't want him stopped. I just want his dispatch bag . . . borrowed, so I can read the letters.'

"Well," said Dodd, "all the papers go into a bag in Richard Bell's room where it's sealed and then one of Lowther's boys carries it to Newcastle, riding post. He usually waits there for the return bag and then he brings it back. If the seals were broken he'd know . . ."

"There are ways of opening dispatch bags without breaking the seals."

"Are there?" asked Carleton, "What are they?"

"Well, you could unpick the stitching at the bottom and take the papers out that way."

"Nay sir," said Dodd, who had carried them on occasion and done his best to satisfy his curiosity, "They're double, and the outer one's oiled canvas."

"Damn," said Carey, "I suppose Walsingham will have advised him how to do it. Well, that leaves Richard Bell."

"The little clerk," grunted Carleton. "Ye could threaten him, I suppose."

Bell was quite a scrawny specimen, but he was also tall and gangling rather than small. However, Barnabus had noticed that fighting men invariably referred to clerks as "little".

Carey shook his head. "That would send him straight to Lowther or Scrope. Can he be bought?"

"I dinna ken," said Dodd, "nobody's tried."

"Are you joking?" demanded Carey, clearly shocked. "Are you seriously telling me that nobody's even tried bribing him for the dispatches?"

Dodd shook his head. "I suppose we wouldn't know if they had, but if he's been bribed he's very canny about it, his gown's ten years old at least."

"He'll have had livery for the funeral, though?"

Carleton shook his head as well. "He's not been invited into the procession."

"Why not? He served the old Lord Scrope for years?"

Dodd and Carleton exchanged embarrassed glances. It seemed that Richard Bell had been left out.

"Well," said Carleton, shifting in the chair, "ye hardly ever notice him, he's that quiet, I suppose they forgot."

Carey was genuinely appalled. "Well, that's simply not good enough. Where would he be now, do you think?"

"Scrope's office," suggested Carleton.

"I'll go and talk to him, if you'll excuse me, gentlemen."

Dodd and Carleton took their leave. Carey picked up his hat and headed for the door, then turned to Barnabus.

"I've an errand for you, Barnabus."

"Yes sir?"

"I want you to go down to Madam Hetherington's and find Daniel Swanders. Tell him I lost his pack and wouldn't advise him to go to Netherby to get it back for a while until things have cooled down there. If he doesn't mind the risk, he might try in a month or so. In the meantime, here's three pounds English for him to buy new stocks and the five shillings I made while I was doing his job with the ladies at Netherby."

"What about his clothes, sir?"

"Oh Lord, I think Goodwife Biltock burned those. He'd better keep the suit he's got on: he'll get a much better class of customer with it."

"Sir . . ." Barnabus, who had had his eye on that suit for Simon when he finished growing, since it was entirely the wrong size and shape for himself, was very aggrieved. "It's worth more than the pack by itself."

"Considerably more," agreed Carey.

"You'll only have three left."

"Don't fuss," snapped Carey, "I can get something made up in wool when Scrope pays me. Now go and do as I say, and get back here before the gate shuts."

"Yes sir," said Barnabus, sadly.

"I'll see to the walnut stain myself. I suppose the hair colour will just have to grow out."

"Yes sir," said Barnabus, "unless you want to go blond." Carey gave him the piercing blue stare that told him he was pushing it. He added hurriedly, "If you let me cut your hair short, it'll be quicker."

"In the morning."

They went down the stairs together and Carey hurried over to the keep.

Saturday, 24th June, evening

Carey found Richard Bell still standing at his high desk, his pen dipping in the ink bottle and whispering across the paper in front of him in the hypnotic dance of a clerk, with a triple candlestick beside him to light his way through the thickets of letters.

Carey stood and waited quietly until Bell carefully cleaned his pen on a rag, put it down and stretched and rubbed his fingers with a sigh. He caught sight of Carey and blinked at him.

"I'm sorry, sir, I didna see ye."

Bell was as thin as a portrait of Death and yet didn't look unhealthy or consumptive: it seemed natural to him. His shoulders were a little rounded, his eyes blinked against the flicker of the candles. He and Scrope made a matched pair, in fact, although Scrope was better built and looked stronger and might even run to fat in a few years.

"How can I help you, sir?"

"Mr Bell, I heard something that astonished me a moment ago, and I hope you can clarify it for me."

"Yes sir?"

"I heard that you were not to be a part of the funeral procession."

Bell said nothing and looked at the floor. Carey stepped a little closer.

"Is it true?"

Bell nodded. "Did you refuse a place . . .?"

"No sir," said Bell, then looked up shyly. "I have been very busy with the arrangements, and I suppose it . . . er . . . slipped the Lord Warden's mind."

"If you were offered a place, would you accept?"

"Yes sir, of course, I would . . . I would be honoured."

Carey smiled. "How are you with horses, Mr Bell?"

Bell looked confused. "Not bad, I like them. I've carried

dispatches in the past, when they were particularly urgent and the man had already gone."

"No problems walking a couple of miles?"

Bell smiled. "No sir. I'm not as weak as I look."

"Excellent. Let me talk to Scrope and see what I can do. I'm sorry you seem to have been passed over, Mr Bell."

Bell studied the paper before him.

"Sir Richard . . ." he muttered. Carey raised an eyebrow. "Sir Richard Lowther said he would see to it." Bell explained.

"I'm sure he meant to," said Carey generously, "but I expect it slipped his mind with all the press of business. Don't worry, Mr Bell, I'll see my brother-in-law now and talk to him about it."

Sunday, 25th June, 2 a.m.

There was hardly any overnight pause at all in the frantic activity of the castle. Carey, finding his ribs griping him and his face at its sorest, got up, shaved himself gingerly by candlelight and threw on his green suit to go out and see how the preparations were progressing, leaving Barnabus snoring by the door. He found the yard lit by torches and crammed full of horses. The baleful duo of Carleton and Dodd were supervising the garrison as they groomed their hobbies' coats and plaited their manes and tails. In the corner was Bell, who could not have been to bed at all, carefully polishing the flanks of old Scrope's handsome chestnut gelding and feeding him carrots. Boys ran around underfoot, imperiously commanded by Hutchin Graham, lugging gleaming harness and saddles.

Carey wandered through the noise and spied the erect figure of Elizabeth Widdrington going into the castle kitchens which leaned up against the walls of the keep. He followed her, ducking automatically past strings of garlic and onions and the hams that were to be served later, and found her by the long table in the kitchen watching as two of the scullery boys heaved kid carcasses onto the empty spits by the vast fire. The baker was already pulling bread from the oven next to the fire, slamming in batches of penny loaves at a terrible rate. Half the produce of Carlisle market was heaped up in baskets by the larder door waiting to be turned into sallets and pot-herbs while Goodwife Biltock stood by the cauldrons hanging on the brackets over the flames, stirring mightily, her face verging on purple and her hair escaping from her cap in grey strings.

The small round greasy creature Carey knew as the Carlisle cook was sitting on a stool watching stale bread being turned to crumbs by two kitchen girls. He was the idlest man Carey had ever met outside the Court, rarely out of his bed before eight, but it seemed Lady Widdrington had impressed him with the importance of the occasion . . . Terrorised was perhaps a better word to describe the way he looked at her.

Carey turned to go, but Elizabeth caught sight of him and came bustling over, wiping her hands on her clean white apron, and smiling.

"How are you, Sir Robert?" she asked. "Is Lady Scrope up yet?"

"I don't know," Carey admitted, "I can wake them if you like."

She nodded. "Scrope's body-servant has the new livery for the boy and a decent gown for Bell. Any luck with the wine?"

Carey shook his head. "If Barnabus can't find any, nobody can. I expect Bothwell had all the good vintages in Carlisle."

"Can't be helped. I don't suppose anybody will notice and there's plenty of beer and ale. I'll soon need two strong men to help me carry the raised pies into the hall."

She gestured at the table along one wall where three enormous pies, complete with battlements, stood waiting.

"They're a little greasy, so don't send anyone who's wearing his mourning livery."

"What happened to the sweetmeats?"

"They're in Philadelphia's stillroom, drying out. They can wait though: the less time they spend in the open for flies and boys to get to them, the better. How are your ribs?"

"Well enough . . ." began Carey, but Goodwife Biltock came up to him with a mug of ale, looking stern.

"You're as pale as a sheet," she scolded, "and bags to hide a pig in under your eye. Drink that, it's spiced and has medicine in it."

"What sort of medicine?" Carey demanded suspiciously.

"Something to prevent a fever. Let me see your face."

She reached up, took his face between her rough hands and turned it to the light from the fire.

"Jesus," she said, "you look a sight. I wish I could have got to your face with a few leeches when that was done . . ."

"Goodwife . . ." began Carey.

"And an axe for the man that did it to you."

"I don't . . ."

"Drink your ale."

He drank.

"What do you think, Lady Widdrington? Will Lady Scrope . . .?"

"I'm sure," said Elizabeth, still smiling at him. "Anyway, it can't be helped and most of Carlisle know what happened."

"We don't want anyone laughing."

"They won't."

"When did you last wash behind your ears, Robin?"

For God's sake, he didn't have to take this any more. "Last night," said Carey repressively, "with your verjuice. It's the best I can do without lemons. I'll go and wake the Scropes if they're not up already, my lady."

As he left Goodwife Biltock tutted and said "Temper! Temper!" but he pretended to be deaf and carried on out the door, up the stairs and through the hall where trestle tables were set up and Scrope's steward was shouting at a girl who had dropped a large tablecloth in the rushes. She put her apron over her head and howled as Carey slid by, climbed the stairs to the Scrope private apartments. He hid a grin as he knocked: it seemed the preparations for elaborate ceremonial were identical wherever you went. He almost felt homesick for Westminster.

Scrope was already awake and Philadelphia was in her

smock and fur-trimmed dressing gown with her hair full of curling papers, her back eloquently turned to her husband.

"Philadelphia, my dear," said Scrope nervously. Philadelphia sniffed. Carey was irresistibly reminded of a kitten sulking at being refused a second helping of cream, or no, hardly that, perhaps at having her tail trodden on. "Your brother's here." Scrope rolled his eyes eloquently at Carey who tried to look sympathetic. Philadelphia came over and kissed him on his good cheek.

"Robin, you're here, that's splendid," she said. "How is Elizabeth doing?"

"I wish we had her supplying the English troops in the Netherlands," said Carey gallantly, and then balked because Philadelphia was leading him to her dressing table. "What . . .?"

"Now don't fuss, didn't Elizabeth say why I wanted you?"

"No, she . . . What the devil are you doing? No, I don't want to sit there, I have seven men to . . ."

"Oh hush, Robin, this won't take a moment." Philadelphia pushed her stool up behind his knees so he sat automatically in front of the mirror. She chewed meditatively on her lip and then darted forward and picked up a little glass pot.

"What the blazes . . ."

She started dabbing the cream onto his bruised cheek. Carey caught her wrist.

"Philadelphia, what are you doing?"

"I'm going to cover up all the black bruising so you don't look like a Court jester, now let go."

"I'm not wearing bloody face-paint at a funeral . . ."

"Yes, you are. Come on, Robin, did you never wear anything at Court?"

"I most certainly did not, who do you think I am, the Earl of bloody Oxford? I never heard anything so ridiculous in my . . . Ouch!"

"Don't move then. Honestly, I've seen horses easier to deal with than you. Nobody will know if you let me . . ."

"Goddamn it," growled Carey, looking round for moral support. Scrope had disappeared into his little dressing room.

"There now. A bit of red lead, I think, just a bit . . . Your skin's hard to match, Robin, it's lucky you're not a woman. At least you got most of the walnut juice off, what did you use?"

"Verjuice, but . . ."

"No wonder you smell like a meat pickle. Smear a bit of this on, it's a musk perfume, might hide the worst of it. Now then, perhaps a little . . . Yes, that's better. Hm. Much better. Look in the mirror."

"Oh."

"I can't do it round your eye because it'll get sore. We'd better set it . . ."

She picked up a feather pad and dabbed it in powder, brushed it over his face. He sneezed.

"Now," said Philadelphia with satisfaction. "Don't touch your face, don't rub your eyes, and when Barnabus cuts your hair, put a towel round your head so you don't get clippings on it, but I think you'll do. And be careful if you change your shirt as well. There, lovely. You look as if you've been in a fight, but you don't look as if you lost it any more."

"Philly, I . . ."

"That's all right, you don't have to thank me. Now I expect you've got a great deal to do," she added with emphasis, "I certainly have."

Barnabus had the sense not to make any comments when Carey climbed back up the stairs of the Queen Mary Tower to his room. Carey conscientiously protected his face with a towel while Barnabus snipped at his curls.

Once the sky began lightening he examined his face very carefully in the mirror while Barnabus was tying his doublet points and there was no denying the fact that he looked a great deal less like someone who had recently been given a kicking by an expert. His skin felt stiff and odd and he wondered how people like Oxford and even Essex stood it day after day. The Queen wore triple the thickness but women were used to it, he supposed, as he put on his rings.

He complimented Barnabus on his boots which were gleaming and slipped on a pair of wooden pattens to keep them decent until he could mount his horse. He had forgotten to give orders about his sword, but Barnabus had seen to it anyway, and it was glittering and polished. He left the lace-edged ruff off until after he had eaten the breakfast of bread and beer Simon brought him, knowing the magnetic attraction white linen had for crumbs and brown stains, and once that was on and his hat on his head, he was ready. Looking in the mirror again brought a private unadmitted lift to his heart. Not even the Queen could find fault with his elegance, though no doubt she would shriek and throw slippers at the smell of verjuice disguised with perfume. Otherwise he could have attended her in the Privy Chamber with no worries at all.

When he ventured out into the courtyard again the chaos had given place to a semblance of order. There was a row of men pissing against one of the stable walls, and Dodd and Carleton were already mounted. Simon ran to the row of horses, brought out Carey's best horse, Thunder, and led him over. Carey thought about it, joined the row of men to relieve himself, refastened himself carefully because one of his recurring nightmares while serving at Court had been attending the Queen with his codpiece untied, then went over to his horse, slipped off the pattens and mounted up carefully. Dodd lifted his cap to him, replaced it with his helmet and followed him as he rode down the short row of his own six men.

Carey went all round them in silence, eyes narrowed, while the horses shifted nervously and their riders did their best to stare stolidly ahead.

Bell was also waiting, watching out of the side of his eyes as he held Henry Lord Scrope's old horse. It had been the work of two minutes to make the younger Scrope thoroughly ashamed of forgetting Richard Bell and secure him the position of honour, leading the riderless charger behind the bier. Carey approved of the fact that Bell had groomed the animal himself. He came round in front of the men again.

"Archie Give-it-Them," he said gently.

"Ay sir," said Archie nervously. Somebody had put him under the pump: his hair was still wet.

"You look fine. You could attend the Queen herself." He addressed them generally. "In fact you all could." This was stretching the truth slightly as the Queen insisted on handsome men about her at all times, and these looked like the thugs they were, but never mind. "I'm very pleased with your turn-out. You look like what you are, the best men of the garrison." He paused to let that sink in. "Now a few words about processions. Firstly, don't be in any hurry, especially as you're near the front. For some reason, the natural tendency of a procession is to spread itself out and the rear is always in a hurry to catch up. So keep your horses down to as slow a walk as you can. Secondly, be alert because something always goes wrong." There went Philadelphia and Elizabeth in their black finery, followed by half a dozen servants almost hidden under the weight of gowns for the paid mourners waiting by the gate. And Lowther had arrived. He ignored the man and continued.

"Dogs get tangled up in them, horses take a dislike to each other, people fall off their horses, women faint, children make rude remarks. With luck we won't find a nightsoil wagon with a broken axle barring our path as we did at an Accession Day parade I took part in once." Most of them sniggered at that. "It doesn't matter. If it concerns you directly, sort it out quietly. If it doesn't, ignore it and try not to laugh. If some idiot child gets himself trampled, and his mother is having blue screaming hysterics in the middle of the road, Red Sandy, Bangtail and Long George are to clear the path and join the tail end if they can."

He smiled and caught young Simon's eye: he was carrying the big drum. "Let me hear you give the double-pace beat, Simon."

Simon blushed, dropped a drumstick, picked it up and banged a couple of times.

"Can you count?" asked Carey patiently. The sun was up, the Carlisle gate was open, the crowd of mourners, some of them drunk, were putting on their gowns, and the draft horses were hitched to the empty bier. In about two minutes the Carlisle bell would start tolling.

"Y–yes sir." said Simon.

"Try again. Count one, two, one, two."

"One, t–two, one, two . . ."

"Bang on the one." Simon did so. "Better, much better."

Two more boys with drums came running up and looked at him. One of them had his cap over his ear. Carey sighed. "Can you remember that, Simon?"

Over in the corner Lowther was trying to shine the trumpeter's instrument with his hankerchief.

"Don't think of anything else. Say it to yourself: bang, two, bang, two."

"A–ay sir."

"And keep it slow. We're not going into battle."

That got a laugh. High overhead the bell at the top of the keep made its upswing and came down with a deep solid note. Normally sounded in the middle of the night when raiders came over the border, it was eery to hear it in the morning. The trumpeter snatched back his trumpet, made an accidental raspberry and began blowing an abysmally untuneful fanfare.

As they waited their turn to go out the gate, Carey nodded to himself. Dodd had done as he asked, though he suspected wheels within wheels, since one of Lowther's men had a burst lip and Dodd had fresh grazes on his knuckles. His men were clearly smarter than Lowther's and while he doubted anyone except himself really noticed that, still it pleased him . . . Oh Lord, he'd forgotten to put on his gloves.

Just as he finished drawing them on, it came his turn: he let Lowther and his men have precedence, followed with his horse on a tight rein. Thunder had been ridden in plenty of processions before but was apt to get overexcited at drumbeats and bells. Normally Carey was wearing full tilting armour and the extra eighty pounds on his back kept Thunder subdued. This time . . .

Somebody waved a wooden rattle right by Thunder's head. Carey used the whip to stop the crow-hopping which jarred him painfully, and caught Lowther's face turned over his shoulder expectantly. Damn, the man was a complete pillock.

Like all processions that one became a blur of sunlight,

faces of crowds, drumbeats, horse tails, creaking and a jam of bodies waiting at narrow places like the gate. All the time the trumpeter valiantly kept up his corncrake blowing and the Carlisle keep bell tolled, to be joined in counterpoint by the Cathedral bells, telling out the age, sex and rank of the deceased. The bell-ringers knew their business, which they should do with the amount of practice they got. And somehow Simon and the two other drummer boys, kept the beat firmly so it was easy to match paces to it.

Once at the cathedral, they filled up the battered old building from the back. The churchyard was packed just as tight, with puffing blowing horses investigating each other's necks and four of Lowther's men set to guard them and keep the lesser Borderers from temptation to the sin of horsetheft.

Within, Carey stood, hat in hand, grave reverence on his face, long practice filtering out the mendacious eulogy of the bishop while his mind wandered where it would. There was Philadelphia behind her husband in the front pew, pert and handsome in black with her ruff slightly askew. For all the rehearsed wailing of the paid mourners, there was not a wet eye in the house. Old Scrope had been respected, but not loved, particularly not by his eldest son whom he regarded, rightly, as a fool. His younger son, a solid, pleasant man, had had less expected of him and earned less of his father's impatience: he at least looked sad.

The cathedral choir managed the psalms well, if a little sharp, and the pall bearers succeeded in not dropping the coffin, now closed. In the rush to mount up again outside and form the procession once more, Carey was braced for disaster, but it all went astonishingly smoothly.

They were halfway down the road to the citadel when Carey suddenly knew that something was going on behind him. There was an odd yowling and the crowd was laughing at the bier.

He turned his horse, caught Hutchin Graham's expression of panic and murderous outrage, looked past the glossy draft horses with their black trappings at Carlisle's only bier where the coffin was and wondered how black velvet had become tawny . . .

There was a ginger cat tangled in the armorial cloth over the coffin. Wishing his ribs weren't so sore and fighting not to grin, Carey brought Thunder alongside the bier, reached in, grabbed the cat by the scruff of its neck and hauled it out. It tried to bite his hand, was foiled by leather glove, and lashed a paw full of needles at his face.

"Jesus, does everyone in Carlisle want to spoil my beauty . . ." muttered Carey, holding the cat out in front of him. A little girl's face swung into his vision, with her eyes full of tears and her arms out, so instead of simply wringing the cat's neck as he was tempted, he jumped off his horse, rammed the aggressive bundle of fur into her hands and vaulted back into the saddle again. As he settled and found the stirrups, he suddenly knew that his girth strap was either loose or cut.

Thunder side-stepped slightly, Carey had him lengthen his stride and came up alongside Dodd again.

"My girthstrap's been cut," he muttered out of the side of his mouth at Dodd, whose long face blinked in incomprehension and then rage. "I know, I know. Take a look at it."

Dodd looked. "It's hanging by a thread."

"Wonderful. Let me check yours."

Dodd's was also half-severed. All the rest of his six men had half-cut girthstraps. Clearly, the men Lowther had left to guard the horses had spent a happy hour of sabotage. If he hadn't been so furious with them and himself for not thinking of it first, Carey would have found the situation funny. Dodd's expression was a picture.

"Straighten your face, Dodd," he hissed, "don't let Lowther know we've spotted it. We're supposed to fall off when we mount up after the burial."

"God rot the bastard . . ."

"Shut up. This is what we do . . ."

At the grave side he listened as the words of the burial service were intoned by the bishop, dropping like pebbles of mortality before them. The coffin was lowered into the grave, Scrope and his brother scooped earth on top of it.

Carey backed away from the grave immediately, followed quietly by his men. At the edge of the graveyard were the horses with their reins looped around the fence posts. Choosing their mounts carefully, Carey had his men in the saddle, lined up just outside the gate in two rows, with their helmets off. As they left the burial, Scrope and the gentlemen of the March would pass between them. He kept his own head covered. When Scrope went by, he took his hat off and bowed gravely in the saddle. Scrope beamed with pleasure.

Carey looked through the lychgate to see Lowther furiously trying to stop his men from mounting.

"The Lord hath delivered him into my hands," he intoned piously to Dodd opposite him, who snorted. In the graveyard there was a sequence of thuds, yells and complaint as eight of Lowther's men discovered what had happened to the girthstraps of the horses that were left. Thunder was there, over by the fence, neighing at him reproachfully while the lad who had taken him slid slowly sideways into the mud.

"Tch," said Dodd, "nae discipline."

"Now follow."

The gentlemen's horses were on the other side of the gate, with grooms waiting to help the ladies into the saddle. There was a flurry of mounting. As the cavalcade rode off back up English Street to the waiting funeral feast, Carey and his men followed meekly, leaving confusion behind them.

Sunday, 25th June, noon

Carlisle castle was packed with gentlemen and attendants: the common folk got their meat and bread and ale in the barracks, while the gentlemen and their ladies filled the hall of the keep and attacked the carved beef, mutton, kid, venison and pork with gusto. In the centre of the main table was Philadelphia's artistic subtlety of a marzipan peel tower under siege, only made more realistic by patching here and there where kitchen boys' fingers had explored it.

The various headmen of riding surnames south of the Border were shouting and talking: lines of tension sprang when the heads of two families at deadly feud happened to cross each other's paths, and Richard Graham of Brackenhill and William Armstrong of Mangerton were moving among the throngs, not overtly unwelcome, but watched covertly wherever they went. There was, of course, an official truce until sunset the following day to let everyone get fairly home.

Scrope came up to Carey busily.

"Robin," he said, clearing his throat and hunching his shoulders under his black silk gown, "that was well-done at the churchyard, quite a compliment, eh? Whose idea was it?"

"Mine, my lord."

Scrope looked sideways at him and smiled nervously. "Well, thank you. Very graceful. Er . . . Lowther seems to think there was some kind of mischief, but I'm not clear what."

Does he indeed, thought Carey, who had felt honour was satisfied by swapping the horses and hadn't planned to make any more of it.

"Yes, my lord," he said blandly, "despite Lowther's guard on the horses outside the church, somehow our girthstraps were half-slit."

"Oh dear. Very difficult for you. Any idea who did it?"

"No my lord," lied Carey. "Perhaps Lowther had a better notion. It was his men who were supposed to be guarding the beasts, after all."

"Ah. Whose girths, exactly?"

"Mine and those of my men."

"Ah. Oh." Scrope sidled a bit, then reached past Carey's elbow to grab a sweetmeat off a tray as it went by. The boy holding it skidded to a halt, and stood waiting respectfully, one cheek bulging. "Wonderful comfits Philadelphia made, do try one."

"No thanks, my lord. My teeth won't stand it."

Scrope was full of sympathy. "Dear me, was it Jock . . ."

Carey smiled. "No, they survived Jock well enough. It was the Queen feeding me sugar plums and suckets every time she thought I looked peaky that ruined them."

Scrope laughed and then caught sight of someone over Carey's shoulder, hurried away to speak to another gentleman.

Carey spoke to everyone once, even passed the time of day

with Mangerton and Brackenhill. Armstrong of Mangerton was a tall quiet man whose carrotty head had faded into grey. Graham of Brackenhill could not have been anything except a Graham, with his long face and grey eyes, though he was twice the width of Jock of the Peartree his brother.

"Brought your pack, eh, peddler?" he asked and guffawed.

"It's still in Netherby," said Carey equably. "Would you go and fetch it for me, Mr Graham?"

Graham laughed louder. "God's truth, Sir Robert," he said, wiping his eyes and munching a heroic piece of game pie. "Ah niver laughed so much in my life when I heard what ye did tae Jock. Wattie still hasnae forgiven ye for the damage to his peel tower. Bit of a tradition in your family, eh, damaging peel towers?"

"I hope so," said Carey with a little edge, "I'd like to think I could be as good as my father at it if I had to."

Graham of Brackenhill stopped laughing. "Ay, he burnt mine an' all in '69. Took fifteen kine and four horses too. But it's a good variation, eh, having us break 'em down ourselves?"

Carey smiled at him. "You may speak truer than you know."

"Eh?"

"If I had my way, I'd make you cast down every tower in the March."

"Nae doubt ye would, but we canna do that with the Scots ower the border. Even the Queen must ken that."

"Have you thought, Mr Graham," said Carey softly, "of what will happen when the Queen dies, as she must eventually, God save her?"

Clearly he hadn't. Carey left him with the thought and decided he needed some fresh air. The London fashion for drinking tobacco smoke hadn't travelled this far north yet, but still the air in the keep was thick enough to stick a pike in it.

Out in the castle yard you might have thought it was a wedding, not a funeral, with the folk milling about and the queue for beer at the buttery. By the castle gate was a table, guarded by four men, piled high with weapons.

On an impulse, Carey wandered over to it. There was a hideous array of death-dealing tools, most of them well-worn and extremely clean and sharp. In a neat pile over to one side was a collection of dags and calivers.

"Whose are these?" he asked one of the men guarding the table, a Milburn if memory served him.

"What, the guns, sir?"

"Yes."

"They're the women's weapons, sir. Brackenhill's women. All of them carry firearms when they're in Carlisle."

"Good God, why?"

"The Grahams dinnae like their women to be raped, so it seems." said the man and grinned.

"But the recoil would knock them over."

The man shrugged. "Most of them are broad enough."

Carey was staring open-mouthed at the weapons, with his mind spinning. Somebody took his arm and drew him to one side. It was Elizabeth Widdrington.

"Mary Graham had hurt her wrist," he said, seeing the pattern of it all fall into place. "She was there when Sweetmilk challenged Hepburn. Mary Graham shot Sweetmilk?"

Elizabeth nodded. "To save her lover."

"Who then sent her back to Netherby so he could get rid of the body on Solway Moss."

"And would have nothing more to do with her."

"When did you know?"

"When I heard Thomas the Merchant's tale. Sweetmilk would never have let Hepburn get up behind him, but Mary . . ."

"Why didn't you tell me?"

Elizabeth flushed. "I wasn't sure. I didn't know the Graham women carried dags. I might have made a mistake – all I had was guesswork."

Carey nodded. "And you felt sorry for her?"

Elizabeth didn't answer. Then she added firmly, "And sorry for Jock of the Peartree too. He's lost a son, why take his daughter?"

Carey stared at her. "For justice. Because she killed her brother."

To his astonishment, her face twisted into a sneer. "Oh yes, justice," she said. "I'd forgotten. She's sixteen, she's with child, she's a fool who lost her heart to a man, and we must put her on trial and bring witnesses and get her to confess, and then when her babe's born, we must hang her."

"Yes," said Carey simply.

Elizabeth turned, walked away from him.

Sunday, 25th June, evening

Carey found himself put in charge of dealing with the leftovers when all the various gentlefolk had gone, or been carried, back to their lodgings in the town. He delegated it on to Dodd who was still fairly sober, and as the heels of the pies and the unusable remains of the carcasses and bread were carted down to the castle gate to feed beggars (some of them very well-dressed), Goodwife Biltock descended on the hall with an army of women with brooms to sweep out the rushes and scrub the floor clean of spiced wine stains.

Carey went upstairs to the cubbyhole next to Scrope's office used by Richard Bell. One of the boys had come to him in the afternoon asking if he would care to do so, and he went, wondering if Bell meant to thank him.

Richard Bell was, as usual, writing when he came in. He wiped his pen and put it down at once, and came over holding some papers.

Feeling tired and very sore, Carey leaned against the wall by the closed door, took the papers with his eyebrows raised, and skimmed through the Secretary script still used by Bell.

"Lowther's letters," he said neutrally when he's finished.

"Ay sir."

"Not very flattering, are they?"

"No sir. I have a second . . . er . . . draft of the letter referring to you."

Carey took that one, glanced at it, read it carefully and smiled.

"Very subtly done, Mr Bell," he said, "Burghley will make

the same response to this as he would to the other if he disagreed with it." He waited.

Bell looked down at his desk. "Sir Robert," he said, "I will be frank with you. I served the old lord faithfully and I will serve his son in the same way. If the lord Warden writes a letter like that to my lord Burghley, you will never see it and nor will I . . . er . . . improve it as I have with this. However, Lowther is not my lord and . . . I would rather be your friend than his."

"I already regard you as a friend, Mr Bell," said Carey, his heart lifting. Surely it couldn't be as easy as this, surely the man would want money?

Bell smiled at him, a remarkably sweet smile for such a skull-like face.

"May I have the other letters back, then sir?"

Carey handed them over, keeping the one that described, in withering terms, his doings of the Friday. Before his eyes, Richard Bell put the three letters into the dispatch bag and sealed it.

"May I keep this?" he asked, waving the paper.

"I hope you'll burn it."

"Naturally, I will," said Carey, "but I want to be sure I've understood it properly."

Bell shrugged. "These are the only letters dictated by Sir Richard," he said, pointing to the dispatch bag. "That one in your hand must be a libellous forgery."

Carey tucked the paper into the front of his doublet and grinned.

"Of course it is," he agreed, "I'm in your debt, Mr Bell."

"No sir," said Bell, as he put the dispatch bag on a hook, "I regard this as fair exchange."

"Well, good night Mr Bell."

"Good night, Sir Robert."

Back in his chamber in the Queen Mary Tower, Carey bit down on his rage and forced himself to read again what Lowther thought of him. It wasn't at all complimentary. In fact, there might have been a disaster if the Queen had seen it. Lowther described Carey as an impudent, ignorant young puppy, an unprincipled gloryhound, whose ridiculous, irresponsible and foolhardy attempt to spy out what Bothwell was up to at Netherby had imperilled Lowther's clever intelligence work et cetera, et cetera.

Carey committed it to memory as a way of drawing the sting of his anger, then watched with satisfaction as his candleflame caught the edge and curled the whole epistle into a little pile of ash in the grate. But Elizabeth's astonishing defence of Mary Graham kept rising up in his mind causing confusion and irritation, and when Barnabus arrived with a bowl of rosewater and a pile of cloths to take the white lead off his master's face at last, he was snarled at. That night Carey lay for a long time staring into the darkness of the bedcurtains, listening to the snoring of his servant and the Carlisle bell telling the hours, unwilling to risk his ribs in turning over. He wished he could put his arms around some warm cuddly girl, bury all his doubts in her, perhaps even ask her what she thought . . . No, perhaps not.

Even when he slept at last, Elizabeth Widdrington haunted his dreams with her hand bandaged and her gun smoking.

Saturday, 1st July, morning

The week had passed with breathless quiet, since all the worst raiders among the Armstrongs and Grahams were busy deep in Scotland and the hay harvest was in full swing. After the hurry of the days before the funeral, Carey took life easy for a while and spent some of the time, once he felt more comfortable on a horse, riding out across the rough hills and learning how they lay. He even got in some hunting with dogs, since all the falcons were still in moult, though they returned empty-handed.

It was Young Hutchin Graham who came to Carey as he stood in the castle yard at dawn on the Saturday following Scrope's funeral, and muttered that if he chose to ride up to the ford at Longtown, he might find some horses. This confirmed everything Carey had heard about Young Hutchin from Barnabus, but he only narrowed his eyes and said, "Anything else?"

"Ay," said Young Hutchin, "if ye go alone, there might be someone to meet ye there."

"Will that someone be alone as well?"

"Ay. He gives ye his word on it."

"I'll be armed."

Young Hutchin grinned. "So will he."

Probably I shouldn't do it, Carey thought, as he shotted both his guns and put them in their carrying case, probably it would be wise to have Dodd and the men follow at a distance.

In the end he did take Dodd and the men, but he told them to wait for him a mile down the road and come if he blew on his horn.

Longtown was alive with horses, most of them too tired and footsore to do more than crop the grass ravenously. He rode through them and found Jock of the Peartree sitting in a tree by the ford, with the Widdrington nags tethered to the next bush.

"Good day to you, Jock," he said.

"Now then, Courtier."

"How was the raid?"

"Och, it was beautiful," said Jock, showing the gaps in his teeth. "The horses . . . Ye told naught but the truth, I never saw such magnificent animals before."

"How many of them did you get?"

"I'm not sure. About five hundred, give or take a few."

"And the King?"

"He's well enough. He was a wee bit upset when we banged his door in and he still canna understand it how the sixty men he had with him in the house managed to drive off two hundred Borderers. He thinks it was God saved him, though Chancellor Melville did his best when ye sent him word."

"Is that all, a wee bit upset?"

"Well, he's verra upset, to tell ye the truth. I hear he's on his way to Jedburgh with 3,000 men to do some justice."

"And Bothwell?"

"Gone north to the Highlands. He's worn out his welcome here and he knows it."

They looked at each other in silence for a moment, Carey wondering if he dared ask.

"Ay," said Jock, "I dinna like his way of doing things. About Sweetmilk."

"Yes."

"I know who killed him."

"Oh?" said Carey carefully. "Did . . . er . . . did Mary tell you?"

Jock spat. "Not a peep out of her and I broke a stick thrashing her."

"Then how do you know?"

Jock stared off into the distance, one hand on the bough beside him.

"All the time we were conversing on top of Netherby tower there was something about your face that was troubling me, Courtier. I didna mind me what it was until we'd let ye go and then it came to me. It was the cut on your cheek."

Carey had forgotten all about it, though he put his finger to the scar now. "What about it?"

"I spent a full night before he was buried, looking at my Sweetmilk's poor dead face," said Jock, "and it was sorrowful what the crows had done to it, but none of the peckmarks had bled. Except one, the one on his cheek, like yours, that had bled, ay and clotted too. It was the same shape, ye mind, like a star, made by a fancy ring."

Jock's mouth worked. "I asked the Earl if anyone hit ye while ye were at Netherby playing at peddlers. He said it was Jock Hepburn that struck you for not calling him sir. Nobody else until I got to work on ye. And Hepburn had a ring like a star, with emeralds on it."

"Had?" asked Carey, feeling hollow and tired.

"Ay, had," said Jock, "I asked him, he admitted he hit Sweetmilk, he admitted Sweetmilk called him out. He denied shooting my son in the back, but he lied."

"Did he have a trial?" demanded Carey, his voice shaking

with a sudden surprising rage. "Did he get a chance at justice?"

"Justice? There ye go again, Courtier, you're ower impractical. What justice did he give my Sweetmilk? If he'd killed him honourably in a duel, ay well, it would have been sorrowful, but what he did . . . He's had all the justice he deserves."

It was on the tip of Carey's tongue to tell Jock the truth about his daughter, but somehow the words stuck there. The silence broken by horse noises was all around him while he tried to decide: would justice truly be served by her hanging? Would Jock even believe him? Mary's death would bring back neither Sweetmilk nor Hepburn. Perhaps Elizabeth was right; he remembered her anger, which had puzzled him. At last he said, "Where is Hepburn now?"

"His soul's in hell, but ye'll find his body where he left Sweetmilk's, if you've a mind to go fetch it. I wouldnae bother, myself. It's no' very pretty, ye follow."

"You could have waited, Jock," said Carey tightly, "I was planning to arrest the murderer. You could have waited for a trial and proper justice."

Jock shrugged. "Why?" he asked. "Ye're begrudging an old man healing his heart? Besides Hepburn could likely buy his way clear – who cares about the killing of a reiver? This way Sweetmilk can rest quiet."

"Very neat," said Carey bitterly.

He turned his horse away to return to Dodd and start the long wearisome job of rounding up the horses, sorting them out by brand and knowledge, and take them back to their rightful owners. Jock called after him, "I'm in debt to ye, Courtier. I'll mind ye if we meet in a fight and if ye need aid from the Grahams, ye've only to call on me."

Carey turned back.

"God forbid," he said, "that I should ever need help from the likes of you."

Jock was not offended. "Ay, perhaps He will. But if He doesna, my offer stands. Good day to ye, Courtier."